Savage Love
A Dark Mafia Romance

The Savage Trilogy

M. James

Elena

Elena,

If you're reading this, I've left for New York. I'm sorry for the early departure, but I think we said everything that could be said last night. I meant it all—you deserve better than me, better than someone carrying the weight of a former life on his shoulders, who can't be all the things to you that you should have.

Despite that, I do care for you, Elena. I think you know that. And I want to leave you with that, at least, so that you don't wonder. In time, you'll see that it's better this way, as I do. You'll find more happiness without me than you would by my side, even if you don't realize that now.

I wouldn't change what happened. But it needs to remain in the past. I want only the best for your future—and I hope you understand that's why I'm gone.

We shouldn't see each other again. In time, it will hurt less. I promise you that.

Goodbye, Elena. I'm grateful to have known you.

–Levin

. . .

I've read the letter so many times now. I could probably repeat it from memory if I wanted to.

I don't.

I never knew what heartbreak felt like before. I've read about it plenty of times, in all the romance novels I devoured in my bedroom back home. In those books, the heartbreak never lasted. Eventually, the hero always comes back. He realizes he was wrong and begs the heroine to forgive him. Some of them make the hero grovel more than others, but in the end, he's always forgiven, because he loves her so much. Because he can't live without her.

Clearly, Levin can live without me.

And I was an idiot to ever think otherwise.

I don't know how long I sit on my floor, sobbing. I thought I was going to cry last night when I went to bed before everyone else—that I'd finally be alone in my new room and all the stress and worry, and fear of the past weeks would explode all at once.

That's not what happened, though.

I couldn't cry. I laid there awake in the darkness, staring up at the ceiling, faintly hearing the sounds of Isabella and Niall and Levin's voices from another part of the house, and I waited for the tears to come.

They never did, and I finally fell asleep, until I'd woken in the middle of the night, mouth dry and wide-awake.

I'd gone to the kitchen for water and saw Levin in the backyard. I'd gone to him, of course, because how could I not? He was leaving in the morning, and I wanted so desperately for him to stay. For him to change his mind in the last moment, the way the heroes of romance novels sometimes do, when they realize what a terrible mistake they're about to make.

After all, everything had worked out so far, hadn't it–despite all odds? We survived a plane crash. We dodged bullets through Rio de

Janeiro, and Levin won money in poker games to keep us afloat. I kept him alive when he was nearly murdered after one of those games, stabbed in the side.

I killed men to keep him alive.

At the very end, he won the game that got us our way out of Rio. And when that went upside down, he fought through men who wanted to kill him in order to get me safely home.

How could that not end in a happily-ever-after for us?

I didn't feel naive or innocent anymore, after everything that had happened. But now I do, sitting on my bedroom floor, clutching Levin's goodbye letter to me. I feel stupid.

You don't have to be alone forever, you know. What we had was real. I know you know that—it doesn't have to be over.

You know it does, Elena.

Did you feel anything? Did you love me at all?

Remembering the conversation makes my heart ache like I'm the one who's been stabbed. I'd put myself out there one last time, but it hadn't been enough. He's so sure that I should be with someone my own age. Someone *like me.*

But there isn't going to be anyone like me here. Not anymore—not after what I've seen and done. I'm not the same girl he thinks I am.

My job was to protect you. I've done that. There's nothing more I can do for you. You deserve better than a man nearly twenty years older than you, who's lived a hard life and can't love someone the way you deserve to be loved. The only thing I can still do is protect you, by going far enough way from you that you can get over what we had and have your own life. And tomorrow, that's what I'm going to do.

And you? Are you going to get over it?

I want to believe that he's not going to get over it. That he never will. But I don't know what I believe any longer.

A soft knock at my door startles me out of my miserable train of thought. I wipe at my face, suddenly alarmed at the thought of Isabella seeing me like this—or whoever is on the other side of the door. No one other than Levin and I know what happened between us—and I planned on keeping it that way.

"Yes?" I call out, trying to keep my watery voice from shaking, but I don't do a very good job.

"Elena?" It's Isabella, as I expected. "Are you alright? Can I come in?"

"Um—sure." If I tell her no, she'll be even more suspicious that something is really wrong. I wipe harder at my eyes and face, getting to my feet and folding the letter up in my hand, looking for somewhere to put it.

She opens the door before I can.

"Elena?" She stands in the doorway, her pretty face creased with concern. I've always thought my sister was the more beautiful of the two of us. She has sharper features, an ocean of thick dark hair, and the most perfect figure I think anyone could ever be blessed with. I'm softer in some places than I'd like to be, but Isabella is a vision. She's also much more fiery than I am—all it takes is one look at her narrow dark eyes to see that she takes absolutely no one's shit.

I used to not be that way. But some things have changed.

"What's wrong?" She steps into the room, closing the door behind her. Her gaze sweeps over my face, and I see instantly that I haven't done a good enough job of hiding that I've been crying. I'm not surprised—my face *feels* puffy and swollen. Isabella has always been quick to pick up on things like that anyway, especially when it comes to me. "Is it—did something happen?"

Her gaze flicks to the letter in my hand. "What's that?"

"Nothing." I swallow hard, walking quickly to the nightstand and depositing it there. "It's no big deal."

"You've never lied to me, Elena. I wish you wouldn't start now." She purses her lips. "You know *papa* called me. He told me to make sure I took care of you. That was weeks ago—when you were supposed to be coming straight here from Mexico. We've had no idea where you were. I've been so worried. If it wasn't for Niall keeping me calm—"

"If I could have gotten in touch with you, I would have." I look at her apologetically. "There wasn't any way—"

"I know that. I've been through something similar, remember?" Isabella lets out a small, sharp breath. "But if something happened to you in Rio, something that's bothering you—"

I haven't gotten to talk to my sister very much since she left. But I can't imagine she likes thinking about what happened to her—about being kidnapped by Diego in a very similar fashion, nearly forced to marry him, and sent to the bride-tamer to be broken to Diego's will. If it weren't for Niall, she might be back home still, trapped in a horrific marriage to the man responsible for so much of our pain. I'd be back there, too, probably on the verge of my own arranged marriage. I would never have met Levin. And Isabella—

She wouldn't be here, in this cozy house, with her devoted husband and my little niece.

I know Isabella well enough to know that she's the kind of person who would prefer to look forward instead of backward. But I also know she would understand at least part of what I've gone through.

I just don't think she'll understand about Levin.

"I'm fine." I take a deep breath, trying to force a smile onto my face, but I can see she's not buying it.

"Who is the letter from?" Isabella narrows her eyes at me. "I'm not trying to parent you, Elena, but when I come in your room and find you sobbing—"

"I'm not sobbing—"

"You were." She steps past me, reaching for the letter. I try to block her, but she's too quick. I should have known she'd go for it—Isabella has always been a bit of a bossy older sister. She's always believed she knows best—and a lot of the time, that's true. But now that our parents have told her to look out for me, I have no doubt that she's going to take that far too much to heart.

She opens the letter before I can snatch it away from her. I see her face go from concerned to angry in an instant, and she looks up at me, a furious expression in her sharp dark eyes.

"What the hell, Elena?" Her fist crumples around the letter, and it's all I can do not to snatch it away from her. If I do, it'll tear, and it's all I have left of him.

Just thinking that makes me feel so pathetic I can't stand it.

"What did he do?" Isabella's lips are pressed together, turning white at the edges, and I'm not sure I've ever seen my sister so angry. She's not angry at me, I don't think, but if Levin were here, she'd be flying at him. It's him that I think she's pissed at.

"*He* didn't do anything—"

"It sure sounds like he did!" Isabella tosses the letter onto the bed, crossing her arms over her chest. "It sounds like he took advantage of you."

"He didn't!" I shake my head, trying to think of how to make her understand. All of my emotions feel frayed, my mind foggy. "I–I initiated most of it. He tried to tell me no, but I insisted–"

Isabella's mouth twists. "He's nearly forty," she spits out. "He should have had more goddamned self-control."

"Like Niall?" I glare at her, and from the look on her face, I almost regret saying anything. But I'm upset too. "I know how things went between the two of you, Isabella. I just took a page out of your book and made my own choice–"

"Don't try to make this about me." Isabella crosses her arms, a mirror of me. "Niall didn't know who I was. Levin knew very well who you were and what his job was. It was to protect you, not…not—"

"Fuck me?" I supply helpfully, and Isabella's eyes widen.

"Elena—"

"We were stranded on a beach. We'd been in a plane crash. We were eating fucking barbecued snake meat that Levin shot, for fuck's sake. We had no idea how long we were going to live—and I didn't want to die a fucking virgin!" I stare at Isabella, willing her to understand. "Are you telling me you wouldn't have done the same thing?"

"That's not the point—"

"Then what is?"

"He should have—"

"What?" I burst out, feeling tears well up in my eyes again. "He should have stayed? I wanted him to. But he's telling the truth when he says that he let me know what this was from the start. It's my fault for—"

I can't finish the sentence. I can't put into words what I feel for Levin, because it hurts too much. If I say it aloud, it will be too real.

I can't stand that, not with him gone forever.

Isabella lets out a sharp breath. "I can see you're upset," she says finally. "We can talk about this more later. If you don't want to come out for breakfast—I can bring you something. Just take some time until you feel better."

She looks at me, her teeth worrying at her lower lip, and then I hear a baby's cry from somewhere else in the house. "I need to go help Niall," she says, looking torn. "Elena—"

"It's fine. I'll come out in a little bit. Go take care of Aisling," I tell her encouragingly, and Isabella lets out a sigh.

"I'll be back," she says finally.

I sink onto the edge of the bed, looking at the crumpled letter next to me. A part of me wants to read it again, but I don't.

What's the point, anyway? It won't change anything.

I sit there, feeling numb, until I hear raised voices from down the hall. It's Isabella and Niall, and I know I shouldn't eavesdrop. But I have a feeling it has to do with me, and I can't contain my curiosity.

Listening in on a conversation is far from the worst thing I've done recently.

I step out of my room, leaving the door cracked as I inch down the hall toward their room. The house that they live in is small in comparison to the one we grew up in—five bedrooms and three bathrooms, two stories, and an attic. The outside is grey-painted clapboard, with shutters and pretty window boxes and a picket fence around it, a landscaped backyard that overlooks the water with a huge deck in the back. It's the kind of sweet suburban home I imagined when I thought about Boston, and it doesn't disappoint. Isabella said last night that it was Niall's childhood home, inherited from his parents, and it fits him. He's not much like the other men that I've met—he's more ordinary, down to earth. He reminds me of Levin, in a way—rougher and earthier than someone like Connor or our father.

This is a house, not a mansion, and I like it that way. It doesn't feel too big, like I'm rattling around inside of it.

"What the fuck was he thinking?" As I creep closer to the door, I hear Isabella hiss from inside the room. "Taking advantage of her—"

"He wouldn't have hurt her, lass," I hear Niall's deep, Irish-accented voice. "If that's what happened between them, then it must have been her choice—"

"Are you blaming *Elena* for this?" Isabella's voice is outraged.

"No, lass, I'm saying there's likely no blame to be had. Remember when we—"

"Oh, for fuck's sake! I'll tell you the same thing I told Elena, this isn't about *us*. You didn't know who I was—"

Niall chuckles. "Lass, if I'm being honest? I can't tell you if it would have made a difference. You in that red dress—"

His voice turns husky, and my cheeks flush. This is a conversation more intimate than I should be hearing—but it makes my chest ache, too. I want to hear Levin say that to me—that regardless of the circumstances, he'd make the same choice. I'll never get that from him now.

"Stop that." Isabella clearly isn't having any of it, not right now. "He should have known better. His job was to protect her, not deflower her!"

Niall chuckles again. "*Deflower* her? Lass, I didn't think you subscribed to all that bullshit. If Elena wanted to make her own choice, didn't she deserve that too? After all—"

"She's young. Innocent. They were in a situation where they thought they were going to die, and he didn't tell her no! He had all the power—"

"I know Levin," Niall says reassuringly. "I guarantee you he spent a lot of time turning Elena down before anything finally happened between them. And whatever *did* happen—it wouldn't have happened without her consent. That's not the kind of man he is. So whatever occurred between them—and I'm hesitant to say it's anything other than their business—it was—"

"I don't care," Isabella snaps. "I don't want him anywhere near my sister. Is that understood? I don't want him in this house. I don't want to hear or speak to him again."

Whatever Niall says in response to that, trying to mollify her, I don't hear. I back away from the door, tears welling in my eyes, because I've heard enough of the conversation. Whatever comes next doesn't matter, because Levin isn't coming back. Isabella doesn't need to worry about that.

I go back to my room, tears sliding down my cheeks as I crawl onto the bed, curling on my side into a tight ball. I never knew anything could hurt this badly. It feels like a physical pain, like someone has reached into my chest and strangled my heart, like I can't breathe.

Levin left me because he thought I deserved someone else. Someone *better*.

But there isn't ever going to be anyone else for me.

I wish he understood that.

I wish he cared.

Levin

Being without her is excruciating.

It's penance. It's what I deserve, for letting things go as far as they did. With every mile I put between us, I'm more and more aware of how out of hand I allowed all of it to get.

I should have told her no so many times. Even if what happened on the beach was unavoidable, born of the thought that we were going to die. There was no future beyond that night; I should never have let it happen again once we were off the beach.

Everything that happened in Rio shouldn't have. And the number of times I fucked her without protection, telling myself that I'd say no next time—

Christ, I was a fucking idiot.

I was the one with the age, responsibility—and hell, supposedly the fucking wisdom—to tell her that it was a bad idea. That we couldn't give in, no matter how either of us felt about it.

I'm supposed to be past the age of thinking with my dick, and I'm beyond ashamed of myself that I apparently am not. At least when it comes to Elena.

It doesn't matter. There's enough distance between us that she'll forget about me soon enough. Time heals the majority of wounds—and so does space.

There are some that no amount of space and time can ever heal, but I tell myself that this isn't one of them. That Elena will be fine, in time. I'll tell Viktor that I can't go to Boston for a while, that if there's anything else that needs handling with the Kings, I'll either do it from a distance or he'll need to send someone else. I've been loyal to him long enough that he'll trust that I have good reasoning.

And as for me—

I fucking miss her. Sitting on the plane on the short flight from Boston to New York, the silence feels cavernous without her to fill it. It's hard to believe there was a time when I found her endless optimism irritating, that I thought she was anything but a ray of much-needed sunshine in a dark and difficult world. That there was ever a time when I thought she was too naive to survive.

I take a deep breath, closing my eyes. There's guilt in that, too. Elena's hands are bloodstained now, marked with the deaths of five or more men, most likely, because I wasn't there to take care of it for her. Because I got myself stabbed in the gut in a poker game meant to buy our way out of Rio, and she had to save me.

I'd be dead now if she weren't far more capable than I ever gave her credit for.

I know, from the things she said to me after, that she thinks that means she's earned a place in this world. That she's proved she's able to be a match for someone like me. But what she can't seem to understand is that I never wanted her to have to be that at all. That I don't want her to find out all the small ways this life chips away at your soul until you find yourself looking for any way you can to prove to yourself that you still have one.

I want her out, before she gets sucked in so deeply that she can't ever escape.

The worst part is, I can fucking *hear* what she'd say to that in my head. *I was always a part of this life. I was born into it—I would have been married to a man in one of the cartels if I'd stayed at home. So why can't I choose my place in it?*

And my answer would always be the same—that she has a chance to be almost entirely free of it now. Niall, her now brother-in-law, is an enforcer for the Kings, true, but it's not the kind of thing that will keep her tied into all of that. Niall, of all the men I know, is the best at keeping what he does away from his family—and I know for a fact that he's been clear with Connor and Liam that he wants Isabella kept away from all of it. There will be no arranged marriage for Elena, and the Kings will do their best to make sure that what Niall does won't come back on his family. There's never a perfect guarantee in this life—but of all the places Elena could land that would give her the best chance at a normal life, her sister's new home is the best.

That means keeping myself out of it. And I intend to do that, no matter how much it hurts.

I go straight to Viktor's offices when I land. I find him behind his desk, flipping through a file, and he looks up at me the moment I step in.

"Levin!" He stands up, coming around to greet me with a quick, one-armed hug. After so many years, Viktor is more like a friend to me than an employer, someone I trust above anyone else. "It's good to have you back."

"It's good to be back." I sink into one of the leather chairs in front of his desk, rubbing a hand over my face. "I hope you don't have a job for me in Rio, because I don't plan to go back for a while. Maybe not ever, if I'm being honest."

"I don't blame you. After what Vasquez pulled, I don't think we'll be putting down any roots there, either. Not that I really had any plans to." Viktor sits back down behind the desk, turning to take a bottle of vodka and two glasses off of a shelf to his left. "I would have honored that deal if you'd made it, though. That was good thinking."

"Well, it would have worked out if Vasquez had honored his." I take the glass from him after he pours, sipping the vodka. It's the highest quality, but it still burns a little going down, just how I like it.

Viktor shrugs. "It ended well, at least. Elena is in Boston, safely with her sister. You did what needed to be done. And now you're back home." He lifts the glass towards me. "A job well done."

I nod, tilting my own glass towards him, and Viktor looks at me appraisingly.

"There's something else to it, though, isn't there?" He sets the glass down. "Something to do with Elena?"

He's too perceptive, that's for sure. I'm not surprised he's picked up on my mood or what might have caused it. We know each other too well by now. But I'm not about to delve into all of it—not now, and probably not ever.

I've gotten through most of the past years by trying to not think too often about what's in the past for me to miss, and grieve. If I didn't, I'd have given up long ago. This is no different.

"Connor mentioned to me that there seemed to be a—closeness between the two of you," Viktor adds, swirling the vodka in his glass. "I assured him that you're a more focused man than that these days. He wasn't happy about the possibility—something about how Ricardo Santiago might change his mind about the deal that was made if he thought you'd taken advantage of his daughter. But I told him it was ridiculous."

I can see the plausible deniability that he's giving me. I nod, taking another sip of the vodka. "It was a job," I say finally. "And it's finished now."

I'm not going to lie to him. But neither do I need to come out and say what actually happened.

Viktor nods. "Well. That's where we'll leave it, then. I assume you'd rather not go to Boston for a while."

"I think it would be for the best."

"I've got plenty for you to do here." He shoves a stack of files toward me. "Recruits being sent over to us. You can look them over and see who might be worth your time. Nico is taking on some of the firing range training, working with those that we might contract out as bodyguards. I'd rather have you working with the mercenaries."

"That's certainly in my skill set." I look at the files, feeling a bit as if I've been relegated to desk duty, but I have a feeling that's just another part of my penance. "I'll let you know my thoughts in a few days."

"No rush." Viktor leans back. "You've earned some time to yourself, after what you've been through. Getting Elena back to Boston safely was a huge success for all of us. You can take all the time you need."

"I appreciate it. I like to keep busy, though." I finish the vodka, setting the glass down, and reach for the files. The stitches in my side pull and ache as I stand up, and I know Viktor's not wrong about the idea that I could use some time off.

But 'time to myself' also means time to think. Time in my own head. And that's the last fucking thing I need right now.

I consider going to a bar, out to a movie, anything I could come up with to keep from being alone in the silence of my apartment. But instead, I go straight there, the files tucked under my arm as I ride the elevator up to my floor and walk into the sterile quiet of the small one-bedroom that I've called home for a while now.

I could afford a house. Hell, I could afford a nicer apartment if that's all I wanted. But I've never really seen the point. I meant it when I told Elena that it was just a place to eat and sleep and fuck—though I left that last part off. Now, I'm not so sure it applies any longer.

What, you're just going to be celibate at thirty-eight? Who the fuck do you think you are, Maximilian Agosti? And even he found a woman he couldn't resist eventually.

I drop the files on the kitchen counter, open the refrigerator, and look for a beer. There's half a six-pack left and nothing else in there. I let out a long breath as I consider the merits of grocery delivery versus just ordering food in. The latter is likely to win out, as it usually does.

The thing is, I'm fucking *aching* already for a release. It's been three days since I was with Elena last, and I already feel frustrated and restless, as if it's been much longer. But the thought of going out and finding someone to bring home—my usual solution to feeling this way—is the last fucking thing I want.

There's no one that I could find that I wouldn't wish was her. No one who I wouldn't have to grit my teeth against calling her name in bed. No one that could measure up right now.

I want *her*. And right now, even though I know that in time I'll likely feel differently, the wanting feels endless.

It feels like I'll never be able to want anyone else again.

I tilt the beer back, drinking it in a few long gulps as I stride to the bedroom and strip off my clothes, tossing them in the hamper and heading for the shower. The apartment is neat and clean to the point of feeling more like a hotel room than a home—someone comes once a month if I'm on a job to clean it, and once a week if I'm here, and they do a pristine job—and that just makes me think of Elena, too, of all the hotel rooms we stayed in over the past weeks. Most of them were shitty, and yet she still never complained.

It was like she was happy no matter where we were, as long as I was there too.

The thought brings an almost physical pain. I turn on the shower, rubbing my hand over my face, trying to exorcise the thoughts of her. It won't solve anything. It won't make anything better. And yet—

I'm not as ready to let go of it as I told her I was.

I ignore my stubborn arousal as I shower, refusing to give in. *I gave in too many times when she was there with me.*

What, now you're never going to jerk off again, either?

I grit my teeth with frustration as I rinse off, still ignoring my cock. I know I'm acting like an idiot—like a teenager with a first crush on a girl he can't have, rather than a man who's lived enough life to be practical about things like this.

My self-imposed punishment after the shower is to sit with the remainder of my beers and the files, going through them. I'll have to wait a few days before I let Viktor know what I think—I don't feel like listening to him lecture me about how I need time off—but it keeps my mind occupied. There's a handful of recruits that I think are promising, including one dark-haired, petite woman who, unfortunately, turns my thoughts back in the direction that I'd been trying to steer them away from.

Anna Lindovna. I run through her file as quickly as I can before setting it aside—it goes in the pile of potential recruits, as much as I'm tempted to turn her down based on how much she makes me think of Elena. Which is ridiculous—the only thing they actually have in common is dark hair and a shorter stature—Anna Lindovna is sharp-featured and thin, with a lean hardness to her that suggests from just a glance that she could fuck any man up who tried something with her.

Elena does *not* suggest that at first sight. But she'd proved to be dangerous anyway—both for others and for me, in a different sort of way.

Once I've finished the beers, I switch to vodka until I've at least glanced through all the files and have a pleasant, warm buzz that fogs up my mind enough that I think I'll be able to sleep. I retreat to my bed, sinking into it and trying not to think about the space next to me, how empty it is, or how good it would feel to have Elena there, warm and soft and sweet in my arms.

Unfortunately, my dreams don't allow me that luxury.

I dream about Rio, muddled flashes of that rainy night when she came out to stand with me, and we ended up against the motel wall, her mouth on mine as she pressed her hands against me, pinning me while she showed me exactly how much she wanted me. I dream of how it felt to stumble back inside, falling into the bed, of how she arched under me, warm and eager and begging for me, and how I gave in.

I dream about all of those times I gave in, tangled together like we were in beds across Rio. I wake in the middle of the night with the sheets sweaty and twisted around my hips, my cock hard and aching, demanding relief.

Half awake and still partially lost in dreams of her, I don't have the control to deny myself this time.

I reach down, my hand wrapping around my aching shaft, eyes closing as I slip back into the fantasy of having her here with me. I think of tying her up in my own bed, the way I did in that room, of silk shibari ropes around her wrists instead of my leather belt, of her ankles, tied up too, holding her legs open for me. I think of all the ways I could torment her with pleasure, all of the ways she would beg for me, and my cock throbs in my fist, wanting her instead of the lesser pleasure of my hand.

I want to taste her again. My other hand clenches into a fist against the sheets, remembering the warm, silky feel of her inner thigh against it as I held her open, spread for my tongue, the way she arched against my face and writhed, begging for me to make her come.

My thumb presses into the base of my cockhead, feeling the drip of my pre-cum as I stroke my hand up and down. That first morning in Rio, when I'd come out of the shower, and she'd gotten down on her knees, her hot mouth enveloping me—the way she moaned as she licked up my arousal–

I groan aloud, hips jerking as I fuck my hand faster, imagining it's her mouth, that I'm getting to the very edge before I thrust into her, filling her up with my cum. I can imagine her begging for it, pleading to taste me, moaning as I insist on fucking her. I can imagine how she would feel, how she would pulse under my fingertips as I make her come–

After that first night on the beach, I thought she would be shy. I'd never been with a virgin before her, but I'd imagined that she would be hesitant, innocent, that she wouldn't know what she wanted. That she would only know the barest mechanics of sex, that she would be shocked by all the filthy fantasies that I could have described to her.

Instead, I found out that she had the same types of fantasies. That she was willing and eager to tell me *exactly* what she wanted, when, and how. That she wasn't shy at all about it.

That, more than anything, had made it impossible to tell her no. That had broken my self-control over and over, how eager she was, how much she wanted me. How little she cared about what she was *supposed* to want.

My cock throbs again, pulsing in my fist, and I remember her lips tightening around it, her nose brushing against my abs, the feeling of her throat clenching around me as she took me all the way down—

That sends me over the edge. I groan, my head tipping back as the memory of my cum flooding her mouth fills my thoughts, pleasure sparking over my skin as I drag my hand hard and fast up and down my aching shaft, feeling myself spill onto the taut flesh of my abs, spurts of cum streaking my skin as I imagine that it's coating her tongue instead, her lips, her breasts. That I'm covering her in it, instead of lying in my own bed, fantasizing about something I'll never have again.

My hand drops to my side, my wilting cock against my thigh, and I close my eyes. I don't mean to fall asleep like that, but exhaustion floods me in the wake of my orgasm, and I'm fast asleep before I realize what's happened.

When I wake again in the morning, daylight streaming through the half-open blinds, I feel foggy and more than a little ashamed. I'm in need of another shower; the sheets are still tangled around my ankles along with my boxers, the way I left them last night when I passed out. I have a headache and the vague memory of jerking off in the middle of the night, dreaming about Elena. I let out a long breath through clenched teeth, asking myself what the fuck is wrong with me.

The time I spent with Elena was passionate, incredible, and more special than it ought to have been. But it's over.

No more nights like this. No more indulging in thinking about her like that. What I told her in Niall and Isabella's backyard rings true for me as well—in time, this will pass. In time, I'll stop wanting her so badly, if I don't continue to entertain it.

In time, I won't miss her any longer.

For now, I just have to keep believing that's actually true.

Elena

I hate being sick.

In all my life, I've only been *really* sick a couple of times. Food poisoning once, from a restaurant we went out to when I was much younger, on one of the rare occasions when the family left the house. Pneumonia, as a teenager. Both times I recall being miserable, but it's so far in the past that right now, sitting on the fluffy blue mat next to the shower with the toilet in front of me, I'm convinced this is the worst I've ever felt.

It's been nearly a month since I arrived in Boston, and for the last few weeks, I've felt varying degrees of sick. When it started, we chalked it up to exhaustion from everything that had happened. I can still hear Isabella's voice in my head—*a plane crash, running all over the city, sleeping in uncomfortable motels, trying to get back home. Of course, you don't feel well. You've probably barely slept in weeks.*

I didn't tell her that for a lot of those nights, I'd slept perfectly well, tired and satisfied after Levin and I were finished or nestled up next to him. That wouldn't have helped anything, because if there's one thing I figured out very quickly, it was that Isabella was determined to blame Levin for anything that might have gone wrong, or was wrong with me.

From what I gathered, overhearing a few conversations, Levin and Niall were quite close. Isabella knew him slightly less well, but there wasn't any indication that once upon a time, she hadn't liked him well enough. It was just that once he had something to do with me that she didn't approve of, she decided there must have been something off about him all along.

I'd tried to tell her that I was fine, to get her to focus all that motherly instinct on Aisling and not on me. Still, she took our parents' insistence that she needed to take care of me very much to heart. It wasn't all that strange—Isabella has always taken care of me, all our lives…but it was dialed up to eleven after this. As I steadily started to feel worse, she became more and more concerned.

For the past week, I've been certain I have a stomach flu. I've barely been able to keep anything down, throwing up after every meal, only able to manage to drink a protein shake here and there, water, and the occasional bland soup. Isabella has pestered me nonstop to go to the doctor, worried that I picked up some parasite in Rio or an exotic disease, but I haven't wanted to go. I've convinced her to put it off again and again, telling her I'll go if I don't feel better next week—and I know it's at least partially because, in the back of my mind, there's another worry as to why I might be so sick.

I'm surprised Isabella hasn't latched onto it yet.

The thought reoccurs just as I'm forced to lean over the toilet again.

"I'm making you a doctor's appointment."

Isabella's voice from the doorway makes me jump, just as I'm reaching for a piece of toilet paper to wipe off my mouth. "You scared me," I gasp, standing up unsteadily, and she lets out a sigh.

"I knocked, but you didn't hear me. Elena, this is the eighth day straight I've heard you puking from the moment you wake up. You've got to go to the doctor."

"I hate doctors." I reach for the mouthwash, feeling exhausted. I also hate throwing up. I feel like every ounce of energy has been drained out of me.

"I know, but Elena—" Isabella runs one hand through her thick black hair, and I can see shadows under her eyes. It makes me feel guilty, because I don't think it's just from Aisling keeping her up. My niece is a surprisingly good baby—she sleeps through the night more often than not, from what I can tell. "When was your last period?"

There it is. I turn to see Isabella giving me a narrow look, and I know she's been hanging onto this question for a while, waiting to see if it needed asking. I guess, at this point, she's decided that it does.

I try to think. *Surely it hasn't been that long?* But I hadn't needed anything for it the entire time we were in Rio. I didn't need anything before then. I can't recall where I was in my cycle when Diego kidnapped me or when Levin and I finally—on the beach….

My cheeks flush red as I think of the many, many times we had sex without protection. I'd told myself it was fine every time, that surely it was harder to get pregnant than it seemed, that my mother had always said women needed to be in an exact point in their cycles to conceive, something she'd told us to keep in mind if we wanted to plan out the children we had with our husbands. And truthfully, at the moment—I had never been able to make myself care. The pleasure of the moment with Levin had always been what I wanted —the possible consequences were something for a future version of me to worry about.

Well, now you're that future version of yourself. And it's probably time to start worrying.

"Elena?" Isabella prompts, and my cheeks flush deeper. I hear her sigh, and I know she can see how hard I'm blushing. "Was it only the one time, on the beach? When you thought you weren't going to make it off?"

I should tell her yes. That we only did it once. That if my reason for puking every morning *is* the reason I'm most afraid of, it was because of one split-second decision made when we both thought we were going to die. But I take too long to answer, and my sister isn't an innocent virgin any longer, either. She knows enough to know what happened in Rio.

"I'm going to kill him," she says through gritted teeth. "Please tell me he at least bought condoms, when the two of you—"

My silence tells her everything she needs to know. When I finally find the nerve to look up at her, the furious expression in her eyes tells me that she's found another reason to be utterly and completely pissed at Levin.

"You've got to be *fucking* kidding me," she grinds out through her teeth. "He didn't use a fucking *condom*? Sweet Christ, Elena, he pulled out at least, right?"

"I really don't want to talk about this—" I'm blushing so hard it feels like my face is going to melt.

"It's past the point where you get to be shy about this." Isabella crosses her arms over her chest. "That time was when you were staying in hotel rooms with a man almost *twenty years older* than you—"

"Are *you* my mother now?" The words come out more sharply than I mean for them to, but I feel like warmed-over death, my stomach doing flips again despite the fact that there's absolutely nothing left in it for me to throw up. I'm so tired of Isabella hating Levin for something that I pushed him to, again and again, something that I wanted every bit as bad as he did, despite how convinced she seems to be that he must have taken advantage of me by virtue of his age and experience, no matter how much I had a say in it too.

"No," Isabella says tartly. "But it seems like you're about to be one."

The two of us face each other from opposite ends of the bathroom counter, and the silence stretches out for several long moments, the words hanging between us.

Isabella lets out a long breath finally. "I'm sorry, Elena," she says, leaning against the doorway. "It's just—this isn't what I wanted for you. You know it's not what our parents wanted for you when they sent you here. We're supposed to be talking about enrolling you in college classes in the fall and if you want to start going to yoga with me, not—"

"You hate yoga." I feel my lips twitch in what might be the start of a smile, and I wonder if I'm going to laugh or cry.

"I do hate yoga," Isabella admits. "But I hate cardio more, and after the baby—"

It's an absolutely ridiculous thing for her to say—she looks every bit as perfect as she always has, and from that one conversation I overheard between her and Niall, I'm certain he thinks the same. I look at her, feeling my eyes burn with the start of tears, wondering if, in eight or nine months, I'm going to be thinking the same thing.

Only I have no idea where Levin will be in that equation.

"We don't even know if it's really a thing yet," I say quietly. "I might just be sick. All that bad takeout food in Rio, all the anxiety—it could just all be catching up with me."

"Yeah." Isabella looks at me, her lips pressed together. "It could be that."

There's another of those heavy, drawn-out silences. "But," she continues finally, "we need to find out, one way or another."

"I don't want to go to the doctor—"

"Well, you might have to soon. But for now, we'll start with the more usual way of figuring this out." She motions for me to follow her. "Come on. We'll see if you can keep a smoothie down while we're at it. I'm starving. Niall doesn't have anywhere to be this morning; he can watch Aisling for a little while."

I get dressed while Isabella goes to tell Niall that we're going to go grab breakfast, promising not to say anything to him until we know one way or another. I feel like I'm in a daze as I fish out jean shorts and a t-shirt, part of a new wardrobe that Isabella helped me shop for just after I got here.

That whole experience had been the first time I'd felt really happy to be here. I'd managed to put Levin out of my head for almost an entire day while Isabella and I had gone out to lunch, shopped, and then met Niall for dinner, just the three of us, with a sitter at home to watch the baby. I'd tried on everything I liked without our mother there to suggest that any of it was too tight or too short, or too revealing. For the first time in my life, I'd gotten to pick out my clothes entirely on my own, without any input beyond what I asked for from Isabella.

Everything had felt strange at first, after spending all my life sheltered and mostly locked behind the high walls of our family compound, only going out in bulletproof SUVs with security and at least one of our parents, if not both. Isabella and I went out in her car, a white Mercedes that she said she bought shortly after she and Niall were married, without any kind of security. I'd asked her if it wasn't dangerous, and she laughed.

"It could be, I suppose," she said with a shrug. "But things have calmed down a lot here, and neither Niall nor I want to live feeling as if we're afraid all of the time. The truth is—accidents happen all of the time. They're just not targeted. But I could die in a car crash or a shooting at a mall or be mugged or any number of things that have nothing to do with Niall's job. If there's something that the Kings feel poses a threat, then we'll lock things down. Until then, I drive myself, and I go where I want, and I don't feel unsafe."

It had surprised me that Niall was fine with that, and that had made Isabella laugh, too. "He doesn't tell me what to do," she said. "We're a team, Elena. A partnership. We make decisions together. And this is one of them."

That idea had seemed so foreign to me. Our parents had what I would consider a decent enough marriage by the standards of the world we lived in, but it wasn't a partnership.

But in marrying Niall, Isabella subverted all of that. And she had told me to expect the same. "I know *Papa* probably told you that you might go home eventually," she said over lunch that day. "But as far as I'm concerned—and Niall feels the same way—you can and should stay here. You can go to college, pick a career, get married if and when you want to, to whomever you please. You can get your own apartment when you're ready. You can live your own life like I am. It's worth it, Elena, even if it's scary at first."

Her knock at my door startles me out of the memory. "Elena? Are you ready?"

"Almost! Hang on." I grab the soft red t-shirt I pulled out of the drawer and drag it on over my head, shoving my feet into a pair of sneakers. It's already getting to the point where it's sticky and humid in Boston for the summer, and I'm glad to be able to wear shorts.

When I come out, Isabella has changed out of the leggings she had on when she found me in the bathroom into jeans and a black tank top, her long hair tied up in a ponytail atop her head. I wonder for a moment if the change in outfit had something to do with Niall, if that's what took her so long, and I feel a sudden, unexpected flush of jealousy.

Not over Niall—he's attractive, but I would never have the slightest thought like *that* about my sister's husband, my brother-in-law. The jealousy is entirely centered around the thought of having someone like that at all—and not just someone, but the someone that I miss. I have a deep, aching sense of loss, of missing Levin, and not just what we had, but everything we *could* have had.

I'll never go find him on some random morning to tell him I'm going out for breakfast, only to have him delay me with kisses or more, stripping off my clothes so that when I go to meet whoever it is that I'm having breakfast with, I'm wearing something else altogether. I'll never share another quick, private moment with him, never have an even deeper intimacy than what we had before, the kind of intimacy that I imagine develops between husbands and wives over time.

Whatever chance we had at that is gone, along with him.

I follow Isabella out to the car, numbly buckling myself in, the buttery leather cool against the backs of my thighs. Isabella puts music on, something bright and cheery, but I barely hear it. All I can think about is that my life might be about to change forever, and Levin isn't here. He can't share in my worry and anxiety or help ease it, because he's hundreds of miles away, completely oblivious.

And *he* chose that, not me. I wanted him to stay. I would have wanted him to be here, right now.

Isabella takes us to the smoothie shop closest to the house, letting me stay in the air-conditioned car while she goes in. "I know what you'll probably be able to keep down," she tells me, disappearing inside while I sit there, trying to calm my riotous thoughts.

Would I actually have done anything differently, if I thought this was how it was going to turn out? I try to imagine myself *not* trying to spend as many nights in bed with Levin as I could, or asking him to buy condoms, a thing that would have almost certainly brought him to his senses and stopped any chance of anything more happening between us. Our entire relationship was predicated on the idea that every time we slept together, it wasn't going to happen again. Buying condoms would have suggested that it *was* going to happen again, any number of times, and Levin would have simply—not.

You could have asked him to pull out. My face flames red again at that, imagining Levin inside of me, the sound of his groan in my ear as he came close to the edge, the way he would bury himself inside of me as if he couldn't get close enough, and I know there was never any chance of that. Again, everything between us always happened because he lost control—and I wanted to make him lose it. Regaining that control would have stopped everything.

My eyes fill with tears, and I hastily wipe them away as Isabella returns with two smoothies, handing me one of them. It looks green, and I peer at it suspiciously.

"It's green tea and almond milk," she says reassuringly. "It settled my stomach a lot when I was pregnant with Aisling, believe it or not. It might work for you, too."

I sip at it tentatively as Isabella drives us to the drugstore. By the time we're there, it's patently clear that green tea smoothies are *not* the solution to my upset stomach. I end up in the bathroom, once again throwing up while Isabella looks for pregnancy tests. When I emerge, I feel dizzy and weak-kneed, and I wonder how anyone manages to reproduce if the process is this miserable.

Isabella glances at me as she puts two boxes into the basket she's holding, and I see a flicker of sympathy on her face. "I think you're having a harder time than I did. But if it is what we're hoping it's not, then it will get better. I promise."

I can't even respond. I'm too busy trying to convince my stomach that everything I've consumed today has already come back up, and there's no point in continuing to press the issue.

The store clerk has a very knowing expression as she rings us up, looking at the boxes, and then at my pale face and red-rimmed eyes. It feels a little condescending, and I think Isabella feels the same way, because she shoves her card at the woman pointedly, giving her a look that clearly says we're in a hurry. Which we are, because I can feel my throat tightening up again, and if I'm going to vomit again, I'd rather do it in Isabella's guest bathroom that smells like lavender and has a rug on the tile floor.

"You said the smoothies were fine when you were pregnant," I protest weakly as we go back out to the car. "So maybe it *is* just a stomach bug since I can't keep *anything* down."

"We'll find out soon enough," Isabella says darkly as she starts the car.

I don't want to take the tests with her hovering over me, as well-intentioned as I know her worry is. I know she's trying to take care of me in the absence of our mother, that she's trying to be a good older sister and protect me. But I need some time with my own thoughts before I can handle anyone else's.

"Can you wait somewhere else while I do this?" I ask her as we stand in the hall, the plastic bag containing the boxes in my hand. "I just—I need some privacy."

Isabella presses her lips together. "Won't you need help figuring it out? I mean, I've done it before—"

"I can manage. Just—please. You can come check on me in a little while. I need to do this by myself."

What I don't say, because I know what her reaction would be, is that the only person I want waiting with me while I find out whether or not I'm pregnant is Levin. But he's hundreds of miles away—and he made it very clear that he doesn't think I should contact him again.

The act of getting ready to take the test is oddly comforting. There's an intensity to it, a means of focusing on something other than my own anxiety as I read the instructions. It's simple enough. I tell myself that it's nothing, that I just drank some bad water in Rio, or I picked up the flu from someone else—even though if it was the flu, surely someone else in the house would be sick by now. I take the test, and then I stand at the sink, staring down at it as if I can convince it to be negative just by wishing hard enough.

One pink line appears almost instantly. I sink my teeth into my lower lip, willing that to be it. Willing it not to change further.

And then another line appears.

It doesn't seem real at first. I convince myself that it's not real, that it must be an error. A bad test. There are two boxes in the drugstore bag, four tests total, and I take all of them before I find myself sitting on the tile floor in front of the same sink, the tests scattered around me, all of them with the same result.

Added up, eight pink lines in total. All of them are bright and clear and without the slightest doubt.

I'm pregnant.

Tears well up in my eyes, both from the shock and complete unknown of it as well as the sharp, piercing knowledge that Levin isn't here. He'll find out at some point—whatever my decision is, I'll need to let him know. I can't go my whole life keeping that a secret from him, even if I never see him again, and I don't want to. I *want* to tell him. But we'll never have the moment where I open the door and show him the result, for good or for ill. There was no chance of him standing in the bathroom with me, watching the lines appear.

For this, I'm all alone.

I know I won't be, whatever comes. If I want to keep the baby, Isabella will help me. Niall will tell me to stay for as long as I want or need to. I have family here, safety, security, and support. It's more than a lot of girls my age, in my position, with the kinds of expectations my family had for me would have. I know I'm lucky. If I had wanted Isabella in here with me, she would have been.

But I wanted Levin. And he's the only thing I can't have.

I crack the door open a little and call for Isabella. A few moments later, I hear her footsteps hurrying down the hall, and then she pushes the door open, looking down at me with her hair starting to come out of her ponytail, a little loose around her face.

"Elena—" She starts to say my name, as if to ask me the question that I know she's been waiting to ask for half an hour now, and then she sees the look on my face and the tests scattered around me. "Oh, Elena."

That's what does it—what tips me over the edge into tears. I let out a small, strangled sob, tears welling up in my eyes and spilling down my cheeks. Isabella instantly comes into the bathroom, shutting the door behind her and sinking down onto the floor next to me, her hand wrapping around mine.

She sits there with me for several long moments in silence, her thumb rubbing back and forth against the back of my hand, while I cry. I cry and cry, until I feel entirely wrung out, even more so than I had this morning. Then I wipe my other hand across my face, blowing my nose as Isabella hands me a wad of tissue.

"Let's go sit down somewhere more comfortable," she says finally, "and we'll figure out what to do."

I don't realize that Niall is still home until we go out to the living room, and I catch a glimpse of him in the kitchen as we pass, Aisling in her high chair as he feeds her bites of cereal. I wince, because I don't really want him to know about this yet, but there's nothing for it now. He's going to find out—and he would have eventually, anyway, so I don't suppose it really matters.

Isabella goes to the living room with me, sitting me down on the couch. "It's going to be okay," she tells me, squeezing my hand. "I'll be back in a minute."

I think she means for me to not hear their conversation, but it's hard not to, as angry as she is. I can tell that she's trying to keep her voice down, but Isabella has never been good at hiding her emotions or keeping them in check.

"You need to tell him to get the *fuck* back to Boston," I hear her hiss angrily. "He…irresponsible…now Elena…*kidding* me?"

I only catch snippets, but it's enough to guess at what she's saying and just how pissed she is. Even Niall has a terse edge to his voice, but I hear him trying to reassure her, to talk her down.

"How do you think Aisling got here, lass? We weren't exactly careful, either–"

"*Stop* making this about us! This is about my *sister*, and that man was meant to protect her. You and I were never—"

Her voice lowers then, and I don't hear what comes after that, but frustration wells up in me, mingled with the aching sadness that seems to have settled into a yawning pit in my chest.

When I had thought about what it would be like to have children, I had determined that I wanted to be a good mother. But I hadn't really ever thought about what that would look like. What it would *mean*.

Isabella's voice is still raised, telling Niall to call Levin *today*, not to tell him why, just to get him here so that I can tell him myself. It's what I want, I think—to tell Levin in person, but I'm still more than a little annoyed that Isabella didn't actually ask me. She just decided that was how he should find out.

It doesn't matter. You have bigger things to worry about right now than your sister being a know-it-all.

Like what I'm going to do.

"We'll figure this out." Isabella's voice from behind me makes me jump, as if she read my mind. "You obviously can stay here for as long as you want or need. If you want to stay here forever, well, then Aisling will just grow up with her little cousin. It's going to be okay, Elena. I'll take care of you."

My eyes well up with tears all over again–tears that I really thought would have run dry by now–both because for all my sister's high-handedness, I appreciate her being here for me, and because as much as I *do* appreciate it, it's not her that I want taking care of me right now.

I want Levin.

"Niall is going to call him," Isabella says, once again as if she's read my thoughts, coming to sit down next to me. "He'll be here just as soon as he can get on a plane, if he knows what's good for him. And then the two of you can have a talk."

She squeezes my hand, leaning back on the couch next to me, and goes blessedly silent for a moment. I want the quiet, the chance to try to unravel my racing thoughts, but it doesn't do much good. I have no idea what comes next.

A part of me, a small, secret part that I can't admit to anyone, feels a thrill at the idea of him coming back. I want to see him again more than anything in the world. Before today, I would have said that I'd give anything, do anything to make that happen.

Now, I might change that to almost anything. The thought of seeing Levin walk through the front door, here to see me, sends a flush of excitement through me like the buzzing of electricity, turning me into a live wire of anxiety and anticipation.

But this wasn't how I wanted it to happen. This wasn't what I wanted the reason to be for us seeing each other again—something that makes him have to come back. If he came back for me, I wanted it to be because he couldn't stay away. Because he needs me as much as I need him.

What if this could change things? What if this could make it so that we can be together—so he can see that we could be happy?

As soon as I think it, I push it away. I don't want him to think that I somehow did this on purpose, that I ignored everything he ever told me about how he couldn't commit to someone again after losing his wife, about what I learned from Vasquez that his child died with her, that I didn't care about any of that and instead decided to make sure I could have what I wanted.

I don't want us to be together because he thinks he doesn't have any other choice. But if we could be—

I don't really think Levin will see this as some kind of trap—but I feel embarrassed anyway, for not anticipating it, for letting myself pretend that we could keep being reckless without there ever being a consequence. Even as innocent as I am, I knew better. I just didn't let myself think about it. I wanted him more than I wanted to be smart about what we were doing.

I should have guessed this would happen. It feels like a shock, but I know it shouldn't. We weren't careful, not even once. And I was an idiot to think I'd get away with it scot-free.

I just never imagined that this was how the story was going to end.

Levin

"I didn't have any intention of coming back to Boston for a while—"

I'd picked up the phone immediately when Niall called, assuming it had either something to do with Elena or Kings' business—unsure which one I hoped it was. I wanted to hear about Elena, but something told me that he wouldn't call unless something was wrong, especially considering her sister's opinion of me. From the tone of his voice, I have a feeling that's the case—especially since he won't actually tell me what's going on.

"You need to get here." Niall's voice has a touch of urgency in it that I rarely hear, and it sends a wave of unease through me.

Is Elena alright? The question is on the tip of my tongue, and I have to bite it back. Asking so urgently would only raise suspicions that won't do either of us any good. If it is about her, I'll find out shortly. Not the time to drop the poker face, Volkov.

"Is there a problem?" I sit down heavily on my couch, looking at the stack of files staring at me from across the coffee table. So far, over the past weeks, Viktor has taken my recommendations and given me new ones to peruse without actually giving me much to *do*. I've spent some time training recruits at the firing range and on the martial arts floor in the gym, but it hasn't approached the rigorous schedule I used to keep. I know he thinks I need a break, but it's been too long. I'm ready to be finished with the vacation part of my return to New York.

"Things aren't good," Niall says darkly. "Just—come to Boston, Levin. The first plane you can grab. Hell, Viktor's plane, if he'll let you. You need to be here."

"Is this Kings' business? If so, I should tell Viktor what's going on—"

"It doesn't concern him. You'll get your questions answered. Just *get* here, alright?"

It's not like Niall to be so cagey. I feel certain it has to do with Elena, which leaves me with a sick pit in my stomach as I hang up and go about starting to book a flight—I'm not about to ask Viktor for the use of his plane and deal with all the questions that would go along with that, especially since I don't actually have any answers. I know Niall well, and his manner has me feeling as if all my fears have been confirmed.

Is she sick? Something worse? I know it was difficult for her to accept that I was leaving, but I was certain that she would get over it in time. More quickly than she thought, even. Boston is a huge city, full of diversions, friends for her to make and men for her to date, and although the thought of her with anyone else for a dinner out made me feel possessively, furiously angry, let alone—

I cut off that thought before it can go any further, as I have every time it's come up over the past weeks. I have no right to jealousy, no right to think of Elena as anyone other than someone in my past, who has every right to a future of her own. Certainly not someone I get to be possessive over. Not when she was never really mine—and I made that clear to her.

It can't be about Elena. I tell myself that it must be some Kings' business as I throw clothes into a duffel, something that Niall has been told not to talk about over the phone, something that is being kept quiet until I can speak to the McGregors in person. I ignore the voice in the back of my head that tells me that if that were the case, if it were business that important, either Connor or Liam would have called me themselves, not delegated it to Niall. That if it were that important, they likely wouldn't have called me at all and would have gone straight to Viktor.

I ignore it, because if it's not about the Kings, then it's about Elena —and if something is that serious, then she's either horribly sick, or...

It can't be that. But even as I think it, I know it can.

We weren't careful. And if it is that, it's entirely my fault.

The thought haunts me all the way to Boston. I tell myself over and over that it can't possibly be, that Niall will meet me and take me to talk with Connor and Levin, that this is business—but I can't shake the feeling in my gut.

It only gets worse when Niall greets me with a serious expression, his face warning me that whatever this is about, he meant it when he said on the phone that it wasn't good.

"We're going to the house," he tells me without preamble as we head out to the car. "And be warned, Isabella is *pissed* with you. She has been, ever since she found out—"

"Since she found out what?" I demand, feeling that knot of dread in my stomach again. Isabella finding out about my relationship with Elena would be bad enough, but this feels worse. Niall wouldn't drag me all the way to Boston over Isabella finding out that I slept with her sister, unless Connor is actually that furious about it, and it's both something having to do with Elena and Kings' business.

Niall glances toward me. There's no judgment in his expression; I hadn't expected that there would be. After all, he and Isabella weren't meant to be together, either. He'd fallen for her by accident, without realizing who she was, and their road to a happily ever after had been as fraught as most of the couples I know, however happy they are now. But I can see from the look on his face that he's concerned.

"You should have told me," he says finally as we get into the car. "I could have—I don't know. Warned Isabella ahead of time. Prepared her so if it did come out—if Elena told her, it wouldn't be such a shock."

"She didn't want anyone to know." I stare out the window at the city as it goes by, lighting up the darkness. "She covered for me with Connor—I think he picked up that something was going on. She told him nothing had happened between us. That made me think she wanted to keep it between us."

"So you just left." There's still no judgment in Niall's voice—it's a flat statement of fact, but I can tell he doesn't entirely approve of how I handled things. "As I recall, you headed out so early we weren't even up yet."

"I thought it was better that way, for Elena. I had already said goodbye to her, the night before that. I didn't want to put her through another one."

Niall nods silently, as if he's considering that. "You know," he says finally, "you still could have talked to me. I've had my own share of —questionable entanglements."

I know what he's referring to. There had been a time when he'd been in love with the woman who is now Connor's wife, when they had very nearly had something together, back when Connor and Saoirse were nothing but a marriage of convenience. I remember very well how difficult that had been for him. "It's not the same," I say quietly. "Saoirse was older. A woman who knew her own mind. And Isabella—"

"I think Elena knows her own mind just as well as either of them," Niall says wryly. "But I also think you already know that."

He pulls up in front of the house, and I see the warm light flooding out from the windows, out across the lawn. It looks soft and homey, like an embrace in structural form, and I feel a strange sort of longing in my chest, one that I haven't had in a long time.

Lidiya and I never had a house like that. We never got that far. The bed I found her dead in was in an apartment we shared together, one that we had shared since the day we got back from Tokyo, and I went to make things right with Vladimir. She had spent that first day apartment hunting in Moscow—*something to take her mind off of worrying about me*, she had said. When I came back home that evening with a bloody nose but fewer fears about recrimination, she had shown me the glossy pamphlet with pictures of the high rise that would eventually become our home.

We had talked a number of times about buying a house. When she told me about the baby, the idea of it started to feel more like a reality. Like something we should actually do—a place meant for raising a family, instead of the crisp and architectural apartment we lived in at the time. We had imagined what it might look like, talked about whether we wanted to stay near Moscow or go somewhere else altogether. We had talked about moving closer to her grandmother, far from the city, somewhere peaceful and quiet. I had told her I was leaving the Syndicate. We could do that. It wouldn't matter anymore. I could live whatever life I wanted—whatever life *we* wanted.

And then I came home to sheets drenched in blood, and I knew that was always a fool's dream for me. There would be no cozy house, no nursery, no home that we would make together.

That was never written in the cards for me.

What if it could be now?

The thought sends a flood of guilt through me as I walk into the house after Niall, towards the living room. I see the tops of both Elena and Isabella's heads over the sofa, and then I see Isabella turn, her face sharpening instantly when she sees me.

She gets up immediately, crossing the room before Niall and I can walk in, standing in the doorway. "I'm glad to see you made it so quickly," she says crisply. "I thought it might take you a lot longer to make your way here."

"Why would it?" I frown at her, trying not to rise to the bait. "I don't even know what's going on, Isabella. Niall was very circumspect in his information. He just told me to get here as soon as I could, and since he's not in the habit of asking me to do things like that frivolously, that's what I did."

"Well, you're about to find out." Isabella crosses her arms over her chest. "It's not exactly the sort of thing you should hear over the phone. Of course, it shouldn't have happened at *all*—"

My gut clenches at that, and Niall steps forward, putting his arm through his wife's and guiding her out of the doorway. "Let him talk to Elena," he says quietly, and I glance into the room, seeing Elena still sitting stock-still on the couch.

The moment I step through the door, she turns, and her entire face lights up when she sees me. Whatever is wrong, whatever it is that I've been brought here to find out, it's as if it doesn't exist for a moment. There's an expression of such absolute happiness on her face for that brief moment that I feel a wave of guilt for having ever left her—and an equally strong following wave of it for having made her feel this way about me at all, knowing I couldn't return it.

She gets up from the couch, making a beeline for me, and I see her face crumple as she reaches me, flinging her arms around my neck. Her cheek presses against my chest, and my arms go around her automatically, holding her to me as I feel a shudder go through her.

My first instinct is always to protect her, no matter what. That has never changed, and never will change.

I just wish I knew what I was going to need to protect her from, this time.

I realize after a moment that she's crying. I can feel her tears seeping through my shirt, and I hold her for a moment before gently steering her toward the couch and sitting down with her.

"What's wrong?" I ask her, my hand reaching to wrap around hers, and Elena looks up at me, bright-eyed with tears, as her mouth opens, but no sound comes out.

"You can tell me." I'm very aware of Isabella and Niall somewhere near the back of the room, but I don't look to see where they are. Something tells me that Elena needs all of my focus to be on her right now, whatever it is that's happening.

"I–" She swallows hard, and her hand tightens around mine, her nails biting into the back of it. "I'm—"

I know what she's going to say before she finishes the sentence. I don't hear it entirely at first, the blood roaring in my ears as my heartbeat speeds up past what's probably healthy, and then she repeats it, in the same small, watery voice, as if she can't quite believe it either.

"I'm pregnant."

"What do you need from me?" The words come out automatically, before it can fully sink in. I don't know how long something like this *takes* to sink in. I don't feel as if it's real, but from the look on Elena's face, it very much is. "Whatever you need from me, I'll do. What do *you* want to do?" This feels a little like the times I've been in shock from an injury—I'm technically aware of what's happening, but none of it really feels like it's sinking in. My mind immediately clicks into gear, trying to figure out what's needed, how to solve it, shutting emotion out of the equation.

It's what I've been trained to do, but I don't think they had this sort of circumstance in mind when I was taught these lessons.

"Did you hear me?" Elena looks at me curiously. "I'm pregnant, Levin."

I let out a sharp breath. "I heard you. That doesn't change what I said—what do you need? Whatever kind of support you need from me—"

"You're not angry?" She bites her lower lip, and it's my turn to stare at her.

"Elena, why would I be angry? It's my fault. I—"

"It's not your fault." Her voice is sharp, vehement. "I wanted you. I came on to you, over and over. You remember that night—"

Someone clears their throat somewhere in the back of the room, and Elena breaks off, her cheeks flushing. "I wanted you," she whispers again. "I convinced you. It's not your fault—"

I can hear the *hmph* noise that Isabella makes from where she's standing.

"Be that as it may," I tell her gently, "I was responsible for you. For your well-being. Even if I didn't turn you down—and we can argue later about whether I should have or not—I should have been more careful. That was my responsibility to you, Elena, and I failed you."

The guilt I feel as I tell her that is immense. I've thought it many times before—that I was irresponsible, that I could have protected us both from these potential consequences and didn't—but saying it out loud sends it crashing over me anew. It strikes me fully just how irresponsible I was. How I've potentially taken the future that I fought so hard for her to have away from her, out of my own selfishness and lust.

It's unconscionable.

"You're not happy about this, though, are you?" Her teeth worry at her lower lip. "I remember what Vasquez said to you. About your baby—"

I don't hear if there's a reaction to that or not from our own personal peanut gallery of Niall and Isabella. The blood rushes in my ears again, both from the unpleasant memory of speaking with

Vasquez and the thought of Lidiya and our child. My chest aches, the pain as sharp and fresh as if it just happened, and I feel a fresh torrent of guilt for the one moment when Elena said she was pregnant, and I *did* feel happy. Before it started to sink in, there was no guilt or worry or shock, just happiness.

It's not that I've always been against the idea of a wife, or children, or a family. But long before Lidiya, I knew I lived a life that wasn't conducive to it. Letting myself believe otherwise led to tragedy. And now—

Now I know I don't deserve it.

"What matters is what you want," I tell her as delicately as I can, and I see her face fall a little. I know she was hoping for a different response, but I'm not going to lie to her. There's no picket fence in our future, no picture-perfect family. "Whatever you choose, Elena, that's what we'll do. This is up to you."

"I don't know if Elena has had enough time to think about it," Isabella interjects, and I feel Elena flinch.

"I do know what I want to do." Her voice is quiet but firm, and her hand tightens around mine. "I want to keep the baby."

I can't begin to untangle the emotions that flood me at that. I don't know where to start—what part I can play in all of this that could possibly make her happy and be the best thing for our child. Right now, I feel as if the best thing for both of them would be if I disappeared and were never seen again. But I know Elena won't want that—and if I'm being honest, neither do I.

The thought of another man with her was hard enough to stomach, but I'd forced myself to live with it, knowing she deserved better. The idea of another man raising my child–our child–feels unbearable.

So I settle on the one thing I know I *can* do—be there for her. I don't have to understand how I feel, or even decide what I'm going to do yet, in order to do that.

"Alright then," I tell her calmly. "Then that's what you'll do. And I'll do whatever you ask of me."

Niall clears his throat, closer to where the two of us are this time. "You know what you need to do," he tells me pointedly, and it's the closest I think Niall has ever come to giving me an ultimatum—or even direct advice.

I know what he's talking about. And despite the fact that I know he's right—that it's the honorable thing to do, the only thing to do if I'm going to keep my word and protect her, be there for her—I feel an instant and immediate aversion to the idea.

I swore I'd never get married again. The thought of it feels like a worse betrayal of Lidiya than anything I've done so far—worse than wanting Elena for herself and not just for the pleasure she offered me, worse than the fact that I didn't want to leave her, worse than the feelings that I have for her that I refuse to put a name to and make them a reality.

I've stepped over line after line—but making vows to another woman was one I never planned to cross. Not for anything.

Elena looks between Niall and me, her expression confused. "I don't understand. What are you talking about? What does he need to do?"

Niall lets out a long breath. "He's going to marry you, lass."

Elena

"Marry me to *who?*" I ask in a startled rush, before the words sink in, and I realize what Niall meant. I look at Levin, wide-eyed. "Wait. *We're* going to get married?"

"It's what he's suggesting," Levin says slowly. "And he's right. It's what we should do, Elena. It's what I should do for you, to do right by you."

He says it as if it's the most obvious thing in the world. And maybe it should be, considering how I was raised—but I hadn't even considered it. All I'd been able to think about was how Levin would react to the news about the baby. I hadn't gotten to anything else.

It takes me a moment to be able to speak again. I'm torn between feeling utterly amazed that Levin is so willing to even consider being whatever I need at this moment that he's considering doing the *exact opposite* of what he'd been so insistent on, and wondering why he's even entertaining the possibility of changing his mind so quickly. I feel like everything I'd expected has been turned upside down.

It's not that I expected he would be angry or cruel. I know Levin could never be that. But I thought he might be upset. That he might suggest I not keep the baby. That he would place the blame equally on me, if not more so.

But he hasn't done any of that, and I don't know how to react. I wasn't prepared for this.

"Can we have a little time alone?" I ask, glancing at Niall and Isabella. "Please? I–I need to talk to Levin alone."

"Of course," Niall says gruffly, before Isabella can say anything. "You're not our ward, lass. You and Levin can discuss how you want to go about this." He reaches over, clapping Levin on the shoulder, and then he turns back to Isabella, his hand on the small of my sister's back as he guides her out of the room.

"Just give them time," I hear him say quietly to her, and then they're both gone.

Levin turns back to face me. His face is still and silent, and his hand is still wrapped around mine. It hasn't moved since he sat down.

"You don't have to marry me," I say in a small voice.

"I don't *have* to," he agrees. "Although I think your father might have some demands in that regard. But Niall is right, Elena. It is the right thing to do."

The right thing to do. Not what he wants to do, just what he should do. I can hear what's not being said just as loudly as if he'd spoken it. "I know you don't want to get married again. Not after—"

Levin pauses, as if he's considering what to say next. "I'm not sure that what I want factors into this, Elena. This is your choice. I made mine when I took you to bed without taking the consequences into account. Now I need to do whatever's necessary to make that right. You say you want our baby. Now I need to know what else you want. You could raise our child here, with your sister and brother-in-law to help, and you could allow me to be as much a part of it or not as you choose. Or you could tell me that you want marriage, and if we do that, then I'll be here for all of it. Well," he amends. "I'll be here for all of it regardless, if that's what you want. As for marriage—that's…"

He trails off, as if he's unsure how to finish the sentence, but I think I understand. He doesn't want to hurt me, and saying outright that he doesn't want to get married would only be another knife in my heart. But I know very well that he doesn't. That if this baby weren't a reality, I would likely have never heard from him again.

But I also think that if I say that I want our baby to have him here as a father and as my husband, as a nuclear family with paperwork to bind us together, he'll do it. He'll do anything if it means making what he sees as another mistake in a long list of them right.

I don't think Levin understands how well I know him, after the time we spent together. I might not know everything about him, all the fine details that make up a person, but I've seen into parts of him that I think I understand very clearly now. And what I don't know is if telling him that I do want him to marry me is taking advantage of him in some way—taking advantage of his guilt and sense of honor to trap him into something that might never make either one of us happy.

Is that what I want to do? I don't know what I want. It's as if everything I thought I wanted is being handed to me on a silver platter—but in all the wrong ways. I hadn't envisioned myself marrying Levin—I just wanted to be with him. The end result of that hadn't mattered to me, so long as we were together. I'm sure I would have wanted that, in time, but now—

"Do you love me?" The words come out small, quiet, in no small part because I think I already know the answer.

He takes a breath, and I close my eyes. For a moment, I'm not sure I can look at him. I don't want to see the truth on his face any more than I want to hear it.

"It has to be enough that I'm willing to consider marrying you," he says gently, his hand still around mine. I have the sudden urge to pull it away, but I don't. I have the feeling that if I do, he might not touch me again, and I don't want that, either. "I said I would never get married again, Elena. I meant that. If I choose to do it anyway, because I care for you, it's because–

"–it's the right thing to do," I finish for him, hating the hint of bitterness in my voice but unable to keep it out. "You *care* for me. You don't love me."

"Elena." There's a hint of pleading in his voice that I've never heard before. "I meant what I said the night before I left. I would still mean it, if things hadn't changed. It would be better for you if we weren't together. You would get over me, eventually. But things *have* changed. And if you want this baby, if that's your choice–" He lets out a long, slow breath, as if he's come to a decision within himself. "If you feel like it's what you want—then we should get married. I should be there for both of you. There's not anyone who won't agree with me. Niall has already said so. Your father will feel the same, as will Connor and Liam–"

"So all of the *men* will agree with you." Now I do pull my hand away, knotting both of them together in my lap, feeling my nails bite into my palms. "I wonder what my sister would have to say about it. My mother—"

"I don't know your mother well enough to say," Levin says slowly. "But I think I know what your sister's answer would be." He takes a deep, slow breath. "The only answer that matters to me, Elena, is yours. I won't force you to do anything. I will only do what you want me to."

"You can't do that." The words come out as a small, desperate whisper, and I hate myself for them as soon as I hear it, because it feels pathetic. "You can't love me, and that's what I want."

"You don't love me." He sounds so sure, so certain. "You don't, Elena. You love a fantasy that was created in a very trying time for both of us. You love a version of us that existed in a circumstance that doesn't any longer. You don't know me—the day-to-day version of me—well enough to love me."

I swallow hard. "You can tell yourself that if it makes you feel better. I *know* how I feel."

Neither of us says anything for a long moment. The offer hovers between us—Levin's proposal that isn't really a proposal at all. A marriage of circumstance, much like the kind of marriage I would have been pushed into at home, if I'd stayed.

Except this is so much worse.

"What does that look like?" I ask softly. "You being a father to this child, us getting married—what does that look like to you? You live and work in New York; I'm here. Where would we live? What would we do? I—"

"Well—" Levin lets out a slow breath. "What do you want?"

It's never been so hard for me to be asked that question. I should be thrilled that he's asking it, that he's taking my opinion so much into consideration. No one else ever has. But at this moment, I have no fucking idea what I want—and the things I *do* know, some of them I can't have.

I want to keep my—*our*—baby. That is a decision I can make.

I want Levin to love me. That, I can't choose for him.

I want him to stay—and he's offering that, but with terms that make my heart twist in my chest with a fresh, aching pain.

"I want to stay in Boston," I say softly. "Isabella is here. The only family that I can be close to. My niece is here. I wouldn't know anyone in New York other than you."

Levin nods, as if it's the easiest thing in the world for him to agree, to give me what I've asked for. Everything except the one thing I want the most.

I think I would move to New York, if he said he loved me. If he meant it and gave me that to hold onto.

"Viktor and I will have to work some things out," he says. "But it can be arranged. It's not as if it's that far, anyway. I may have to go to New York for work sometimes, but I have access to plenty of ways to make that a quick and easy trip. If you want our home base to be here in Boston, near your family, then that's what we'll do."

Just like that. I look at him, feeling as if I'm entirely adrift. As if I have no idea what to hold onto.

"So we're getting married?" I ask in a small voice, and he hesitates, then nods.

"Unless you want to tell me no," he says gently. "I will never force you to do anything. But yes, I–I think that's what we should do."

It's not the proposal I always dreamed of. I can hear the hesitation in his voice even now. But the truth is—I never really dreamed of one at all. I never imagined a world in which I chose who I married. So I'm not sure that it really matters.

If I'm going to have this baby, then Levin should be a part of it—especially if he *wants* to be a part of it. And that appears to mean getting married.

"Alright." I stand up, a little unsteadily, feeling my heart beating in my throat. "We're getting married, then."

I can't read the emotion on Levin's face as he stands up, too. I can't tell if it's happiness or not. I can't tell whether it's regret, worry, or just resignation. He reaches for my hands, and for one brief, wild moment, I think he's going to kiss me.

I want to kiss him. I look up at his chiseled face, at those lips that I know so well, that have been all over every inch of my body, and I want to kiss him so badly it hurts. I'm *aching* to touch him, and I take a step forward, trying to close the distance between us. It seems like a proposal, even one like this, should end with a kiss.

He steps back. "I need to go back to New York," he says, clearing his throat. "I have a hotel for the night—I didn't expect that your sister's hospitality would extend to me any longer, after what Niall said about her feelings towards me, and I didn't want to put him in the position of offering anyway. I'll be going back in the morning, but you'll have my number. Call me or text me if you need *anything*, Elena. I mean it. Anything at all."

His hands are still holding mine, but I feel cold. I hear what he's saying, but I can't get past the fact that a moment ago, I tried to kiss him—and a moment ago, he pulled away. Backed up, as if touching me that intimately would burn him.

"I'll be back for your first doctor's appointment," he assures me. "And whatever kind of wedding you decide you want, I'll make sure it's paid for. Whatever you and Isabella plan. Big, small, it doesn't matter. You have free rein, Elena." He pauses, looking down at me, and I can tell he means it. The problem is—that doesn't matter to me. A wedding doesn't matter. He's promising me all the wrong things.

"Whatever makes you happy, I'll do," he says softly. I can tell he means that too—or at least, he thinks he does.

The problem is—the thing that would make me happiest, he can't give me.

And it seems like he never will.

Elena

My sister is the furthest thing from thrilled about the wedding that I can imagine, but she tries to rally. "What do you want to tell our parents?" she asks me over breakfast the next morning, between eating bites of her own and spooning bites of cereal into Aisling's mouth. "You're marrying *Levin*. The man they sent you off with to protect you and bring you here. They're not going to be thrilled, especially since it's a shotgun wedding."

"Do we have to tell them that?" I can't eat. I know it's all going to come right back up, and I'm beyond exhausted.

Saying I didn't sleep the night before is an understatement. I laid awake, thinking about Levin. About the idea of being married to him, having a child with him—what all of that *means*. It doesn't feel real, even now. None of it does. I press my hand against my stomach, and it feels like something someone else made up.

I feel like I'm trapped on an awful merry-go-round of emotion. I think of the fact that I'm marrying Levin, and I feel a rush of excitement, of happiness. He came back. We're going to be together forever. And then I remember why, that he's marrying me out of hesitant obligation and nothing more. That if it weren't for our baby, which also makes me feel torn between excitement and fearful dread, Levin would have never come back from New York.

"If we don't," Isabella says flatly, "they're never going to agree to you marrying him. You get that, right? The *only* reason they're going to go along with it is because you're pregnant."

It's as if she heard everything I was thinking and decided to twist the knife deeper. I know she doesn't mean to hurt me, though, and I also know she's right. Levin isn't the sort of man my father would agree to me marrying. He doesn't fit the requirements for the kind of man that my father would arrange a marriage to, and he's not the kind of man that they would understand me marrying as my own choice. The baby is the only reason that they'll say yes.

I could do it anyway—but the consequences of that aren't worth it, not just to avoid the awkwardness of admitting why I'm marrying him.

"What about the wedding itself?" she continues, glancing over at me. "You should have a big wedding. This is your only chance to experience that."

"You didn't have a big wedding," I point out, and Isabella lets out a huff of frustration.

"Stop comparing all of this to me," she says firmly. "This is nothing like my relationship with Niall, and your wedding doesn't need to be small because mine was. Small is what Niall and I wanted. *You*, on the other hand—"

"What if I want a small wedding? What if Levin wants one?"

"Levin will want whatever you want," Isabella says, with a vehemence that tells me not to argue with her. "What do *you* want?"

"I don't know. I don't think I—"

"I think you deserve a big wedding. After everything you've been through, under these circumstances—you deserve that. Something to be excited about, something to plan…and a day that's about you. One that you can make however you want—"

"I don't think that's what I want." I keep my voice as calm as I can, trying not to get frustrated or emotional. "I think—why don't we compromise? We'll do something in between. Not just going to the courthouse—we'll get married in a church, we can shop for a dress, all of that. But not a huge wedding, either. I don't want to have to talk to a bunch of people I don't know and pretend that this is all perfect. I don't want to have to put on a show for a crowd—that doesn't sound like the kind of wedding I would want even if this were—"

I break off, feeling my throat catch. *If this were real*, I almost said—but it is real. All of it is real, just not in the way I hoped.

"We'll make dress shopping our first priority, then," Isabella says firmly. "Along with reserving a date for the church. Niall can talk to Father Callahan." She stands up, gathering my plate and hers as she leans down, kissing me lightly on the top of the head. "I'm going to make sure you have a wedding that will make you happy."

Even if I don't like who you're marrying. She doesn't have to say it aloud for me to know what she was thinking. But the fact that she's participating at all, rather than simply leaving me to it and glowering at Levin and me throughout the entire process, is something.

Out of everything I might want for my wedding, being able to share it with my sister is something that does matter to me. Isabella has been difficult throughout all of this. Still, I love her, and I know her protectiveness is because she loves me too. I want her to be a part of this, to help me. I want her with me through all of this; it's why I insisted we stay in Boston.

We end up going to a bridal salon that afternoon. "This is the same place I bought my dress," Isabella tells me, her voice bright and cheerful as she shifts Aisling onto one hip and pushes the door open. "Anything you want, you can try on here. They have so many options. An overwhelming amount, actually." She smiles brighter as a pretty woman with long, straight blonde hair approaches us. "Madison! You're here."

"Isabella!" The woman smiles at her, turning her attention immediately to Aisling and cooing at the baby. "And this is—"

"This is my sister, Elena." Isabella nudges me forward. "She's getting married. Elena, Madison helped me pick out my dress. She's fantastic; she'll help you figure out exactly what you want."

I see Madison's gaze flick to my left hand, but if she's confused by the lack of a ring, she doesn't show it. "Where are you getting married?" she asks, and I let out a quick breath, relieved for a question I can actually answer easily.

"The Cathedral of the Holy Cross," I tell her, and her eyes widen.

"You need an *outstanding* dress then for that venue! Something fit for a princess, with a train—"

"It's not a big wedding," I amend quickly, before she can get too excited. "Just a few family members and close friends and colleagues. We—compromised on the venue."

"It might not be a big wedding, but you should fit your surroundings!" Madison beams at me. "Why don't I bring you a few options in different styles? Something grand, something a bit more casual, something in between. We'll try them on and see what you feel comfortable in. Now–lace or satin or silk?"

I stare at her. I don't have the faintest idea how to answer. Again, I had never gotten far enough in envisioning my future marriage to think about my dress. All of my dreams of romance and weddings were for the characters in the romance novels I read—the ones where they actually got their happily ever after, instead of being married off to someone they didn't want. I assumed my mother would have opinions about my dress, and that I would probably agree with them, to save time and frustration for us both.

"I–don't know. Um–lace?" I like the idea of a lace wedding gown. I wonder what Levin would prefer, and my heart skips a beat in my chest, imagining him watching me walk down the aisle in a wedding dress.

And then I remember that this isn't the kind of marriage where something like that matters, and my heart sinks.

"Sleeves or no sleeves?" Madison chirps, and once again, I have no idea what to say.

"It's a summer wedding," Isabella chimes in, saving me. "I would think either short sleeves, straps, or strapless. Just–bring some options, and we can narrow it down."

"Of course!" Madison bustles away, and I stand there, feeling a bit dizzy.

Isabella looks at me a little sympathetically. "It's overwhelming at first. But it's a lot of fun, once you narrow it down to a few choices. And I'm here to help you pick."

I can tell she's enjoying this—wedding dress shopping with her little sister, and I resolve to try to enjoy it too. Much like what happened in Rio, nothing will be gained by *not* enjoying the parts of this that can be fun.

Madison brings me a heaping armful of dresses, hanging them up one by one in the dressing room, and then pushing the pink velvet curtain aside so that I can come in. She waits expectantly while I strip down to my underwear, and then pulls the first dress off of the hanger, holding it out for me to step into.

This one is smooth white silk, heavy and thick, with finger-wide straps and a v-neckline that shows off my shoulders, collarbone, and cleavage to a nice effect. The waist nips in, the skirt billowing out in heavy pleats, and it's very flattering, if a bit plain. I hold my hair to one side as she zips it up and pins it in place to give me a better idea of how it would fit my shape.

"Oh, that's gorgeous!" Isabella exclaims as I step out, her eyes widening as I walk to the three-way mirror and turn this way and that. "What do you think?"

"It's pretty. A little plain." I'm not entirely sure what I think of it. I'd never really envisioned myself in a wedding dress, so I can't say if it's what I pictured. "I think I would like something with some lace, maybe? I'm not sure—"

"We'll try something with some lace, then," Madison says cheerfully, bustling me back to the dressing room.

We try on so many dresses that I lose track, in every silhouette I can think of. Big, Cinderella-style ballgowns, sleek sheath dresses, mermaid gowns so tight that I don't even know how I would walk down the aisle. I try on silk and satin and taffeta, gowns with varying amounts of lace, and something called *Swiss dot*, but eventually, I come back to a dress I tried on about halfway through the appointment.

"I want to put this one on again," I tell Madison, finding it in the sea of silk and chiffon and lace hanging from the hooks in the dressing room. She beams at me as she pulls it down and holds it for me to step into again.

"This one looked absolutely *stunning* on you," she says firmly. She's said that about every dress, so I'm not sure how much stock to put in it, but as she tugs it up to my shoulders, zipping and buttoning and attaching the clips to the back so it fits me the way it will after it's been tailored, I know it's the one.

Tears spring to my eyes, which only makes Madison's smile even bigger when she catches a glimpse of it in the mirror—but they're not for the reason she thinks. The dress is perfect—I know it is the moment I look at it again, but I don't want to wear it for this wedding. I want to wear it to marry Levin—but in a world where this wedding is our choice outside of any other influences, where there are no obligations and no danger in making that decision for us.

This is the only time I'll ever get married. The only day where I'll get to wear a dress like this and walk down the aisle, the only day that I'll make those vows. I'm torn between buying the one that feels right and choosing something else because if the marriage isn't going to be what I want, why should this be, either?

"Is something wrong?" Madison peers at me over my shoulder, and I suck in a breath, smoothing my hands over the lace skirt.

There's no reason to make this harder than it actually is. And some small, foolish part of me; a part that belongs to the girl who read romance novels and dreamed of handsome princes and fairytale knights, the girl who existed before that plane crash—still hopes that Levin will see me walking down that aisle and that in that moment, everything will change.

That he'll realize he's loved and wanted me all along, and we would always have ended up at the altar, no matter how we got there.

"No," I tell her with a smile, forcing it onto my face. "It's perfect. Let's go show Isabella."

I want that small hope to be true. But I have a feeling that I'm about to be facing a lifetime of forcing smiles that feel as if they don't belong on my face.

As if, at least when it comes to the man who is about to be my husband, all of the happiness that I was ever going to feel is already behind me.

Elena

The moment I see Levin sitting in the living room, my heart leaps into my throat. I know I shouldn't let myself be as happy as I am—it's a road that is only going to lead to my getting hurt. This isn't going to be the kind of marriage that I want to imagine it will be.

But I can't help the way it makes me feel, seeing him there.

Isabella walks in, going over to Niall to scoop Aisling up and give him a kiss, and Levin turns to see me. I think I see a flicker of emotion in his expression, and then he stands up, walking towards me before I'm very far into the room.

"Elena." He hesitates, and I have the briefest of moments where I think he might be about to kiss me, before he tenses, and nods towards the hall. "Can we go outside? I thought we should talk."

"Um–sure." I glance back at Isabella and Niall once before following him out, feeling unsteady. It's never felt as if there were so much distance between us before, even before what happened on the beach. I've never felt so off-balance with him, like I'm not entirely sure what to say or what's coming next.

I follow him to the kitchen, out of the back door, and into the backyard. There's a small, pretty garden to one side of the house, with flowers planted everywhere, and a bench towards one far side of it. Levin leads me there, his hand wrapped around mine, and for a moment, I just let myself savor the feeling of him touching me, his broad palm pressed against my smaller one.

I miss touching him, in so many different ways. This doesn't feel like enough, but it's what I have.

He takes me all the way out into the riotous array of flowers, and then, on the small winding stone path that Isabella placed among them leading to the bench, to my utter shock, he goes down on one knee.

I stare down at him as he fumbles in his pocket, my lips parting, startled beyond being able to speak. When he opens the black velvet box in his hand, it makes it even more impossible for me to come up with a single thing to say.

The ring in the box is beautiful. A sparkling oval diamond on a rose gold band, with two deep red stones on either side—either garnets or rubies, I can't be sure which. It glimmers in the evening light, and I feel tears well up in my eyes as I imagine Levin choosing this for me, hand-picking it, trying to decide what I might like.

It doesn't make sense. With things as they are, why would he buy me a ring?

The question comes out before I can stop it.

"Why are you doing this?" I blurt out. "If you don't love me—why? I don't understand."

I think I see a flicker of hurt on his face, but I can't be sure. I know better than anyone how excellent of a poker face Levin has. He's employed it often with me.

"I do care for you," he says softly, and somehow that burns worse than ever.

"I know you think that helps," I tell him, taking a step back, feeling my heart ache in my chest. "But every time you say it, all I hear is what comes after. *I do care for you, but I don't love you.* I can hear the words you don't say just as well as the ones you do."

"I'm sorry." He stands up then, still holding the open box in his hand. I see his other hand twitch, almost as if he's going to reach out and touch me, and then he stops himself. "I want you to have everything you deserve, Elena. You're losing out on so much of that, because of me. Because I didn't protect you from my own lust. Your life will be entirely different now on account of this. All of it has changed, like that." He snaps his fingers, and I flinch, my heart aching with every word. All I hear is obligation. "So I wanted you to have a real proposal, and a ring. You deserve to experience all of this, and I—"

"Did you propose to her?" Once again, the question comes out before I can stop it, and it's Levin's turn to look stunned. I've rarely asked him about his late wife, and never so bluntly. "Did you buy her a ring? You must have. It wasn't like this, was it?"

Levin swallows hard, and his hand closes around the ring box. "Is this you telling me no, Elena? Are you not going to marry me?" I can't tell if I hear relief or disappointment in his voice, or if there's neither. I'm only making it up because I want him to feel something strongly, something besides acquiescing to my desires and what the right thing is.

Tears burn at the back of my eyes. "I'm going to marry you," I tell him quietly. "But I'm marrying you for the sake of our baby. I'm not going to accept a proposal or wear a ring that you give me that isn't because you love me."

This time, I do see hurt on his face. I'm not happy about it; I don't want to hurt him, but at the same time, I'm glad to see some emotion. I want him to understand that this isn't what I want, either, not like this.

He takes a deep breath, pocketing the ring, and then he sinks down onto the bench, his elbows resting on his knees.

"Lidiya and I got married under strange circumstances," he says finally. "It was to save her. The job we were on together—it went bad. There was an issue with one of the cartel bosses. The only way to keep her safe from him, *really* safe, was for us to get married."

"Did you want to marry her?" I don't know why I'm still asking the questions. Hearing the answers is only going to hurt. But if I'm going to be with Levin forever, I feel like I need to know.

He looks up at me, and I wonder if he's deciding whether to tell the truth or not. If he's weighing his options.

"Yes," he says finally. "I wanted to marry her. She wasn't so sure. I had no idea if it was going to be a real marriage, or if she was going to have it annulled when we got back to Moscow. But we had to lay low for a little while and go to Tokyo first. And by the time we got back—"

He breaks off, whether because he doesn't want to say more or he's sure I don't want to hear it, I don't know.

"That doesn't answer your question, though," he says finally, after a long moment of silence. "I didn't propose to her before we were married. I didn't buy her a ring. But I did, in Tokyo. I didn't ask her to marry me, exactly—but I asked her to stay my wife. To try to make some kind of life with me—to trust me with our future."

Levin's head bows forward, his shoulders slumping, and in that moment, I can see the weight of everything that's happened, and how heavily it rests on him. It makes me feel guilty for having brought it up, knowing how much it must hurt.

But I need to understand.

"She trusted me with her future," he repeats. "And I failed. I am doing my best, Elena, since a certain future has been decided for us. But I have been trying to warn you, again and again, not to do the same. This isn't going to be a marriage of love. This is me trying to do right by you–and trying not to fail, again."

"There is *some* future, though. There has to be." I press my hand against my stomach without thinking, feeling the ache spread through me. "We have to figure it out together, Levin. It's not enough for you to just *be* here. I need you to be a part of this."

"I'm going to do my best." He looks at me, his lips pressed tightly together. "I was supposed to have a child before, Elena. You heard what Vasquez said. And you know what happened."

"Were you happy about it, then?" Another question that I don't know if I really want the answer to, but it's there anyway, out in the open. "Did you want—"

Levin lets out a heavy sigh. "I was afraid," he says flatly. "Fucking terrified. And then, once I came around to the idea–I found that I didn't mind it. But it doesn't matter," he adds, pushing himself up from the bench. "This is the past, Elena, and—"

"A past that clearly still affects you now." My arms are wrapped around my middle despite the warmth of the evening, and I feel a chill settling through me. "It's coming between us, whether you want for it to or not—"

"Elena." This time I *can* read the emotion in his eyes. It's sympathy, and I hate it more than I've hated indifference or frustration or anything else he's ever felt toward me that I didn't like. "It has *always* been between us. It's been between me and every woman I've met for the last twelve years."

Tears burn in my eyes again, because I can hear what I think are unspoken words—*you're not different. You're not special. You're not going to change that.* He doesn't say them, and I can't even be sure that he's thinking them, but it's what *I* think, what comes into my head as I look up at him, and it hurts so much that for a moment, I feel like I can't breathe.

I'm in love with him. If I had ever wondered whether or not I was before, I know now. I love him, and I want him; I can see that marriage or no marriage, he's going to keep his distance. This wedding is, plain and simple, because he believes it's the right thing to do, and for no other reason.

I have to live with that—and I honestly don't know how I can.

Levin spends the night at the house this time, evidently on account of the fact that we're now engaged. Niall felt that it would be horribly rude to expect him to get a hotel, which Isabella reluctantly agreed to. There's no question of us staying in the same room, which leaves me lying awake in my bed yet again, staring up at the ceiling and missing him next to me with a palpable ache.

Will we sleep in the same bed after we're married? Or is he going to want to have separate rooms? The thought of that makes me feel like breaking down into tears all over again, the prospect of years and years of a marriage where I don't even sleep in the same bed as my husband. It makes me realize, more than ever, that I really don't know what this looks like for Levin. He keeps telling me that he'll do whatever I want, whatever makes me happy—but when it comes down to it, the things I want are the things he can't give me.

I get up after a little while, padding softly down the hall towards the bathroom, considering a hot shower in the hopes that it might enable me to sleep. I walk past the guest room where Levin is sleeping, expecting to hear light snoring, but instead, I hear a low groan that stops me in my tracks.

Arousal floods me instantly, and my thighs squeeze together. I know that sound and what it means—I've heard Levin groan in my ear in exactly that way before, night after night. My pulse leaps into my throat, my skin heating, and all I can think of is how much I want to be in bed with him, hearing that groan as he slides into me, filling me up again after what feels like an interminable amount of time without him.

It's been a month, and it feels like six. More, even. I want him in a way that feels like a physical ache, and I gently push the door open a crack, wincing as I wait for a creak that will give me away.

There's no sound, and as I peer around into the room, Levin is too occupied to notice the door opening. The sight in front of me makes my thighs clench together all over again, a wave of arousal soaking the thin cotton of the shorts I wore to sleep in, causing them to cling to my skin.

The blankets are pushed down around his thighs, and he's in only his boxers, his muscled and tattooed chest bare in the sliver of moonlight coming through the curtains. He freed his cock at some point, sliding it out through the fly of his boxers, and his hand is wrapped around it, sliding up and down the straining length as his head tips back, his jaw tight.

He's thinking of me. I know he must be, and the idea of it makes my heart race in my chest, until I feel like I can't breathe, weak-kneed with desire. The thought of Levin lying in bed, his cock swollen and hard as he thought of me a few doors down, wanting me the same way I had been lying there wanting him, so badly that he had no choice but to slide his cock out and stroke it himself, wishing it was my hand or mouth or—

It could be. I know I should go back to my room, that if Levin really were going to take me up on any kind of offer, he would have come down the hall to me, knowing that I always want him. I know I'm only setting myself up for disappointment, but that thought doesn't seem to register in time to stop my feet from propelling me into the room, my heart pounding as I push the door closed behind me and start to pad towards the bed.

Levin freezes, his hand stuttering on his cock, his eyes snapping open as he stares at me. For one brief second, I'm treated to the sight of him stunned and still, his gorgeous cock held tightly in his hand and almost all of him bared to my view—and then he snatches the blankets up, letting go of himself as he sits up halfway, his forehead creased.

"Elena, what the hell are you doing?"

It's not unlike the night I caught him on the beach, before we ever slept together. He'd been upset at me then, too–but the difference now is that we've had sex. I'm not a virgin any longer, and we're going to be married. It feels ridiculous to pretend that we need to be chaste.

"I was–in the hall, and I heard you, and—"

"And you thought it was a perfectly fine idea to just walk in?" He sounds almost outraged, and I blink at him, feeling off-balance.

"I thought—" *you might want help.* I can't say it aloud. It sounds small and foolish to me now, standing here like this, with him looking at me as if he can't believe I ever had a train of thought that led me to think walking in here was a good idea. Now, in this situation, I'm having a hard time believing it too.

And that makes *me* feel upset, because this isn't the kind of marriage I want. I know that for sure.

"When I caught you like this on the beach, we hadn't slept together yet," I tell him, swallowing back the lump in my throat. "So I get it–why you were so upset. You were trying not to touch me–to take care of it yourself. But Levin, this is ridiculous."

"What is?" He frowns at me. "It's normal for men to jerk off, Elena. I know you don't have a lot of experience, but—"

"No–I know that. But—I was right down the hall."

"Sleeping, I thought," he points out. "I was hardly going to come wake you up. And besides—we're not doing this, Elena."

"At all?" I stare at him. "I mean it, Levin—this is ridiculous! I get not wanting to wake me up, but then being upset at me for coming into your room? I'm literally pregnant. What is the point of us not touching each other? That ship has sailed."

Levin lets out a sharp, frustrated breath. I'm sure it has no little part to do with the fact that I interrupted him, leaving him hard and probably close to the edge, but right now, I can't find it within myself to care all that much. "That will only make things more complicated," he says finally. "I'm trying to make this *less* so—"

I can't believe the words that are coming out of his mouth. "So you're just going to jerk off for the rest of your life when you have a perfectly willing wife?" Aloud, the words sound absolutely insane coming out of my mouth, and I hope he can hear it too. But instead, his face just settles into stubborn, irritated lines, and I can tell that it's only made things worse.

Is this our first real fight?

"This marriage is about raising our child together," Levin tells me firmly. "That's *all* it's about, Elena. Our child, and doing right by you and them. Nothing else comes into play. I thought you understood that already, but if not—"

I'm so close to bursting into tears, and I hate myself for it. I want to be angry with him, *furious* even; I want to shout at him that it's not fair to me either, that I didn't want to sign up for a marriage of celibacy. But for all I know, he'll calmly tell me that I'm welcome to find pleasure outside the marriage if I need to, or that he plans to do the same. I know beyond a shadow of a doubt that I can't handle that right now. I'll fall apart.

"You asked me what I want," I whisper in a voice that sounds too small, without the emphasis I wish it had. "I want to be in that bed with you. I want you to ask me to come join you, and I want us to finish what you started. I want you to want me enough to do that."

"I do want you, Elena." Levin's voice is deep, roughened with frustration, and it sends a thrill of desire through me even under the circumstances. "But this isn't about *want*. This is about what's best for—"

"Don't say that." I shake my head, cutting him off. "I don't want to hear you say that you know what's best for me."

"I was going to say for both of us," he finishes quietly. "But you can take it as that, too, if you want."

We stare at each other for a long moment, and I don't know what to say. I feel as if my heart is cracking open in my chest all over again, as if he's never going to stop breaking my heart; that feels worse than ever, knowing that we're going to spend the rest of our lives together.

I thought watching him walk away was the worst thing that could happen. But somehow, this feels worse than him not marrying me at all.

Levin

When I'm called to the Kings' offices the next day, I assume it's because the news of the wedding has reached Connor, and I'm about to be chastised for hiding my relationship with Elena in the first place. But instead, I'm faced with much worse news.

"Diego has made contact with connections he has in Boston. Connections we weren't aware of." Connor is sitting at one end of the table, his eyes narrowed, and mouth pinched around the edges. "I'm sure you can guess what it is that he wants."

"Something to do with Elena?" I keep my voice calm, but inwardly I can feel my gut clenching with a particularly heated mixture of rage and worry. Elena was meant to be safe here. We'd been assured that Diego had no connections in Boston and no way to reach her. If that's not true, and Elena isn't as safe as we expected—

"He's demanding her return." Liam leans forward, steepling his fingers as he rests his elbows on the scarred wood of the Kings' table. "Of course, we're not inclined to comply with that request."

"I would certainly fucking hope not." I drop down into the chair opposite Liam, jaw tensing. "How the fuck did these *connections* slip past us?"

Connor shrugs, looking more irritated than concerned. "We haven't been in the business of dealing with the cartels for long. I can't say that we have the best network for sussing out every possibility. We did our due diligence, but clearly—"

"Clearly not." I glare at him, and Connor raises one thick auburn eyebrow.

"You're a little more on edge about this than I would think you should be, Volkov. Especially considering that your part in this is meant to be finished. You completed the job you were given. What are you doing in Boston, anyway? Just a social call with Niall?"

From the expression on his face, I know there's no point in bullshitting him. It'll all come to light soon enough anyway—no one here is stupid enough to be at my wedding to Elena and not put two and two together.

"Do you need me to spell it out for you?" I ask him flatly, and Liam chuckles.

"We already figured it out," he says, leaning back in his chair. "Elena tried to cover for you, but she's not that good of an actress. It was obvious there was something between you; we just weren't sure how far it had gone."

"That wasn't a part of your job," Connor says icily. "I can't imagine how Ricardo Santiago would feel if he knew that you deflowered his daughter. Which I assume is what you did, since she must have been a virgin if Diego wanted her in the first place. You put this entire deal in danger, Volkov. It would come down on *our* heads if Santiago decided to take offense that the man we vouched for to bring his daughter back here safely chose to take advantage of her instead."

I don't argue the point. Elena would have flown into a fit over the idea that I *took advantage* of her in any way. However, I still feel some guilt over the whole situation. "I'm willing to take responsibility for my part in it," I tell Connor calmly. "I understand that what I did was not a part of the job I was given, and that I was out of line to give in to temptation. But Santiago will know soon anyway—Elena and I are getting married."

"Oh fuck, man." Liam shakes his head, blowing out a sharp breath as he looks at me. "What the fuck did ye do?" His accent thickens, his voice taking on a tinge of surprise. Connor, on the other hand, only looks even more irritated.

"I clearly gave you more credit for intelligence than I should have." Connor crosses his arms, glaring at me. "Well, we won't be calling on you to do any more rescue missions for the Kings anytime soon, not unless they're men or old, dried-up crones."

"I intend to be faithful to my wife," I tell Connor stiffly. "As for why I'm marrying Elena, I think your first suspicion is likely the correct one. But I am marrying her, regardless. And as for anything else regarding her family, I think that will be between the two of us."

"If Santiago threatens our deal on account of this—"

"I think that, since I intend to do right by his daughter, that won't be an issue," I tell Connor, an edge creeping into my voice. "And, as I said, my marriage to Elena is between her and I."

"Not when it affects Kings' business—"

"I think he's right, Connor," Liam interjects. "He is, as he said, doing right by her. I think that will be enough for Santiago. And if it's not—" He shrugs. "It can't be undone, brother. There's no point in castigating him for it. What can be done is being done."

Connor grunts but says nothing else, and Liam turns his attention back to me.

"However," he continues, "when is the wedding meant to take place? Not too soon, I imagine, since neither of us has seen an invite."

The statement is pointed in Liam's own way, and I nod. "You would, of course, receive an invite. But you're correct. We were thinking three months, maybe? The end of summer? I believe Niall is contacting Father Callahan about a date."

"It'll need to be sooner than that," Connor says sharply. "If Diego is reaching out to whatever contacts he has here, that means he's considering his moves. Elena needs to be protected. I wasn't going to suggest marriage to *you*, but since that's already beyond my decision to make, the wedding needs to be moved up. The sooner, the better," he adds. "As soon as the arrangements can be made. Diego can be told no, if she's married. To you, it will be a bit flimsy, but you are at least an official part of Viktor's Bratva. He won't be able to take her from you by negotiation or demand, which only leaves force. We will hope that one girl and his bruised ego isn't worth so much to him that he'll reach so far by violence."

"I hope not." I press my lips together, considering. I hate the idea of telling Elena what's happening—that even in this place, the danger is reaching out to snag her. But at the same time, I know she wouldn't wish to be left in the dark. And she won't be able to be for long—especially with the wedding being moved up. Isabella wouldn't hear of it, unless there were circumstances like these. "I'll take care of letting her and Isabella know. I'm sure Niall can speak with the Father tomorrow. As soon as the arrangements can be made, it will be done."

Well, that's that. I don't know whether to be relieved that there's no backing out now, that the decision has effectively been made for Elena and me, or filled with dread. Up until this moment, there had been a possibility that either of us could have changed our minds. Elena could have told me that she didn't want the kind of union I offered her—one built around raising our child, not love or desire— or I could have told her that I was willing to be a father, but that I couldn't make vows to her after all, if the guilt and grief became too much to bear before we made it to the altar. But now it's clear that marriage is necessary to protect her from Diego. It will be me—or

Connor and Liam will choose someone else for her. Someone powerful enough to protect her.

Someone who, if they're talked into taking on a deflowered woman with a bastard child, would not allow me any part in that child's life.

All it takes is that thought for me to know that regardless of my feelings about marriage, I can't walk away from this. Not in those circumstances.

"And consummated," Connor adds. "There can be no questions. The marriage has to be ironclad."

"She's pregnant," Liam says with a snort. "I think the time has passed to wonder about her innocence—"

"It doesn't matter." Connor crosses his arms, glaring at me. "I would assume that will be no issue for you, considering the girl's state, but just in case you had any ideas in your head about a marriage of convenience—the wedding night has to be consummated. After that, you can do what you like."

You assume wrongly. I had no intention of touching Elena on our wedding night. In fact, I had reconciled myself to a marriage without any intimacy at all, for the sake of not hurting her further. I don't think Elena is the kind of woman who could continue going to bed with me, feeling as she does, and not be hurt by it in the end.

And the last thing I want to do is hurt her any further.

But I know in this, at least, Connor is right. There can be no question, nothing to make anyone think that Elena's marriage could be annulled, no loophole for Diego to slip through in his continued pursuit of her.

"Has the pregnancy been confirmed elsewhere?" Connor continues, eyes narrowed. "A doctor's visit? Or is it only her family that knows?"

"Only Isabella, Niall, and myself. And now, the two of you."

Connor nods. "Then keep it that way. Her parents can know if they must, but they'll need to understand that, for all intents and purposes, Elena will be presented as having gotten pregnant after her wedding night. You'll need to fake blood on the sheets. No doctor's visits or evidence of it that can be recorded until after the wedding—which is, of course, all the more reason to do it as quickly as possible."

All of it pisses me off. The secrecy, the lies—and the need for it at all. Diego and his machinations were meant to have been left in Rio. Boston was supposed to be a safe place. This was supposed to be over for her.

But it's not. And as tired of Connor's sanctimonious attitude as I am, I know he's right about this.

"I understand," I tell him, as calmly as I can manage. "I will make sure to relay all of that, just as soon as I'm back at the house."

"See that you do," Connor says curtly, getting up from his chair and striding abruptly from the room, Liam following in his wake a moment later—leaving me to sit there and think about how quickly everything has been turned upside down.

—

The worst of all of it is seeing Elena's face that evening, when I tell her what Connor told me.

"You've got to be fucking kidding me," Isabella spits. "He's following her *here*? Why can't he just fuck off?"

Niall reaches out, smoothing his hand along her arm in an effort to comfort her, but I can see sparks flying from her eyes. It's clear she's furious.

"I thought it was over," Elena says in a small voice. "I thought we were safe."

"I thought so too." I reach out for her hand, but she pulls it back, wrapping her arms protectively around herself. "Elena, if we'd known—"

"You'd what?" Her lips press together thinly as she stands up, her face taut with anxiety. "Take me where? If he has contacts here, where else does he have them? You couldn't have left me in Mexico. Surely he has people in New York, too. It feels like nowhere is ever going to be safe."

"Elena—"

She shakes her head, backing up. "I need to be alone," she blurts out, spinning on her heel and rushing out of the room.

"They had no idea?" Niall asks, running a hand through his hair, and I shake my head.

"According to Connor, they didn't. They thought Boston was clear. But—"

"But it's not, and you led them straight to us." Isabella's voice is sharp and caustic. "Both Elena *and* I are in danger, if Diego is reaching out to contacts here."

"She's right." Niall rubs a hand over his mouth. "I'm going to need to talk to Connor and Liam tomorrow and see what their plan is. It's not just Elena that could be affected—it's my family, too. Not that Elena isn't—" He lets out a long, frustrated breath. "I'm sure they're already thinking of how to deal with this. And in the meantime, we'll make sure the wedding happens as soon as possible."

I nod, but my thoughts are already elsewhere, following Elena. I want to go after her, comfort her, but I'm not sure if that's the right thing to do. After our fight, I'm not even sure she wants that from me any longer.

But I go anyway, drawn after her as I so often am. I have a feeling she's gone out to the garden, and that's where I find her, standing on the path with the soft glow of the lamp on the side of the house illuminating her in the darkness.

She looks up as soon as she hears my footsteps. "I said I wanted to be alone," she says tightly, and I stop where I am, watching her from halfway down the path.

"I can go inside if you want. But Elena, I wanted to make sure you were alright—"

"How could I possibly be alright?" She turns to face me, and even in the dim glow, I can see that she's been crying. There are spots of red high on her cheekbones to match the raw edges of her eyes, and she looks exhausted. "I thought I was safe here. I was *promised* it would be safe here. And now I'm pregnant—it's not just me in danger. Fuck—I led him right to Isabella, too! And Aisling—"

"Shh." I stride towards her despite her protest, putting an arm around her shoulders and pulling her against my chest. "It's going to be alright, Elena. I promise. Connor and Liam will come up with a plan, along with Niall and I. We're going to keep you safe. This affects everyone. And the wedding—"

"What will the wedding do?" She crosses her arms, pulling away from me. "You think Diego will care if I'm married?"

"There's politics to this, Elena. You know that. If you're married, then you're no longer worth as much to him. Revenge might still be worth something, but he'll have to weigh that against inciting the wrath of the Kings and the Andreyev Bratva, and decide if it's worth the risk. Not only those factions, but their allies as well, like the Romano mafia. I don't think it's going to be worth it to him."

"You can't be sure of that," she whispers, and I nod.

"You're absolutely right. I can't be sure. But all we can do is take whatever steps we can now to mitigate the situation. And the first and most important one is for us to get married as soon as possible. That's your best protection against this." I let out a long, slow breath. "Elena—there's no choice about this any longer. Or there is —but it's a choice between you marrying me and marrying someone else chosen for you by the Kings, to protect you, the alliance, and Niall's family. That's what Connor and Liam will do if you were to decide not to marry me. Whether or not to be married isn't an option any longer."

She swallows hard, tears filling her eyes as her arms tighten around herself, and I reach for her again, pulling her into my embrace.

"I promised to protect you, Elena. That's not changing. I'll protect you, and I'll protect our child." I reach down, tilting her chin so that she's looking up at me. "You believed in me in Rio. If we could manage it there, we can manage it here, where we have more resources."

She nods slowly, biting her lower lip. "It was easier when it was just you and I that I needed to worry about," she says softly, and I feel something in my chest clench.

I know it's not what she means. But all I can think is that she doesn't trust me to keep our child safe—and why would she?

She knows what happened before.

I feel things for her that I have no right to, that I don't deserve. I want to keep her in my arms forever. At the same time, I want to undo every decision that led us here, so that she can have the life she was supposed to have—the life her father sent her away in hopes that she could make for herself.

I want to kiss her. I want to gather her in my arms and kiss away every fear that she has, every worry that I see in her dark eyes. I want the Elena back that I knew before, the girl who found a reason to believe that we would prevail in every situation, who kept me stronger than she knew.

But instead, I let go of her chin, pulling her against my chest instead as I rest mine atop her head, one arm around her shoulders.

"Whatever happens," I tell her quietly as we stand there in the warm darkness, "I'll keep you safe."

I hope that this time, it's a promise I can keep.

Elena

My wedding day dawns as beautiful and bright as I could possibly hope—and the exact opposite of my mood.

I wake up earlier than I meant to, feeling anxious and fraught with nerves, lying in bed with my pulse beating rapidly in my throat. Levin stayed in a hotel last night, since Isabella felt like it wasn't right for us to be under the same roof, even though he wasn't all that keen on leaving me with only Niall for protection; a phrase which it was clear Niall took some exception to.

Connor and Liam have had security doing rounds, visiting Niall's periodically to check for any sign of disturbances, but they don't have a permanent post. I think it's meant to make us feel as if the situation isn't so bad yet—that we don't need round-the-clock security—but it's only heightened my anxiety, and I think Isabella's, too. I've heard Niall and Levin discussing the wedding and reception, and I know there will be security there.

It's not that it's strange to me—all my life, I've been surrounded by guards watching my every move, keeping me safe. But having had a taste of freedom here, what it's like to choose where I go and when without anyone watching me, it's hard not to feel eyes on me again, and feel as if I'm being caged.

All I want is for Diego to leave Isabella and I be. The thought that he's still posing a threat, that even Boston wasn't far enough away to run, makes me want to curl into a ball and hide. I'd put so much faith in the idea that this was a safe haven, and it feels as if it's been suddenly ripped away.

Isabella knocks on my door at eight. "I brought you breakfast in bed!" she tells me cheerfully, walking in with a tray filled with French toast, fruit, sausages, and a mimosa perched on it.

"You didn't need to do that," I protest, sitting up, and she waves a hand at me, setting the tray down on the bed as she sits cross-legged across from me.

"It's your special day. You should be spoiled today. It's bad enough that it had to be rushed, that it's going to be an even smaller wedding than we anticipated—you deserve everything you can possibly get. You're only going to get one wedding day," she adds, picking up one of the two forks. "So we're going to start with breakfast and mimosas, a virgin one for you, and then I'll help you get ready. Niall is off to help Levin."

I pick at the food, feeling guilty for not eating more, but my stomach is tied up in knots. "What is a virgin mimosa, anyway?" I ask her, and Isabella smirks as I take a sip and realize it's just orange juice.

"I should have known." I roll my eyes at her, but it has the desired effect. It makes me laugh and relaxes me a little, because it's exactly the kind of idiotic prank that she would have pulled when we were just two girls living at home, Ricardo Santiago's daughters, trying to keep ourselves occupied when we couldn't go beyond the walls around our house. It feels warm and familiar, and I take another sip, grinning at her as Isabella drinks her *actual* mimosa.

"What do you want me to do with your hair?" she asks me when breakfast is finished, and I'm sitting in front of the bathroom mirror in my robe, looking at my reflection. "Up? Down? Half and half?"

"Maybe half and half?" I purse my lips, trying to decide. I have no idea what Levin would prefer, and I have no idea if it matters—if he'll even notice one way or another. "Up feels too severe."

"I agree." Isabella fluffs her hands through my thick black hair, considering. "I think we'll do something to amp up the curl a little, and then I'll pull the front back with a pretty comb, and we'll leave the rest loose. It will look gorgeous with your veil."

My stomach knots all over again at the mention of the veil. Somehow that makes it all feel more real and reminds me that when Isabella is done with my hair and makeup, we won't just be getting dressed to go out—I'll be putting on a wedding dress and walking down the aisle to marry a man that is everything I could have ever wanted…and who doesn't want me in return.

Or, at the very least, doesn't really want to marry me.

When Isabella is finished with my hair, sliding a gold and sapphire comb into the pulled-back strands at the back of my head, she circles around to stand in front of me, quickly and expertly applying my makeup. When she's finished, my skin looks perfectly smooth, and my cheeks lightly flushed, a soft rose eyeshadow spread over my eyelids, a thin strip of liner and rose-colored lipstick to match. I look soft and romantic, and something in my chest clenches at the thought that Levin might not care.

That he might look at me and be thinking of how quickly this could all be over with, so he can move on to the next item on the list. The next thing that needs to be taken care of.

I know I'm being cruel, thinking of him like that. Levin has always done his best to be what I need, insofar as what he can actually give me. The problem, of course, is that since the moment he came back—everything he can give me falls so woefully short of what I actually need.

Tears burn at the back of my eyes as I stand up, thinking of tonight. My wedding night—but I have a distinct feeling that it won't be what I hoped for. I don't know if we'll even sleep in the same bed, and if we do, I don't think Levin will touch me.

He's been very clear on that point—that our marriage being anything but one of convenience will only make things harder on us both, in his mind. Which leaves us with only two choices—to spend the rest of our lives in frustrated celibacy, or have an open marriage.

Both ideas make me want to cry, for entirely different reasons.

Isabella has my dress out and hanging in front of the closet door, and as I shrug off my robe and find my undergarments while she takes a few pictures of the dress. "We didn't have time to find a photographer who could do the whole day," she says, glancing back at me. "But you should have plenty of memories from today."

I don't tell her that I'm not sure that I'll want them. That my heart feels heavy and aching, thinking of how I'm going to exchange vows with someone who would never have married me except out of necessity, of how the pretty white lace panties I'm slipping on will likely go unnoticed tonight, that Levin isn't going to weep seeing me walk down the aisle or think of how he wants to take my wedding dress off of me later tonight.

Today is likely going to be a day that I want to forget when it's over. And that makes me feel horribly, achingly sad.

I do my best to hide it, though, as Isabella holds up my dress for me to step into, tugging the sleeveless bodice up over my shoulders and stepping behind me to do up the buttons one at a time. Looking in the mirror, the dress is every bit as stunning as it was when I first tried it on—beautiful embroidered floral lace covering all of it, the neckline a perfect sweetheart, the trumpet skirt sweeping out into a wider short train behind me, satin-covered buttons running from the nape of my neck to the very hem of the skirt. It's gorgeous and romantic and perfect, and I fight back tears all over again, because I want all of this to be so very different.

Isabella attaches my veil to the comb in my hair, the sheer chiffon falling to my fingertips, edged in fragile eyelash lace. She gives me a once-over as I step into my heels, and then helps me put on the pearl jewelry that our mother had sent her for her wedding as a finishing touch.

"Something old, something new, something borrowed, and something blue," she says decisively, stepping back. "You look absolutely stunning, Elena. I still don't think Levin deserves you, but you make an absolutely gorgeous bride."

From there, there's nothing to do but take my bouquet and follow her out to the waiting car, my heart in my throat. The closer we get to the cathedral, the more on the verge of panic I feel, and Isabella reaches for my hand next to me, as if she can hear my racing heart.

She looks beautiful, too, wearing the dark red maid of honor gown that we chose. She's my only attendant, as Niall is for Levin, and I cling to her hand as the car pulls up in front of the cathedral, stifling the urge to run.

Not because I don't want to be with Levin, but because I want it so badly that it feels like a physical pain, and I know he doesn't feel the same way. That if not for the baby that still feels like it's not even real, today wouldn't be happening. He would still be in New York, and I—

Connor has made no secret of the fact that he wanted to marry me off to someone else, someone with more status, someone who could not only protect me from Diego but also further their own ends. It did nothing to make me like him more—I hadn't come to Boston to simply walk into the same fate that would have been the one decided for me back home—but I also know that I wouldn't have had a choice. I need their protection against Diego, and so does Isabella. Niall would side with his wife, but breaking with the Kings would be no small thing, and he wouldn't do it lightly. None of us should—I'm smart enough to know that.

The baby made things simple. Levin was willing to marry me, and the pregnancy made it so that as long as he was willing, no one could say otherwise to force me to marry someone else. But at the same time, I can't find it in me to look forward to what comes next —not when I know how he feels about it.

The nave of the church is cool and smells of incense, a familiar, nostalgic smell. I have a brief flash of memory, especially with Isabella next to me—the memory of us kneeling for the rosary in a church very like this one, of lighting candles for dead ancestors, of saying prayers memorized since we were old enough to speak. The scent and the memory calm me, and for a moment, I no longer feel as if my heart is about to beat out of my chest.

And then the bridal music starts, and I'm flooded with panic all over again.

"Just breathe," Isabella murmurs, looking at me sympathetically, and then the doors open, and she turns to lead the way down the aisle.

Even under these circumstances, even with Isabella's caution, the sight of Levin standing at the altar takes my breath away. He looks beyond handsome, dressed in a perfectly tailored charcoal suit that fits him in ways that makes my mouth go dry, a dark red tie at his neck to match Isabella's dress and the roses in my bouquet. It makes me think of the ring he tried to give me—the rubies set on either side of the diamond—and my throat tightens as I start to walk, unable to keep looking at him as I follow Isabella.

Niall is standing next to him, and his gaze is focused solely on his wife, his face soft with memory as if he's imagining their wedding day all over again. My eyes well up instantly, because there's nothing in the world that I long for as much as Levin looking at me like that —with that kind of soft, aching love in his eyes that I've never known—and now never will know.

My life is going to be altogether different from what it was once supposed to be, and from what I had hoped it might become.

I'm glad for the veil over my face that gives me a moment to gather myself as I reach the altar. Isabella takes my bouquet and steps to one side as I walk up to Levin and take his hand. We agreed that no one would give me away, as Isabella patently refused to formally hand me over to Levin, and nothing else felt quite right.

I chose to give myself to Levin on that beach. I'll choose to give myself to him today, as well.

The choice might not be exactly the one I wanted, but it will at least be mine.

Levin's hand wraps around mine, broad and warm and strong, and I want to lean into that strength, as I have on so many other occasions. I want to trust him with all of me, with my future—mine and our child's.

But I can't stop thinking of how he cautioned me not to. How I have to guard my heart so much more carefully now, because I have a lifetime ahead of me of facing, day after day, that the man I'm going to share that life with doesn't feel the same way about me that I do about him.

I hear Father Callahan speaking, as we turn towards the altar. I hear *dearly beloved* and *join this man and this woman together,* and *if anyone has any reason why they should not be,* and a part of me wonders dizzily if someone will stand up, if my sister will speak up, if Levin himself will say something.

I can't marry this woman because I don't love her. Because I can't ever love her.

No one says a word. The church is silent, and Father Callahan waits a few seconds longer before he continues, his voice filling the cavernous space.

"Do you, Levin Josif Volkov, take this woman—"

I see Levin's lips moving, repeating the words. I search his face, trying to understand what he's feeling, what he's thinking—if he's here with me, or if he's remembering another wedding day to another woman, a marriage just as quick and unexpected as this one, but one that he *wanted*. If he feels guilty or angry or upset or anything at all—but I can't read him. His face is carefully closed off, and that feels worse, because he's about to be my husband—

and I've never felt further away from him than I do in this moment. I know he's keeping his feelings hidden to spare me, but it doesn't spare me anything. It fills me with hurt and confusion and dread, and my mind goes to the worst possible scenario, that he's wishing he were anywhere but here, with someone who isn't me.

"I do." The words, when they come out of his mouth, sound sure and certain, as if he's never questioned them in his life. I should take comfort in it, but I can't even do that, because I know Levin is a man who, once he's made up his mind to do something, finishes it. His certainty isn't because he wants me or this, but because he's set his mind to it. As far as he's concerned, there's no going back, and so there's no wavering.

"Do you, Elena Guadalupe Santiago, take this man—"

I see a flicker of something over Levin's face, a glimmer of interest, and I realize he's never heard my middle name before. I open my mouth to tell him that it's my mother's name, and then I remember that I'm meant to be listening to the priest, and I stammer when I say my vow.

"I–I do."

The curiosity in Levin's face turns to worry, quickly smoothed away, and my chest aches. *He's going to think now that I faltered. That I wasn't sure. That for a second, I thought of refusing him here at the altar.*

"Have you brought rings to exchange?" Father Callahan asks, and Isabella steps forward with Niall, each of them handing us the ring for each other. Two gold bands, one thicker and one thinner, and Levin and I face each other again, my heart hammering in my chest. I don't know why, but this feels like the part that solidifies it the most. Like that ring, combined with these vows, means more than all the rest.

Suddenly, a memory flashes into my head of Levin on that hotel bed after he'd been stabbed, of my hands frantically holding a bloody towel against him as I begged him to stay with me, to hold on. *Do you take him in sickness and in health,* Father Callahan had asked, and what I should have said is *I already have.*

For richer or for poorer, in sickness and in health, for better or for worse. We've already been through all of that. And what I want to say, what I want to *shout* at Levin as he starts to say the words that go along with the thin gold band in his fingertips, is that I was the one who wanted to stay, even after all of it. Who wanted *him* to stay.

He was the one who left.

"Elena Guadalupe Santiago—" Levin begins, one hand holding mine as the other holds the ring poised at my fingertip. "Take this ring as a sign of my love and fidelity—"

I have to swallow back the emotion that wells up in my throat. I hadn't realized how much it would hurt to hear him say *love*, when he so clearly doesn't mean it. When he's said to me, in private, that he can't love me. That he doesn't believe I love him. I want to shout at him that he can't stand here, in front of a priest, and lie. That he can't say *love* when what he means is *care*, that word that I would gladly never hear him say again.

The ring slips onto my finger, cool against my skin, settling at the base of it. Levin gives my hand one small, light squeeze, and then it's my turn.

I can hear how strangled my own voice sounds when I start to speak.

"Levin Josif Volkov, take this ring as a sign of my love and fidelity—"

I mean it. I can't *not* mean it. He might think how I feel is built on a fantasy, but I know better. I *know* what I felt in that hotel room when I kept him from bleeding out, when I went in search of what I needed for even a chance of saving his life, when I killed men for those things. I know what I felt every minute of every day that I spent with him. I know how it grew and changed, from the curious desire that I'd felt when I first saw him in my father's office to what bloomed between us in the darkest and most desperate parts of those nights in Rio.

I'm not too young or too innocent or too naive to know how I feel. And I mean what I say when I slip that ring onto his finger.

Levin's gaze catches mine, and I wonder what he sees in my face. I wonder what he thinks of it. I wonder, and I miss what else Father Callahan says, until Levin reaches for my veil, and I realize that we've gotten to the *you may kiss the bride* part of the ceremony.

He lifts the veil over my head, tossing it back, and draws me closer. His hands are around mine as he leans in, and I crave his touch, this kiss, more than I ever knew possible. I want his hand against my cheek, his lips pressed against mine, the heat of his tongue in my mouth, and the depths of the disappointment I feel when he chastely brushes his lips over mine feel unfathomable. So much so that I have to blink back tears, fighting the flood of emotion that threatens to overwhelm me at the slight kiss.

I think he knows how I feel. But he doesn't let on. We turn towards the guests as Father Callahan announces us as man and wife, and as we start to walk down the aisle hand in hand, I know that the hardest part of the night is yet to come.

The charade that is going to be the rest of my life begins now—and there's an entire party to get through.

One that I can't even drink during to take the edge off.

Elena

I'm glad that I told Isabella that I wanted a small wedding and reception. Even so, there are enough guests milling in the reception space as Levin and I get ready to make our entrance to make me feel anxious all over again at the idea of talking to them, making conversation, and pretending to be an overjoyed, happy bride for most of the night.

As if he can hear my thoughts, Levin squeezes my hand lightly, leaning in to murmur in my ear. "Everyone here is accustomed to arranged marriages, Elena. No one expects you to be the absolute picture of happiness."

A part of me softens at the idea that he knows me well enough to know what I was thinking—and another part aches at hearing him call it a marriage of convenience, that he *expects* me to be unhappy.

"Well, I'll just have to do my best," I tell him tightly as the music increases in volume, and I hear our names announced as the new bride and groom, telling us that it's time to walk in.

Levin doesn't let go of my hand. His fingers stay threaded through mine as we walk in to the sound of our guests clapping for us, all the way to the sweetheart table at the head of the room. The space is beautifully decorated in pinks and deep reds and cream, greenery scattered throughout and a dance floor in front of where the musicians are set up. It's all gorgeous, everything I could have ever hoped for—and I don't remember planning any of it. It all feels like a daze, and I'm fairly sure that Isabella handled most of it, because I wasn't in any state to decide what I wanted for a wedding that felt like it was occurring in a fever dream.

It still doesn't entirely feel real. I sit down next to him, nudging the bustled skirt to one side, and look out over the ballroom filled with guests taking their seats for the meal, too. A server comes around, pouring Levin a glass of wine and then swapping it for sparkling cider for my glass—another reminder of why we're here.

"I've never been much for wine," he says in a low voice to me with a hint of a grin, taking a sip. "I'd prefer vodka, but that's for later tonight."

I know it's not what he means, but *later tonight* sends my stomach into knots, wondering what's going to happen. He was so clear that night when I walked in on him that this marriage isn't going to be a physical one—that he had no intention of touching me again—but I can't help but wonder if that's changed now. If anything at all has changed.

A part of me wants him to be so overcome by desire for me that he can't help it—and the rest of me knows that we can't do what we did in Rio forever. Our whole lives can't be that back and forth, that tug of war between desire and guilt. It will tear us both to pieces—and I can't bear it.

The food is delicious, but I barely taste it. It's a trio of entrees, a small portion of each—a duck thigh in a berry sauce, a filet medallion with some sort of red wine glaze, and delicately cooked salmon with lemon. There are whipped potatoes with crumbled Gorgonzola sprinkled over the top, a salad with berries and vinaigrette, and roasted vegetables, but it all might as well have been microwaved pizza. It feels like dust in my mouth, because all I can think about are the rest of the motions that Levin and I have to go through tonight—and then what happens, or doesn't happen, after we leave.

Dinner is over before I know it, and then it's time to cut the cake, a towering confection of creamy frosting with fondant flowers and greenery that match the decor of the ballroom perfectly cascading down it. Levin stands next to me, his hand over mine as the knife slides through to reveal a soft white cake with a raspberry cream filling. As I lay a piece on the small china plate in front of me and reach numbly for a piece to feed to him, he does the same.

Am I going to have to fight tears all night tonight? I can feel them burning against my eyelids as his fingers brush against my lips, vanilla cake and raspberry exploding over my tongue. I bite back a small moan of pleasure—the cake is absolutely delicious—feeding Levin his bite. His tongue brushes against my fingertips as I nudge the cake into his mouth, and I feel a shiver of desire go all the way down to my toes.

I wish that I didn't want him as much as I do. I wish that he didn't make me feel like this—and I wouldn't give up knowing what it felt like for anything.

Not even if I knew that we'd end up here from the start.

We return to our table as the servers pass out the cake, and I nibble at mine, wishing with every sip of sparkling cider that it were actually wine and looking enviously at the glass of expensive red sitting next to Levin's plate. He finishes his cake, glancing over at me as the dinner comes to a close, and the guests start to get up and move about for mingling and dancing.

"I'm going to have to go and make my rounds," Levin says quietly. "But I won't be gone too long. I don't want to leave you alone if you won't be alright—"

"I'll be fine," I tell him, a little more sharply than I intended to. I want to remind him of everything we did in Rio, everything *I* did—that I think I can handle being left alone at a dinner table for a little while, even at my own wedding reception, but I bite it back. "Just come find me when it's time for our first dance."

Levin hesitates, as if he's thinking of saying something, but nods. I wait for him to lean in, to kiss me even on the cheek, but he doesn't. He pauses almost awkwardly for a moment, then backs away and walks towards where Connor and Liam are standing near the bar. I see who I assume must be Connor's wife standing near him—a tall, beautiful red-haired woman in an emerald silk dress, with the elegant bearing of a queen. She glances at Levin and at me, murmuring something to Connor, and he says something back before she shrugs, kisses him lightly on the cheek, and trails off toward another table.

I feel my face flush, wondering what she said. Isabella has mentioned her to me before—her name is Saoirse, if I remember correctly. She and Isabella don't get along all that well. According to Isabella, they've learned to bury their differences, but the fact that Isabella married the man Saorise once wanted is never entirely gone. I can't help but wonder what she thinks of me now that I'm here.

Most of the wives are a mystery to me. Isabella doesn't spend as much time with them as they do with each other. I get the impression she's not overly fond of most of them, although she's only had good things to say about Liam's wife, Ana. I feel another knot in my stomach, wondering if I'll have to make friends with them. Levin is Viktor's right hand in New York, but here he's not a man of any high ranking in these organizations. I have a small flicker of hope that, like Isabella, I won't be expected to be one of them all that often.

As promised, Levin comes back to the table in time for our first dance. He holds out his arm for me as I get up, the perfect gentleman, and escorts me towards the dance floor as the music starts, a pretty instrumental song heavy on the strings. I hadn't picked out a specific song for our first dance—I couldn't think of what I would possibly find that would fit our relationship. The thought of choosing a song for Levin and me in our current circumstances hurt too much. Isabella had told me she'd pick something instead, and I'm happy with the choice. It's beautiful and easy to dance to. As Levin puts one hand on the small of my back and the other on my arm, I'm glad that it is, because I can't focus on the steps beyond the muscle memory of all the dance lessons I've had, not with him touching me again.

The pressure of his hand on my back feels hot, like it's searing through the lace, my entire body flushing with being so close to him again. We're nearly brushing against each other as we move through the steps, his hand sliding down my arm as his fingers interlace with mine and spin me, bringing me back in, and when the front of my body brushes against him from chest to thighs as we start to move again, it takes my breath away.

I want him so much it hurts. He looks so handsome in his charcoal suit, perfectly tailored to every inch of his muscular body, his tattoos peeking above the collar on his neck and out from the wrists of his shirtsleeves and jacket, the ink covering the backs of his hands. Most of the Irishmen and Kings here have similar tattoos, as do the Bratva members in attendance—although Viktor is notably not as inked as many of his men—but on Levin, they seem particularly sexy to me. Maybe it's because I'm so intimately familiar with them, because I've traced so many of the patterns with my fingers and lips, and the thought sends another flush of heat through me, my heart beating rapidly in my throat as Levin and I move across the dance floor.

It's finished all too soon. I hear, faintly, cheering from the guests as the music slows, and Levin pulls me in, the pressure of his hand on my back and his body suddenly fully against mine making me feel dizzy as he leans down, his lips brushing over mine.

I hadn't expected a kiss. I know he's playing to the guests, and it's no more of a kiss than the one at the altar was—the faintest graze of his mouth over mine, but it makes my knees go weak. I want to hold onto him, to deepen it, but I know I can't. I let go as he breaks the contact, and I see a flicker of what looks like regret in his eyes as he takes my arm and leads me away from the dance floor.

What he's regretting—the end of the dance, the kiss, the marriage itself—I don't know, and I'm not sure if I want to. But I don't have time to consider it, because he's leading me towards Viktor, who I haven't formally met before.

He's sitting at a table with a tall, slender, dark-haired woman who is leaning close to him. He looks at her with the same kind of adoration that I saw on Niall's face when he looked at Isabella during the ceremony. It makes my heart ache all over again, to see a man with so much power who looks so obviously in love with his wife.

"Viktor." Levin stops at the table, nodding at his boss. "May I introduce my wife, Elena."

Viktor stands up, as does the dark-haired woman next to him. "It's lovely to meet you in person, finally," he says genially with a smile, taking my hand and lifting the back of it to his lips. "This is my wife, Caterina."

There's a genuine smile on her face. "It is lovely to meet you," she agrees. "The next time I'm in Boston, we'll all have to spend some time together. All of us wives get together at the McGregor estate every few months or so, and Isabella has been joining us. You should as well."

I nod, my throat tightening with anxiety. "I'd love to," I manage, and I think it comes out sounding sincere.

"Don't let us keep you," Viktor says kindly. "I'm sure the two of you want to get back to enjoying your party."

Levin nods, and we head back into the crowd of guests, winding our way toward the bar so that he can get a drink. He's good at making small talk, commenting to those we pass as we walk by, but all of it feels like a fog to me. I can't focus on anything for too long. The time is ticking by until the evening and whatever that might hold, and then tomorrow—

Tomorrow our life together starts. We have to start thinking of what our future looks like, where we want to live, how we're going to do this. It all feels vast and overwhelming and unknown, and not even tonight's festivities can make it better, because that just feels like a harbinger of what's to come.

I don't know whether to be relieved or anxious when it's time to go. There are sparklers set off as we leave the venue, hand in hand, headed towards the car waiting at the end of the steps, and my heart is in my throat as Levin opens the door for me, and we slide inside.

My head is full of questions. *What happens now? Where are we going? How are you feeling?* I don't ask any of them, because I don't know if I'm ready for the answers.

I know that when Levin was married before, he didn't have a wedding like the one we had today. It was a ceremony in a church, but a quick one, and they left after. There was no reception, no party, no guests to cheer and celebrate. A part of me wants to know how he felt about all of that, how it made him feel to have had that experience with *me*—and a part of me knows that the answer is too likely to be one I don't want to hear. As for the rest of the night—

I know what I want to happen, but I'm not sure that it will. And I'm not sure that my heart can handle the rejection just yet.

We pull up in front of a gorgeous hotel. Levin gets out first and opens the door for me again, waiting while I carefully slide out, my skirt gathered up so I don't trip over it. I follow him into the lobby, which is gorgeously done in an Art-Deco style, all black and gold, and brass. Levin checks us in, and I see the woman behind the desk beam, her eyes lighting up as she sees me in my dress.

"The honeymoon suite is already prepared for you, sir. There's champagne, vodka, and the flowers you requested waiting."

Flowers? My throat tightens as Levin thanks her, taking the matte keycard that she offers and leading me towards the elevator. I hadn't let myself expect anything tonight. The idea of a honeymoon suite with flowers is wonderfully romantic, and I have to fight back the urge to cry.

It's even harder when Levin opens the door for us, and I step into the room.

The room itself is gorgeous—a huge bed taking up most of the center, with double doors leading out to a balcony on one side, a long velvet sofa along the other side, and a gilded room service cart sitting next to the marble and gold coffee table with the aforementioned bottles of champagne and vodka chilling, as well as a plate of fruit. But what catches my eye the most are the flowers—vases of roses on the dresser, in white and pink and red and yellow, at least five dozen of them, filling the room with the thick perfume of fresh flowers.

"I thought it would brighten up the room," Levin says quietly, seeing where my gaze ends up. "Do you like it?"

I can't speak. My throat feels closed over with emotion, and I can't ask the one word that comes to mind, *why*, because I don't want the answer—especially if it's pity, which is what I'm most afraid of. Levin has spent his whole life feeling as if he needs to pay for the presumed sins of his past, and now I can see a future where he spends it paying for what he feels are the wrongs he's done to me. It's not what I want for either of us.

Levin clears his throat, stepping over to the room service cart as he reaches for a glass to pour himself a vodka. "Elena, we—" he breaks off, sucking in a breath as if he's trying to think of how to say whatever comes next. "We have to consummate the marriage tonight. Connor was very clear about it. You're already pregnant—but he doesn't want to leave anything to chance. So—"

I stare at him, dumbstruck for a moment. I'm not sure what feels worse, the thought of him not touching me at all on our wedding night, or the idea that he's under *orders* to.

"I hope it won't be too much of a chore," I choke out, looking at him from across the room, and Levin turns sharply towards me.

"Being with you could never be a chore," he says gently. "I only meant—"

"Is this the only time?" I swallow hard, trying to keep my voice even, to not let the riot of feelings threatening to choke me flood out. "Are we really going to have a celibate marriage other than this one night?"

Levin sinks down onto the edge of the couch, pressing the fingers of one hand against the bridge of his nose as he takes a deep swallow of his vodka before looking up at me again. "I meant to talk to you about this later, Elena. But if you want to have the conversation now, we can."

"You told me that you had no plans to touch me ever again," I tell him flatly, every word weighed down by hurt. "What conversation is there to have?"

"The one where I planned to tell you that after tonight, no, we won't have a celibate marriage—unless that's what you want, and I don't think you do. I intend to be faithful to you, Elena, and a part of that, I've come to see, is keeping you satisfied inside of our marriage. It's not fair to you otherwise, especially as I can't stand the thought of another man's hands on you." A muscle in his jaw tightens and twitches as he says it, and I feel a small bit of gratification that he feels that at least— that he doesn't want me with anyone else. That it hurts him as much to think of that as it does for me to think of him with another woman. But I still can't shake the awful feeling that he's doing this because he has to.

I press my lips tightly together, fighting back the emotion that threatens to close my throat up past the point of speaking. "Is that the only reason you're going to do this, then? Out of a sense of obligation to me and to make sure I don't fuck anyone else? That's so romantic."

I don't mean for it to come out as bitterly as it does, but I can't stop myself. Somehow this feels worse than if he'd simply told me we were going to sleep.

He swirls the last of the vodka in his glass, letting out a heavy sigh. "I told you before, Elena—and nothing has changed—I can't love you. Not the way you want for me to. I care deeply for you, and I will do anything I can to protect you, to make you as happy as I can. But I can't be the kind of husband I was before. I said I would never marry again for that reason. And now—"

"I know." I cut him off before he can say anything else, feeling my stomach knot with a heavy sadness. I don't know how to do tonight, feeling like this—but at the same time, I still want him. Even now, even after everything, I can't stand across the room and look at him and not want him.

Even as devastated as I feel with every word he says.

"I almost think I would rather have ended up married off to someone I knew I could never love," I say softly, wrapping my arms around myself. The lace of my dress chafes against my arms, feeling scratchy now rather than soft. "At least then I could have turned all my emotions off and just stopped feeling. But now—I feel everything. It's too much, all of it. You say you're trying to make me happy—but what I need, you can't give me. You've said over and over again that you never will. I want to say that I don't know how we got here, but I do. And I–I still feel like I would do it again."

The tears start to spill over then, snagging on my lower lashes, threatening to smear my carefully done makeup. Levin stands up, setting his glass aside and crossing the room to me in a few quick strides, his hand pressed against the side of my face as he quickly brushes them away.

"I don't want to hurt you, Elena." There's pain in his own voice, but I don't know if it's for me or for the memory of what he used to have and lost. "God, all I've wanted all this time was to keep from hurting you. And I can't seem to fucking stop, any more than I could stop—"

His words catch at that last, and I can see his face go taut with desire, a look so familiar that it fills me with hope and hurt all at once. "All of this is my fault," he says softly, his other hand settling on my waist, pulling me closer. "And even knowing that, I still think about the rest of tonight, and I want—"

He doesn't need to tell me what he wants. I already know, and even as hard as all of this is, even though I'm torn between anger and tears, I want it too.

Levin's hand on my face slides into my hair, his fingers sliding through the strands beneath where Isabella pinned the first half back. He tips my chin up, his hand cupping the back of my head, and he lowers his mouth to mine.

The kiss is soft at first, but still different from the way he kissed me in the church or on the dance floor. This kiss feels like a promise of more, his lips brushing over mine lightly, remembering me. It feels like it's been so long since he kissed me like this—and it has been weeks. Weeks without the feeling of his hand tightening against my waist, the steadily increasing pressure of his mouth, the way his tongue finally flicks out across my lower lip, urging my mouth open for him as I breathe in sharply and he pulls me closer.

His hand slides to the back of my dress and finds buttons instead of a zipper, and the low groan I hear deep in his throat makes a laugh bubble +up out of mine. "They don't take as long to undo as it seems," I manage, and Levin narrows his eyes at me as he pulls back.

"I'll be the judge of that," he growls, turning me so that my back is to him, and when his hand slides across the upper part of my shoulders and the nape of my neck, brushing my hair aside, a shiver runs all the way down my spine.

I feel him undo the first button, and then another, and another. His lips brush across the nape of my neck as the buttons slip free, and my eyes flutter closed, tremors of pleasure electrifying my skin as his fingertips graze down the center of my back with each button.

Why does he have to be so good at this? It would be one thing if he weren't, if the sex were quick and perfunctory, if he didn't care about my pleasure, about making every second of it so excruciatingly good. *But then again, if that were the case, we might not have ended up here.*

The dress begins to slide down my shoulders as the buttons come undone, and Levin's mouth brushes a little lower, his fingers still sliding over my skin. My breath catches in my throat as he reaches the last button at my lower back, and then I feel his hands press against me, his palms sliding upwards to my shoulders as he pushes the dress off and down my arms.

"You're so beautiful," he murmurs softly, his lips finding the side of my neck. "So fucking beautiful—"

There's a longing in his voice that shouldn't make sense, but to me, it could. It could if it means that he's wishing that this could be more, that he could give me what I want, that this doesn't have to be the way he's made it. That's what I want it to mean, and what I tell myself that it does, as the dress slides lower to my hips and his hands skim up my ribs to cup my breasts.

My head falls back against his shoulder as his fingers toy with my nipples, his lips sliding up my throat to find the soft spot at the corner of my jaw, and my lips part with a gasp as he sucks softly at the skin there.

"Levin—" I breathe his name, my back arching as I press myself into his hands, wanting more. His fingers skim under the curve of my breasts, teasing my nipples until they're stiff and hard and aching. I both want him to go faster and to never stop because suddenly, I don't want tonight to be over. I'd forgotten that we might not have been doing this at all if he hadn't been told to, that a short while ago, he told me that he had planned not to touch me again. Later I'll remember, but for now, it's washed away on a tide of desire, and as my pulse quickens, all I want is more. More of him, more of the pleasure, more of *everything*.

His tongue trails over the shell of my ear, his breath warm against it, and my breathing turns to soft panting. "Please—"

"Please, what, *malysh?*" he murmurs against my ear, and that's when I know he's lost too, when I hear the whispered endearment.

He turns me in his arms then, his lips capturing mine again as he pushes the dress down my hips, leaving me in nothing but white lace panties, standing in a sea of more white lace. His hands slide down my waist, my hips, and I gasp softly as he sinks to his knees on the floor in front of me, his fingers sliding down my thigh and over the curve of my calf as he reaches for the straps of my high-heeled shoe.

No one has ever made me feel as worshiped as Levin does. It's as if, once he decided to do this with me tonight, he gave himself over to it—or, as I think is more likely the case, he couldn't stop himself. He couldn't stay detached, couldn't hold me at arm's length, and that's never more clear to me than when his lips slide up the side of my leg as he lifts it up, drawing my shoe off and tossing it aside.

He repeats the same motion with the other shoe, my other leg, and then he leans up, his fingertips hooking in the white lace of my panties as he draws them down my thighs.

I don't need to hear his low groan of arousal to know I'm soaking wet. I can feel it, the ache settled, throbbing between my legs as his mouth slides upwards, tongue trailing a pattern on my skin as it reaches the apex of my thighs and his fingers spread me apart, his tongue finding my clit as I cry out and my hand wraps in his hair.

My knees feel instantly weak. The moment his mouth presses between my legs, it's almost too much. It's been too long, and I've needed this every second that he's been away, ached for it and dreamed about it, and imagined a moment I thought would never come again. I gasp again as his tongue circles around the most sensitive spot, fluttering, licking, not keeping the same rhythm for too long, as if he's purposefully keeping me on the edge.

His other hand is on my hip, trying to steady me, but it's not enough. When he sucks at my clit, drawing the sensitive flesh into his mouth, my knees nearly buckle, and Levin pulls away.

"Maybe we should do this in the bed," he murmurs. "As much as I enjoy being on my knees for you, *malysh*."

I suck in a sharp breath as he scoops me up into his arms, carrying me to the huge bed. He lays me back against the pillows, and I get one glimpse of his straining erection against the front of his suit trousers before he follows me onto the bed, the sleeves of his dress shirt pushed up and baring his inked, muscled arms as he spreads me wide for him, like a feast he can't wait to devour.

His hands grip my inner thighs as he delves between them again, his tongue running up my pussy from my entrance to my clit and back down again, pushing inside of me as I let out another cry of surprised pleasure, my nails grazing his scalp. His tongue is stiff as he pushes it deeper, licking me, his nose bumping against my clit as he fucks me with his tongue, and it's a sensation that's shocking and pleasurable all at once. It's not enough to make me come, but it's enough to drive me crazy, pushing me higher until he finally slips his tongue free and slides it upwards to where I need it most again, fluttering it over my clit as I gasp with relief.

My head falls back against the pillows, my entire body tightening as I feel his tongue exactly where I need it the most, right on the perfect spot, and as he sucks my clit into his mouth again, the orgasm crashes over me with a force that feels as if I'm unraveling.

I buck against his mouth, writhing as I ride his tongue through my climax, my hand gripping the back of his neck as if I want to hold him there forever. I feel as if I'm coming apart at the seams, the pleasure that I needed so much crashing over me again and again. I cry out his name, gasping and moaning as he keeps going, not stopping until every last second of my orgasm is wrung out of me.

And then he slowly pulls back, trailing his tongue once more over my throbbing clit, and he leans back on his knees as his fingers go to the buttons of his shirt, and a lustful expression curves the edges of his glistening lips.

He's rock hard, straining against the fly of his trousers, and my entire body tightens all over again at the knowledge that he'll be inside of me very soon.

It's everything I want. *He's* everything I want.

And I know that isn't going to change.

Levin

It's like I'm possessed when I'm with her.

Even once Connor had given me the clear instruction that our marriage was to be consummated to the letter, even once I had made the decision that, if she wanted me, I would give her what she needed within our marriage, I had planned to keep some level of detachment. To make the time I spent with her in bed more like what I've been accustomed to these past years—pleasurable, but not lingering. Sex for the sake of release, not what Elena and I have done more times than I care to remember now, because it led us here.

It's as if that's impossible for me. For *us*.

As soon as I touched her, I couldn't keep that distance. I wanted to savor her, draw it out, taste every inch of her, and build up the pleasure slowly, taking my time across her lips and her skin and her perfect body until I finally gave her what I knew she needed, what I knew she'd been craving. And now, as I look down at her in the middle of the huge bed, the taste of her still on my lips and my cock straining for my own relief, I feel more lost than ever.

Her legs are still parted for me, her pussy swollen and glistening from her orgasm, and I can see every inch of her sensitive flesh. A rush of desire floods me, my cock aching, and I yank at the buttons of my shirt. I'm half-inclined to drag down my zipper and fuck her without any further undressing, just so I can be inside the tight, hot grip of her, but I want to feel her skin against mine.

"Let me help." Elena's voice is a soft breath as she pushes herself up, kneeling nude in front of me as her hands go to my shirt buttons. She leans in, kissing me, and the thought that she's tasting herself on my lips is enough to make my cock drip pre-cum, throbbing dangerously on the edge of release.

One delicate hand slips inside my shirt as she deftly undoes the buttons, fingers trailing over the muscled flesh, and a shudder of need ripples through me. It feels like I can't ever get enough of her, like no matter how many nights I spent in bed with her, I'd still crave her like air to a drowning man.

I haven't felt that way since—

I shove the thought out of my head. I made my decision to do this tonight with her, and I won't think of anyone else while I do. It's not fair to her. And if I were being entirely honest with myself—it's not what I want, either.

She reaches up, pushing my shirt off my shoulders, and her breasts brush against my chest as she leans in to kiss my neck.

My cock jerks, and I reach down to thumb open the button at the top of my trousers, desperate to get them off. I shrug off the shirt, one hand on her waist to pull her in closer as she trails kisses up my neck, her hands sliding over my arms, her body so close to mine that I can feel the softness of her skin everywhere, and I feel as if it's driving me a little mad.

The moment I shove my pants down my hips, I lean forward, spilling her back onto the bed, kicking them the rest of the way off as I lean over her and capture her mouth with mine.

She arches up into me, breathless and eager as her tongue tangles with mine, and my cock brushes against her inner thigh, throbbing with the need to be inside of her. I'd planned to go more slowly, but I'm beyond that now. I reach between us before I can even think, guiding myself to her entrance, and the moment my swollen cockhead slides through her slick, hot wetness, I have to struggle not to lose control on the spot.

It feels so good. My head swims as I push forward, the tip sliding into her effortlessly. She's beyond aroused, her body welcoming me without the slightest strain, and her legs lock around my hips the moment she feels me press into her, her pleasured moan swallowed up in the kiss as she tightens around me.

Fuck. She's hot and wet and tight, everything I've imagined in the nights I've spent between our last night in Rio and now stroking my cock and desperately trying—and failing—not to think of her as I did it. The reality is better than any fantasy could ever be, her body dragging me deeper—*all* of her pulling me closer, her legs around me and her nails digging into my shoulders, and her tongue tangled with mine, as if there's nothing more in the world that she wants than for me to sink into her as deeply as I possibly can.

"Levin—oh *god*, Levin—"

She pants my name against my lips, and it drives me insane. I thrust into her, sinking every inch of my aching cock into her welcoming heat before I can stop myself, unable to slow down. She arches under me, every inch of her pressed tightly to me. I break the kiss, my lips dragging down her throat, biting and sucking as I thrust into her again and again, chasing the orgasm I so desperately need now.

"God, you feel so fucking good—" I groan against her throat, hips snapping against hers, lost in the pleasure. I feel her suck in a breath, writhing beneath me, and I grind my hips down into her with every thrust, rocking against her clit as I try to make her come again, too. I want to feel her come on my cock, want to feel her spasm and squeeze me, and I want to fill her so full of my cum that she tastes it when I do. I want it dripping out of her; I want—

My mind is a blur. All I hear are her gasping moans, her heated skin sliding against mine, the bite of her nails in my flesh as she thrusts back every time I sink into her, and I can't think about anything other than how fucking good it is, how I want to come more than I've ever wanted anything in my life, and how at the same time I never want to fucking stop.

"More, oh god, don't stop, *please*—" she moans, bucking underneath me, her body tensing, and I know she's about to come. I can feel it, and my balls tighten, ready to come with her as soon as I feel it—

"*Levin!* Oh *fuck, fuck*—"

She shrieks my name, and I'm almost certain she draws blood as her nails drag down my back, but I don't care. She tightens around me, a hot, spasming clench that holds me inside of her, and I drag backward against it, slamming my cock into her once more as I arch into her, and my own orgasm crashes over me, unraveling me as it does. I fill her with spurt after spurt of hot cum, and I'm convinced, as I bury my face in her throat and breathe in the sweet scent of her, that there's no more exquisite feeling in the world than Elena Santiago coming on my cock while I fill her up with my cum.

I shudder against her, holding myself inside of her as deeply as I can, until she goes limp and gasping underneath me, and my cock slowly stops throbbing, the fluttering of her pussy around me suddenly almost too much against my oversensitive flesh. I slide out of her reluctantly, feeling the hot spill of my cum around my length as I do. As Elena sinks back into the pillows, I feel what I'd been dreading, in the aftermath of my pleasure as reality comes crashing back in.

Guilt.

Overwhelming, crushing guilt.

I do my best to hide it, keeping my face as carefully blank as I can as I roll to one side. Elena starts to move towards me, as if to cuddle up against my chest, and then she freezes, looking at me.

"I'm not supposed to do that, am I?" she asks in a small voice. "We're not going to—"

I let out a sharp breath. In truth, I know it would be better if we didn't. No good will come of holding her afterward, of cradling her against me and letting her feel what it would be like if I could give her everything, if I could love her the way she deserves. But tonight, of all nights, I can't bear to break her heart all over again by telling her that.

So I don't say anything at all. I reach for her, pulling her against me as I roll onto my back, my arm circled around her as she hesitates, and then lays her head against my chest.

"I missed that," she whispers, her voice cracking a little around the edges. "That was—"

"It was," I agree, and I force the guilt out of my voice, force the memory of a different wedding night back, because that's all gone now. There's nothing that can possibly be gained by letting those ghosts join Elena and me in our wedding bed.

I smooth my hand over her hair, pressing a kiss to her forehead, and I feel her relax against me. I wait until I can feel the gentle rise and fall of her breathing that tells me that she's asleep, and then I slowly slip out of her embrace, taking the cashmere throw blanket from the end of the bed and laying it over her so she doesn't get chilled.

My pants are hanging off the foot of the bed, and I slip them back on, going to pour another glass of vodka before I quietly walk out onto the balcony, closing the doors behind me. Beyond the railing, the city is lit up, still alive at this hour, with people out drinking and dancing and enjoying the last bit of their night. I let out a heavy sigh as I take a deep gulp of my vodka.

Fear and guilt, and shame fill me all at once, in the hollow space left behind by the absence of my now-satisfied desire. I think of Elena lying in the middle of that enormous bed, delicate and beautiful, and now all mine whether she should be or not, and all I can think of is the possibility that I'll fail to protect her, too. That one day I'll come home, and I'll find her dead in blood-soaked sheets, and the past that I've fought so hard to keep at bay will have repeated herself.

And it's my fault. *All my fault.* If I'd been stronger, more resilient, if I'd resisted her no matter how much I wanted her, we wouldn't be here now. It's my fault we're at this point, that Elena is in that bed with my ring on her finger and my child in her belly, and there's no argument against that. She can tell me all she wants that she seduced me, too, that she wouldn't leave me alone, that she battered down my defenses—but I was the one responsible for her. It was my job to keep her safe. And now, not only has her life changed forever because of me—she's still in danger, too.

There's the shame too, hot and thick, burning through me along with all the rest—because a part of me, one that I can't bury, is *happy.* I've felt it all day, from the moment the church doors opened and I saw her standing at the end of that aisle in the most beautiful wedding dress I'd ever seen. I saw her, and I felt a burst of happiness. I watched her walk towards me, and had a vision of her months from now, pregnant with our child, and felt excitement. I thought of having a family, of the thing that I've spent nearly forty years of my life believing I would never have and didn't deserve, and I felt joy.

With that joy comes the shame, because I still don't deserve it. How can I? Lidiya and our child are dead, and I don't deserve to move on. I don't deserve the happiness they were denied, because of my failures. And what's worse, because I don't deserve it, Elena will be denied it, too.

I know she won't ever be truly happy unless I can love her, unless I can move on with her and be utterly devoted to her and our family. I want so much to make her happy, and as she's pointed out again and again—I can't.

I stand out on the balcony for a long time, finishing my vodka, until it's gone, and I walk quietly back into the room to set my glass down. Elena is still sleeping, curled on her side facing where I was before I left, and when I undress again and join her in the bed as carefully as I can, her eyes flutter open anyway, just a bit.

A small smile curves her lips, and my heart aches all over again seeing it, because I know she's still half asleep, only awake enough to know I'm there, and not enough to remember all the reasons why that shouldn't make her happy.

Her hand reaches up, brushing over my chest, and before I can catch it, it drags lower, down my abs, as she squirms closer to me. Her body presses against the side of mine, from breasts to calves, every inch of her warm and soft against me. As her fingers slide down the ridges of my abs, my cock jumps, instantly hard from the feeling of her touch and her so close to me. It bumps against her hand, and her eyes flicker open, her fingers immediately wrapping around me, her thumb brushing underneath the tip and sending a hot burst of pleasure through me.

"Elena—"

"It's still our wedding night." She leans in, pressing a kiss to my shoulder, and her hand slides downwards, tightening around my cock.

I feel myself pulse in her grasp, pre-cum already pearling at the tip as she starts to move down my body, fluttering kisses across my chest as she moves between my legs. She looks so beautiful, her perfect naked body kneeling over me, her waves of inky dark hair spilling over my thighs as she leans down, and her tongue flicks out, licking up that drop of pre-cum before it can slide down my shaft. It feels like electricity through my veins when I watch her drag her tongue over my cockhead.

I can't speak. All I can do is groan as she smiles, wrapping her lips around my swollen flesh, hand stroking downwards as her fist presses down into the base, her lips traveling down to meet it, and it's an entirely different kind of ecstasy.

She moans around my cock, and I bury my hands in her soft hair, not to hold her down onto me, but just to feel it sliding through my fingers. Her tongue slides up the underside of my length, teasing the swollen veins, pressing just beneath the head and sliding down again as she tightens the suction around my cock, her other hand pressed against my thigh as if to hold me there so she can pleasure me with her mouth.

"God, you look so fucking beautiful with my cock between your lips." The words spill out before I can stop them. I reach out as she slides up, letting go of me for just a moment to catch her breath, my fingers under her chin as I press my thumb into her swollen, reddened lower lip. Her eyes are glistening from the effort of taking me all the way to the back of her throat, her lips puffy, and she looks so fucking gorgeous it hurts.

"Do you want more?" She flicks her tongue out, the words soft and husky as she licks up another droplet of pre-cum from my tip, and my cock jerks, slapping lightly against her lips and making her laugh. "I think that's a yes."

This time, she doesn't go slowly. She wraps her lips around my tip and sucks, hard, sliding down so that I'm in her throat before I realize it, her head bobbing as she fucks me with her mouth, her hand sliding under my balls to cup them gently while the fingers of her other hand press into my thigh. I feel dizzy from pleasure by the time her nose presses against my abdomen, my cock swallowed up almost entirely between her soft, plush lips.

"I'm—oh god, Elena, I'm going to come in your mouth if you keep that up—"

She slides up again, my cock slipping out of her lips with a faint *pop* as she watches me, her gaze hazy with desire. "Is that what you want?" she asks softly. "Or do you want to come inside of me again?"

Fuck. I know what she's doing. She wants to hear me say that I want her, *what* I want from her. And I can't blame her for it. It's her wedding night, and what bride doesn't want to hear her new husband say how much he wants her and whisper his fantasies to her?

I push the guilt aside, and I give her that, at least. Because *god*, I fucking know what I want.

"I want you on top of me. *Fuck*—" I groan as she circles her tongue around my cockhead again, licking up the steady drip of pre-cum leaking from me now. "I want you to ride my cock while I play with your clit, and I want to feel you come on top of me while I fill you up again—*oh god*—I want to fuck you while you're still full of my cum from before, and—"

I lose track of my thoughts entirely as Elena leans up, her hand wrapping tightly around my shaft as she straddles me, her legs on either side of my hips as she drags my cockhead along her entrance. I feel how wet she is, a mixture of her arousal and my cum dripping out of her from earlier, and the thought makes me throb in her grasp as she leans back a little, sliding the tip of my cock against her clit.

"That feels good," she murmurs, rolling her hips against me. "Just like that—"

It's more than good. The sight of beautiful, once-innocent Elena atop me, rubbing my cock between her legs, against her swollen, glistening clit, my pre-cum mixing with her arousal as she tips her head back and moans—it's almost enough to make me come on the spot. I imagine my cum spurting over her skin, soaking her clit, streaking over the taut flesh of her belly, and I feel almost dizzy with the need for release.

"I want to come like this," she murmurs, her words broken from the pleasure. "Do you like this?"

There aren't words to describe how much I like it. "Yes," I groan, my hands on her hips, letting her go at her own pace, but feeling the way she moves against me in more ways than one. My balls are so tight it hurts, but I hold back, watching as she rubs herself against me, more of my pre-cum dripping out over her clit as she gets closer to the edge and her thighs start to tremble.

"I'm so close—" her voice is a soft whimper, her legs spreading a little wider as her hips jerk against me. My cockhead flares and throbs, spilling more slick, pearlescent fluid over her skin as I watch her suddenly go stiff, her mouth opening on a cry of pleasure as her back arches and her hand squeezes my cock hard, her hips rubbing herself frantically against me as she comes on the tip of my cock. I can see all of it up close; one of the most erotic things I've ever seen in my entire fucking life.

When she arches up, sliding me inside of her still-fluttering depths and sinking down onto my cock, I think I've died and gone to heaven.

She feels incredible sliding down onto me, grasping me tightly, hips rolling as she takes me inside of her, and my back arches, thrusting up into her. Her head tips back, her breasts trembling above me as she rides me, and she looks so fucking gorgeous it takes my breath away. Everything about her is perfect, and I reach up, cupping one breast in my hand, rolling my fingers over her nipple and pinching it lightly as she slides down on my cock again, gripping me every inch of the way. She moans, her hips twitching at the sensation, and I reach up with both hands, playing with her breasts as she bounces atop my cock.

I want her to come again, one more time before I do. I want to see her come on top of me. I slide my hand between her legs, stroking my fingers over her slick, throbbing clit as she gasps, her hair spilling around her face as her eyes close and her hands press against me.

She leans forward, her hips bucking against my hand, grinding on my cock as her mouth finds mine. I slide my fingers back and forth over her sensitive flesh, feeling each time she gasps and moans, the sounds swallowed up by her lips pressed to mine, and I thrust hard inside of her, my other hand on her hip now dragging her down onto me each time, until every inch of me is buried inside of her with each thrust.

"Levin!" She cries out my name against my mouth, her back arching as she starts to tremble, her body pressed against mine. One hand is against my cheek, the other gripping my shoulder as her hips keep rolling atop me, and I feel her starting to clench, pulling me deeper inside of her each time, and the sensation is too much.

"Fuck, *malysh*—I'm coming too, oh *fuck*—"

The climax is even better the second time. I'm still sensitive from the first orgasm, and my cock feels as if every sensation is amplified, the slight soreness in my balls somehow only adding to the pleasure as I grab her hip and keep stroking her clit with my fingers as I feel her pulse and writhe, her cries vibrating against my lips as her pussy ripples along my length, and my cock explodes inside of her all over again.

She drives her hips down onto me hard once more, as if she's trying to get every bit of my cum that she can, her breath warm against my lips, and my hand on her hip grips her ass, squeezing the soft flesh as the memory of her begging me to fuck her in the ass in a Rio hotel room suddenly comes back in a flash.

I'm sure as hell not going to do that tonight, and probably not ever. But the thought intensifies my orgasm, the thought of Elena's tight, untouched ass clenched around my cock while I take the last of her innocence blazing through my mind, and while I know I'll feel guilty as hell for it later, right now it sends another electric jolt of pleasure through me as I fill her up with my cum for a second time, feeling the heat of it dripping out between us as she moves atop me, her hips slowing as both of our climaxes ebb.

She rolls off of me, panting, her hand brushing against my hip. It's much later now, and we're both exhausted. So tired that, when she rolls towards me to snuggle closer, I don't let myself worry about whether it's a good or bad idea. Right now, I want the warmth of her against me while I sleep, too. I want to feel her softness curled into me, and I tell myself that tomorrow we can go back to what this is supposed to be. After all, this is our wedding night.

It's an excuse, certainly. But right now, it feels like a damn good one.

Elena

I wake in the morning in the huge bed next to Levin, feeling sore, confused, and exhausted.

At some point in the night, I rolled over to my other side, and I can feel him behind me. He must have followed me in his sleep, and his arm is slung heavily over my waist, his breath warm on my shoulder, his body pressed against the back of mine. I can feel his cock, hard and hot, against my bare back, and I can't stop myself from arching back into him.

I want him to wake up and slide himself inside of me again, despite how tender I feel after last night after we hadn't been together for weeks. I want him to slide his hand along my thigh and guide himself into me, his lips on the back of my neck as he fucks me slowly from behind.

Briefly, I consider sliding under the sheets and waking him up with my mouth on his cock. I have a feeling it would disarm him enough to mean that we might get to have sex once more before we leave—and I have no idea how long it will be before he's convinced again. He said he planned to keep me satisfied within our marriage, but what does that *mean?*

If it means as often as I want it, we won't leave the bed for a number of days. But I don't think that's what he means. Knowing Levin as I do, and his commitment to both *doing the right thing* and also trying his best to make me happy within the confines of that, he meant a reasonable amount of times that will mean neither of us goes insane from deprivation.

I'll be lucky to get him in bed once a week, under that definition.

I can't help squirming a little against him, just in case. I can still faintly feel the stickiness of him between my thighs from last night. The thought of him filling me up again has me squeezing them together, my clit pulsing with the desire to come all over again.

He shifts a little behind me, his cock rubbing against my spine, and I bite my lip to keep from moaning. *How is it possible to want someone this much all the time?*

Gently, I slide my hand down between my legs, brushing my fingers over my clit. It's swollen, my pussy drenched from both my arousal and Levin's cum, and my hips rock forward a little, giving me the friction I want so badly. The pleasure shivers over my skin, my body instantly rousing even more, and as Levin's cock throbs hotly against me in his sleep, I close my eyes and try to remind myself that last night at least won't be the last time.

My fingers are still moving against my clit. I don't even fully realize I'm rubbing myself until Levin stirs again, his cock brushing against my ass as he pushes himself up on one elbow, and I hear him let out a low groan behind me.

"You're insatiable," he says, his voice low and raspy from sleep, and I let out a soft breath, desire flooding me all over again.

"I want you," I whisper, unable to stop myself, glancing over my shoulder. My fingers have stopped moving, but Levin's cock is still pressed to my ass, and my hand is still between my legs. "One more time, before we leave." I arch back against him, as if to make my point, and Levin's eyes close briefly. I can see him wishing for strength, and disappointment starts to replace the desire.

I reach over, taking his hand and placing it over mine, and I shift my fingers against my clit. "You could help me," I whisper, and I see his jaw tighten, the taut desire washing over his face for a moment before he stiffens, and then he pulls away.

"We need to check out soon," he says, sliding away from me and pushing the blankets back. "And we both need a shower, I think."

There's a forced lightness in his tone, but it doesn't make me feel better. I close my eyes against the threatening tears, the feeling of rejection sending all of my arousal vanishing in an instant as I pull my hand away, a cold, sinking feeling replacing the throbbing heat I'd felt only a moment ago.

Our wedding night is over. He's made that very clear. And while he might be prepared to go to bed with me enough to make sure I don't feel neglected, it's also clear that sex the morning after our wedding, when we fucked twice last night, is something he considers to be a luxury beyond that.

"I'll get in the shower after you," I manage, trying my best not to sound as if I'm about to burst into tears.

"Are you sure?" Levin glances at me, and I nod. I can't bear the thought of being in the shower with him right now, seeing him naked and wet and gorgeous, wanting to touch him and knowing he'll push me away, remembering all those nights in motels in Rio when we did so many things in those showers that he'll stop me from doing now.

"Alright. I'll make it quick." He gets up, and I can't stop myself from stealing a glance at him as he does. He's handsome as ever, his bare, muscled ass flexing as he stands up, the tattoos on his back trailing down a bit past his lower back. My palms itch to slide over his skin, to trace those patterns with his fingertips. I want to kiss every inch of him, drag him back to bed, and keep him here until it's dark again. We should be leaving on a honeymoon, getting ready to spend days in bed, only leaving to eat and explore a little, and we're not doing any of that.

I lie there as I listen to the door to the bathroom close behind him, the water turning on shortly after that, and I try not to imagine him naked in the shower. I have the privacy to finish what I started now, but all the desire has fled. I don't want to lie here touching myself until I come. I want Levin's hands and mouth on me, and if my own fingers are going to make me come, I want it to be while his cock is inside of me at the same time.

I want my husband, and it feels monumentally unfair that I can't have that.

You made this bed, too, I remind myself, brushing away the tears that start to slide down my cheeks. *You kept convincing him to sleep with you in Rio, and you ignored the risk, even though he told you it wasn't going to become anything more.* I can't pretend that Levin wasn't honest with me from the start. He always has been. I just didn't listen.

Now I'm married to a man who will be my husband in the most technical sense only. And as much as I want to bitterly tell myself that I won't go to bed with him if he's only doing it to satisfy me when necessary, I know that's not true. As ashamed as it makes me feel, I'll take whatever of him I can get.

The shower is as quick as he promised it would be, but it still feels like an eternity to me before the door opens again, and he steps out, a towel wrapped around his waist. I feel a flash of what almost feels like anger at him for coming out like that—*couldn't he have gotten dressed in the bathroom, and not teased me?* It feels strange, because I don't think I've ever really been angry at Levin before. I'm not quite sure if I am now, but it feels like the closest I've come to it.

He opens the closet door and pulls out a thick terrycloth robe, handing it to me. "If you want," he says as he drapes it over the bed next to me, walking over to the leather duffel by the dresser that's very similar to the one I saw him use in Mexico when we stayed at Diego's mansion after the party. That duffel, of course, is at the bottom of the ocean now with the rest of the plane's wreckage, but I'd never know it from the look of the new one if I hadn't been on the plane myself. *A man of habit.*

I reach for the robe, trying to avert my eyes as Levin picks up the duffel and sets it on the end of the bed. There's really no point in playing coy—he's been inside me in almost every way that's possible by now. We know each other intimately, and I shouldn't need a robe to go to the shower. But I can still feel the sensation of his hands on my skin last night like a brand, the stickiness of his cum between my thighs, the marks on my breasts where he nipped and sucked at my flesh. I feel like I don't want him to see the evidence that he touched me last night, when he pushed me away this morning.

So I awkwardly half-slide out of the bed, tugging on the robe as I try to keep the sheets around me as much as possible. It doesn't really matter—I can see in my periphery that he seems to be avoiding looking at me as much as I'm trying not to ogle him—and I tie the robe with a jerk of my hands, forcing back a fresh wave of disappointed tears that threaten to well up as I walk across the room to the shower.

With the door to the bathroom firmly closed behind me, I lean against it and close my eyes, trying to get my emotions under control. It doesn't help that the room smells like him, the masculine scents of piney shower gel and citrusy shampoo filling the humid air. He must have brought his own things with him instead of using what the hotel provided. It feels like I'm surrounded by him, all the scents that I've come to associate with having his body close to me, bare skin against mine and hair beneath my hands, and his face pressed against me filling my nostrils. I'm enveloped with it, and the ache in my chest spreads through me, until all I feel is a hopeless sense of hurt.

I shouldn't have done this. It's the first time I've ever thought that, and I try to fight it back. I don't want to regret any of it, not the beach or Rio or our marriage. I want to believe that in the years to come, something will change. That time and intimacy and our family that's beginning now will make a difference.

You're a fool. If he hasn't moved on in twelve years, he won't in another twelve. It doesn't matter what you do.

The thought weighs me down. My steps feel leaden as I walk to the shower, turning it on and letting steam fill the glass enclosure. When I step in, I pour a healthy amount of the orange blossom and honey shampoo into my hand, lathering it and letting it run under the water out between my fingers until that scent starts to fill the air, and not what's left from Levin.

And then I lean against the tiles, the heavy spray of the water drowning out the sounds, and I let myself cry.

It's the morning after my wedding, and I'm sobbing in the shower.

It's been a long time since I've felt so alone.

―

Since we're not going on a honeymoon, and we don't have a place of our own yet, we're headed back to Niall and Isabella's house. "I offered for us to stay in a hotel," Levin tells me as he drives us back. "But Niall thought it was bad hospitality, and Isabella wants you close. So that's that, I suppose."

I know what he's not saying—that Isabella wants *me* close, and that if it were possible to have me stay without Levin, she'd jump at the opportunity. But regardless of how anyone feels about it, Levin is my husband now, and asking him to stay elsewhere would be the height of rudeness.

Isabella was raised the same way I was—rudeness to guests is an impossibility. At worst, you can be cold to those you don't like, while still offering them hospitality. I have a feeling she'll be frosty with Levin until we can find a place of our own—and before, I might have taken issue with it. Now I'm not feeling all that happy with him myself.

No matter how many times I remind myself that I knew what I was getting into, that this is as much my fault as it is his, I can't stop the hurt that seems to have settled into my chest and taken up residence there for now. *He could try*, I keep thinking, and then I remember, over and over again, that this *is* him trying. That he's done all he can to make me happy within the bounds of what he can manage. It's not his fault that it's not enough, any more than it's mine.

Levin parks in the driveway, turning off the car. "We're back home," he says neutrally, looking at the grey-painted house in front of us. "For now."

I twist my fingers together in my lap, feeling anxiety rise up and turn into a lump in my throat. "When are we going to look for our own place?"

He looks over at me, and I see a hint of sympathy in his blue eyes. It's not unfamiliar. I can't sit here and pretend that I don't know that Levin cares about me. It's not his fault that's not enough for me. That I want *more*. "Whenever you want," he tells me. "We can start looking tomorrow, or we can wait a bit until you're ready, if you're more comfortable here."

"You'd do that for me?" I blurt out, before I can stop myself. I know he doesn't particularly like staying here. How could he, when my sister is so clearly disapproving of him? Isabella might not turn him away, but she hasn't—and won't—go to any great lengths to make him feel welcomed.

"Elena." Levin reaches out, his hand covering mine, stilling them where they're still wringing in my lap. "I will do anything I can to make you happy. To make this easier for you. If that could have been my wedding vow, it would have been. If that means staying here until you're ready—"

"Just a day or two." I cut him off before he can say anything else. I don't know anymore what hurts worse, rejection or these moments when he tells me he wants to make me happy, and I know that if he could give me everything, he would. It just underscores the fact that he's not doing this maliciously, and therefore, there's not anything that can likely change it.

If Levin had a heart left to give, it would be mine. That's what he's been trying to tell me all this time, I'm almost sure of it. But according to him, he doesn't.

And I'm no longer sure that he's wrong.

"A few days is fine," Levin agrees. "We can look for an apartment or a house to rent, whatever you want—"

I nod, swallowing hard and reaching for the door handle. I know it's unfair, but if I hear him say *anything you want, anything I can do to make you happy,* one more time, I think I'm going to scream.

Levin is out of the car almost immediately, coming around to open my door the rest of the way for me. I step out and try to bolster myself as we walk up the path to the house.

I almost feel like knocking, but of course, I don't need to. This is my house, too; Isabella has made that clear, for as long as I need it to be. Levin hangs back as I open the door and follows me inside as I call out.

"Isabella? Niall? We're back—"

Niall appears almost instantly, looking a little frazzled. "Isabella will be out in a minute. Sorry, Aisling is having a bad day." He glances at the two of us. "The bigger guest room is made up for you both now, lass. Isabella moved Levin's things in there."

"Thank you." I don't know why I'd thought I would be going back to that room—the one I'd been staying in since Levin brought me here from Rio—alone, and that Levin would be staying in the other room. *You're married now. Of course, you share a bed.* But nothing else about our marriage is normal. I'd somehow thought that wouldn't be, either.

As it turns out, sharing a room isn't enough to make it feel normal. When we emerge from putting our things away, Isabella is up and about, my fussy niece propped on her hip. She hugs me and gives Levin a curt nod, and goes about finding lunch for us. For the remainder of the day, she dotes on me and seemingly pretends

Levin isn't there unless necessary, which means for a great deal of my first day as a wife, Levin is off with Niall, and Isabella and I spend time together.

"I'm glad you're back." She glances down the hall as she finishes feeding Aisling her lunch, her own sandwich still mostly ignored next to her elbow. I can see a lot of that in my future, depending on how fussy my own baby is. "I wasn't going to move Levin's things into your room, but Niall said I should. That you'd probably intended on sharing a bed." She glances at me. "I'd thought he would leave you alone—it being a marriage under duress and all of that."

"I think—" I press my lips together, not knowing how to talk about this with my sister. If it were any other man, any other marriage, I could see myself sitting here with her the morning after, gossiping about my new husband. But I feel protective over Levin. I know how much she dislikes him, and I don't want to give her more reasons to feel negatively about him. "I think he's going to do his best. It's not easy, Isabella."

"It's not easy for you, either." Her voice crisps around the edges, tight and irritable, as she stands up and takes Aisling's small plate and spoon to the sink. "Being married to a man who wouldn't have come back unless you were pregnant. Who got you in this position in the first place."

"It took both of us, Issie. You know that as well as I do."

I see Isabella soften slightly at the use of my childhood nickname. I haven't called her that in a long time, and I see her grip the edges of the counter, her head tipping forward for a moment as I see a long sigh go through her before she turns back to me.

"Be that as it may," she says softly. "Things were supposed to be different for you here. You were supposed to marry someone you loved, if you decided to get married. There was supposed to be a whole life that you wouldn't have had back home. That's all going to be different now. And Levin—"

"Is not entirely at fault," I tell her firmly. "I was a part of this too. Don't take away my agency in this, Issie. Don't make it not my decision. You know how that feels. You made your choice; consequences be damned. I have that same right. And I—"

Isabella looks at me, her dark eyes suddenly very sad. "You love him, don't you?" she asks, resignation there too. "You really do."

I swallow hard, nodding. "Yeah. I think so. Levin keeps saying I have feelings for someone who doesn't really exist, but I don't agree."

Isabella snorts. "For once, he and I agree on something. I wish it was on a different topic. Like him being an absent husband in New York, while you stay here."

"I don't want that either." I give my sister a pleading look. "I'm not a child, Issie. And Levin isn't making these decisions for us. I'm making them too. *I* told him I wanted to stay in Boston, that if we got married, we'd be in Boston together. I wanted to stay near you and Aisling and my new brother-in-law. Levin is letting *me* make the choices for us."

"Because he feels guilty."

I shrug. "Be that as it may, he's still letting me make them."

"How long are you staying?" Isabella sits back down, reaching for her sandwich as Aisling absentmindedly chews on a teething ring. "At the house here, I mean."

I pick up a potato chip, crumbling it between my fingers. "I told Levin I wanted a few days before we look for a place. And then after that—however long it takes for us to find somewhere we like, I suppose."

"Do you know what you want?"

I shake my head. "I'm going to look at some things today online. And think about it from there."

It's not entirely true, but the conversation isn't one I really want to have. I know Levin and I aren't looking to buy a house yet, but I want to look at houses to rent. He told me that he and his late wife lived in an apartment, that they'd never had a house together, because she'd died before they could decide where they wanted to raise their family. I want to start our life the way I hope it will continue, in a small house like the one I'm sitting in now. Maybe something that eventually, if we like it enough, the owners could be convinced to sell to us. Something that could be our home.

Isabella doesn't push further, and I'm glad. She doesn't press me about too much, not this afternoon and not in any of the ones that follow, over the few days that Levin and I stay until I feel ready to start looking for a place of our own.

He doesn't touch me again. Not like that. I tell myself every night when he kisses me lightly on the cheek and rolls over in bed that we wouldn't have done more than sleep anyway, not in my sister's house, but I don't entirely believe it. There's something sneakily romantic about the idea of stealing quiet kisses and slow, hushed sex, about having to bite back moans and stifle our sounds of pleasure because someone might hear. I want that—having to keep quiet because we want each other so badly that we can't wait—but it's not going to happen. I'm sure of it after the first night.

It's made more difficult because every morning, I wake up with Levin pressed against me. He makes an effort to put distance between us at night—moving over to his side of the bed as he turns off the light. I got a glimpse of what I think is his nightly routine the first night—he changed into pajama pants and a t-shirt, slipping under the covers with a book, and read for about an hour before setting the book aside and glancing over at me.

"A lot of nights, I have work that I take to bed with me," he said wryly. "Papers Viktor wants me to look over, files, reports. This almost feels like a vacation."

What that told me was that he typically read *something* in bed before switching out the light. *On the nights when no one else is in bed with him.* I had to force that thought out to keep from going misty-eyed, imagining some strange woman in bed with him. *Was there anyone in New York, after he left me here?* It's not a question I can ask him, if he'd slept with anyone between bringing me here and when Niall had called him to tell him he needed to come back. Even if I felt like I could, I don't think I want to know the answer.

I'd set my phone aside when he switched off the light, and Levin had leaned over. For one wild moment, I had thought he was going to kiss me, that despite the fact that we were in my sister's house, he wanted me enough to not care.

And then his lips had grazed across my cheek. "Good night," he said softly, then rolled over, half an arm's length between us, as my chest tightened and the lump in my throat nearly choked me.

The two following nights were the same, as was every morning. No matter how careful Levin is to put space between us when he goes to sleep, I wake with him spooning me, his broad chest against my back and his hard cock wedged against my spine, his arm slung over me as if in his sleep, he can't stop himself from holding me close.

That hurts more than anything else—the realization that subconsciously, Levin wants me. That he wants more than what he's so carefully cultivated into the beginning of our marriage—something courteous and caring, but ultimately detached.

I don't say anything about it. Every morning, I squirm away from him, out from under his arm and over to my side of the bed before he wakes up. I'm not entirely sure why, exactly. A part of me thinks that it's because I'm afraid that if he knows, he might start sleeping in another bed. It might be because I'm afraid that in his sleep, he thinks it's someone else that he's holding. Or maybe—

I can't really put my finger on why. I just don't want him to know. So I savor the feeling of being in his arms for just a moment—the heat of his body sinking into mine and the safe, secure sensation of his arm wrapped over me, before I move away from him and return back to reality.

The morning of the fourth day after our wedding, I get up after I slip out from under his arm. We have houses to view this morning; the realtor that Isabella contacted gave us the lockbox key number for each of them—and we're supposed to set out in a couple of hours. I leave Levin quietly snoring in the bed while I pad down the hall to shower, throwing on my robe afterward before coming back to what I've started to think of as *our* room, no matter how hard I try not to.

Soon, I'll be waking up in *our* house. The thought fills me with a strange mixture of dread and excitement, because it's not something I ever thought I'd have with him. Even when I'd imagined the arranged marriage I'd expected to have, before all of this, it would have been me going to my husband's house. Not *ours*. Not something I would have chosen with him.

This is a new experience for me.

Levin is awake when I come back in, sitting halfway up in bed and rubbing a hand over his face. He's wearing a t-shirt with his pajamas, as always—I think it's more a means to keep us from doing anything he's trying to avoid rather than how he actually usually sleeps—and I can see his muscles flex under it, making my mouth go a little dry.

Four days since our wedding, and it feels like a lifetime since our wedding night. I feel wound tight with desire, aching for him. Spending every night in bed with him and not doing more than sleeping feels like torture, and I can't help but wonder what he would say if I told him that. Once again, I wonder what constitutes *satisfied?* I'm not sure what would satisfy me when it comes to him. I've never once felt like I had enough of him.

I wish he felt the same about me.

"House-hunting day?" Levin glances at me, looking at the slim black pants and cream-colored peplum silk blouse I slipped on with a pair of sandals and pearl earrings, fancier than what I usually wear during the day. "You look like you're going to an interview."

I shrug. "I don't know what you're supposed to wear to something like this. I thought I should look nice."

"You look beautiful."

His voice is sincere, and I freeze with my hand halfway to my ear, one pearl stud still clutched between my fingers. I look at him, a flood of emotion rushing through me.

"Thank you," I whisper, not knowing what else to say. I want to hear him say it again. I want him to get out of bed and walk over to me and kiss me, whispering it against my lips. Instead, we stare at each other over the gulf of space between the bed and where I'm standing, and my chest aches all over again.

Levin gets up, but he doesn't walk to me. He walks past me, collecting clothes out of the dresser, and I can envision him doing that in our own bedroom, wherever that ends up being. *This is going to be my life, every morning, for the rest of it.* It should make me the happiest woman in the world. Instead, it makes me feel as if I'm drowning. Not because I don't want it to be Levin that I spend those mornings with, but because I *do*.

"I'm going to shower. I'll meet you for breakfast." He glances at me, and I see the flicker of a moment where he almost moves towards me, as if he instinctively wants to cross to me for a kiss.

And then he's gone, disappeared into the hallway.

I sink down onto the edge of the bed, the pearl stud still in my hand. *Don't cry,* I tell myself firmly. I can't spend every morning of my life crying. I have to find a way to make this not hurt so much, because I won't make it otherwise.

It will be easier when the baby comes, I tell myself. *You'll have something to occupy your attention, then. Something that demands so much of it, you won't even notice when Levin walks past you without a kiss. It won't hurt so much, then.*

I just wish I really believed that.

Elena

By the time we walk through the third of the five houses we have on our list to look at, I don't know how we're going to pick one.

I've never been house-hunting. I had it in my mind that we'd decide on something today and told Levin as much when we left to go to the first one. "I don't want to spend a bunch of time going back and forth," I told him firmly. "I just want to decide on something, so we can move in and be done with it."

Levin had shrugged. "I'm not picky," he told me. "I've lived in the same apartment for a long time. Other than a room I can turn into an office, I don't need much."

I don't know why his answer made me feel disappointed. I didn't want him to argue with me, exactly. I just wanted—I wasn't sure.

For him to have an opinion about it, maybe. To care.

I never thought I could feel so fed up with someone telling me that I could have whatever I wanted all of the time. I know it sounds ungrateful. But what I really wanted was for him to have an opinion, too.

The first house was far too small. Three bedrooms technically, but only one was even decently large enough to be ours, and the other two would have been a tight fit each for a nursery and an office. "I think it would be nice to have a guest room," I tell Levin tentatively as we leave for the second house. "I don't know who would visit, but just in case—"

"Why not?" Levin shrugs. "It would be nice. And who knows? Maybe your parents will come to visit one day."

It sounds nice to hear him say it, not that I think my mother would stay at either Isabella's or my house, wherever the latter ends up being. I know Isabella has avoided showing her very much of her home with Niall, knowing that our mother sees it as a huge step down from what we grew up in and what she sees as what we deserve.

Still, who knows what the future holds? I might make friends who might need a place to stay over some nights after staying up too late. Levin might know someone. It feels hopeful to have a spot for guests. *And a place to sleep if it ever gets too hard to lie in bed next to a man who doesn't really want to be there.*

I don't let the last thought linger. The second house is pretty, and larger, but it doesn't feel quite right. Neither does the third, although I can't put my finger on exactly why. There's nothing wrong with them on the surface, but as I tell Levin over lunch before we visit the fourth and fifth houses, it just didn't feel like home.

"We don't have to rush," he tells me gently, setting down the burger he ordered. I have a salad with dressing on the side in front of me, because it's one of the few foods Isabella and I have determined through unpleasant trial and error that I seem to actually be able to keep down without any issues. "I know you said you wanted to choose something today, Elena. But we have time. Isabella has been trying to be more welcoming with me, I can tell. It's nice to have the time to catch up with Niall—I hadn't seen him in a while before this. And you're comfortable there with your sister. We're in no hurry."

I nod, jabbing at my salad with a fork and no real desire to eat. I don't know how to explain to him that to me, it *does* feel like we're in a hurry, like the sooner we get out of this strange liminal space where I'm living in my sister's house with my new husband, the sooner our marriage might shift into something that feels more real for both of us. I can't find the right words to tell him, because I know that whatever I say, he'll likely remind me that this is what our marriage is going to be. For better or for worse—no pun intended—this is it. This is our life together.

"We'll look at the last two," Levin says encouragingly. "If one of them feels right to you, we'll move forward. And if not, we'll find some others to check out. We'll find the one you want eventually."

It doesn't make me feel as hopeful as I know he means for it to. I have half a mind to say we just head back to Isabella and Niall's after lunch, but I push forward, getting into the car as Levin looks up the directions for the fourth house—and when we pull into the gravel driveway, I'm glad I did.

The moment I look at it, I have the feeling that I didn't with any of the others—like this is our home, and I just didn't know it until now—the feeling that I was hoping for. The house itself is situated about fifteen miles or so away from my sister's house, not on the water, but nestled up against trees that, from my vantage point in the passenger's seat, I can see lead to a trail that goes further back into the forest. I picture myself walking out there with a stroller, maybe a dog on a leash, or going for a run in the cool morning air later on, when our baby is older and has already been dropped off at school.

I realize in a rush that in seconds, I've been able to picture a future here. *Maybe we can buy it,* I think to myself as I get out of the car, walking up the gravel drive. The house itself is a similar style to Niall and Isabella's, made of the clapboard that's popular here, two stories high with an attic window and a gabled roof. The house is painted white with navy blue shutters, pristine and crisp against the greenery of the trees. As Levin unlocks the door and we step inside, I once again have that feeling of coming home.

The house is empty of furniture or decorations, a blank slate for us. The floors are all gleaming, smooth wood, dark with white walls to accent them, ready for us to paint or wallpaper in any color or pattern we choose, if it becomes ours for good.

After one walkthrough, I know it's perfect. And I also know that if I tell Levin I want it, he'll smile and tell me *absolutely. Anything you want.* But I want *him* to want it, too.

"Let's go through it one more time," I tell him when we make our way back down to the foyer. "I really like this one."

"I do too." Levin rubs a hand over his face. "It feels spacious, but not *too* big. Not like we'd rattle around in here until the baby comes, and even after."

Something catches in my throat at that. I don't think I've heard him say it so casually before like that. *Until the baby comes.* For just a moment, there's no guilt or hesitation in his voice. He says it like it was always supposed to be like this—him and I and our child. And maybe more, one day.

I have to stop that train of thought before it goes too far. We haven't talked about it, and I haven't let myself think about whether we'll want or have more children after this unplanned baby. But I think about how much Isabella and I love each other, how devoted we've always been to each other, and it feels like it wouldn't be right to deprive our baby of that—having a sibling.

We'll talk about it another time, I decide, looking down the hall. *We don't need to decide today. There's no hurry.*

"It's all so open." I lead Levin down the hall to the living room, which is one of the biggest rooms in the house, with a huge stone fireplace and double French doors leading out to the tree-lined backyard. "The light in here is beautiful. The windows are so big— we could put a reading nook there—" I point to one of the larger bay windows, with a gorgeous view of the backyard. "And I love the fireplace mantel. Can you imagine it all decorated for the holidays? And how cozy it'll be in the winter?"

Levin warned me, one of the nights we spent in Rio, what northeast winters are like here. It sounded exciting to me—something new to experience, and he'd shaken his head at me. *It's just like you to find a reason to be excited about it, instead of dreading it. We'll see how you feel when you're calf-deep in snow and feel like it's all the way down in your bones, just to go to the grocery store.*

The memory sends a tangled thread of emotions through me. I'd barely heard anything that he said that night after *we'll see how you feel,* because, in that moment, that had implied that he would *be here* for my first winter. Not in New York, far away from me and whatever my reactions might be.

Now he is going to be here, for my first winter and all the winters after that—and the feeling is so bittersweet that I have to swallow back the urge to cry, as I have to so often these days.

I clear my throat, walking through the living room to the kitchen. "I don't know how to cook," I tell him with a laugh. "But with a kitchen like this, how could I not learn?"

It's half the size of the living room, with a light grey granite island, cupboards everywhere, and a range stove. All of the appliances are shiny and new. The windows overlook the backyard where the stove is, and the side of the house where the sink is located, with a view of the garage and the other section of the yard. It's bright and airy, and I can see myself spending time in here, cooking breakfast, and learning to make dinners for guests to come over and enjoy.

Levin chuckles. "I'm not much for cooking either," he admits. "Live alone long enough, and takeout becomes the best solution a lot of the time. But I could learn, too." He grins at me, and I see a moment where his guard slips, and he's his most natural self. "Can't let you do all the housekeeping. Gotta pull my weight, too."

My teeth sink into my lower lip as I fight back another well of emotion. I had a reason for wanting to walk through the house again—I wanted to look for something in each room that could be a part of our future here, to show Levin here what our life could look like. I had *wanted* this, to see a glimpse of him the way he would be if this were something we had both wanted all along, not something we're stumbling blindly through, trying to find a way to make it work.

I had, if I'm being honest with myself, wanted to see what he was like when he *had* wanted this. Before he had decided he would never have it again.

I don't know if it helps or hurts now.

"Come on." I clear my throat, walking back out into the hall. "That room can be your office," I tell him, pointing at the room with an open door that's down from the guest bathroom. It's a medium size, with a window that looks out on the other side of the house. "You can do whatever you like with that—decorate it however you want."

"Giving me permission?" Levin grins at me again. "I'd already decided you could make all the decorating decisions, but I'll take one room."

I narrow my eyes at him, enjoying the playful lilt to his voice. "Depending on what your taste is, maybe more than one room. And the bedroom down here can be the guest room."

"Sounds fine to me."

We walk back upstairs, where the other three bedrooms are and a second extra bathroom. There's a big master suite and then two good-sized bedrooms with a bathroom between them. "This one should be the nursery," I suggest when we step into the first room. "It's the closest to ours."

"That makes sense." Levin turns around, looking. "Plenty of room in here. What color were you thinking of painting it?"

My throat closes up again, a lump threatening to choke me. "I don't know," I manage finally. "I haven't gotten that far. I thought something neutral. Yellow maybe—something sunny and bright."

"Or sage green?" Levin suggests, turning back to face me. "I always liked that color."

I'm so startled by how easily he's contributing to the conversation that I can't answer for a second. My hesitation seems to spark his, and a strange look passes over his face, as if he's realized what he's done. That for a moment, he forgot to be anything other than excited over the possibility of decorating our baby's nursery in this room.

"What about the other room?" He turns away, looking towards the door, and I feel my heart sink again. I can feel the tension emanating off of him, *feel* him closing himself off again. Frustration wells up in me, making me grit my teeth.

I don't want to be angry with him. Not today, and not over something I decided to do myself, knowing that it would likely be a lost cause. That Levin will always defer to me when it comes to decisions about our life—at least these kinds of decisions, like what house to live in and where—because it's more my life than his. Because he's going to spend all of it trying to make up for what he thinks he's taken from me.

When, in fact, he's given me so much that I wanted.

"The other room—" I hesitate. "I don't know. Maybe a room for the baby when they're older. In case—" I swallow hard. "In case we need the nursery for another one."

I see his shoulders tense, and I wince. Having one child was never in Levin's plan, so I can't imagine he's given much, if any, thought to a second. "I loved having a sister growing up," I whisper softly. "Our baby might like that, too. Or a brother."

He lets out a long, slow sigh. "Maybe," he says finally, still not looking at me. "We'll just have to see what happens, I suppose."

It's not the definite *no* that I'd been afraid of, but it's not what I wanted to hear, either. He steps out of the room, opening the door, and crosses the hall to the master bedroom, and I follow him, trailing a little behind as I try to keep a grip on my emotions.

"We could put another little reading nook in here," I suggest. Anything to try to steer the conversation away from things that make me want to cry. "It would be so cozy in the winter, especially with the fireplace—"

The room is huge, with another of those big bay windows overlooking the backyard, and a little balcony leading off of it. There's a fireplace, something I've never had in a bedroom before, and the idea of cozying up here in the cold with a book and a warm fire sounds heavenly. There's an attached bathroom with a large whirlpool tub and a separate shower, as nice as any hotel suite we've stayed in. I try not to summon the memory of Levin and me in the bath in that last hotel room in Rio.

He's silent for a long moment, staring off into the distance, turned away from me. "Levin?" I ask finally, my voice a hesitant whisper, and when he turns to face me, his expression cuts me to the core.

It's so conflicted that I can't stand it. I can see everything that he's struggling with in the brief moment before he manages to clear some of it away—and I realize that he *does* want this. That standing here with me, imagining our future in this house, is making him happy.

And it's also making him feel so guilty that it's tearing him apart.

I know I'm not supposed to go to him. He hasn't so much as kissed me, other than on the cheek, since our wedding night. But I can't stop myself. Seeing him like this is tearing *me* apart, because regardless of what he or Isabella or anyone else thinks, I do love him. I know it down to the core of my being, with a certainty that I'm not sure I've ever had for anything else. I love him, and I can't stand to see him in this kind of pain, any more than I could stand to see him in pain in Rio when I nursed him back to health.

So I cross the distance between us, my shoes clicking on the wooden floor, and before he can stop me, I go up on my tiptoes and press my hand against his cheek, my lips brushing over his.

"This is our house," I whisper softly against his mouth. "This is the one I want."

This is the one I want. I mean something other than the house, too. I mean him, and our life, and our baby—everything that I have with him, and I'm not sure at first if he realizes it. I feel him stiffen when I kiss him, and I brace myself for the moment when he pushes me away, when he tells me that we can't do this.

That *he* can't do this.

I feel a shudder go through him, and I know what it means. I've felt it so many times before, the physical way that he fights with himself when he's trying not to give in to me, in to what he and I both want.

But it's a battle that I want him to lose.

When his hands land on my waist, I know he's losing it—if he's not already lost.

His mouth presses against mine, slanting over my lips. I can feel him hesitating, trying not to kiss me. I can almost hear the wheels in his head turning, demanding that he back away, coming up with all of the reasons why he shouldn't and all of the reasons that he should.

Please don't stop. I slide my hands up his chest, fingers sliding into the small gap above the top button, where he left two undone. I press my fingertips there, against his warm skin, and I trail my tongue over his lower lip.

He breaks the kiss, just a little. "We have one more house to see—"

"This is it." I lean in, brushing my lips over his again. I haven't pushed since our wedding night. I've been too afraid of the possibility of him rejecting me, of how it would feel, how much it would hurt. Too afraid that I don't know how much time he thinks is supposed to pass before we go to bed together again. "This is our house."

"It's not ours yet." The words are murmured between our mouths, his breath warm on my lips, and a flood of desire rushes through me.

"It will be." I undo one of his shirt buttons, and another, and another, kissing him between each one, my tongue trailing over his lower lip, my teeth nipping at it. "Levin—"

I know he knows what I want. His hand tightens on my waist, his hips moving against mine, and I can feel how hard he is. He wants me too, and I decide at that moment to make it as difficult as I can for him to turn me down this time.

"You said you wanted to give me what I wanted," I whisper against his mouth. "I want you. Here. Now. Please—"

"That's not fair." Levin's voice is hoarse, and I feel his hands squeeze my waist, as if he's struggling with whether to pull me closer or push me away. "Not even a little bit, Elena—"

"I know."

I close my eyes and kiss him harder. I reach up, sliding one hand behind his head, and I crush his mouth to mine as I keep undoing the buttons of his shirt with my other hand, until it's hanging almost entirely open, and I feel him shudder again as my fingers brush down his abdomen.

When I feel him give in when his mouth opens and his tongue tangles with mine, my knees go weak. It's been less than a week, but it feels like it's been an unbearable amount of time since he last kissed me like this, and I curl my fingers into the edges of his shirt, pulling him closer.

I feel him groan against my lips, the vibration tingling against my skin, and his hands slide down to my ass, squeezing, gripping, pulling me closer too. I slip the last buttons of his shirt free, breaking the kiss to drag my lips down his throat, flicking my tongue in the hollow of his collarbone as my hands drop to his belt.

Every moment is one where he might remember that he feels like we shouldn't be doing this, where he might stop me. I grab every second of closeness with him that I can, tucking them away for all the days and nights when I know he'll remember his self-control, savoring him while I have him under mine. I trail my lips down his chest, down lower still, sinking to my knees in front of him as I pull down his zipper.

"Elena, the floor—"

"I don't care." I slide my hand inside the opening of his trousers, and he's so hard that he springs into my hand instantly, hot and throbbing. I hear Levin bite back a groan as I slide my thumb over the damp tip of his cock, already dripping for me, and his hand strokes over my hair.

"*Fuck*, Elena—"

"I want you," I breathe, my lips very close to his cock. "Please—"

He chuckles a low, dark, deep sound. "You're on your knees with my cock in your hand, and you're the one begging *me*." The irony in his voice is thick. "Goddamn it, Elena, do you have any idea what you do to me?"

There's so much in that one question. "Sometimes," I whisper, and then, before he can answer, before the moment can get dark and sad and turn into something that could keep us from doing this, I slide my hand down the length of him and wrap my lips around the tip of his cock. I feel the tremor that runs throughout his entire body as his hand presses against the back of his head.

I know him well enough now to know what he likes. What he wants. What will drive him crazy with desire. I know the taste of him, the way he loves when I swirl my tongue around his tip, licking up the pre-cum there, salty and thick on my tongue. I know he likes when I slide my hand down slowly, my lips and tongue following, letting him watch as I take him inch by inch, all the way into the back of my throat, looking up at him wide-eyed.

I can see the moment when he's no longer fighting it, when he gives up and gives in to the pleasure. His fingers slide through my hair, his expression softening as his eyes go hazy with lust, watching me as I suck his cock.

"You look so fucking beautiful," he murmurs, his fingers sliding along my jaw as I take him a little deeper, and he groans. "Such a good girl. You take my cock so well."

A shiver runs down my spine, my thighs squeezing together at the praise. His voice ripples over me like silk, and I'm aching to have him inside of me, to feel him fill me up again. Nothing could ever feel as good as he does when he's inside of me; I'm certain of that.

I slide down all the way, until my nose brushes against his skin, and his head tips back. "Oh *fuck*," he breathes, and I hold him there as long as I can, my throat tightening around him until I have to come up for air.

When I slide off of his cock, gasping a little for breath, the look on his face makes it hard to get any at all. He's looking down at me with an expression of such blatant lust that it makes me feel as if I'll never breathe again. I see his other hand clench at his side, as if he's trying to stop himself—and he can't.

He sinks down onto his knees in front of me, the hand in my hair tangling it around his fist as his mouth comes crashing down onto mine again. In an instant, I go from being the one seducing him to the one being taken. He leans into me, pushing me onto my back on the hard wooden floor as he growls against my lips, a harsh, desperate sound of need.

"You drive me insane," he groans, his forehead pressed against mine as his other hand finds the button of my pants, jerking it open. My entire body arches when I feel his fist close around the waist, yanking the fabric down, his hand sliding between my thighs, and I moan when his fingertips slide between my folds. "Oh, *god*, you're so fucking wet—"

It's an understatement. I'm drenched, aching for him, and when he pushes two fingers inside of me, more roughly than usual, with his thumb on my clit, I feel like I might come on the spot. I arch my hips into his hand, thrusting back as he fingers me, his thumb rolling over my clit in the same rhythm over and over until I'm so close to unraveling.

When he kisses me again, I sink my teeth into his lower lip. He grunts, a deep sound of surprise, and thrusts his fingers into me harder still, driving me towards a rough, quick orgasm, as if he knows exactly what it is that I need—and it shouldn't surprise me any longer. He's always known what I needed.

His tongue pushes into my mouth, tangling with mine, and he drags my pants lower on my thighs with his other hand, leaning over me. I feel his cock brush against my inner thigh, ready to take the place of his fingers the moment I come for him, and that pushes me over the edge.

I grab the back of his head, nails digging into the nape of his neck as my scream of pleasure is swallowed up by the kiss, clenching around his fingers as his thumb grinds into my clit. My vision blurs at the edges as I come, my entire body convulsing as I finally come, the orgasm I've needed for days crashing through me like a tidal wave, again and again, as I hold his mouth against mine, my other hand shooting down to grip his wrist and hold his hand against me as if he might stop at any moment.

I squeeze around him, riding his fingers until the orgasm starts to ebb, and he wrenches his hand free from mine. I cry out at the loss of friction, the moment when I feel empty and hollow again, but it's not for long.

He shoves his pants down his hips, and I catch a glimpse of his hand wrapping around his long, thick cock, his fingers still glistening from my arousal. The sight is so frankly lewd that it sends another jolt of pleasure through me, and I moan as he leans forward, the swollen head of his cock pushing into me as I arch upwards, my hand gripping his ass.

"Fuck me," I gasp, my nails biting into his skin. "Please fuck me—"

I can't wrap my legs around him. My pants are tangled around my calves, tugged down just enough for Levin to get my legs far enough apart that he can thrust into me. I feel half-restrained beneath him, desperate to get him closer and entirely at his mercy. It's maddening and arousing all at once, and I drag my nails up his back, bucking underneath him as he starts to push himself deeper.

"Please—"

"Easy there." His hand cups my jaw, tipping my head up so he can look down at me. "This is what you want, Elena?"

I stare up at him, feeling half-dizzy with need. *Is he really asking this right now?* The head of his cock is inside of me, but he hasn't pushed deeper, holding me pinned beneath him. I clench around him, rolling my hips for a little of the pressure and friction that I so desperately need, and I see his jaw clench as he struggles for control.

"You want me to fuck you on the floor, like this?" His other hand is braced next to my head, his eyes dark with lust. His hips move, and he pushes another inch of his cock into me, making me moan with a desperate sound that would make me feel embarrassed at any other moment, but right now, I don't care. I need more.

"Yes—" I drag my nails higher up his back, twisting my hips under him, but his muscled bulk holds me in place. "*God*, Levin, please!"

"You have no idea what you do to me." Another inch and I still need more. I squeeze helplessly around him, needing him to thrust, needing the hot slide of him back and forth inside of me, making me come again. "You have no idea how you make me feel. Every fucking day, Elena—"

He thrusts forward another inch. I cry out, shuddering, and he groans.

"You confuse the hell out of me. You have, every fucking day since I met you. God*damn* it, Elena, you make me *want*—"

His hips snap forward as he bites off the last word like a curse, slamming his cock into me harder than I think he ever has before, and I shatter underneath him.

He starts to thrust as I come, each slide of his cock dragging through my clenching muscles, and I cry out again, the sound suddenly swallowed up by my mouth as he kisses me hard. Both of his hands grab mine, his fingers curling around my wrists as he pins them up over my head, and I'm reminded of the night in the motel when he tied me up with his belt, when he made me beg for him.

I feel like I'm going to spend the rest of my life begging for him.

Levin has me pinned, my legs trapped in my tangled pants, and my wrists clasped in his hands, and I lose track of where my orgasm ends, and the next one begins. All I can feel is the heat of his skin, burning through the thin material of my shirt, the pressure of his lips on mine, the hot, inexorable slide of his cock into me again and again, driving deeper every time, as if he wants to imprint himself on me. His hips grind into mine, his groan vibrating against my mouth, and I feel him shudder as he reaches the edge, too.

"Fuck, *malysh*—I'm going to come—"

The words are groaned into my mouth, cut off by my teeth grazing over his lower lip, my tongue tangling with his as I arch up into him. I want it. I want to feel him come inside of me. I want to feel the heat of him filling me up, and I want to tell him, to urge him on, but I can't stop kissing him long enough to say it. His fingers feel almost bruising around my wrists, his hips grinding down into me with a mad desperation as he presses me down against the hard wooden floor. Then I feel every inch of him go rigid, his cock thick and hard and swollen inside of me in an instant before his hips buck, and I feel him flood me with the hot rush of his cum.

Pleasure washes over me again, electric and jolting over every inch of my skin. I shudder helplessly under him, moaning his name as he buries his face in my neck and his hips roll against mine, his cock throbbing as he comes hard.

For a long moment, neither of us move. I feel the knot of dread in my stomach, knowing this is the moment where he comes back to himself, where he remembers what he thinks of all of this, how he feels every time he loses control. I can *feel* it when he starts to shut down, his hands unwrapping from around my wrists as he pulls back, his cock slipping free as he turns away from me.

"Jesus, Elena." He runs one hand over his hair as he stands up awkwardly, tugging his pants back up around his hips. "Fuck, we probably made a mess—"

"I'll deal with it." My clothes are in even more disarray. I pull them back into place, my chest aching hollowly as I wish for him to turn around, to look at me, to give me *anything* other than what feels like regret. "We have to rent the house now, right? We fucked in it."

It's a terrible attempt at a joke. He stays facing away from me for a long moment and then slowly turns, holding out a hand to help me up from the floor.

"If it's the house you want, it's the house we'll get," he tells me, just as I always knew he would. But it's not just the house that I want.

I stand there looking at the man I love, his face a careful blank again, and I want to tell him that I'd live anywhere if he would just stop looking at me like that, if I could have even one more day where he could just be himself with me, and not throw up every wall he has after letting them down without meaning to. If I could not feel as if every time we're together, I'm clinging to every second I get, because I never know when I'll have another one.

"This is the one," I tell him softly, and once again, I'm not just talking about the house. I stand there, watching as he buttons up his shirt, and I want to go to him so badly it hurts. I want to kiss him and run my hands through his hair and tell him how much I love him, and I swallow it all down, along with the hurt burning in my chest. I force a smile, and I watch him as he straightens, settling back into the careful version of himself that I know so much better than I want to.

"Well then, I'll call the realtor." Levin smiles, but it doesn't quite reach his eyes. "You should text Isabella. We should all go out to dinner to celebrate."

"That sounds nice." I follow him out of the room, reaching for my phone, but my heart isn't in it. I should feel like celebrating, but right now, I don't.

I don't know how to make any of this bearable. I don't know how to spend the rest of my life living for the moments in between, when Levin forgets how much he hates himself for everything he blames himself for. I don't know how to make a life for us both.

I don't know how to love someone who's forgotten how.

Levin

The day after Elena and I settle on the house, I'm called back to the Kings' headquarters to meet with Connor and Liam, along with Niall. I suspect, from the tone of Connor's voice, that it won't be good news, but I'm glad for a moment away to collect my thoughts.

I know Elena is frustrated with how distant I've been since the day before. I can feel it emanating off of her, no matter how hard she tries to hide it. It feels like we're two people locked in an endless battle with ourselves—me with my lingering guilt and grief, and her with her need to take responsibility for the situation we've found ourselves in. She's determined not to blame me, and a part of me wishes that she would.

At least then, we'd be on the same page in regards to that.

The meeting gives me something to focus on, a job to do. I might not have been able to protect Elena from myself, but I can do my damndest to protect her from the lingering threat of Diego, and I intend to do exactly that. I didn't see the threat coming the last time. I was complacent, certain that I knew what the future held. Now I have some idea what's coming, and I intend to be prepared for it.

He's not getting anywhere near her or our child, if I have anything to say about it.

Boston was supposed to be a safe place for her, and I'm going to keep it that way, if it fucking kills me.

Connor and Liam's faces are grave when Niall and I walk in. I can feel the tension thrumming through Niall as he stands next to me, and I've known him long enough to know when he's angry. He's served the Kings for a long time, much more closely than I've ever been with them, and I know he's as afraid for his family as I am for Elena and our unborn child.

"What do you know?" Niall demands the moment we're in the room, not even bothering to sit down. "I want to know what's going on."

Connor's face tightens, as if he's about to castigate Niall for his tone, but Liam holds up a hand, giving his brother a pointed look. "Diego is furious," Liam says carefully, "as we expected he would be. From what we've heard, he feels as if he's been outwitted by Levin's marriage to Elena."

"So I'm guessing that your next words aren't going to be that he's decided to cut his losses and focus on something else?" Niall asks caustically, before I can even get a word in. I'm not sure I've ever seen him so angry. His arms are crossed over his chest, his jaw tight as he glares back and forth between the two brothers—one of whom is his best friend. But right now, I can tell, he's not a man having a conversation with a friend.

"Just have a seat," Connor interjects sharply. "We're not keeping anything from you, Flanagan. We know you're worried about what this means for Isabella. Just as we know Levin is concerned for Elena—though him keeping his distance from her might have made all this simpler."

I narrow my eyes at him. "Are we going to keep retreading this old ground forever, or—"

"If I'd been able to marry her to someone with some actual fucking influence—"

"Alright!" Liam slaps his hands down on the table, shaking his head. "What's done is done. Elena and Levin are married. There's no changing any of it or rewriting what's happened. Now we deal with it." He looks at me, his shoulders squaring as he takes over the conversation, ignoring his brother's murderous look. "Diego is taking this personally. He doesn't want Santiago continuing to trade with us and gaining strength that could be used against him, but this is more than that. Both of the daughters have been taken out from under his nose now, and the fact that it's been because of men working with the same factions that are allied with Santiago rubs salt in the wound. There are layers to this."

He pinches the bridge of his nose, looking tired. "His point of view is that we've had men working with us deny him both of the Santiago daughters on purpose, as an additional insult to add to the fact that we're allying with Santiago and not him. That's not true, of course—both of these situations were borne out of the girls' rebelliousness—"

"I'll thank you to keep your opinions about Isabella's nature out of your mouth," Niall says sharply, and Liam gives him an exasperated look.

"Niall, we're friends. Don't sit across the table and act as if we don't both know how all this transpired. I'm not going to pretend that I haven't made reckless decisions in pursuit of Ana. We're not here to rehash old choices made out of emotion, but it *was* Isabella's choice to take matters into her own hands and Elena's choice to pursue Levin that got us here—"

"You're not going to blame her for it," I interject, and Connor rolls his eyes so hard that they look as if they might disappear for a moment.

"We fucking get it," he snaps. "You're both protective over your wives. Liam and I would feel the same about Ana and Saoirse. But put your goddamn hackles down for one second, and fucking *listen*."

He stands up, running one hand through his hair as he braces the other against the back of his chair, glaring at us both. "There are threats that Diego is going to move into Kings' territory and attack. He clearly has enough resources here in the States, resources that we weren't aware of, to do so. How many? We're unsure. But he's not going to let this go. Personally, my opinion—and the opinion of my brother—is that he's a fool to think he has the slightest chance at taking over Kings' territory. But he's clearly pissed enough to think he can try."

"We met with the rest of the Kings." Liam rubs a hand over his face, exhaustion marring his features and making him look closer in age to his brother. "They're in agreement that we'll defend against this, but we're going to bide a little longer and see what moves he makes."

Niall's expression darkens instantly. "You've got to be fucking kidding me," he snaps. "*Wait and see?* That's the tactic you're taking with this?"

"You need to remember your fucking place, Flanagan," Connor returns, his tone hardening, but Liam shakes his head, holding up a hand.

"A direct assault will get people killed, Niall, you know that. Especially since we don't know exactly what numbers Diego has and where or what he's planning. We need time to gather intelligence. Beth is on it, and we have Nico, and some of Viktor's espionage recruits looking into it as well. When Alessio returns from Italy, Luca will have him take point on clearing out some of Diego's cells of resources, if Diego has made any moves by then."

"If we hold our ground, he may back down." Connor looks at us both evenly. "He has a lot to lose, trying to infiltrate our territory like this, for two women who have little value to him outside of a grudge." He holds up a hand before either Niall or I can say anything. "I'm not suggesting that *I* think they have no other value, and you fucking know that, before either of you come back at me. But to Diego, their value is in salving his hurt pride. Our hope is that he'll think better of that before it can escalate."

"In the meantime," Liam continues, "we're going to put added security at your house—" he nods at Niall, "—and yours as well, once you're moved in," he tells me. "Elena and Isabella shouldn't go anywhere without security with them. We're all aware of the kind of tactics that can be used against them. I know Isabella is protective of her freedom, but I'm sure that she'll see that this is for the best. With any luck, this will be resolved soon, and things can go back to normal."

He nods to both of us. "The best thing you can do is stay close to your families and keep them safe. If you're needed for anything else, we'll make you aware."

Niall looks as frustrated as I feel, but neither of us argues. We both know Connor and Liam well enough to know that when they've made a decision in this capacity, it's difficult to get either of them to back down—especially Connor, who is always on a knife's edge of contention with Niall anyway. But neither of us wants to be sitting and doing nothing while we wait. It goes against everything either of us have ever done for our entire lives.

The ride back to the house is a quiet one. Tension is radiating off Niall, and he grips the steering wheel hard, his knuckles whitening around the edges.

"I promised Isabella she wouldn't have to worry about this shite anymore," he says finally, when we've stopped in the driveway. He runs one hand through his hair, his jaw working, and I can tell he's holding back his rage by a thread. "That all that fucking nonsense she grew up with, all the danger she was in, was fuckin' over. She's supposed to be fucking *safe* here. Both of the lasses are." He slams one fist against the dashboard, hard, his mouth pressed so thinly that his lips have vanished. "I swear to fuckin' *Christ*, if that man lays a hand on her—"

"I know." I take a deep breath, hanging onto my own anger and frustration by a similarly slim margin. "I promised Elena this was a safe place, too. The man is a fucking blight on all of us."

"He needs to be put in the fuckin' ground." Niall grits his teeth, his hand still running through his hair, a nervous tic. "I love Liam like a goddamn brother, but he and Connor are going to sit on their fuckin' hands until all this burns down."

"Maybe not." I glance over at him. "I'm as angry as you are. And I don't like waiting and seeing any more than you do. But we can't singlehandedly start a war, and we can't take him out, just the two of us."

"Like hell, we can't." Niall stares straight ahead, and I can see the wheels turning furiously in his mind. "We—"

"Need to wait," I tell him firmly. "As much as it fucking pains me to say it. You know what I've lost, Niall. You know how close to home this is. But we've both done this shit all our lives. We need to think of it the way we would any other conflict, not differently because of how closely it touches us. If we go after him on our own and fail—where does that leave Isabella and Elena? If we start a war, when he might still back down?"

"You really fucking think he's going to back down?"

"No," I admit, honestly. "But I think he might slip up. He's angry, Niall, and his pride is wounded. Angry, prideful men make mistakes. If he acts recklessly, he'll open himself up to a way for us to put an end to this—with backup. Let's not do the same, and give him that option."

Niall lets out a short, harsh breath. "You're right, as usual," he mutters. "But *fuck*, I want to put a bullet through that man's head and end this for all of us."

"As do I. And who knows?" I offer him a tight, grim smile. "We might still get the chance."

Elena

On the day of my first doctor's appointment, I'm incredibly anxious. It's like an addition to the ever-present nausea of my pregnancy, except for brief moments of time I forget, only for something to remind me of the things I have to worry about. Adrenaline floods me, making my palms tingle and my heart race, a cycle that's been repeating for days now.

It feels like everything has gotten crammed into a small space of time. We're moving into the new house in two days, and the mess of packing and stress doesn't help my mood. Added to that is the claustrophobic feeling of having the Kings' security what feels like *everywhere*. Although Levin has handled the conversations of how much security there will be at our house and where, I still hate every second of it.

Isabella's house felt like a safe haven when I was brought here, but now every time I go anywhere—to the kitchen for a glass of water, to the living room to watch tv, to the backyard to try to get a moment's peace—there are security guards everywhere. Liam and Connor said there would be a few, but I don't think they know the meaning of that word. Added to that is the fact that I can't even go into the room I share with Levin to get away from them without being reminded of the impending move from the boxes scattered across our floor—something that should excite me, but instead reminds me that soon I'll be learning how to share a life with someone else for the first time. How to live with someone, just the two of us—and that someone doesn't actually want that life with me.

Until today, the pregnancy hasn't felt entirely real. Nothing has really changed about my body yet, aside from sore breasts and constant nausea, which has started to taper off a little. I could have had a bad period or the flu, and had similar symptoms. But the appointment makes it real. And with that comes the reminder that it's not just me that's in danger from Diego any longer.

I have something more to worry about, and sometimes it feels overwhelming.

Levin is waiting in the living room when I walk in to find him, and the moment I see him, that familiar longing rushes back in. It never changes–it never stops. I can't see him and not want to be near him, touching him—and I can't help but wonder if it will ever stop. If I'll ever feel differently.

He hasn't touched me again since the afternoon in the house we chose. I know that it's not that he doesn't want me—it's that he wants me too much—but it doesn't make it easier. If anything, it makes it all feel so much worse, knowing that my husband wants me, but is forcing himself to stay away.

He's intent on punishing himself for the rest of his life, it seems, and I've been caught up in it.

I ask Isabella to come to the appointment with me, too. I want Levin there, of course, but I want someone there who's done this before to help with my nerves. She readily agrees—I think she would have been hurt if I *didn't* ask—and she offers to drive us, something that's quickly cut off by the tall, muscled bodyguard near the door.

"I'll drive you," he says flatly. "Kings' orders—you ladies don't drive yourselves."

Isabella gives him a withering look, and I glance at Levin. "Can't you drive us?"

He glances over at the guard, who looks perturbed. "I've got it," he tells the black-clothed man. "I think I can still manage to keep an eye on them."

I'd gotten a glimpse of what it's been like for Isabella to live without that constant shadow, the feeling of someone watching her at all times, following her every step. She's had a measure of freedom since coming here that neither of us ever had, and now that I've had it too—the ability to simply go where we please without an escort, to live without the reminder that danger lurks around the corners and we need to be protected from it—it feels awful to go backward. As if all of the efforts we've gone through to be safe have meant nothing in the end.

My nerves only get worse on the way to the doctor's office. Levin glances over at me, and I see him give me a sympathetic look, his hand reaching out to rest on my thigh. A shiver goes through me at the feeling of his hand on my leg, when he hasn't touched me in days, other than the brush of his lips over my cheek before bed. I know he notices, but he says nothing, though his hand stays comfortingly on my leg.

"It's going to be fine," he finally says quietly to me, when he pulls into the space in the parking garage outside the doctor's office. "There's no reason to think anything will go wrong. Just routine. I know Isabella told you that, too."

I nod, swallowing hard. Levin is worried about everything around us that could hurt me or our child—Diego, the people coming after us, someone who might still hold a grudge against him from his old life —but I'm afraid of the smaller things, of the ways my body might betray me, that we might lose our baby for some reason that I can't control, and it will be my fault that he's lost a child all over again. I can't say it out loud, but the closer it's gotten to the appointment, the more that's kept me up at night.

The doctor is the same one that Isabella went to when she was pregnant, and Isabella is friendly with the receptionist. She goes up to check me in while Levin guides me to a seat at the back of the room, his hand brushing against the small of my back as we walk. I can feel him sticking protectively close to me, and it makes me feel a little less scared of all of it.

"I'm glad you're here," I murmur quietly to him as we both sit down, my heart leaping a little in my chest from nervousness as I say it. I'm always afraid to let slip how I feel, worried that it will be too much, that it will upset him, that he'll pull away even more if he feels me getting closer. But he just reaches over, his hand sliding around mine, and I feel myself relax a little more.

Isabella joins us a moment later, and I see her gaze flick to where Levin is holding my hand before she comes and sits down next to me. "It shouldn't be long," she tells me, reaching for one of the magazines on the glass coffee table in front of us. "They're always pretty prompt here."

The entire office is done in soft pinks and creams, meant to be soothing and cozy. The office is empty other than the three of us, and I can't help but wonder if it's just a slow morning, or if someone has intentionally cleared the schedule so that there wouldn't be anyone else here. As worried as Connor and Liam seem to be about the situation—hell, as worried as I know *Levin* is—I wouldn't have put it past one of them to have made sure that my appointment was the only one on the schedule for the morning for added safety.

When we're called back, I can tell that everyone is immediately trying to put me at ease. The nurse is chipper and friendly, and the doctor, when she comes in, greets me with a pleasant smile. "So I hear this is the first one," she says, glancing at my chart. "And this is—"

She looks at Levin, and I introduce him nervously. "This is my husband, Levin." It's the first time I've introduced him to anyone as that, and I feel a flurry of emotion run through me, making my chest ache. I want to be happier, saying that aloud. I want to not feel as if it's a loaded sentence when it comes out of my mouth.

"Nice to meet you." The doctor glances over my chart again, and I can feel the tension coming from Isabella. She's standing on one side of me, Levin hanging back a little on the other, and I know he's giving her space to be the one being supportive of me. It's sweet of him, but knowing that the reason that he's doing it is because he doesn't feel that he deserves to have this at all makes me feel as if I might start welling up with tears all over again.

He's taken a backseat in everything so far, deferring to me, to Isabella, and even to what Niall thinks. I know it's not the kind of man he usually is, and I know it's because he doesn't believe that he's supposed to have any of this.

I wish there was someone who could convince him otherwise.

The appointment itself goes so much easier than I thought, even if it is a little embarrassing to be poked and prodded and examined, especially in front of Levin. He offers at one point to step out if I want him to, which Isabella immediately agrees might be for the best—*so I can relax*—but I tell him firmly that I want him to stay. I want him here with me for this.

When we hear the faint sounds of a heartbeat on the monitor, I feel my eyes well up with tears. Isabella gasps softly, her hand squeezing mine, and I feel Levin's hand rest on my shoulder lightly. I can't look up at him at first, or I know I'm going to start sobbing.

When I finally find the nerve to look up at his face, he's staring at the monitor, his expression softened in a way that I've never seen. It makes me feel as if I'm melting, my heart aching as I reach up to touch his hand, and he wraps his around mine without his eyes ever leaving the static. There's something almost like awe on his face, and for a moment, there's absolute silence before he clears his throat.

"So everything is fine?" he asks the doctor, and she nods, smiling at him.

"Everything looks great. The kind of nausea that Elena said she was experiencing is on the more extreme side, but plenty of women have that issue, unfortunately. You said it was getting better?" she asks, glancing at me, and I nod.

"I've been able to keep more down. Mostly bland food and smoothies, but it's better than it was."

"Good. Test it as much as you're able—slowly incorporate what you can. We'll keep an eye on your nutrition—I might have you come back a little sooner, just to check, but overall I think there's nothing to worry about." She gives Levin a reassuring smile. "We have fathers come in here all the time that are more nervous than anyone else, and I tell them all the same thing—there's no reason to worry until we have one. I can't see anything wrong right now."

"That's good to hear." I can hear the relief in Levin's voice as the doctor steps away.

"You can go ahead and get dressed. I'll come back with the paperwork for you to check out and schedule your next appointment. It was lovely to meet you both."

Isabella exhales as the doctor leaves. "Well, that's good news." She smiles at me, and I offer a small smile in return. "Sounds like we'll have to come back sooner than I did, but—"

"I think next time, maybe it will just be Levin and me?" I bite my lip, looking at her hesitantly. "I needed the support for the first time, but I think—"

I break off, seeing the flicker of hurt on her face. "We can talk about it at home," I tell her quickly, reaching for my clothes. "I'm ready to get out of here."

I don't know how to explain to her how much I wish, now, that it had been just Levin and me when we heard our baby's heartbeat. That I feel like there was a moment there that could have brought us closer together, and having the buffer of my sister in the room kept it from being as intimate as it could have been. I feel guilty, because I know she just wants to be there for me. But I also need any opportunity I can find to try to make things better between Levin and me.

I know she's hurt from how silent she is the entire ride home. I follow her into the kitchen when we get back, noticing that Levin slips away, murmuring something about going to find Niall.

"We don't need to talk about it," Isabella says crisply, in a tone that I know she only uses when she's trying to pretend she doesn't care about something. "Of course, it should just be the two of you."

"Issi—"

"Stop." She shakes her head. "You don't need to try to smooth it over. I get it."

"Do you?" I bite my lip, sinking down onto one of the barstools at the island. "I was glad you were there today. Really glad—I mean it. But when we heard the heartbeat—I feel like if it had just been the two of us, it would have been more intimate. Something we just shared together. And I need all those moments I can get, if Levin and I are ever going to—"

I break off at the surprised, almost pitying look on Isabella's face. "Oh, Elena." She leans back against the counter, looking at me. "Do you really think that something is going to change? That's why you're doing this?"

"It could." I cross my arms under my breasts, feeling suddenly self-conscious. "He's trying. I know he is."

"I don't see that." Isabella frowns. "I see a man who is letting everyone else around him make the choices for the life that he's supposed to be building with his wife. Hell, Niall would have argued if someone else had tried to come along to our appointment. He would have *wanted* it to be the two of us. And I'm not saying that your or my wishes shouldn't win out in the end, for something like that, but Niall would at least have had a fucking opinion about it—"

"Levin can't." I blurt it out, before I can stop myself. "He can't have an opinion, because he doesn't think he deserves any of this. He doesn't think he's supposed to have it, so he's letting it all happen around him, because he's afraid it's going to disappear if he takes an active part in it. And he feels guilty, but he has to be here, because it's the *right thing to do*." I mimic Niall's accent, and Isabella almost laughs, before she looks at me in confusion.

"Elena, what the hell are you talking about?"

"Levin's first wife died."

"I know that." Isabella runs her hand through her hair. "Elena, I get it—and that's horrible. It really is. But I also know it was a long time ago. People lose their spouses. That doesn't mean he's not allowed to get married again."

"She was pregnant." I look at Isabella, willing her to understand. "They—what they did was awful. They killed her, and they—"

I can't finish the sentence, but Isabella has lived in the world of cartels and mafia and Bratva long enough to guess how it ends. I see her face pale a little, and her hands grip the countertop more tightly.

"Oh," she says softly. "I didn't know. I—" She swallows hard. "That's horrible. I'm so sorry."

"I didn't know until recently." My teeth sink a little deeper into my lower lip. "And he feels like it was his fault. He was trying to leave the Syndicate, and some of the other members were angry that he was getting out. They blamed her. So they murdered her to try to keep him from leaving—or just out of malice, I don't know for sure. I don't think Levin does either, or he hasn't said for sure which. But they're dead now, too."

"I can imagine they are." Isabella still looks pale. "So he blames himself for it."

I nod. "He thinks if he'd just left her alone, if he hadn't fallen in love with her, then she'd be alive now. He has this habit—" I take a deep breath. "He always seems to feel that these choices are made in a vacuum, I guess. That he alone could have walked away and made the choice for both of them. I've tried to tell him that maybe that's not what she would have wanted. That maybe their life together was worth it for her. I can't know one way or another. *I* don't know how I would feel, if it were me, if I knew I was going to—"

Tears well up in my eyes, and I rub my hand across them, trying to wipe them away. "I've told him over and over that it wasn't just him that wanted this. That I didn't think about the consequences, either. But he's so convinced that if he had just told me no, he could have changed all of this. Just like he thinks that if he had kept himself from falling for Lidiya, all of that would be different, too."

"It's hard to say what would be different, if you change something." Isabella sighs. "I'm sorry, Elena. I didn't know about all of it. But I still don't really see that he's trying—"

"He is," I insist. "He wants to make me happy. He thinks the way to do that is by letting me have whatever I want. And all I want is—"

"I know." Isabella frowns. "These aren't easy men to love, Elena. Niall and my relationship didn't come easy, either. He fought against it, too. But he didn't have to contend with what Levin does." She lets out a slow, measured breath. "I still think that if he hasn't moved on in all this time, it's not going to change, Elena. What you have is what you're going to get. And I don't think that is going to make you happy."

"I've thought the same thing," I admit softly. "That this is probably how it's always going to be. But I have to try, right? If I reconcile myself to it already—then there's no chance. Maybe I have to accept eventually that nothing will ever change, but I have to give it a little time. And do what I can."

"Like going to the appointments, just the two of you. I get it." Isabella gives me a small, forced smile. "I just want to be there for you. I feel like you don't have enough support."

"I feel like I do. You're doing a great job."

"I'm glad you think so. Which reminds me—several of the other wives are in town for a board meeting. They're getting together tomorrow night at the McGregor estate, and I'm supposed to go. Do you want to come?"

It's on the tip of my tongue to say no—I briefly met the other wives at the wedding, but I didn't talk to them extensively, and the idea of getting to know essentially a group of near-strangers sounds exhausting. But I also know that they all know Levin, at least a little—and it might be a chance to get to know him through the eyes of others. To find out things about him that he wouldn't tell me, or that I might not know otherwise.

And besides that, Isabella can't be my only friend here. It's not fair to her.

I give her a small smile, and nod. "Sure."

Elena

I've never been to the McGregor estate before. Isabella told me to dress casually, so I did—leggings and a long chiffon tank top and sandals—and then immediately felt self-conscious when our car pulled up to the estate, despite the fact that Isabella had dressed similarly.

"I feel like I should have put in more effort," I hiss at her as she tells the security guard who drove us here that she'll call him when she needs him to come back. I can hear the terseness in her voice—having the security around us is chafing at her. After being able to go where she pleases and do what she wants without anyone watching her, having a shadow all of the time is making her feel even more claustrophobic than it makes me.

"It's fine," she reassures me as the car pulls away, and we walk up the driveway. "Everyone else will be casual, too. Just–brace yourself. Everyone is probably here already. We're running late."

An hour late, precisely, because Aisling had been furious that her mother was leaving, and Niall hadn't been able to get her to calm down. It wasn't until Isabella had managed to finally get her to stop crying that we were able to leave, and I saw Levin watching with a nervous expression on his face that made me want to laugh.

I know Levin has seen things that would terrify most of us, spent his whole life doing a job that requires calm and self-possession in the face of extreme danger—and the only time I've seen him look really unsettled is when faced with a crying toddler.

He'd seen me looking at him and chuckled, shrugging. "Not something I've had to deal with yet," he said with a twist of his mouth, and I'd had a flush of momentary happiness, a feeling that we were in on some shared joke.

And then the moment passed, as it always does, and I was left feeling like I wanted to hang onto it by my fingernails, if need be.

"It's going to be fine," Isabella repeats as we walk up to the door. "Look, Saoirse doesn't really like me, and I still manage to enjoy these little get-togethers just fine. Everyone else will be really friendly, and Saoirse will probably be as friendly as she ever gets with you, too. You're not the one married to Niall."

"You're going to have to tell me the rest of that story one day," I tell her as she rings the doorbell, and Isabella makes a face.

"I'd really rather not."

Saoirse is the one who answers the door, dressed in slim dark jeans, an emerald green blouse that brings out her bright green eyes, with her red hair up in a high ponytail. She looks as effortlessly beautiful as when I saw her at the wedding, even dressed down like this, and I immediately question my choice of clothing all over again. I'm also impressed that Isabella doesn't seem to care. I think my sister always looks beautiful, but she chose to wear something very similar to me…black yoga pants and a tank top, with her hair left down.

There's the briefest of seconds where I see Saoirse's mouth twitch in a semi-unpleasant expression when she sees Isabella, and then she smiles at me. "I'm so glad to see you again, Elena. Come in, both of you."

I can hear the chatter as we're led through the wide foyer to the massive living room. There's a picture of Saorise and Connor on their wedding day above the mantel, and the entire room is luxuriously appointed, decorated like the inside of an interior decorator's catalog in neutral tones and plush textiles. The other wives are scattered across the room—I immediately recognize Caterina, Viktor's wife, from the wedding. She's sitting on one of the long sofas, wearing jeans and a long-sleeved cranberry shirt, her hair tied back in a messy bun. There's another pretty, dark-haired woman next to her, talking animatedly about something.

"Maggie, can you get the drinks—oh, thank you!" Saoirse calls out as a woman emerges from the kitchen with two bottles of wine in one hand. She looks different from the others in a way that I can't exactly put my finger on—all of the wives of the men who run the organizations have a polish to them that can't be rubbed off, even when dressed down. But Maggie looks as if she's never anything but casual. She has shorter, wildly curly hair, twinkling blue eyes, and she's wearing denim shorts and a white t-shirt, without a spot of makeup on her lightly freckled face.

"I've got the first round right here," she says with a grin, in an accent that sounds very much like anyone we've encountered in the city who's lived in Boston for a long time, or is from here.

"Ana should be down in a minute. She's putting Brigit to bed." Saoirse waves us into the living room, and I feel instantly like running back home when everyone turns to look at Isabella and me. If Isabella weren't there as a buffer, I think I might have.

I've never been the most social person. Isabella has always been much better at it. I hated when our family hosted dinner parties, hated big gala events, when I could have been in my room reading and left quietly alone. Now I'm faced with an entire room of vaguely familiar faces, and my heart races instantly with anxiety.

A blonde girl that I remember introducing herself as Sasha at the wedding gets up, waving us over and giving me a sweet smile. "I'm

Sasha. I don't know if you remember me. We met briefly at the wedding."

"You're—Max's wife?" I fish for the name, and she nods, motioning for me to sit down.

"That's right." She points around the room. "You've met Saoirse and Maggie—Maggie is her best friend. That's Sofia, she's Luca Romano's wife—and she's close with Caterina, who I know you met too, since Levin works for her husband. Ana—Liam's wife—will be down in a few minutes." She smiles at me. "It's a lot of new people, I know. It was a lot for me to take in when I first came here. But everyone is really friendly, I promise."

I nod, still at a loss for words. Isabella is talking to Maggie, something about schools, and I try to focus on what Sasha is telling me, especially as a tall, thin blonde woman walks into the room who I know must be Ana.

"We all know Levin," Sasha says, and I glance at her, feeling my heart skip over itself a little. "I think we were all really happy to know he's found someone."

He hasn't. I don't say it, though, feeling the momentary leap in my chest sink down again. "How do you know him?"

She shrugs lightly. "He helped Max find me. It's a very long story. But he has a penchant for helping people who are in trouble—especially him and Max and Liam. He's a good man—without him, I don't know if I would have made it out. Ana would say the same about how he helped Liam find her. He really is one of the best."

My chest tightens at that, and I give her a small smile. "I know."

That's the hardest part of it. I *do* know. I know better than anyone how good he is, how brave and honorable and good. He was so good that he broke a promise to himself to never marry again in order to make sure that I and our child have the best possible future.

I wonder how many of the women here know about that. I think they all know something about his past—with Maggie maybe being the exception, since she doesn't seem to be as much a part of this world as on the fringes of it due to her close friendship with Saoirse.

"I'm a teacher," she explains to me as she brings me back a glass of sparkling flavored water to make up for the fact that I can't have the wine. "Saoirse and I have been close friends since college. I don't know much about what they all have going on here—" she waves her hand at the other wives, shrugging. "But Saoirse has me on the board of her foundation to give a different perspective, something a little closer to the heart of what's going on here. And I've made some good friends, being a part of it."

Ana is as effusive about Levin as Sasha was, repeating the same thing that Sasha said—that Levin helped Liam and Max find her when she was in trouble. No one has a single bad thing to say about him, which doesn't surprise me at all. What does surprise me is that Caterina is the one who corners me in the kitchen when I go for a refill of my drink, smiling at me as she refills her wine glass.

"How have you been, since the wedding?" she asks, and I look at her, a little startled.

"Fine?" There's a question at the end of the word that I don't mean for there to be, but it comes out anyway, and Caterina gives me a sympathetic look.

"An unwanted marriage isn't an easy thing to deal with. Believe me, I know."

I stare at her for a moment, almost letting my glass slip through my fingers. "What makes you think it's unwanted?" My voice is sharper than I mean for it to be, sharper than it *should* be when I'm talking to the wife of Levin's boss. But I hate hearing that word come off of her lips.

Caterina purses her lips, setting her glass down before glancing over to see if anyone else has walked in. "Elena—Viktor and I talk about everything. And I know Levin very well, too. I know he wouldn't have married again outside of these very—*unique* circumstances. *Unwanted* might be a strong word, but it's the best one I could think of. What I'm trying to say is that I know things must not be easy for you right now."

I don't know what to say. Everything that comes to mind is either something that I don't know Caterina well enough to say out loud to her, or something that I know is too sharp and acerbic to say out loud. The silence goes on for a few beats, and then she sighs.

"How well do you know him, Elena?"

I blink at her. "I'm married to him."

Caterina laughs softly. "You and I both know that in our world, that doesn't mean knowing someone. I was married to Viktor for quite some time before I knew much about him as a person."

"And you know Levin better than I do? I'm his wife."

Caterina tilts her head, looking at me with a patience that makes me feel slightly ashamed of my tone. "I'm not trying to start a fight with you, Elena. I'm trying to reassure you. I know things are hard right now. The first months of my marriage to Viktor were incredibly difficult, and he is—and was then—a much different man than Levin. What I'm trying to tell you is that—I hope in time, Levin will come to see how lucky he is to have you."

That stops me in my tracks. I look at her, still unsure what to say. "What do you mean?"

"I've seen, personally, the violence that Levin is capable of when someone he cares about is threatened. I also know that he's lost everything, and that he blames himself for it—that when those closest to him needed him, he couldn't protect them, no matter how violent of a man he's been in the past. He's terrified of that future repeating."

"I know." I press my lips together, feeling a too-familiar ache spread through me. "And I can't convince him that it's not going to."

The words surprise me as soon as they come out. I hadn't meant to say it aloud, especially not to someone I don't know all that well. But

I see from Caterina's expression that she understands, at least a little, and it makes me wonder if maybe it was a good thing that I did say it.

"Be patient," she tells me. "I know your sister has probably told you that, too—"

"Isabella isn't his biggest fan. I think she'd rather I just tell him to leave."

"I'm not surprised by that." A small smile plays over Caterina's lips. "Isabella is very protective over you, I'm sure."

She reaches over, taking a sip of her wine before glancing back at me. "Things work out in time, Elena. I know it seems that Levin isn't going to find his way out of the grief he's kept himself mired in for such a long time. But he hasn't had anyone to give him a reason to." She smiles at me, a little sadly. "He deserves happiness, and so do you. I think the two of you could find it in each other, if you're willing to give him time and patience."

"I hope that's true." I swallow hard, willing myself not to let too much emotion out. I don't want to cry in front of her, and I don't want her to see just how difficult it's been. I don't know her that well yet.

But at the same time, the conversation itself feels like a hand extended in friendship. I've never had friends, other than my sister. This feels like the beginning of a chance to change that.

"Thank you," I tell her quietly. "I'm sorry I wasn't all that receptive at first. You're right—it has been hard."

"I know." Caterina gives me another of those small, reassuring smiles. "Let's go find the others." She picks up her glass. "They're going to think we've disappeared." She glances at me, "You'll find that everyone here will want to help you when things are hard. We all take care of each other—this world we live in isn't an easy one. You'll find friends here."

She leads us both back toward the living room, then, and I follow. I'm not entirely sure how I feel. Everyone has been more welcoming than I expected them to be, and I hadn't thought Caterina, of all people, would be the one to reach out and give me advice about my marriage. But it makes sense when I think about it. She's Viktor's wife, and he knows Levin best out of anyone.

Give it time. It seems like such simple advice.

Doing that is much, much harder. All I have with Levin now is time. But I don't know how best to use it, to make our future into something that could make us both happy.

Elena

For the first time since I came to Boston, I'm going home to the new house and not back to Isabella's. We got the keys this morning, and I'd asked Levin if I should stay home, since everything was being moved in—all the furniture we picked out, our personal possessions. He'd told me no, that we'd hired enough people to handle it, and that I needed to make friends. He had plans to go out with Liam and Niall, once the movers were finished.

I have no idea if he'll be home or not when I get there. I toyed with the idea of sending him a text a half-dozen times between leaving the McGregor estate, dropping Isabella off, and getting close to the house, but I didn't. I wasn't sure if that was a thing we did. *Do we send each other messages, letting the other know we're on the way home?* It seems like something a married couple should do, but I still have no idea what kind of married couple we are.

I don't really think either of us do.

There are lights on when I get out of the car, shining a warm glow through the windows. I feel a small leap in my chest, the way I always do when I think about Levin, or hear him mentioned, or talk about him. I wonder, as I brush past the security and put my key into the lock, if it will ever go away—either because of the passage of time or because I've had to find a way to put it to rest, to keep my heart from being broken over and over again.

I open the door, stepping inside. It's the first time I've come home to this house, and as I slip off my shoes, the smooth wooden floor cool under the bare soles of my feet, I find myself hoping that we stay here. That we get to keep all the memories that I hope we'll get to make, if I give it *time*, the way Caterina seems to think that I should.

"Hello?" I call out as I pad down the hall, wondering if Levin is home, or if he just left the lights on—or if one of the security did.

"Elena?" I hear his voice from the living room, a little blurred around the edges, as if he's a little drunk. I feel that leap in my chest again, remembering the last time I saw him drunk—in a hotel room in Rio, and how that night had gone. A game of *never have I ever* that turned into much, much more.

I close my eyes against the memory of his hands on me in the small, uncomfortable bed, the way I hadn't cared because everything else felt so good, the memory of coming to talk to him outside, with the scent of smoke hanging around us and the sound of rain beating down against the pavement, the wall of the hotel rough against my back as he'd kissed me.

Rio feels like an entirely different world now, a place where we were other people. Where I was someone more like the person I think I'd have liked to be—free and careless and adventurous—and now I'm expected to go back to being the person that everyone else knew.

I know I was reckless back then, too. That I didn't think about the consequences of my actions—the potential consequences, anyway. But for the first time, I'd been living in the moment. I hadn't been trying to do anything except hold on to the brief moments that I could grasp with Levin, and clinging to some faint hope that if we spent enough time together, he'd realize just how good we were.

I hadn't ever thought it would spiral into this–still wishing he would realize how good we are together, while I'm carrying his child and we're sharing a home together…a life…a marriage. I could never have imagined that that's what it would lead to.

I walk slowly into the living room, trying to tamp down my emotions. To not think that tonight will go like that drunken night in the motel, when I know how unlikely that is.

Levin is sitting on the sofa, dressed as casually as I've ever seen him in joggers and a black t-shirt, a slight flush to his skin from drinking. He looks up as soon as I walk into the room, setting his phone down, and watches me as I walk towards him, stopping at the edge of the couch.

"I thought about sending you a text. I wasn't sure if I should let you know how late I'd be or that I was on my way—"

"You don't have to. It can't hurt, though. I didn't worry, though, knowing you were at the estate."

I don't know if that makes me happy or not. It's not that I *want* to worry him, but I like the idea of him thinking about me, wondering when I'll get home. I had hoped that maybe he would've anticipated our first night in the new house, in some way, although I'd guessed that him having both of us go out was a way of not making a big deal out of it.

"How was your night?"

Levin shrugs. "It was fine. Nice to spend some time with Niall and Liam."

"It wasn't awkward with—" I frown. "Everything going on? Even with Liam being in charge of the Kings, and—"

Levin chuckles. "We're good at compartmentalizing that sort of thing. Liam and I won't ever be as close as he and Niall are, but we're good friends. We know how to keep that and business separate. Connor is another story. I've got no idea where he made himself scarce at while you ladies enjoyed the estate, but it wasn't out with us."

"I imagine between home and work, Liam gets enough time with his brother."

"Especially when his brother is Connor." Levin chuckles again, and then cocks his head. "What about you? How was your night? Did you enjoy it?"

The questions come out in a quick string, and I blink at him. "Yeah–I think I did. I didn't get to know anyone that well at the wedding; it was all so fast. It was nice to meet everyone without all that going on."

"They were nice to you? I know Saoirse and Isabella haven't always been on the right foot."

"They were all wonderful." *And they all had wonderful things to say about you.* It's on the tip of my tongue to tell Levin that. I can't help but wonder if he realizes that no one else seems to see him as the failure that he thinks he is, someone constantly in need of redemption. I haven't known a single person yet who knows him that's said anything like that. Even Connor seems to have respect for him, even if they didn't appear to get along all that well the one time I saw them both in a room together.

"That's good." Levin shifts on the sofa, looking at me curiously. "Do you think you'll be happy here? That you might be able to make friends?"

Slowly, I come to sit on the couch next to him, still an arm's length away. I feel too fragile, too vulnerable right now to be closer. The night has been a lot to take in, and I want things from him that I'm not sure he's going to be willing to give me.

"I think so," I tell him tentatively. "I hadn't expected them to welcome me in so soon, but I'm not unhappy with it. It's not all that different from what I would have expected if I'd stayed in Mexico and married someone picked for me. I would have gotten to know the other boss's wives and their son's wives, and there would have been similar evenings—dinner parties and get-togethers and all of that."

"Instead, you ended up with me." There's what looks like a smile on his face, but I can hear the self-deprecation in his tone, and I know he doesn't mean it positively. I know I should let it go, but I can't. Especially not tonight, when I'm so tired, and it's our first night in our new home, and I wish with a kind of exhaustion that seems to be settling into me that things were different.

"I wouldn't be happier in a situation like that," I tell him flatly, and Levin looks at me, his gaze sharper than before, the smile gone.

"You can't possibly be happy with a husband who can't love you." His words are still blurred at the edges, and I have a feeling that he's only saying this because his defenses are a little lowered.

I wish that had resulted in something other than this conversation.

"I always expected that." The words stick in my throat. "I was always going to be married to someone I didn't love and have to find a way to be happy in spite of it. What I didn't expect—"

I look at my husband, at his handsome, chiseled face and his blue eyes, at the man that I ache for all of the time, and the rest of the sentence comes out without my meaning for it to.

"—I didn't expect to have a husband I was in love with, who didn't love me."

The moment I say it, I feel myself flinch, startled. I want to grab the words out of thin air and drag them back, unsay them, because I never meant to tell him like this. I never meant to tell him at all.

The silence between us feels especially thick and heavy. I feel my cheeks turning red, flushed and heating, and I push myself up from the couch, wanting to be out of the room, anywhere else. As far away from this particular moment as possible, because now I've said it, and I know I won't hear it back.

I'm halfway up from the couch when his hand closes around my wrist, pulling me back down, much closer to him than I was before. A flood of heat fills me, my entire body tightening at how close he is to me, and I hate myself a little for it, that no matter what happens, I can't seem to not want him.

"I'm sorry." The words sound thicker now, coming out of his mouth, emotion wrapped up with alcohol, and I can see the apology in his eyes. His hand is still around my wrist, holding me there, and I know if I tried to pull away again, he'd let me go.

I don't want him to.

"I'm sorry, I can't." His other hand reaches for my waist, pulling me closer. I can feel the warmth radiating off of him, the tension in him as he fights with what I know he wants, especially right now, when his self-control is already frayed. "I'm sorry. I'm so fucking sorry, Elena, I'm sorry—"

He keeps repeating it, over and over, his hand tightening around my wrist, like a litany, like a prayer, until the words stumble over each other, and I can't take it any longer.

I love him, and I want to take away what hurts him and I can't.

So I lean forward and kiss him instead, swallowing up the apology spilling from his lips, because it's all I can do.

I feel him tense, a ripple of need going through him, and then as my lips press against his, he spills me backward onto the couch, his hands suddenly *everywhere*.

"Elena—"

His forehead presses against mine, and I can taste vodka on his mouth, *feel* the way he's beyond being able to tell himself what he should and shouldn't have. His hand pins mine above my head, his broad palm and long fingers wrapping around my wrists and holding them together, his muscled body pushing me down into the couch cushions. He's hard against my thigh, pressing hotly through the layers of fabric between us, and a rush of desire fills me with an intensity that makes me feel dizzy.

"Tell me no," he whispers, his lips moving against mine. "Tell me you don't want me, Elena. Tell me that I'm not what you need."

Tears blur behind my eyes. "Why would you want that?" I whisper, my nails biting into my palms as I clench my hands, held in place by his grasp on my wrists. "Why would you want me to tell you no?"

Levin sucks in a deep, shuddering breath, his hips moving against me, and I can feel the weight of his desire, how heavily all of it weighs on him, how much he wants this. As much as I do—and I think at that moment, as I feel him tremble atop me, that he feels what I do, too.

He just can't admit it, and it's tearing us both apart.

"Then I wouldn't have to fight it," he murmurs. "If you didn't want me, I'd leave you alone. There'd be no question about it. But you fucking *do*, and every day, I have to—"

I cut him off with another kiss, arching up into him, my hands grasping at nothing as I slant my mouth over his. "I can't tell you that," I whisper against his mouth, kissing him again. "I wouldn't lie to you."

He groans, hips grinding into me again. "I can't stop," he murmurs into the kiss. "*Fuck*, Elena, I'm fucking *aching* for you—"

"I don't want you to stop." I graze my teeth over his lower lip, following the same spot with my tongue. "But I do want you to take me upstairs, so we can do this in our own bed."

He's so fucking hard that I can feel him throbbing against my inner thigh, his hips jerking again at that. "I have a better idea, first," he murmurs, and then his hands let go of my wrists as he slides down my body, his fingers catching in the waist of my leggings.

I know what he's going to do before his lips brush between my thighs, but I still let out a sharp, startled cry of pleasure when his tongue drags over my clit. I'm surprised every time by how good it feels, how the heat of his tongue soothes and builds the ache in me all at once. His hand is on my inner thigh, holding my legs apart as the stubble on his chin scrapes against my soft flesh, making me moan as he traces circles around my clit with the tip of his tongue.

He's not as careful or as practiced as he usually is. I've been with him once before like this, drunk and less certain, and I forgot how good it was to have him like this, the edges of his control softened and his desire bleeding out around them, making him forget to focus only on me. What *he* wants is to devour me, lashing his tongue over my clit and sucking my sensitive flesh into his mouth, his fingers tracing the outside of my entrance as he holds me open for his lips and tongue to explore, and I fucking *love* it. I want him to do what he wants with me, and that's exactly what it feels like.

He drags my leggings the rest of the way off, pushing my shirt up with the flat of his hand on my belly, fingers twisting in the material as his tongue slides over me again and again, making me shiver and tremble from the pleasure electrifying every inch of my skin. It feels so good, the raw desire that I can feel in the way he presses his mouth against me, as if I'm all he wants to taste, to feel, to make *his*, and I can forget for just a moment that this is temporary. That this side of Levin, the side that wants me without reservation, will disappear again.

"Come for me," he murmurs against my heated flesh, the words vibrating against my skin. "I fucking want it. I want to fucking *taste* it—"

His tongue drags over me again, wet and hot and insistent, his fingers pressing into my thigh, and he slides his tongue lower, pushing it into me as he thrusts, curling it as if he wants to taste as much of me as he can.

"Levin!" I gasp his name, hips writhing, my suddenly neglected clit throbbing with the need for pressure, friction, *pleasure*, and he thrusts his tongue inside of me again before he slides it free and gives me what I so desperately need.

It's enough and not enough all at once. I feel the orgasm unfurling inside of me, the tremors starting in my legs and crashing over the rest of my body as my muscles tense and I flood his tongue with my arousal, but I clench hard, wanting to be filled, wanting *more* as I come for him, bucking against his tongue.

"*God*, yes–" Levin moans, and then he sucks my clit into his mouth, rolling his tongue against it, and it sends my orgasm into a fresh cascade of pleasure, the friction against the oversensitive flesh making it so that I feel as if I can't speak, can't breathe, can't think of anything but how fucking good it feels. My toes curl so hard that my feet nearly cramp, my hips bucking against his mouth, and he holds me down, his tongue still sliding over me until I'm lying, limp and gasping and twitching under his hands.

He stands up, a little unsteadily, and I can see the outline of his cock against the soft material of his joggers, jutting out hard and thick and ready for me. I reach for him, wanting the feeling of him in my hand, my mouth, *anywhere* I can have him, but Levin moves out of reach, his hands sliding around my waist as he lifts me up off of the couch.

"You said you wanted to go to the bed," he murmurs. "So that's what we'll do."

I'm ludicrously half-naked and as tipsy as he is, I'm not sure he should be carrying me up the stairs, but I can't seem to make either of those thoughts stick. My head feels fuzzy with pleasure and lingering desire, and as Levin scoops me up and heads for the stairs, all I can think about is our bed, and all the things I want to do to him in it.

I haven't even seen it in person yet. I don't have time to take it all in when he pushes open the door to the bedroom, not to notice what our bedding looks like or how the furniture has been arranged, because he carries me directly to the bed, spilling me onto it and following me, his still-clothed body leaning over mine as he drags my shirt up over my head.

"You're wearing…too many clothes…" I gasp as I hook my fingers in the hem of his t-shirt, pulling it upwards. I want it off of him, to see all that smooth, muscled, tattooed flesh, and Levin gladly complies. For once, there's no arguing, no pausing for him to ask if I'm sure, to struggle with himself over what comes next. He sheds the t-shirt without a thought, throwing it aside, his own hands shoving his joggers down his hips, and I gasp as his cock springs free.

"You act like it's a surprise," he says with a half-grin on his face, leaning over me as I reach for him. "It's not like you haven't seen it before—*ah—*"

His words break off as I stroke my hand down the length of him, feeling him throb hot and hard against my palm, pre-cum streaking damply against my skin as his hips jerk forward, thrusting into my grasp. Everything about him has a slightly desperate edge right now, all those days of self-control melting away with the blurring of the alcohol, and one of his hands grips the pillow next to my head, his breaths coming short and quick.

"*Fuck*, that feels good—" His head drops down, his forehead pressing against mine as he kisses me, hips still moving against my hand as I stroke him. I like feeling him like this, hard and needy, and I want it to last.

He groans my name as I arch upwards, guiding him between my legs, and I hear his hiss of pleasure as his swollen cockhead presses against my drenched entrance, sliding in. I clench around him instantly, tight and wanting, and I feel the shudder that goes through him as he tries not to thrust all the way immediately.

"Not too fast," I whisper, letting go of him as I run my hands down his back, feeling his muscles flex under my touch. "I want—"

I don't have time to say what it is that I want. His mouth covers mine again, his tongue sliding possessively into my mouth as he slides deeper into my body, filling me up inch by inch as he does exactly as I asked, giving me each inch slowly, letting me feel it. I tangle my legs around his, and it feels so fucking good. *He* feels so good.

"That's perfect," I whisper, arching up to take that last bit of him as he slips into me as deeply as he can go, and Levin groans.

"No, you are." He murmurs the words against my hair, his hips starting to move. I feel a well of emotion tightening my chest, feelings that I push away as I grab his arms, bracing myself for the waves of pleasure that roll over me with each delicious thrust.

I dig my fingers into his shoulders, pulling him tighter against me, wanting to feel the hot slide of his skin against me, the sheen of sweat gathering between us, the way his chest catches and heaves with his breath as he thrusts into me harder. I want *this*, all of the time, the way he makes me feel, these moments when he's entirely himself with me and nothing else. I hear him groan my name, his hips shuddering as he pushes all the way into me and holds himself there for a moment, and then suddenly, he's sliding free, hands rolling me onto my side as I moan with frustration at the sudden emptiness.

"Not for long, *malysh*," he murmurs into my ear, his hard, muscled body curling behind me as he pulls me tightly backward against him, one hand sliding under my thigh and lifting it as he guides his cock inside of me again. His other arm slides beneath my head, curled around my body with his fingers stroking my breast, and the position is intensely intimate.

I know he's only doing this because he's drunk, that if he were sober, he'd think twice about this, about the intimacy of it. I can feel his hands *everywhere*, his muscled bulk pressed to my back as he cradles me against him, cock moving in slow thrusts inside of me as the hand, not cupping my breast, slides between my thighs and begins to play with my clit. He rolls my sensitive, swollen flesh between his fingers, making me gasp and my back arch with the jolts of pleasure that it sends through me. I'm on the verge of coming again as he pushes himself inside of me as deeply as he can go, grinding against me as he holds me there.

"Oh god, I—" I gasp as he presses his fingers against me a little more roughly, jolting his hips upwards. My back arches, driving myself back into him as the climax starts to crash over me, consuming me as I feel his mouth press against my shoulder, teeth grazing my skin. I don't want it to ever stop. I don't want *him* to ever stop, and I hear myself moan it as he rolls me onto my stomach, hips moving faster as he thrusts into me from behind, his fingers still rolling over my clit as I come for him in what feels like an endless tidal wave of pleasure.

"*Fuck*, I don't want to come yet–fuck–I can't–" Levin groans from above me, leaning into me, his mouth against my neck as I feel him stiffen and shudder, one hand gripping the pillow next to my head and the other hard on my hip as he starts to come, and I can feel the hot rush of it filling me.

He stays like that for a long moment, pressing me down into the mattress, hips moving in sharp, quick movements, and I don't want him to move. I want him to stay like that, his hot, hard body against mine, the quick sound of his breathing in my ear, the heat of him filling me up.

But it ends. It always ends. He rolls off of me, breathing hard, and as I roll to face him, I brace myself for the moment that he pulls away and shuts down.

"Fuck, Elena–" he breathes my name, and as I hesitantly move towards him, wanting to curl into the warmth of his body, I feel his arm go around my shoulders.

He holds me against his chest, and I breathe in the warm, piney scent of him, closing my eyes as a flood of emotion fills me. We're in our bed, in our bedroom, in our house—and I let myself sink briefly into the moment, wanting to remember this, our first night here.

"Do you like the house?" I ask softly, hooking one of my legs over his, wanting to be as close to him as I can. "I didn't know if you'd get home first."

I feel him press his lips to the top of my head, his fingers trailing through my hair. "I do," he says softly. "You made a good choice."

"I think so too," I whisper, my cheek pillowed against him, but I'm not talking about the house any longer, and I wonder if he knows that. If he knows how many things I want to say to him that I can't.

It feels like a bittersweet moment, lying there in his arms. It's everything I want and everything that I know I'll only have for a little while. *Isn't that better than not having it at all?* I ask myself as I feel his breathing even out beneath my cheek, and I know he's fallen asleep. *You can have a part of him, or nothing at all. Isn't that better?*

There would have been a time when I would have innocently thought that, *of course, it's better.* But now I'm no longer sure.

He knows I love him now, I realize as I lie there. *And I don't think he was so drunk that he'll forget it in the morning.* I feel that flush of heat creep up my cheeks again, even though I feel certain that he won't mention it.

But he knows. I can't take it back, and I wish I could.

I hadn't wanted to be the one to say it first.

Levin

The first weeks of Elena and I living in our new house were not what I expected.

Though I'm not sure what I expected, exactly. The last time I was married—the last time I lived with someone—I was a very different man.

Staying at Isabella and Niall's was easier. After twelve long years of living alone, I'd developed a routine, an ease to being by myself. While staying with them, it didn't feel so different. Elena and I had existed in a kind of limbo, going to bed together and waking up together, but without any of the rest of the responsibilities and routines that come from living together.

Now, that's changed. I've had to learn how to live in someone else's space again, to share it. And with that has come learning things about her that have drawn me closer to her without my meaning for it to happen—simply because it's impossible to live with a person and not have that occur.

I already knew how she looked when she first woke up in the morning, sleepy-eyed with her hair tangled around her face, how she burrows down into the pillow and tries to pretend that it's not time to get up yet. I've already become accustomed to waking up wanting her, my body hard and aching, and forcing that desire away, telling myself that the more often that we're together, the more I give in to what I want, the harder it will be on us both.

I'm starting to wonder if that's true—because it feels just as difficult, no matter what.

Above all else, I want to make her happy. I've never known how to cook, but I make an effort for breakfast at least—the only meal I know how to even begin to manage—because the first morning that she walked in to see my attempt at pancakes and eggs, she smiled in a way that I hadn't seen her smile in days. I bring her flowers when I come back from meetings. I've tried to figure out the things she likes—the type of coffee she has in the morning or the snacks she's started to crave and keep them in the house for her. Anything that I can think of to see her smile or brighten her day.

The fact that she told me she loved me, that first night in the new house, hasn't come up. She hasn't mentioned it again, and I'm sure as hell not going to.

Not when I know I can't say it back.

But with every day that passes, it feels more and more muddled. I've told myself that I can't love her—that I can't ever give her the love she deserves, but every time I do some small thing for her…bring her ice cream or flowers, try to cook a meal or clean up before she comes back from visiting Isabella, every time I take her out to dinner or a movie or a museum or anything else I can think of to show her in the city, a small nagging voice in my head asks *what exactly is this, if not loving someone?*

If someone asked me why I like spending time with her, why it's not a hardship to be married to her or share a life with her, I could list off reasons without missing a beat. *She's funny, intelligent, kind, and sweet, and she has more nerve than some men I've run jobs with.* The last part no one would understand unless they'd spent time in Rio with us, but after what Elena did there, I'd rather have her watching my back than some guys I've worked with—not that I'd ever tell her that. I want her to be able to put all of that behind her. I want her to be able to forget about it.

I tell myself, every time that thought comes up, that I'm doing these things to make the marriage tolerable for her—to make sure that she isn't miserable because I got us both into this situation. That I'm trying my best to be a decent husband, and that it has nothing to do with the way my chest clenches every time I see her smile, the way I look forward to hearing her voice when I walk through the door, the way I feel a sense of crashing relief every time I convince myself that I've waited long enough, and that I should take her to bed.

I told her I'd keep her satisfied. We didn't put a metric on what that meant. For Elena, I think it's a lot more than what I allow myself—*us*—because I know if I took her to bed every time I wanted her, we'd stay there for longer than I know we should…and I'd lose the ability to keep that distance that I know I need.

As the days pass, though, it's harder and harder to remember *why* I need it. Why I've held myself for so long to the idea that I'm not allowed to find happiness or peace in anything ever again. And the thing is—the thing I keep forcing myself not to look too closely at—I can't seem to help it. When I'm with Elena, I'm happy. There's no way around it. *She* makes me feel that way, in every single moment I spend with her.

As for peace, I know the only thing keeping me from that is me. Something that Max and Liam are all too quick to point out to me the next time I get drinks with them, when Max is in town again.

"You're putting yourself through hell for nothing, man," Liam tells me flatly, over pints at the bar we normally frequent with Niall. "I don't know why you hesitated to marry her at all in the first place."

"We both know," Max cautions, his glass of whiskey sitting in front of him. "Give the man a break."

"I'm sitting right here." I glare at both of them. "And you do both know. I can't—fuck, you know I can't make her happy."

"You know my wife spends time with her, right? And her sister?" Liam narrows his eyes at me. "I hear what they talk about secondhand. You *do* make her happy, when you're not living with your head so far up your ass that you can't see what's right in front of you. You're going to spend the rest of your life living half in and half out of a marriage that is clearly a good fit—"

"I'm nearly twenty fucking years older than her—"

"Who the fuck cares?" Liam takes a deep draught of his beer. "You're already married, so that's a null point. You can't change it now. The time for that was way back when you first took her to bed."

"I fucking know that," I growl at him, and Max waves a hand at us both.

"You're being too hard on him," he tells Liam. "I'm well aware of what it means to be so devoted to an idea of something that you miss out on what's right in front of you—or nearly so. But," he adds, looking at me, "I'm also going to say, in a kinder manner, that you *are* missing out on what's right in front of you." He clears his throat, taking a sip of his whiskey. "You might not have lived a life as a priest, the way I did, Levin. But you're doing penance all the same, and you've carried it out long past when you should have put a stop to it."

"I'm just going to hurt her—or get her hurt. She shouldn't be with me at all." I nudge my own beer aside. I've lost the taste for it.

"But she is," Max points out. "There's no changing that. You've married her, and rightfully so. All you're doing is making it harder on both of you."

"From what I've heard, she's not unhappy to be married to you," Liam interjects. "You've got a gorgeous wife who wants you and adores you, a child on the way—you should be enjoying this, man.

Not constantly fighting it like it's a fuckin' punishment." His accent thickens as he speaks, and he takes another deep drink. "Keeping her at arm's length isn't going to make anything better."

"There's got to be a statute of limitations on how long you punish yourself for something," Max says quietly. "Whether it was or wasn't your fault—I know what you believe it was, and we're not debating that—it's been a long time. Priest or no priest, eternal punishment isn't something I believe in."

I can't help but snort a little at that. "You clung to your celibacy with your fingernails, long past when Sasha made it clear she wanted you, and you wanted her back. And now *you're* telling *me* not to stick by something I'd decided for myself? I said I wouldn't fall in love or get married again. Just like you made vows not to kill or fuck. You couldn't help killing, and I couldn't help getting married. But I can do my damndest not to fall in love."

"And how's that going for you?" Liam asks, his expression impatient. Max throws him another glare.

"I made vows," Max says, and I narrow my eyes at him.

"So did I. A vow to myself isn't less important than one made in church."

Max drains the remainder of his whiskey, an expression on his face that suggests he's struggling for patience. "I'm not saying that it's not. What I *am* saying is that I realized clinging to that vow wasn't in my best interest. That it served a version of myself that I no longer was. And you're repeating the same error. You'll hurt Elena with it, just as I nearly hurt Sasha with it—and do the exact opposite of what you've said so often that you're trying to do. Protect her."

It's a convincing argument, and it settles in the back of my mind, long after we've finished up at the bar and I'm on my way home. It only serves to make the question I've been asking myself for a while now press harder—whether or not, after so long, I should allow myself a second chance at happiness.

What's done is done. Max and Liam are both right about that. I married Elena, and there's no undoing it—and the truth that I've struggled with admitting to myself is that if given a chance, I *wouldn't* undo it. I didn't want to leave her when I brought her to Boston, and now, having learned what it's like to share the beginning of a life with her, I don't want to walk away from it, even if I could.

I've told myself that I was doing enough, trying to be a decent husband. Trying to do the smaller things that could make her happy, even if I couldn't give her everything. But the question keeps creeping in—am I being unfair to her still, by only giving her that?

It would be one thing if I didn't care about her. If I didn't want her, like her—if I didn't—

I break off before I can finish the thought, as I pull into the driveway. I can't let myself finish it. *It would be one thing if none of that were true.* I wouldn't lie to her and pretend to feel things that I didn't.

But I'm lying to her anyway, by pretending that I don't feel what I do. What's been steadily growing between us since Rio.

It's not even just desire. Desire can be slaked, fulfilled until it wears out its welcome. But it's more than that, and I know it.

I feel weighed down as I walk inside, tossing my keys on the side table and heading upstairs, knowing that she'll likely be in bed by now. There's no solution to it that I can see. Not one that doesn't either leave me feeling as if I've betrayed a past that I've clung to for years or continue to keep us in this purgatory, where I give her only as much affection and care as I can manage without being overwhelmed by the guilt it fills me with.

I know I'm going to want her tonight. And I'm not so sure that I should try to fight that. I tell myself that I'm considering it because it would make her happy, but—

As I push open the door to our bedroom, I stop in my tracks. Elena isn't asleep, the way I thought she might be, or even lying down, reading or scrolling through her phone. She's sitting up, her arms wrapped around her, staring out across the room as if in shock. After a moment, I realize that she's crying silently, her face paler than I've seen it in a long time.

She looks up at me, and her mouth opens, making the shape of my name, but no sound comes out. And then I see it—something that I think I'm hallucinating for a moment, a throwback to another woman, another bed, another night where my world fell apart in an instant.

The bed in front of her is drenched in blood.

Elena

I look up and see Levin standing there, see his gaze shift to the blood on the bed, and I see the instant panic in his face, the way it goes white as bone.

"Elena, what happened?"

There isn't the anger in his voice that I expected—no recrimination, just fear and worry, the same emotions crashing through me. "I–I don't know, I woke up—"

"How long ago?"

His voice shakes when he asks the question. I realize, numbly, that I've never seen him so afraid. I realize that he's very close to falling apart himself, that he's holding on by a thread so that he can be the one who handles this situation, when I so clearly am unable to this time.

"Not long," I whisper. "I just woke up. There was this sharp pain, and—"

"We need to get you to the emergency room."

"I wanted to stay awake until you got home. I—" I don't finish that thought, that there had been a small part of me that, knowing he was out having drinks with Max and Liam, had hoped that when he came home, we'd have a repeat of the first night we were in our house—that he'd come home tipsy and fall into bed with me. But I'd been too exhausted and fallen asleep.

I'd woken up to a still-silent house, with a cramp of pain tearing through my abdomen that jolted me awake with a gasp, feeling as if I were dying. I'd never felt pain like that, not even after the plane crash. My first thought was that I should get up and call someone. Anyone. Levin, Isabella, the hospital. But I was frozen, in shock, the instantaneous fear that I felt paralyzing me.

I wrap my arms around my waist as I stare at him, gaze flicking between him and the blood-soaked duvet and sheets, all the words caught in my throat as the same thought rushes through my head again and again—I'm going to lose the baby, and Levin will hate me for it. I'm going to lose everything.

Levin steps forward, striding to the bed quickly as he reaches for his phone. He hits a button, and in a second, he's barking into the phone, telling one of the members of our security to bring the car around. "Here. I'll help you downstairs."

"I—" I want to tell him that I can walk, but I'm not sure it's true. My entire body feels numb and shaky. I don't protest again when he reaches down, scooping me into his arms, seemingly heedless of whether I might get blood on him.

I feel like I might pass out, as I cling to him on the way down the stairs, my vision blurring with a mixture of tears and a creeping darkness at the edges. I try to cling to consciousness, afraid of what I'll wake up to if I let myself pass out.

"It's going to be alright," Levin murmurs reassuringly to me as he helps me into the car, still holding me as the man driving us slips into the front seat and pulls out of the driveway. "We're going to get you to the hospital, and it's going to be fine. It's going to be fine."

He repeats it again, and I know he doesn't entirely believe it himself. I know he's saying it to try to calm me—and probably himself—down, and it works, in a way, if only because the sound of his voice is something for me to hold onto, to listen to instead of the screaming fear in my head that tells me everything is over.

That I'm going to lose everything in one night.

The sharp pain tears through me again, making me gasp and press a hand to my stomach, and Levin's broad hand covers my own. "We're not far away," he tells me, and I can hear him struggling to keep his voice calm. "Just hang on, Elena."

I'm not sure what I'm hanging on *to*, what it is that I could possibly do to change this one way or another, but I try to calm myself down. *Panicking isn't going to help*, I tell myself, trying to breathe, my other hand on top of Levin's between mine as I cling to him, taking comfort in the only thing I have right now that makes me feel as if I'm not floating away.

"I'll call Isabella," Levin says. "I know you'll want her here, too."

I want to tell him *thank you*, that, of course, I want my sister, but I can't speak. The pain cramps deep in my belly again, and hot tears swim in my eyes as I try to breathe, clinging to Levin's hand with both of mine. It feels like the car is moving impossibly slowly, as if it's taking far too long to get there, and I have the nonsensical thought that I must be bleeding on the seats, and I *know* how hard it is to get blood out of the back of a car.

It almost sends me into hysterical laughter, because it wasn't all that long ago that I would have never thought that I would know something like that. The idea of Elena Santiago scrubbing her dying lover's blood out of the back of a stolen car with bleach would have been a laughable one.

But I did that, and so much more. And now it all feels like it happened to someone else.

Levin is out of the car in an instant when we pull up to the front of the emergency room, opening my door before the driver can get out and lifting me out of the car. "I can walk," I protest this time, but he shakes his head.

"Absolutely fucking not," he tells me sharply, holding me to his chest as he strides towards the revolving front door.

The next several minutes happen in a blur. Levin carries me straight up to the receptionist, who tells him that there's a wait, and I hear him telling her, *like fuck there's a wait, my wife is bleeding, our baby*—and then I don't hear anything when another wave of pain grips me, and the world turns white around me for a second.

I think I do go unconscious for at least a short time. When I wake up, I'm in a hospital bed, Levin standing next to it, talking to a nurse. I think I hear him tell her the name of the doctor I've been seeing, but the room feels as if it's swimming around me, and I let out a low moan of pain. I feel sore and tender, and bruised, and I want to go home.

"Soon," Levin says, turning towards me, and I realize that I must have said the last part out loud. "She's calling your doctor now. Once we know what's going on, we'll go home. I promise."

He stays there with me as the nurse checks my vitals, his hand wrapped around mine, giving me something to hang onto. He answers the questions that I feel too out of it to manage, and I turn my head to look at him briefly, thinking to myself the words I can't say out loud—*how could you ever think that you're not a good husband? That you don't deserve everything?*

"The bleeding has stopped," the nurse tells us, as she gives me a quick examination while we wait for the doctor. "That's a good sign. I'll start you on an IV, and then we'll wait for her to get here."

I've known what it feels like to be exhausted down to my bones before, but this is a different type. It feels like I'm floating, and I cling to Levin's hand as tightly as I can, because a small part of me feels like I might float away.

Isabella comes bursting in shortly after, looking shocked and pale, her gaze immediately landing on Levin as soon as she sees me. "What happened?" she demands, and I shake my head, lifting my other hand to try to get her attention.

"I fell asleep and woke up bleeding," I tell her numbly. "Nothing really 'happened'—"

"We don't know what caused it yet," Levin says calmly. "We're waiting on the doctor."

Isabella strides around the bed, her cool hand pressing to my forehead as she brushes my hair back, peering down at me. "It's going to be okay," she tells me calmly, her thumb stroking along my hairline. "This kind of thing happens. It doesn't necessarily mean anything."

I can feel the tension in Levin, and I sense, vaguely, that he's not overly thrilled with my sister. That he wants to be the one comforting me right now, even if he's not entirely sure how to go about doing that beyond handling the situation and holding my hand, and I wish I could find the words to tell him that he *is* comforting me, that what he's doing is helping. That having them both here, the two people I love most in the world, is keeping me from spiraling into utter and uncontrollable panic.

But my mind feels too foggy to make the words connect, and I close my eyes, wishing to be anywhere else. Wishing for this all to be a bad dream.

When the doctor does arrive, she says the same thing Isabella did, comforting words about how this happens, how it doesn't necessarily mean the worst-case scenario. She does a thorough examination while Levin holds my hand and Isabella asks pointed questions, and when she's finished, she asks me a few more questions about how my day had gone and what I did.

"Nothing out of the ordinary," I tell the doctor weakly. "I spent most of the day with Isabella; we picked out some things for the house—I cleaned a little bit? I went for a walk on the path behind our house. Nothing that I would think would cause—"

"I'm not saying it's your fault," she says gently. "Just trying to pinpoint if there's something that we should avoid in the future. But it sounds like this wasn't triggered by anything. It's your first pregnancy; you're young—this isn't unusual. But it is early, and I want to take precautions. So I want you on bed rest for a little while. Not full bed rest, you can get up and walk around, go up and down stairs, but try not to do too much. Nothing overly strenuous. Don't pick anything up, no sexual intercourse—" she glances at Levin, and I feel a slight sinking feeling in my stomach. *Well, that gives him an excuse not to touch me.* It's not a fair thought, exactly, but it is there.

"For how long?" I ask weakly, and she smiles sympathetically at me.

"We'll reevaluate at your next doctor's appointment. If all is well and I don't see any signs that anything is abnormal, and there's no further bleeding, then we'll take you off bed rest and see how things go. How does that sound?"

"Does that mean the baby is okay?" I ask, still feeling as if I have to reach down and rummage for every word. "Are they—"

"Your baby appears to be fine right now," she tells me reassuringly. "I can't see anything that suggests that you're in a crisis. It was an alarming amount of blood, I understand, but I don't think there's a need for panic. Just a need for caution. You can go home if you like, or you can stay here overnight—"

"Overnight might be best, so they can watch you—" Isabella starts to say, but I shake my head.

"I want to go home," I say firmly, looking between the doctor and Levin.

"You could come back to the house with me, so I can help." Isabella bites her lip. "Or I can come with you—"

"I really appreciate it." I fumble for her hand, looking at her and hoping she'll understand. "But I just want to be in my own bed, with Levin."

"I'll call you if we need anything. I promise," Levin tells her.

Isabella's lips thin slightly, but she nods. I see a glimmer of our mother's stubbornness in her, but she relents, undoubtedly thinking of the conversation we had in the kitchen after the first doctor's appointment.

It's early in the morning by the time we get home. Levin insists that we go to the guest room on the first floor, since our own bed is still bloody, and he doesn't want me walking up the stairs. "I know the doctor said stairs were manageable," he tells me as he helps me into the room, his hand solidly on the small of my back. "But I think it's better not to risk it."

I want to be in our room, but I'm too exhausted to wait for the bed to be fixed, and I know Levin is trying to help. So I give in, silently thanking my past self for having put in the effort to furnish and somewhat decorate the guest room despite the fact that we don't expect to have anyone staying in it anytime soon.

I want to ask him to stay with me while I fall asleep, but as it turns out, I don't have to. He helps me out of the hospital gown that they changed me into, balling it up and tossing it on the other side of the laundry hamper to be thrown away later, with a particular amount of force that tells me just how closely he's hanging onto the thread of his own stress and fear in order to keep calm for me.

"Do you want to take a shower?" he asks, and I bite my lip. I'm so tired, down to my bones, but I also feel very much as if I need one, especially before slipping into a clean bed.

"I don't know if I can manage it," I tell him honestly, and Levin nods.

"I'll help," he says simply, and gently guides me out of the bedroom and to the hall bathroom, where he turns on the hot water and helps me into the shower. "I'll go get some clothes for you to change into. Just be careful until I get back."

I'm not sure exactly what could happen to me while I'm standing in the shower, but his concern makes me feel soft and warm, soothing away the fear that seemed to settle down into my bones since I woke up in the bloody bed and left me with a constant chill. I stand under the hot water, arms wrapped around myself, closing my eyes against the flood of emotion that threatens to overwhelm me.

I want our baby for more reasons than just to keep Levin with me. It was never intentional, and it was never meant to be a trap. But I can't deny that there's a part of me that's terrified that if I lose our baby, he'll have no more reason to stay. That he'll divorce me or simply go back to New York, and that will be it. There won't be any of that time that Caterina talked about, no more chances for me to be patient and wait to see if he can slowly come around to the idea that he can be happy again.

That I'll lose him for a second time, and there will be nothing I can do about it. That I'll lose *everything*.

It's the same thought that rattled in my head on the way to the hospital. It does so again, repeating until I feel like it might drive me insane, all the way until the door opens and Levin comes back in.

I hear the rustling sound of him undressing, and a moment later, he gets in the shower with me, concern written all over his handsome face. "I'll help you wash up," he tells me firmly, stopping any protest that I might have. "You've taken care of me before; it's my turn to do it for you."

I'm so tired that I can't argue. I let him wash the blood off of me, stand there numbly while he washes my hair and scrubs every inch of me gently, getting the hospital smell out of my hair and off my skin, until there's nothing but the soft honey-almond scent of the shower gel and the tropical aroma of my shampoo perfuming the warm air. Then he helps me out of the shower as he dries us both off.

He helps me into the soft pajama pants and tank top that he brought me, putting on clean clothes for himself, and then we go back to the room. He gets into bed with me without a word, lying close next to me as I close my eyes, knowing I'll be asleep in moments. The exhaustion is all-encompassing, and I want to tell him to wake me up if anything happens, but I already know he will.

Thankfully, I sleep without dreams.

When I wake up to bright daylight, it's with the other side of the bed neatly pulled up, the blankets tucked around me, and breakfast waiting for me on a table tray next to the bed. I take a breath, momentarily wondering if it was all a bad dream, but as I realize I'm in the guest room and feel the tender soreness still in my abdomen, I realize that it wasn't.

Levin is already awake and dressed in dark grey chinos and a fitted v-neck shirt that tells me he has somewhere to be.

"Where are you going?" I manage, pushing myself up a little against the pillows. "Can you stay—"

"I have a meeting with the Kings." There's a crispness in his voice that makes my heart sink, because I've heard it before, and I know what it means. I can see the wall that's gone up around him as if it were a physical thing, a manifestation of what I already know is happening.

Last night, I needed Levin. I *always* need him, but he's best in a crisis, when everyone else is on the verge of falling apart, and one person needs to keep a cool head. Now that that's past, I know he's putting up his defenses, because what happened last night budged up far too close to what happened before.

Whatever progress we might have made—and it was small, maybe not even there yet—has slipped away. I'm almost certain of it, and I blink back tears in the morning light as I look at the breakfast waiting for me.

"I need to go." He clears his throat. "I wanted to make sure you were awake and alright before I left, and had breakfast, but I'm already running late. So I'll–I'll see you when I get back."

He doesn't kiss me goodbye. He pauses, looking at me once more, with an expression almost as if he's making certain I'm still there, but he doesn't cross the room to the bed. He leaves, and the all-too-familiar ache in my chest settles back solidly where it was before as I watch him go.

I understand, and I don't, all at once. I manage to hold back tears until I hear the front door close, and then I press my hand over my mouth, my shoulders shaking as I start to cry. All I can think is that he'll never let go after this, that this reminder of what he stands to lose if he lets me too close will be the thing that cuts me off from him ever loving me forever.

I'm afraid of losing you, too, I want to shout at him, if I could make him come back into the room this minute. *But I can't help but love you. Why can you help it?*

I don't have any answers, and I don't even know if I want them. I'm almost sure that they would hurt too much. But I had thought, ever so briefly, that he was trying.

I don't know how I'm going to stand it if he's stopped.

Levin

"What are we doing to stop Diego?"

The question is out of my mouth before the three of us have even fully settled into our seats—Connor, Liam, and I. "I need Elena and our child to be safe," I tell them sharply, my tone brittle. "So whatever needs to be done, tell me what it is. I'm not willing to let this drag out any longer than it has to."

"He's not backing down," Liam says, rubbing a hand over his mouth. "We hoped that he would see the futility in it, but the man has pride, I'll say that. And he considers it gravely wounded from what's happened with both Isabella and Elena. He wants the Santiagos and anyone associated with them brought down. He seems to be willing to do whatever he needs to—risk whatever and whomever—in order to facilitate that."

"So what can I do?" My jaw is clenched so hard that it hurts. "I need them safe. I need this threat to be finished. Give me something to *do*."

I see the glance exchanged between Connor and Liam. I don't know if they're aware yet of Elena's trip to the hospital, of what happened. I have no doubt they'll find out sooner or later—there's nothing that happens in their orbit that they're not aware of, and rightly so—but I'm not in any mood to explain. As far as I'm concerned, it doesn't fucking matter.

My wife and child are in danger, and I refuse to sit on the sidelines and wait for something to happen. I'm not going to rush headlong in, as Niall was wont to do, but I'm also not going to sit back. Whatever Connor and Liam have planned, I intend to be in on it.

"Elena might be better served to have you with her," Liam says slowly. "If something happens to you, Levin—"

"—then her sister and all of you will see that she's taken care of," I tell him sharply. "I've never sat by in the face of danger, and I don't intend to start now. So *tell me what you need me to do.*"

I have no intention of being told differently this time, and I think they're both aware of that. They exchange another glance, and then Liam nods.

"There's a trade shipment coming in from the Santiago cartel," Liam says finally. "It'll be coming in tonight, and there have been threats made to intercept or damage it. We've got men already assembled to deal with it, but we'll put you on it as well. Jacob is heading up the operation—he's aware of the fine details—but he can fill you in, and you can work alongside him, in charge of the others. How does that sound?"

"That's fine." My voice is clipped, flat. Connor raises an eyebrow at me.

"It's not grunt work," he says coolly. "If Diego sees that he can't so much as get men to damage a shipment without us putting a stop to it, he may back off before trying anything more ambitious. That's the hope, at any rate."

"I didn't say it was. And I'm well aware of why a job like this matters."

Connor and I have never been adversaries, but we're not close, either. I can feel the tension rolling off of him, and Liam, as ever, is the intermediary.

"Go home for a bit, check on Elena," he says in a calming tone that tells me that he's aware of what happened—no doubt because Niall knows and said something to him. "Meet Jacob a couple of hours before, and he'll debrief you while you're getting ready to go. This is nothing for you, I'm sure. Old hat. You'll be back in bed before the sun's up."

I'm sure he's right. A part of me doesn't want to go home, doesn't want to face Elena and all the fears that dredge up. But I also want to make sure she's safe and that there's no repeat of last night. So I do as Liam suggested and go home briefly.

When I carefully open the door to the guest room, Elena is sleeping. I stand there in the doorway for what feels like a long time, watching her. She looks peaceful and lovely sleeping there like that, and it makes all the fear of last night briefly feel like a bad dream.

But I know it wasn't. None of it was a dream. And watching her like this, I feel the desperation to keep her safe, her and our baby, clawing at my throat like nails embedded in my skin. It feels like everything I was afraid of coming back at once, and I stand there, hating the fear of being helpless to stop it again that washes over me.

I can't fail again. I can't watch while someone else dies because of me—or worse, if Diego gets his hands on her. The thought of it is impossible, and I know that it would be the thing that breaks me. The thing I can't come back from.

I'd been close to letting myself consider what Max and Liam told me, whether forcing myself to deny my feelings for her was hurting us both more than it helped. Whether or not I ought to finally, after all this time, allow myself a second chance at happiness.

I don't believe in fate, or in anything higher than my own agency, really, but if there were ever a time when I felt like something seemed to be telling me what to do, it was last night. I'd gone out for those drinks, had that conversation, come so close to coming back home and letting myself fall into Elena's arms without fighting it—and instead, I came home to her staring at me, shell-shocked in a bloody bed.

It felt obvious then, and it feels obvious now. I know what happens when I try to be someone other than the man I was told I would be, over twenty years ago now. I know the price I pay for reaching further than I should and what happens to those I take down with me.

Men in our world aren't meant to have things they love. They're taken away from us far too easily. They're used against us. Men in our world should not have weaknesses. All other weaknesses are within yourself and can be overcome. Fear and pride can be conquered. The skills that the Syndicate needs can be honed. You are a weapon. A weapon should not have something that it can lose except its own sharpness, and that can always be regained.

Vladimir's speech to me isn't one I ever forgot. He repeated it to me when I came back from Tokyo, when I told him what happened with Lidiya, when I told him that I had married her. He warned me what would happen—that it didn't matter that he had decided my punishment, and that it didn't include expulsion or death, or anything that would be done to her. He warned me that someday, someone would come for what I loved. That conversation, too, isn't one I've ever forgotten.

Someday, someone will come for what you love. It's a part of the life you've chosen, Volkov. If you have nothing you love, nothing you hate, there is nothing that can be used against you.

I didn't choose this life. I never did. I was pushed into it.

There is always a choice. You could have chosen to leave. Struck out on your own. You chose to stay. And I've been glad you did. You're one of my best, Volkov. But you have a weakness now. I could exploit it, if I wished to. I won't. But others will.

So I had tried to leave. I tried to walk away, to have the life that Lidiya and I dreamed of. A small plot of land and a house, outside of Moscow, near her grandmother. A place for our children to grow up, for us to grow old. A place far enough away from the ghosts of my past that nothing could touch us. A place without violence.

Vladimir had been willing to let me go. Not because he cared for me, or my happiness, or for hers—but because he knew that a man whose heart was no longer in it was a liability. That if my loyalties were split, I would get myself or someone else killed or incriminate the Syndicate. That I would fuck up, in his words.

He could have had me killed. I had feared that he might, and so had Lidiya. But instead, he had let me leave. Not without punishment, not without another warning. But he had let me go.

It was some of his men, angry and resentful that I had left, that Vladimir hadn't imposed the ultimate punishment on me, who came for Lidiya. Who did, as Vladimir warned me someone would do, when I thought we were safe.

I had wondered if Vladimir was behind it. I knew him well enough to know he told me the truth when he said that he wasn't. He gave me permission to get my vengeance for Lidiya, though I would have whether he allowed it or not. I knew that it wasn't displeasure over her death that meant he gave me that permission; it was his fury at them for having acted without orders. He would have killed them anyway—he just allowed me to be the hand that did it.

He had hoped I would come back to the Syndicate. When I refused to come back in my former capacity, he sent me to work for Viktor's family. And the rest is history.

It all comes rushing back as I stand there watching Elena sleep, and all I can think is that the moment I let my guard down, the moment I allow myself to be a man and not a weapon, those I love are hurt. If I do it again, the same thing will happen.

Last night was an accident. A natural thing, nothing anyone had done. But that doesn't change the way I saw a blood-soaked bed and saw Lidiya all over again, felt that tearing pain in my chest, the memory of her cold hand in mine as fresh as if it were yesterday, and not twelve years ago.

If there is nothing I love, there is nothing that can be taken from me. The words I repeated to myself, over and over in the wake of her loss, an echo of what Vladimir said to me, ring in my head again. I can't stop what I feel for Elena, not now. It's entirely possible that I never could. But I can stop myself from allowing it to take over. To blunt my edges and make me helpless to keep her safe again.

And if nothing else, there's one simple fact, as selfish as it is.

I can't bear to feel the pain of that kind of loss again. I have long believed that there is very little left in this world that could kill me, as skilled and well-trained as I am.

But that would end me, when no one else has been able to.

Jacob is waiting for me when I head back to the Kings' arsenal to get geared up. He glances up at me as he cleans a pistol, giving me a grin. "Good to see you, lad," he offers up amicably, setting it back down on the workbench in front of him. "Connor and Liam said you'd be coming along."

I don't know Jacob well, but I know him well enough to like him. He was Connor's right hand in England, when Connor went by a different name and ran a different organization, before Saoirse and her scheming father dragged him back to take up his mantle as the heir apparent to the Boston Kings. Connor had brought his men back with him and kept Jacob in the same role he'd had before, without any argument from Jacob, it seemed.

What I know of him is enough—that he's a tough and honorable man, someone good to have at your back in a fight. I have no qualms about going into a job side by side with him, and that's all that matters to me.

"Should be a quick in-and-out," Jacob offers up as he sets another gun down. "Shipment is on time; everything else is as it should be. If Gonzalez sends his men to fuck with it, as we expect that they will, then we take them down. No talking, no negotiating, boss says. There's been enough of that with the top guys. Gonzalez knows the consequences of continuing to push. They fuck with us, they find out."

I nod grimly, ignoring Jacob's gallows humor. At another time, I might have been willing to engage in the banter—it's not unusual. I've long since lost the fear of these kinds of situations, and I know Jacob is skilled, but there's always something that can go wrong when bullets start flying. There's rarely been a man I've known who didn't use a little dark humor to deflect that. But right now, with all of my past memories crowding in and the sight of Elena bloodied and pale too close for comfort, I can't find any humor in me.

"Look—" Jacob shifts a little, turning to face me with his back to the workbench. "I know this is personal for you. I'm willing to let you take point on it, if you want. Technically I'm the man in charge of this job, but you've got a hell of a lot of experience on me, and I know it."

"We have different skill sets," I tell him tersely. "You're good at running with a crew. I've worked mostly alone. I'm sure together, we'll do a fine job."

"Still. You've got a few years on me—not many, but a few—and you worked for that bad-ass Russian organization. Trust me, I've heard enough about what you used to do and what you still do for Viktor. My point is—" Jacob runs one hand through his hair, looking slightly uncomfortable. "I trust you to have my back. I'll have yours. And I know this is personal, so I'm willing to defer to that and your experience, to a point. But–don't be reckless. I know how something being personal can cloud your judgment."

I give him a chilly look, and he holds up his hands. "I'm not trying to tell you what to do, man. Just saying—I get it. And I get how this kind of situation can get into your head."

"Do you?" I don't bother waiting for a response. Instead, I cross to one of the weapons cabinets. I have my own gun with me, the one I've been using going on twenty years and prefer, but I'm well aware that it's better to have more firepower than not, in these sorts of situations. This is a job with a crew, a job that will have multiple targets, different from the kinds of missions I used to be more accustomed to tackling.

He doesn't answer, and I don't ask anything further. Whatever he's got in his past that might suggest he knows how a job turned personal can go wrong isn't something I know him well enough to ask about, and I'm not about to offer up my own experience. We both know we're able to keep each other alive tonight, and that's all that matters.

The rest of the men sent with us aren't ones whose names I know. Jacob seems to know them—some of them are men who ran with him and Connor, I think—and I trust that Connor and Liam wouldn't send us with a team that isn't capable.

There's an odd sort of calm that comes before a job like this. The decision to go is made, the team is put together, and the gear is all dispersed. There's a stretch of time when everyone there knows there's a chance that things go wrong, and they don't see whatever tomorrow brings. Some of the men make jokes, some are quiet, as if they're going over their training in their heads, again and again, trying to be so prepared they can't be caught unaware. Everyone has a different method.

Mine has always been to simply exist. I've been at it so long that it's all muscle memory, trained not to be surprised, not to flinch, to know when someone is coming and where they're coming from almost before they do. I don't need to run through maneuvers and training exercises any longer, and I worked alone for too many years to find comfort in joking with others. As far as I've been concerned for a long time, there's a switch that flips off when it's time to go—and if I make it out on the other side, then the rest of me comes back online. It's kept me alive for years, and I see no reason to change what isn't broken.

Tonight is harder.

Like Jacob said, it's personal. Diego himself won't be there, just his lackeys. I won't get to put an end to any of this tonight, not unless Connor and Liam's guess is correct, and ruining his plans is enough to make him back off. I don't think that'll be enough. He's gone too far, and backing down because we kept his men from damaging a shipment would make him look weak.

I don't think he's going to stop until he's gotten what he wants, or he's dead. And that means tonight is just a start.

It's hard to let my mind fall into that easy blankness that it won't come out of until the job is done, because of what this means. Another step forward into a fight that's meant to end with my wife dead or worse, and this time, her sister too. Failure has a higher price tag than just pissing off Vladimir or looking like I'm bad at my job—and either way, no matter how tonight goes, it doesn't help anything, if my impressions are right.

If we succeed, Diego sees it as a step forward into a war. If we fail, it emboldens him. Either way, he keeps coming.

There are other ways I've seen men I worked with keep themselves calm before a job. I've heard them talk about the other shit they've done, the missions they've pulled off, the times they've skirted death and danger, and how it felt. I've made a practice of doing the opposite, and *not* thinking about what I've done in the past. A finished job is just that—finished. I've never seen any point in looking back on it. It's never made me feel better about myself to think about all the blood I've spilled.

But tonight, as the car winds through the roads and down to the back alley where we'll leave it, I can't stop thinking about Lidiya. About how it felt to find her dead. How long I sat there in that room, those blood-spattered curtains blowing in the breeze, looking at the absolute ruin of everything I'd loved.

A worse man would have taken away what they loved, too. They all had something—the four men who killed her. One had a sister. Another had a girlfriend and child of his own. A third had a mother who depended on him. The last one was an older man—old enough to resent a life spent with the Syndicate that hadn't been entirely his own. He had no one, except an ex, that he still visited from time to time. Someone he'd loved and kept at arm's length, the way I should have kept Lidiya. Someone he'd lived a half-life with, seeing them in between pockets of time, when neither of them could avoid the other any longer. Someone he could have had so much more with, if not for the Syndicate.

That was how I knew he was the one who convinced the others to go with him, who stoked their resentment that I was getting out until he got those three men to buy in on his plan to murder my wife.

I could have done to them what they did to me. I could have exacted my revenge on people close to them and forced them to live with it. I've never thought that it made me a better person that I didn't—only that it was a choice, and I chose to kill them instead, directly. Quicker, for the other three, although not as quickly as it could have been. For the old man, the one who planned it, I made sure it took long enough that he had time to think about all the years he could have been doing something else, and regret that time. I made sure he had a chance to think about how things could have been different.

I don't often think about it. Not just because of how much it hurts to think about Lidiya, to remember her, but because those four men are the only ones I ever killed because I wanted to. Everyone else was just a job.

Tonight is just a job. The men Diego has sent to destroy this shipment mean nothing to me. I won't remember what they look like tomorrow, and I won't ever know their names. But I *wanted* to kill those four. I *enjoyed* it. And that's never been who I am, otherwise.

If I get to Diego, I'll enjoy that, too. And I want that to be the end of moments where I look at someone else, and think how good it would feel to have their blood on my hands.

I never wanted to feel that way about anyone. I thought, if I never let anyone close to me again, I'd never have to.

The car pulls into the alleyway, and I try to shake it off. I know this is what Jacob was talking about—how something making it personal can get in someone's head, distract them, and put everyone at risk. I know I'm meant to be better at this than that. So I try to switch off. To sink into that quietness between the beginning and the end of a job where everything is just muscle memory. Where I act on instinct and nothing more.

But I keep seeing Lidiya, and Elena. I keep remembering what it felt like to kill those men. I keep thinking ahead to the moment when Diego is the one at the other end of my gun. And I know, from years of long training and experience, that I shouldn't be here tonight. That I'm too close to being a liability.

It's too late now.

There's always a possibility that the shipment comes in, and everything's fine. That this turns out to be nothing but a patrol.

I don't think that's going to be the case, though—and it's not.

The shipment is half unloaded when we hear them coming. Me and Jacob first, because we're the ones keeping the sharpest ear out, and the ones best trained for this. Both of us already have our guns out, waiting, and Jacob makes a quick motion to the two of our men closest to us, signaling for them to warn the others.

I let Jacob be the one who steps forward as the group of Diego's men approaches. I can see their steps slowing when they see that there are others there beyond just who they expected to be unloading, but they don't stop, and they don't turn to leave. I don't blame them—I've encountered enough bosses like Diego to know that for these men, they're better off coming the rest of the way and dying than going back to whoever is in charge of them and saying they turned around and bailed on the job. Whoever answers to them answers to Diego, and a man like Diego isn't going to reward failure with anything but a slower death than the one they'll get tonight.

Still, Jacob offers them the choice, when they get closer. It's what makes organizations like the Kings think that they're better, more sophisticated, more honorable—that they're willing to be merciful, in some circumstances.

"Get out of here, and we won't shoot," Jacob calls out. "You can go back to your boss and tell him the shipment was already unloaded and cleared out, or whatever keeps your nose clean. I don't give a fuck, lads. But you best get out, or we'll be forced to send you home to Gonzalez one way or another."

There's no response except for the faint clicking of gun chambers being loaded and the low murmuring of one man saying something to another—all what I expected. Once they arrived, they weren't going back.

Jacob waits long enough to see them for certain. To know that they're going to shoot at us. He doesn't wait long enough for them to shoot first, and that makes me respect him a little more than I already did.

My mind almost slips into that quiet blankness as I fire, as the air all around me fills with the sound of gunshots and the greyish smoke, and the smell of hot metal. And then I remember seeing Elena sleeping earlier today, the soft peacefulness on her face, and I find myself wishing that I'd kissed her goodbye before I left again. That I'd told her I was leaving to go do this job at all.

If I die, she won't ever know what I was doing until it's over.

The thought makes me flinch. The thought of not seeing her again distracts me, just for a moment. Not long enough to get me killed, but enough to get me clipped, and the feeling of a bullet grazing my thigh, tearing through the fabric of my pants and spilling hot blood down my leg jerks me back to reality.

I pull the trigger and the man who shot me drops. One of our men goes down, and I fire again, and feel a second bullet graze me, enough to make me reassess the situation.

It goes fast. So fucking fast. Jacob sees what's happening and drops the man who fired at me, and I keep shooting, the rest of the men with us fanning out. My arm and thigh are burning, pain lancing down into my bones, but I learned long ago to ignore it. Pain can be addressed later. It can't be addressed at all if I'm dead.

It's not until all of Diego's men are down that I start to let myself feel it. Jacob is at my side immediately, looking at me with concern. "Are you alright, man?"

"Just got winged, that's all. I'll get home and patch it up."

"I can get you somewhere closer if you want to address it there—"

"I'd rather be home." I grit my teeth, looking around to make sure there's no one else coming that we haven't accounted for. "Let's finish dealing with the shipment and—"

"No, you're done." Jacob whistles, and one of the men comes loping towards us.

"I can stay and finish this with all of you—"

"You're going home." Jacob's voice holds a finality that tells me he's spent time telling other men what to do, and as much as it rankles with me to be given orders by someone who isn't technically my superior—and is, in fact, younger than me—I can still feel the hot trickle of blood down my thigh, and I know he's not wrong.

I need to get patched up. One way or another, I need to get somewhere to do that, so it's either wherever the Kings' men take care of those things, or my own home. If my home is my preference, then—

"He'll take you." Jacob nods towards the man who came hurrying over. "We can call for another car. He'll get you back, and then just report in to Connor and Liam when you can. I'll debrief them after." He pauses. "It was a big help, having you out here. You're as good as I've heard."

"I appreciate the compliment. I'm sure it won't be the last time."

Jacob gives a tight, sharp laugh that tells me he agrees, and then he turns away to deal with the others. I follow my assigned driver back to the car, my mind already turning to how to keep quiet when I get home so as not to wake Elena up. I don't want to worry her.

I'm not so lucky. I'm barely stripped out of my clothes, rummaging for a first-aid kit with one hand holding a hand towel that I'll throw away later to the wound on my leg, when the door clicks open, and I see Elena standing there, her eyes gone wide as she takes in the sight in front of her.

Fuck.

Elena

For a minute, I'm not entirely sure what I'm seeing. It's my husband, I know that, stripped down to his boxer briefs—which is distracting enough in and of itself—but it's the rest that really gives me pause. He has a wadded-up hand towel—one of the new ones that we bought—held to his thigh, which has dried blood streaked down it and more soaking the towel in his hand, and his arm is bleeding, too. The arm wound looks worse—a flap of skin is hanging loose, and the gash is wide, bleeding more than even I know it should be.

I have no idea what the context is, but what I do know is that all of this put together points to my husband having been somewhere that he didn't bother telling me he was going. That, combined with the forced distance, only makes me all the more upset.

I've spent the whole day and night sleeping and crying by turns, feeling lost and hopeless, unsure what to do next—*how* to do this. I spent the hours that I was awake and crying, wondering if *I* needed to start learning to shut myself down, to protect my heart, before it becomes broken past repair.

And now I know he kept something from me today.

"I know I was the one bleeding last night," I tell him coolly, crossing my arms as I face him from the doorway. "But this doesn't have to be a competition."

"Elena." Levin turns to face me, his expression completely startled for a moment before he smooths it over. "You shouldn't be out of bed."

"The doctor said it wasn't total bed rest. What's going on?" I motion to the wounds on his thigh and arm, which don't look nearly as bad as what I helped him patch up after the fight in the hotel, but still don't look *good*.

"You shouldn't be out of bed," he insists again, and I glare at him.

"Stop changing the subject."

"I can handle this myself." He's rummaging through the first aid kit with one hand while trying to keep the compress on his thigh with the other, blood trickling down his arm.

"Do you remember what happened in Rio?" I demand, my irritation growing by the second. "I can *help*. Sit down."

He looks at me as if he's not entirely seeing me for a moment, before he lets out a long sigh, and sinks down onto the toilet, still holding the compress to his thigh as I start to pick things out of the first aid kit.

"Rio would have been easier with one of these," I mutter, pulling peroxide, ointment, bandages, gauze, and anything else I think I might need out of it.

"Rio would have been easier with a lot of things. Elena, seriously—"

"No, you." I glare at him, and he flinches a little. I think he can see how upset I am, because he doesn't say anything else as I start to deal with the wound on his arm first.

If he didn't know, he does when I don't bother warning him that it's going to hurt, when I'm done cleaning off the old blood and press an alcohol-soaked pad to the wound to clean it. Levin sucks in a breath through his teeth, but doesn't say another word or make another move as I clean it out, carefully using butterfly bandages to close the gash before patting antibiotic ointment around the edges and then laying gauze over it, wrapping another bandage around that.

"I can do my leg—"

I ignore him, reaching to tug away the hand towel. The wound on his leg is bigger—still not so bad that it can't be patched here, but enough that it makes me swallow hard when I see it. "These are gunshot wounds, aren't they?"

"Just grazed." Levin looks at me as I clean the old blood away. "I wish like hell you didn't know enough to figure that out, Elena."

"It seems like it might come in handy, being married to you." I press another alcohol-soaked pad to it, and Levin's jaw clenches above me, the muscle there leaping as I finish cleaning it and start to tug the edges together with bandages again.

"You shouldn't be the one dealing with this."

"Who else should be? I'm your wife."

"I'm supposed to protect you. Keep you out of all of this—"

My own jaw clenches at that, and I tug a little harder than necessary at the edges of the wound as I finish bandaging it up. "You've done a good job protecting me. But I've been in all of this for what feels like a really long time, Levin. So let me help you, so at least I'm fucking *doing* something. You, of all people, should know how that feels."

The last sentence is probably, a step too far. But he says nothing, staying silent as I finish patching up the wound.

"What happened?" I ask as I pat the antibiotic ointment around the edges. "Can you at least tell me that?"

"Just a job. Protecting a shipment that Diego planned to hit. Connor and Liam let me go out there with Jacob and their guys."

"*Let* you? So you asked to?"

"Elena, this is my *job*—"

"No, it's not." I press the gauze down on his thigh, feeling too frustrated and full of a cascading torrent of emotions from last night and today to be as careful with my words as I normally would be. "Your job is working for Viktor. This is you trying to *protect* me, when what I actually need is you here with me. *Here*, not showing up in the middle of the night bleeding, because you helped with a *shipment*. That's not what you should be doing." I wrap the bandage around the gauze, trying to summon the strength to say what I want to.

I look up at him as I finish, my hand still resting on his thigh. "I need you here, Levin."

And then, before I can tell myself why it's such a bad idea, I lean up to try to kiss him. I can't *not*, because I love him, and he came back home in the middle of the night hurt, reminding me how easily I could lose him, if things keep going the way they are.

It's just supposed to be a small kiss. Something that any wife would give her husband without thinking. But he stops me, with a hand on my shoulder, gently pushing me back as he stands up and moves away from me.

It feels like I'm the one who's physically wounded. I stop, my heart lurching in my chest and tears instantly burning at the back of my eyes as I look at him, feeling rejected all over again. It hasn't felt this bad since the morning after our wedding, and I stare at him, trying to understand.

"What changed?" I ask him softly, the words slipping out half-choked. "Do you blame me for the scare with the baby? Is that what's going on?"

Levin turns to face me, startled. "What?"

"Is that why you've been different since this morning?"

"I—" He pauses, looking at me with something very close to confusion. "How could you possibly think that, Elena? Of course, I don't blame you. It couldn't possibly be your fault, and I wouldn't blame you regardless, no matter what. I know you would never purposefully—"

"Then why?"

"Why, what?" He leans back against the counter, favoring his injured leg. "I don't understand."

I can't tell, from the look on his face, if he means it or not. If he *really* doesn't understand, or if he's claiming not to, so this conversation can be over more quickly. I've never thought of Levin as being someone who would hide things from me intentionally or deceive me. Still, after how quickly I saw things change this morning, after he left on a job tonight without telling me, I'm no longer entirely sure.

"You were different this morning. Closed off. You were—" I struggle with trying to think of how to explain it. "You were so distant. And I thought—"

"Elena." Levin rubs a hand over his hair. "I warned you before we were married that I'm not going to be able to be the kind of husband you want. I'm not saying it can't be difficult for you, or that your feelings aren't valid because of that, but this shouldn't be a surprise. If I'm distant, then—"

"It doesn't make sense, though," I whisper, feeling the emotion rising up and clogging my throat despite myself. "These last few weeks, you've—" I suck in a breath, trying to keep myself under control. I don't want to burst into tears. I want to *understand*. "You've been bringing me flowers. Taking me out. Helping around the house. Cooking fucking *breakfast*—all these things that were so sweet, and thoughtful, and—"

"Elena." Levin lets out a slow breath. "I want you to be happy. I just can't be the one to make you happy. I do those things because it cheers you up. Because it makes you smile when I show up with flowers, or I tell you to dress up because I'm taking you out to dinner. Because it makes you laugh when I fuck up pancakes, and you appreciate it when I tell you to relax because I'll do the dishes and order takeout. I'm *trying* to figure out how to live in the same house with someone—how to get to know them and share a life with them—while still keeping that distance. I don't want to make you miserable. God fucking knows I don't want to be the reason for that. So I'm doing my best to do the things that will keep you from feeling that way."

"Not because you want to?" I swallow hard. "That's *worse*, Levin. If you're just pretending, just doing those things out of some sense of obligation—like you're reading out of a fucking *manual* of *Keeping Your Wife Happy for Dummies*—do you not see how that's worse?"

"No! Christ—*fuck*—" Levin rubs his hand through his hair again, looking as frustrated as I've ever seen him. "I do want to do those things, Elena. I *like* spending time with you. I like going out with you. I like seeing you smile. I do *things* and bring you *things* because *they* make you happy, when I can't. Doesn't that make sense?"

I stare at him, and I wonder how someone can so clearly seem to feel one thing and be so completely in the dark about it. I don't want to let myself believe that he does feel it, because if he doesn't, and I'm wrong, it will hurt so fucking bad that I'm not sure I'll make it through that kind of crushing blow. But what he's saying, with the sincerity in his voice, sounds an awful fucking lot like someone who *does* love me, and just somehow can't see that actions can say it just as clearly as speaking the words.

That telling himself he doesn't love me doesn't make it true, if all the other signs point that way.

"Don't you see?" I ask him, frustration edging into my own tone. "You *are* making me happy, Levin. You can say you don't love me and can't be a good husband all you want, but what you're doing shows otherwise. You *are* being a good husband, by wanting to make me happy. By doing these things. You don't do all of that for someone you don't love—"

"I care about you, Elena—"

"Oh my *god*." I stare at him, my own hands tightening into fists as I try not to burst into frustrated tears. "I've never known a man so capable who's also so blind when it comes to himself! Unless you're lying to me or faking all of this somehow—which you say you aren't—then you're genuinely trying to make me happy, genuinely enjoying being with me, genuinely *want* me, and all of that points to *love*, Levin! Even if you're not in love with me now, it's headed in that direction, and I don't know why you can't see it! Why you don't see that caring enough about someone to try to build a life with them even when you aren't sure if it's what you want doesn't fall into that category, too!"

I let out a long breath, the words trailing off, and I stare at him helplessly. "You're a good man, Levin. You have been since I met you. And I can *see* what you're doing, how you feel—all you're doing is hurting us both by fighting it. By telling yourself a lie."

There's a long, protracted silence. Levin looks at me, his face drawn and tired, and I see a resignation there that crushes my heart, because I know in that moment that it doesn't matter what I say. It doesn't matter if it's the truth or not. It doesn't matter if I'm right.

He's made up his mind, and Levin is nothing if not committed to a course of action.

"Either way," he says finally, quietly. "I can't let myself give in to it, Elena." He shifts his weight, wincing. "I was out with Max and Liam last night. They said a lot of the same things to me that you're trying to say now. I tried to listen to them as best as I could. I tried to hear what it was they were trying to tell me. I started to question some of how I've been acting, how I've been thinking—but what I saw when I got home was too close to how things went before. I think you know that already. And it reminded me that no matter what, I've got to keep some kind of distance. I've always known that—and the last time I let myself get close, the people I loved paid for it. I'm not going to let that happen to you, Elena. I'm not going to let you suffer because I get too close."

"It's just as bad, living half-in and half-out. How do you not see that?"

"If that's really how you feel, then I can give you your space. Not until Diego is taken care of—I'm not leaving you alone until I know that threat is over—but afterward, I can give you more distance, if that's what you need. I can split my time between Boston and New York—you can have whatever arrangement you want." He breathes in, his shoulders tightening, and I can see the resolve in his face, hear it in his voice. "But I can't lose someone I love again, Elena. I can't let myself close enough to even make that an option. And I'm not going to change my mind. I told you that before Rio, and in Rio, and in Boston before I left. I told you when I came back, and it hasn't changed. It *won't*. So however you need to live with that, tell me, and I'll make it happen."

There's such absolute surety in his voice that I feel like it's going to break me. He sounds so fucking *certain*, and hearing him say that he'll give me space, that he'll split his time between New York and Boston—essentially just being here when he needs to be for our child, makes me feel as if all the wind has been knocked out of me. I sink down, sitting on the edge of the tub as I struggle to fight back the surge of emotion that makes me want to break down just at the thought of it.

"That's not what I want," I whisper in a small voice. "I want you here. I do. I just—"

"Then we have to find a way to live with the way things are, Elena. *You* have to find a way." Levin looks at me, that exhausted expression lining every inch of his face. "I will be sorry for the part I've played in putting you in the position for the rest of my life. If that suffering makes it easier for you—and I hope it does—I'll tell you as many times as you need to hear it. But I can't be more to you than this."

He pushes away from the counter, still favoring his injured leg as he looks at me. "All you have to do is tell me what will make it easier for you, and I'll do it. If you want me to stop trying to do things to make you happy, if you want us just to live in each other's orbit, I'll do that. If you want me to live separately from you—in another house or another state or whatever you want—I'll do that. I will do *anything* to make it up to you, Elena. But I can't give you what you're asking for."

"I don't know what to say," I say softly, and it's true. I don't—because none of the things he's offering *will* make it easier. I don't want him gone. I don't want him to stop doing all of the small things that he's done for me in the weeks since we moved in. I don't want to live in this house and wish he were here. I don't want to long for him every day for the rest of my life.

But I also don't want to long for someone who's standing right next to me.

There's no solution to it. And so I have no idea what I could possibly say to tell him what to do.

"I'm going to bed." Levin looks at me tiredly. "I'll manage to get upstairs. If you need me—"

"Please stay down here with me." I look up sharply at him, feeling a sense of panic at the idea of him going to a different room to sleep. It feels like a turning point, like us going to sleep in separate bedrooms is another wall between me and any chance of the future I want with him. "I don't want to be alone. Please—"

I *hate* begging him. I hate the feeling that I'm pleading for him to stay. But I feel everything that I've hoped for slipping through my fingers, and the pain of having him next to me when he won't touch me or hold me somehow feels better than taking that next step into separation.

Levin looks as if he's considering refusing me. If he does, I have a terrible feeling that we won't come back from that. Even in Rio, even when he was insistent that nothing could ever come of what we had together, we still shared a bed for most of it.

But finally, he lets out a breath, and nods. "Alright," he says. "I'll stay down here to make sure I'm there if anything else happens."

If that's the excuse you need. I don't say it out loud. I just give him a small, watery smile. And then I get up, and walk past him, back to the bedroom.

Elena

For the second doctor's appointment, Levin is running late.

It feels like another symptom of things going wrong. Of them getting worse. Nothing has been the same since the morning after we went to the emergency room.

With me on bed rest, there's been no question of going out. The dates to the museum, the movies, out to dinner—all that stopped. And Levin had a perfectly good excuse—I wasn't supposed to strain myself or even really leave the house unless I absolutely had to. Flowers still showed up in the bedroom, and Levin made sure that I had all of my meals—that I didn't have to get anything for myself. But it lacked something that there was before.

Before, I could *feel* that he was trying to make me happy. That he spent time trying to think of what he could do to make me smile or laugh. There was an earnestness to all of it that was especially sweet coming from a man like him.

Now, it's felt detached. I feel a distance between himself and what he does, as if he's acting on autopilot. It's made me feel like an invalid, and there's a certain small resentment that I've had to struggle against.

This feels like another nail in the coffin. I sit there in the waiting room alone, feeling like an idiot for asking Isabella not to come because I wanted to share this with Levin, just him and I—and now he's not even here.

When he does show up, it's halfway through the appointment. The doctor raises her eyebrow but says nothing, waiting for him to give me an apologetic kiss on the cheek—the first time he's touched me since we argued in the bathroom—and then fills him in on what we'd just been talking about.

"I told Elena that there seems to be no issues with the baby that I can see. You're cleared for all normal activities, and although I'd recommend being cautious, I see no reason not to resume the same sorts of things you were doing before the incident—just don't exert yourself past that…don't take up a new workout routine, for example." She smiles reassuringly at us both. "I know it was terrifying, but I truly see no reason to worry. You both can rest easy."

I don't say anything to him until we've checked out and we're back in the car. I sit in the passenger's seat next to him as he drives us back to the house, trying to find a way to be rational in the midst of the emotions churning inside of me.

I decide to go with the simplest question to start.

"Where were you?" I ask softly as I sit there, my hands knotted together in my lap. "Did you forget?"

Levin shakes his head silently. I see it out of the corner of my eye, but I don't say anything. I let him figure out how he's going to deal with this.

"I had a meeting with the Kings," he says finally. "That's why I was gone earlier this morning, before you got up. It went long. I'm truly sorry, Elena—I told Connor and Liam you had an appointment, but they said it could wait. That part of being married into this life is dealing with some things on your own that you'd rather not, and that you should know that—Connor said that, by the way, and not Liam," he adds quickly. "I got there as quickly as I could. I can't tell you how sorry I am. I wanted to be there for all of it, especially after—"

I don't *want* to believe him. I want to be angry at him. I want a *reason*, a genuine, concrete reason to be angry, to have something that could eat away at what I feel for him, something that doesn't always circle back to *well, he told you it would be this way. You were warned.* I want a reason to think that he's not as good of a man as I've seen over and over that he is.

But I do believe him. That's the hardest part of all of this. I believe that he would have been there if he hadn't gotten caught up in the meeting, that he would have driven me himself. No part of me truly thinks that he carelessly forgot or that he didn't care. There's never been anything he's ever shown me that would make me think that's the kind of man he actually is.

If anything, he cares too deeply, and it's caused him to punish himself for far too long.

His hand brushes my leg, as if trying to reassure me, and my pulse leaps in my throat. It's been *weeks* since we've had sex, and I've been aching for him constantly. It's felt like a certain kind of torment knowing that he's there in bed with me, and we can't. Even I wasn't willing to risk it while I was on bed rest, and I know he certainly wouldn't have.

The doctor cleared you for all normal activities. You could—

We haven't talked about it. I wondered, when he offered to give me space, when he said he'd sleep in another room, if the conversation we had that night changed anything about his decision on our wedding night to keep me 'satisfied' within our marriage. I was afraid to ask, and hear him say that he *had* changed his mind, that it made it too difficult for him to keep that distance. I was equally afraid that he would deflect it, put the conversation off for later, and I'd be left wondering and tormenting myself with it until I finally got an answer.

"We can go back up to our room now," I tell him when we walk into the house. "No more worries about stairs."

"I can't say I feel a hundred percent better about it," Levin says cautiously. "But stairs are fine, I'm sure. So yes, I'll help you move your things back up there. Actually, why don't you go change, and I'll bring them up for you now?"

A plan starts to form in my head the moment he says it. I go up first, while he gets my clothes out of the guest bedroom, and I strip out of the leggings and t-shirt I'd worn to my doctor's appointment and toss them in the hamper. Quickly, before he can come up, I find a pair of the type of panties I know he likes—a silky pair of cheeky boyshorts that shows off my ass to the best advantage...I've seen him react in the past when he's discovered I'm wearing something similar—and a silky tank top without a bra. It's warm in the bedroom, and the silky material clings to my breasts, the outline of my nipples pressing against the thin fabric.

I take down my hair just as he comes into the room, and it *seems* innocent. Like I was halfway through dressing when he walked in. I have no idea if Levin will be fooled or not—but I'm not sure I care. I want him too much.

The moment I turn around, my hair tumbling down around my shoulders, I *see* the heat in his eyes. His gaze flicks down my body in an instant, taking all of it in, and I can see the moment before he catches himself, when there's unbridled lust in his face.

And then he remembers how he's *supposed* to feel, the control he tries so hard to cling to, and his expression goes blank.

"Do you want to rest for a bit?" he asks neutrally, walking over to put my clothes in the drawers. "I can find something to do, if you want some peace and quiet after the appointment—"

"Or you could come lay down with me." I walk over to him, running my hands down his back, over the soft cotton of his t-shirt. "It's been a while—"

I reach up, brushing my fingers over the nape of his neck as I press a kiss to the middle of his back, my other hand sliding under his shirt. My fingers skim over the ridged muscle of his abs, and I feel him suck in a momentary breath before he turns to face me, catching both of my hands in his before I can touch him any further, as if he knew where my hand might stray next.

I don't need to touch his cock to know he's hard, just from that small amount of closeness. When I look down briefly as he turns, I can already see him straining against the fabric of his pants, his cock a thick ridge against the front of them, wanting me.

"It's not a good idea, Elena," he says quietly, his broad hands wrapping tightly around mine. "The baby—"

"The doctor said it was fine. That we can go back to our normal activities."

"I don't know if we should risk it." He takes a breath, looking down at me. "It's not—"

"Not worth it?" I bite my lower lip, looking up at him. "We're going to spend the next several months being celibate? When my doctor said it was fine?" I try not to say what comes into my head next, but I can't help it. "What excuse are you going to come up with after the baby?"

"Elena, that's not fair—"

"You're my husband. I'm your wife. I *want* you, and I know you want me." I pull my hand free of his, sliding it down the front of him, my fingers tracing the shape of his straining cock. He sucks in a hissing breath, his eyes briefly closing, and I feel a small flutter of satisfaction.

"You want it too. You can't fight *everything*, Levin. Why can't we have this?" I arch towards him, my other hand curling in his as I go up on my tiptoes to brush my lips over his. "Not everything has to be so complicated. It's been weeks."

"This has always been complicated." He stiffens as I kiss him, his lips cool and dry, and there's a stab of disappointment in my chest. "*Always*, Elena. But I mean it when I say that I don't know if we should. You were *just* cleared. We could wait a little longer—"

"Then we don't have to do all of it." My fingers trail over him again, my thumb pressing against the swollen shape of his tip through the fabric. "I just want to touch you. I miss it. I want—" I swallow hard, my pulse leaping in my throat. "I want to taste you. I want to *feel*—"

"God, Elena." Levin's voice goes hoarse, the words dragging out of him as I rub my palm over his length. "Do you have any idea what you do to me?"

"I'm getting some idea."

I whisper it as I run my hand over him again, and as I start to sink to my knees in front of him, he grabs my upper arms. I start to protest, opening my mouth to argue with him—and then my breath is taken away entirely as he silences me with a kiss.

It's long and hot and slow, his tongue sliding into my mouth, tangling with mine as he groans, his hips pressed against me with my hand caught between us, rubbing over the straining shape of his cock. I feel him move, the shudder that goes through him, and when he finally breaks the kiss, his eyes are dark with lust.

"If we're going to do anything," he says finally, "we're going to do it in the bed, where you can be comfortable."

I'm not going to argue with that. I let him walk with me to the bed, let him lift me onto it as he follows me, lying down next to me as he brushes my hair away from his face.

"We're not going all the way with this, Elena," he tells me firmly, his voice a deep growl in his throat. "I mean it. I'm not risking that yet. Not when you were only cleared today."

"Alright." I nod, my fingers tracing along his jaw as I tilt my chin up to kiss him again, gently. "I just want—I want to be close to you. I need this, Levin. Please—"

"There you go again." He shakes his head, the words coming out half-strangled with desire as he cups my cheek, moving close enough that I can feel the hard, tense lines of his body pressed against mine. "Begging to pleasure *me*. You say you know what you do to me, but I don't think you have any idea how that makes me feel."

"Then tell me," I whisper, arching closer to him. "I want to hear it."

He groans, his lips brushing against my forehead as my hand slides between us again, tracing the shape of him through his clothes. "It makes me feel like I'm going fucking insane, sometimes. The thought of you begging to make *me* come like you did on the beach, in that fucking hotel, in *this* fucking room—*god*. I think about it sometimes, when I—"

He breaks off, as if he's said something he didn't mean to, and my eyes widen, a flush of heat going through me at the thought of him alone, stroking his cock and imagining me. "That's what you picture when you're—by yourself? Me?"

Levin's eyes close again, and I can see that same inner struggle that he always has, the fight between what he feels and wants and what he thinks he should say or do. "I don't know how to answer that —*fuck*—" he groans as I rub my palm over the hard ridge of his cock. "I should tell you I don't think about it. But god, Elena, of course, I fucking do—*ohh*—"

He moans, the sound catching as I undo his belt and drag the zipper down, now only the thin fabric of his boxer briefs between his flesh and my fingers. I can feel the heat of him through it, burning against my hand, and I wrap my fingers a little more firmly around him, stroking lightly as he gasps.

"I think about you on your knees, your hand around me, pleading for me to let you suck my cock. The way your hair feels in my hands, the way your *mouth*—god, Elena, having someone as beautiful as you pleading to put my cock in your mouth drives me fucking wild. I think about tying you up to the bed like I did in Rio, making you beg for *my* tongue, my mouth, pleading to come—and I feel—"

"If you're going to say *guilty*," I whisper, my fingers slipping inside to stroke the naked flesh of his cock, "then don't. Because I *like* it, Levin. I fucking love it. I think about all that, too. I think about how much I want you—"

I reach down with my other hand, pushing his pants down his hips, and he groans as he strips off his shirt; all of that hard, naked muscle suddenly bared for me as I tug his clothing off, and his cock springs free, slapping against his abdomen and leaving a damp sheen of pre-cum against his skin. He's so hard that I can see the veins throbbing, and as we toss his clothes aside, I push him onto his back, my hand wrapping firmly around the thick shaft.

"Please," I whisper, a teasing smile on my lips as I move between his legs, confident that he's going to give in to me now. "Please let me suck your cock." I rub my thumb over the tip, sliding the arousal there to the soft bit of skin just beneath it, and Levin's entire body jerks beneath me. "I want to taste you—"

"God—" His hand trails through my hair, his chest heaving as he tries to catch his breath. "I should be the one begging you. I want your fucking mouth—"

I lean down, flicking my tongue over the tip, and his hips jerk again. His head tilts back, his mouth opening on a ragged moan as I lick him there, just the head for now, lapping up the pre-cum and swirling my tongue around it until he's nearly trembling, my hand holding him still for me.

"It's been a while since I—" He swallows hard. "I haven't come in a while. It wasn't enough. I wanted—"

A hot flush of arousal goes through me at that, at the idea that his own hand wasn't enough, that all he wanted was *me*. "Can I make you come more than once?" I whisper, looking up at him as I trace the edge of his cockhead with my tongue, my hand slowly sliding along the shaft as I tease him.

"I—maybe—" Levin's voice sounds strangled. "I don't know. *God*, Elena—"

His voice breaks off again as I wrap my lips around him, sucking lightly as I slide down, and then harder as I move my hand down to the base of him, still gripping him tightly as I tease him with lips and tongue. I see his jaw clench, his eyes shut tightly as I slide back up again, enjoying the feeling of having him in my mouth again, seeing him revel in the pleasure I can give him.

Knowing he wants me.

I'm aching for him. My entire body feels like it's on fire, and I can feel how wet I am, the silky material of my panties clinging to my damp flesh, my nipples stiff and begging to be touched. I want him so much it hurts, but I want to enjoy him more, to enjoy the way it feels to be this close to him, to have him at my mercy. It makes everything else fade away, and it feels like, just for a little while, he's actually mine.

Like I could keep him this close forever.

His hips jerk upwards as his hand tangles in my hair, and I can feel him struggling not to thrust too hard into my mouth, not to choke me with his cock. He could if he wanted to, and I'd like it, feeling the thick length of him pushing deeper, forcing me to take more of it. But he lets me set my own pace, sliding down further until both of my hands are braced against his thighs and my nose is brushing against his skin, the pressure of his cock in my throat making me convulse around him for just a moment. I hear him groan at the sudden tightness, his body shuddering, and when I come up for air, I see him look down at me with an expression of such lust that I feel a fresh wave of desire wash through me, drenching me with it.

"God, that feels so fucking good—" Every word catches as he says it, his other hand fisting in the blanket as his fingers wrap in my hair.

I slide my tongue over him as I catch my breath, my hand stroking over his hard, glistening length as I wrap my lips around him again.

"That's so good," he repeats, breathing heavily. "You've learned how to suck my cock like such a good girl, Elena. Just how I like it."

I moan around him, my own body stiffening at that, throbbing from the flood of arousal his hoarse, filthy words sends through me. I love it when he loses control, when he talks to me like this, and I slide my mouth down his cock again, taking him as deeply as I can as I taste his pre-cum on the back of my tongue, filling my senses with his taste and scent and the hard, hot feeling of him as I lose myself in the pleasure of what I'm doing.

I'll never get tired of being with him like this.

"Fuck, I'm so close—" he groans as I take him all the way again, throat tightening around his cock as I wrap my lips around the base, my nails digging into his thighs. I hold him there for as long as I can, before I come back up and suck hard on the tip, looking up at him wickedly.

"Good," I whisper, swirling my tongue around him. "I want you to come in my mouth."

"*Fuck*—" Levin's jaw tightens, his hips bucking as his hand presses against the back of my head. I feel him throb against my tongue in the instant before I feel the hot flood of his cum fill my mouth. I swallow convulsively, still sucking and stroking the base of him as I take everything that he has to give me.

I don't stop until he's twitching and shuddering, the hand in my hair sliding down to cup my jaw and pull my mouth off of him as he gasps for breath. "Elena, it's too much; I—"

"I wanted to try to make you come more than once." I try to capture him in my mouth again, his cock still hard, but he tugs me away, another tremor going through him.

"I'm open to the idea," he pants, rolling me gently onto my back as he leans, naked and gorgeous, over me. "But I need a minute to recover. And you—" His eyes are full of dark, heated lust as they rake over my body, landing on the silky material between my thighs that's drenched through. "It's your turn to come next."

I close my eyes, sucking in a breath as he pushes the tank top over my head, tossing it aside as his hands cup my breasts. *This* is the Levin I want always, the lustful, groaning man who loses his mind when he's with me, who says filthy things and touches me in all the ways I could ever have fantasized about and some that I could never have thought of, who makes me beg and plead and come for him. The man who wants me.

The man who drives me just as insane as he says I do to him.

His lips are on my nipple, tugging and rolling it between his teeth, a sharp prick of pain instantly laved away by his tongue. He sucks more of my breast into his mouth, the other still held in his broad palm, fingers replicating what his teeth and lips are doing to my nipple on the other side. I writhe beneath him, feeling the hard press of his hips against me, the still half-swollen shape of his cock rubbing against my thigh as he teases me until I'm gasping.

His lips drag downwards, over my belly to my hips, his teeth grazing against each hipbone as his fingers slip into the edge of my panties. I hadn't been sure if we'd do this, if he would worry that anything he did to me would be too much, but I should have known better.

Levin is nothing if not generous in bed, and if he isn't going to fuck me, I should have known he still wouldn't let me out of bed without making me come, once he'd decided to bring me here.

"You're so fucking wet," he breathes, looking down at me with an expression that's almost one of awe. He slides one long finger upwards against my folds, groaning at the way I part instantly for him, the slick pool of wetness that his fingertip descends into as my hips arch up, needing more. "And all for me—"

"Only for you," I gasp, hips rolling in a bid for friction, for him to rub against my clit, or slide that long finger inside of me. "Only ever you—"

"I know." He leans over me, his lips brushing against mine, careful not to settle his weight on me as he strokes upwards, adding a second finger as he rubs them over my clit at last, and I let out a small cry into the kiss. "You've only ever been mine, Elena. And I don't deserve you."

I kiss him harder, before he can say anything else, lips pressed against his as I grab onto his arms, clinging to him as the pleasure builds. I've been aching for him, wanting him, and the slightest touch feels like almost enough to push me over the edge, to give me exactly what I've been craving.

"I know you can come more than once for me," he murmurs into my ear as he circles my clit with his fingertips, his lips brushing warmly against the shell. "I want you to come for me, *malysh*. Come as much as you can."

I ignore the sharp stab of pain that the nickname shoots through me, the tender way he whispers it, and I focus instead on what he *is* giving me. The feeling of his fingers, pressing harder now, rubbing in the motion he knows I like, driving me wildly towards my first orgasm, and I know it will only be the first. He'll give me as many as he thinks I can take, and that thought alone is enough to push me over the edge, to make my back arch and my head tip back with a shuddering moan as I unravel against his fingers, the orgasm crashing through me as I buck and keen with pleasure.

He keeps stroking, rubbing, crooning *come for me, that's my good girl,* in my ear as I nearly sob with the exquisite pleasure of it, and I want to beg for his cock. I want to be filled up, to feel him hard and solid and thrusting, driving me towards another climax as he fucks me hard, but I bite it back. I know that's asking too much, and I don't want to ruin what we have right now.

I don't want him to stop.

He doesn't. His strokes slow as my orgasm ebbs, his fingers circling the outer edge of my clit instead of right atop it, his tongue gently sliding lower, teasing the edges of my pussy and down to my entrance to swirl there, letting the sensitivity ease before he begins again, pushing me towards another orgasm. He knows exactly how I like to be touched, exactly what will make me gasp and clutch the sheets, twisting them in my hands as my back arches and I grind against his face.

"I want to make you come again," I whisper, licking my lips where I can still taste him, and Levin chuckles, the sound vibrating against me.

"Come for me again, and I'll let you have my cock in your mouth? How does that sound, *malysh*? A good enough reward for letting me have you come on my tongue again?"

A buzzing, tingling sensation washes over me at that, all of my body, my *skin* feeling alive at the words murmured over my damp and sensitive flesh, his urging, his desire. I can't speak, so I whimper instead, nodding as his tongue slides over my clit and my hips jerk upwards towards his mouth.

He groans, his hands gripping my thighs as he holds them apart, keeping me spread open wide for him to enjoy. He pushes my legs up and back, as wide as I can be, and he pulls back for just a moment, his gaze raking lustfully over the sight in front of him, all of me fully exposed.

"So fucking beautiful," he murmurs, and there's no part of me that feels anything but aroused at the way he has me displayed, the vulnerability of it. I trust him completely, and all I feel at that moment is *wanted*.

It feels as good as any physical pleasure.

His mouth presses against me once more, tightly, his tongue stroking familiar circles over my clit, fluttering, rubbing, and he sucks my flesh into his mouth, pushing me quickly towards the orgasm that he's had me hovering on the edge of. A slow, rhythmic sucking, pulsing my clit in his mouth as his tongue flicks over it, and my thigh muscles tremble as I buck against his face, one hand gripping the back of his head as I give myself over to it.

I know I fucking *drench* his face when I come again. I can feel it, the flood of arousal on his tongue, the way my entire body tenses and shudders, hips grinding shamelessly on his mouth as I twist on the sheets and come hard. I hear myself scream his name, the second orgasm as intense as the first—more so, even—and Levin keeps licking all the way through the climax, sending ripples of pleasure through me until I sag backward against the pillows, boneless and gasping.

He leans back, wiping his mouth lewdly as his eyes sparkle with lustful mischief, and I can see how hard he is again, his cock pressed stiffly to his abdomen, pre-cum sliding down the shaft. I lean up, reaching for him, and he narrows his eyes.

"I'll be fine, Elena. I don't need to—"

"I want to. Come here." I almost growl the words at him, and he has the audacity to *laugh*, the fine lines at the corners of his eyes crinkling as he smirks at me.

"You want it that badly, hm?"

"*Yes*. I told you—"

"Then we're going to try something new, because if you're going to make me come again, then I'm going to make sure you get the same."

I blink at him, unsure what he means, especially when he made it *very* clear that he wouldn't fuck me. He's been swayed before, but in this instance, I don't believe he would be.

He shifts on the bed, one hand on my hip as he rolls me onto my side towards him, and suddenly he's lying parallel to me, his hand lifting my thigh so it's hooked over his head. "You can do as you please with my cock now," he tells me, a hint of playful mischief in his voice that I've rarely heard, "but I'm going to eat this sweet pussy again while you do it."

Am I ever going to stop getting wet at every filthy word that comes out of this man's mouth? I came twice, hard, but I feel myself getting drenched anew at what he says, *how* he says it, my thighs sticky with the evidence as he brushes his fingers over my swollen flesh and chuckles.

"You're so wet for me, *malysh*. I could taste you all day and never tire of having you on my tongue."

His cock throbs as he says it, very near my face, and I see another droplet of pre-cum pearl at the tip. I reach out, rubbing my thumb over his swollen flesh without thinking, and Levin shudders, his cock jerking into my palm as his fingers slip between my folds again, stroking me as I start to tease the head of his cock.

The pleasure jolts through me, newly intense at the novel sensation of him touching me like this while I lie here and play with his cock. I can tell he's matching my pace, his fingers lazily brushing over my clit as I circle his cockhead with my fingertips, dampening it with his pre-cum as I explore him.

It's not new anymore for me, not exactly, but I'm not tired of learning him. I love touching him, finding which spots make him jerk and shudder, which make him groan, repeating some of the same touches and strokes, and trying new ones.

I lean forward, tugging him a little closer with one hand on his thigh as I flick my tongue over the tip of his cock, and I'm immediately rewarded with a similar, small flick of his tongue over my clit.

Oh, so this is the game we're playing. I bite my lip, stifling a delighted laugh, and press my lips against the swollen head, circling my tongue around it as Levin presses his mouth tighter between my legs, his tongue mimicking a similar pattern.

It'll take longer for me to come like this, I can already tell, but I don't care. It feels so good, and there's an intimacy to it, this game that we're playing together. I touch him the way I hope he touches me next, my thumb rubbing the soft flesh just beneath his tip as I lick my way around it, and he rewards me with his pushing against my entrance, his tongue still swirling around my pulsing flesh similarly.

It's a slow escalation, bit by bit. When I wrap my lips around the head of his cock and suck, Levin's tongue speeds up, lapping against my clit in that rhythm that he knows I like. When I start to slide down, taking him into my mouth, he begins to suck it lightly. My thighs jerk, squeezing around his head as I suck my way down his shaft, tongue teasing the ridges and veins as his tongue swirls around my clit, and I feel my entire body shudder as pleasure ripples through me.

His thigh muscles are tight and hard under my hand, and I think of what it will feel like to come when he does, to ride his face while I swallow his cum. Levin must be thinking something similar, because he grips my thighs suddenly and rolls onto his back so that I'm hovering above him, my legs gripped around his head as he drags me down onto his face with both of his hands, groaning with pleasure.

I feel his cock throb in my mouth, coating my tongue with pre-cum, and it sends a fresh burst of pleasure through me, knowing that the taste of me arouses him so much, that he's so turned on by the act of having me on his face like this. I imagine the stubble on his chin and jaw drenched with me, the taste and scent of me sinking into his tongue, his skin. I buck against him, letting my mind run wild with every filthy fantasy I've ever had as I swallow his cock down, reveling in the way his hips jerk as he groans against me.

I'd never imagined doing this, but it feels dirty, erotic, grinding down on his mouth while I suck him harder, my hand sliding between his thighs to cup his balls in my palm, lightly stroking my fingers over them and being rewarded instantly with him throbbing in my mouth. I let myself go, riding his face the way I'd ride his cock if he let me, feeling his tongue slide over me again and again, his fingers digging into my hips, my ass as he holds me there. We're past the point of playing the game now, or if we are, we're both going wild —my lips fastened firmly around his cock as I take him as deeply as I can again and again, his sucking at my clit as his nose brushes against me. I can hear him groaning, hear him breathing in the scent of me as I feel him harden between my lips, and I know he's close.

"Fucking *come* for me, *malysh*," he growls hoarsely against me. "I'm going to fill your mouth up, *krasotka*, come for me, ride my *fucking* face—"

My back arches, pressing me against him as my body obeys instantly, the thought of him coming down my throat as I come on his tongue sending me over the edge. My hips press downwards, forgetting to worry about suffocating him, about if I'm too much. Somewhere in the back of my lust-fogged mind, I know he doesn't care, because he's pulling me down *harder*, sealing me against his lips as he drives me over the edge into a wild climax. I feel him throb and jerk in my mouth, flooding me with his cum as we both come undone together.

It feels incredible. I swallow and swallow, choked moans vibrating around his cock as he sucks and licks at my pussy, dragging out the orgasm for as long as he can as he pours himself down my throat. I feel like I'm coming apart at the seams, the pleasure wracking my entire body as I grip his thighs with my hands and come for him while he comes for me.

"*Fuck*," Levin breathes as he gently disengages from me, helping me slide off of him as he lies there panting. I can't even move to rearrange myself so that I'm lying side by side with him instead of my nose nearly brushing his ankles, a heap of boneless pleasure on the bed as he laughs under his breath.

"That's normally pretty hard to pull off," he says in a rasping voice. "But *fuck* if that wasn't incredible."

"I didn't even think of it," I whisper softly. "It was so good—"

I wait for him to say *we can do it again*, or *we'll try it this way next time*, but he doesn't. I can almost *feel* him receding from me, the armor slowly reattaching itself, as if he's dressing himself in his barrier to keep his heart closed off from me, even while he's still lying naked next to me.

When I can move, I push myself up to lie next to him, reaching over to brush my fingers over his short hair. He doesn't make me stop, but he doesn't return the caress, either. He lays there, his breathing slowly returning to normal, and as the rush of pleasure recedes, I feel my heart starting to sink.

I've got to stop getting my hopes up. Every time, I think things will be different, after. And I'm always disappointed.

After a few long moments, Levin speaks, his voice normal again. Flat, detached even, the lustful playfulness, the hoarse desire all gone from it.

"I'm going to have to go to New York for a couple of days," he says slowly. "I don't want to leave you alone even for that long, so Isabella is going to come and stay until I'm back. I already asked her," he adds. "She was happy to, of course, although I think she'd be happier if I just decided to stay in New York."

I know he's right, but I don't comment on it. I don't want to risk giving him even the slightest indication that I might want that, too, because I don't. I have no intention of taking him up on his offer for 'space' when all this is finished and I'm safe from Diego.

"Is it for business?" I ask finally, and he nods.

"Viktor needs me to come and look over some things in person. Nico is doing a good job of stepping into the physical role that I managed while I was there—training and evaluation—but Viktor wants my eyes on it, too, for a couple of days. He wanted me there sooner, but I convinced him that I couldn't go until the doctor had given you the all-clear to be off bed rest."

I have to blink back tears. *Why doesn't he see?* A man who doesn't love me would have told me that he had a job to do, and had my sister come and watch me while I was on bed rest, just as he's doing now that he feels more comfortable. He wouldn't have put his boss, a man he's worked with for more than a decade, who is the closest person to him, on hold for me. Not if he didn't harbor some feelings for me.

But he can't admit it—or he knows and just doesn't want them. *That could be it,* I think despondently, swallowing back the emotion. *He's hoping they fade, if he gives it enough time.*

"When are you leaving?" I focus on the questions, the logistics, so I won't cry.

"Tomorrow morning. I've got a flight scheduled. Isabella will be here before I leave." He turns his head, giving me a brief smile. "I'm sure that will be nice for the two of you. Some time with the house to yourselves, without me here to bother you."

He says it in a joking way, like any husband to his wife, but it hurts anyway. I want to tell him that he *never* bothers me, that I'd rather have him here, and that anytime he's gone, I miss him. But I don't. I keep all of it to myself, because I can feel a kind of exhaustion creeping in, a feeling of being so very tired that I love him so much, and he's fighting it so hard.

And I know in time, that feeling will turn to resentment. It might even turn to hate. It will drive us apart, and Levin will get what he claims he wants—a marriage of convenience, where we love our child but not each other, and he can protect his heart while it dies inside of him.

If he's very unlucky, he'll realize too late that he wants what I've wanted all along, when I'm the one who can no longer give it to him. It'll be a bitter irony, and the thought makes my chest ache, because I don't know how long we have.

Maybe things will be different when the baby comes. It's the last hope that I have to cling to, and I dig my nails into it, holding on with everything I have.

I love him.

I don't want to give up on us.

But even I can only try for so long.

Levin

When I wake up next to Elena in the morning, seeing her peaceful, sleeping face next to mine, her dark hair tangled around her cheeks, I have an overwhelming sense of wanting to stay.

I hadn't thought it would be so hard to leave. When Viktor had told me weeks ago that he needed me to come and oversee some of the final testing, I thought it might be good for us. Some space for me to work through what I'm feeling, and for Elena to see that she can be happy even when there's distance between us. That she doesn't really need me there as much as she thinks she does. That she might even have enough fun on her own, with her sister, to put some distance between us when I return.

I told myself that would be for the best. That if Elena wants space, it will no longer be me constantly pushing her away, hurting her despite my best efforts.

But when I look at her, lying there for a few moments before I need to get up and get dressed, I feel a pang of fear instead. A *worry* that the days apart will result in exactly that—she'll realize she doesn't want me as much as she thinks she does. That she's tired of trying so hard—that she feels relieved without me here.

That, added to the worry of what could happen with the baby while I'm not here to take care of her, makes me not want to go. To stay here in bed next to her and wake up with her, tell Isabella that she doesn't need to stay and be here with Elena instead. To tell Viktor that I can't do what he needs me to any longer—that I need to be here with my wife.

But I drag myself out of bed anyway, because I have a job to do, and staying here instead won't make anything easier. In fact, it might make it much harder.

Elena stirs as I get up, lashes fluttering against her cheeks as her eyes open and she looks up at me, her expression soft and sleepy. "Leaving?" she mumbles, her hand fumbling across the blankets for me, and an ache spreads through my chest that feels as if it might settle there forever.

"Only for two days," I tell her as I cross the room to get dressed. My phone vibrates, and I glance at it. "Isabella will be here in a few minutes."

"I really don't need a babysitter," she grumbles, her eyes opening a little wider as she pushes herself up against the pillows, her hand running through her hair. She does that every morning, tugging her fingers through the tangled strands, and there's a pang in my chest again at the knowledge of that small intimacy. That I *know* that about her, a thing that only I know. No one else has ever woken up next to her as many times as I have. No one else has seen all the tiny things she does, the small habits that she's formed, and remembered them. She's *mine*, in a way that she never has been anyone else's, and it both makes me ache for her and sends a flood of guilt through me all at once, because she could have been someone's who would love her the way she deserves to be loved.

It's the great conundrum of my life that I can know that, and at the same time feel a flood of vicious possessiveness at the idea of anyone else touching her, a feeling that if anyone were to try, I'd kill them with my own bare hands.

It's a feeling I don't have any right to, but it's there all the same.

"I wish you didn't have to go," she says softly, her teeth sinking into her lower lip afterward, as if she knows she shouldn't have. "I know you do, though," she adds hurriedly. "You're still working for Viktor, after all."

"It'll go by in no time," I promise her, crossing the room to press a kiss to her forehead as I finish buttoning my shirt. I see her gaze flick to it, as if she's considering the possibility of *unbuttoning* it for me again, and my cock twitches against my fly.

I want to fuck her before I go. *God*, I want it. It's been weeks since I've been inside of her, and as good as our afternoon playing in bed as I ate her out and she sucked my cock to a shuddering orgasm twice was, it's not the same as feeling her around me, all that tight, wet heat rippling down my length as I thrust, and thrust—

Fuck. I'm rock-hard in an instant, my cock throbbing almost painfully, and I grit my teeth. Now I'm going to be fighting a hard-on for the entire flight, and I consider whether I might make myself a member of the mile-high club as I retreat from the bed, angling myself so that Elena hopefully doesn't see my erection and get any ideas.

Of course, she does, however. "You can't leave like that," she calls out to me softly as I start to put clothes into my duffel, trying to focus on how many shirts I need instead of the painful throbbing in my groin. "Come back to bed for a minute."

"I just got dressed." I glance at my phone. "Your sister is going to be here in fifteen minutes."

"Then make it ten." I hear a rustling and turn to see that she's pushed the duvet down, her legs spread invitingly as she nudges the loose fabric of the shorts she wore to bed to one side, and I realize with another painful throb that she isn't wearing panties underneath them.

She gives me a small, wicked smile as she spreads herself with her fingers, giving me a mouth-wateringly enticing view of her soft, wet pussy, glistening temptingly as she rubs one finger over her clit. "It's been a long time since you've been inside me," she murmurs, her hips arching up a little, the last word ending on a gasp as she circles her clit with her finger. "You don't even have to take your clothes off. Or mine. Just come fuck me before you go. *Please.*"

That last word comes out on a moan, and a part of my already lust-fogged mind is impressed at how well she's learned me, how she knows exactly what buttons to push to make me question my decisions every time.

"Elena—"

"It's safe. I know it is."

"And if I do, and then leave, and something happens—I'd never forgive myself." My cock jerks against my thigh, protesting. "We can't—"

"We can," she insists. "And now I'm so wet—" She arches her hips up again, sliding her fingers through her folds, and I can see exactly how correct she is. I can imagine her taste, and if we had more time, I'd already be between her legs, licking her to the fastest orgasm of her life.

"I'm going to come one way or another," she purrs, narrowing her eyes at me. "So you can keep packing, and listen while I do it myself, hear how *wet* I am—" she rubs her fingers through her folds again, each word more breathless than the last, playing up the sound of her hand moving against her aroused flesh, "—or you can come over here and make me come with your cock, Levin, and leave me dripping with your cum while you go to New York."

I turn at that, staring at my wanton wife as she rubs her clit a little faster, her teeth sinking into her soft, pretty lower lip. "You like that idea, don't you," she whispers, her voice a husky moan as she reaches down, tugging her shorts to one side with her free hand so that I have an even better view than before. "Getting on that plane, thinking about your cum inside of me all day. How *full* I'd be—"

"God*damn* it," I growl, crossing to the bed in two strides. I'm already undoing my belt with one hand as I grab her with the other, yanking her halfway across the mattress and nearly coming on the spot from the yelp of excitement she makes as I jerk my zipper down and shove my pants far enough down my hips that she won't make a mess of them as my cock springs free.

"Keep those shorts to one side for me while I fuck you, like a good girl," I tell her, my voice thick with lust. "You wanted to get fucked? Then take my cock, Elena."

I don't thrust into her as hard as I want to. Even as overcome as I am by her taunting, I have enough self-control not to slam into her. If not for the baby, I would. I'd fuck her as hard and fast as I could, pound my cock into her to show her just what happens when she teases me to the limit. The part of it that nearly has me spilling into her the moment I feel her heat around me is that I know she'd fucking *love* it. It's what she wants, for me to fuck her with every ounce of strength I have, to fucking *destroy* her, and at this moment, I want to.

But I'm not going to risk her for either of our pleasure. I grit my teeth as I push myself into her, a groan erupting from me the moment I feel her clench around my swollen cockhead, and I'm not sure I'm even going to need ten minutes. "Keep rubbing your clit for me, *malysh*," I murmur under my breath as I slide into her, feeling her tighten around me. "Make yourself come on my fucking cock."

"Yes, yes—oh *god, oh fuck yes—*" Elena moans, her hips snapping upwards, pushing herself down my length eagerly, so that I bottom out inside of her even faster than I anticipated, every inch of my cock buried inside of her wet, tight pussy.

"Such a filthy mouth for such an innocent girl," I murmur against her ear, thrusting into her. Some small part of me still thinks I shouldn't be doing this, that I shouldn't risk it, even if we were told it was safe. But I also don't think I can go months without her.

And you think you can give her space. A separation, if she wants. When a few weeks has you fucking her as if you're just shy of an animal.

It's only the barest thread of self-control that keeps my thrusts measured at all, each hot slide sending jolts of pleasure down my spine as I thrust into her again and again, bringing us both closer to the peak. Elena's hand is trapped between us, rubbing quick, fast circles over her clit, and I can feel from her breathing that she's close.

So am I. And the moment I feel her start to come around me, I know I won't be able to hold back any longer.

"I'm almost—oh—" she breathes, arching up against me, her legs tangled around mine, wrinkling my shirt between us as her hand grips my arm, anchoring herself against the pleasure as she writhes on my cock. "Oh, *fuck*, Levin—"

I feel when she comes. That sudden tightness, the pulsing, the way she ripples and flutters around me, sucking me deeper as she tips her head back and cries out my name again and again, and I'm fucking lost. My cock hardens, throbbing as I come inside of her, and all I can think about is her teasing voice asking me if I want to imagine her dripping with my cum while I'm gone.

Fuck yes. I want to fucking fill her up. I sink into her as deeply as I can, feeling her grind against me as she gasps out her orgasm. I groan into her shoulder as I fill her with wave after wave of cum, the pleasure consuming me as I hold myself inside of her.

It's even harder to leave. I want to stay there, inside her warmth, feeling her pant and shudder underneath me as she clutches me closer to her, her legs trapping me, her pussy still fluttering around my cock. I want to get in bed with her and do it again, over and over, as many times as I can until I physically can't get hard any longer.

I absolutely do not want to get on that fucking plane.

Slowly, I slide out of her, groaning at the lingering pleasure as she tightens around my softening cock. I give myself the pleasure of taking one more glance, seeing the sheen of my cum on her folds, pearling at her entrance, and my cock jerks halfway back to hardness just from the sight of her so full of me.

She slides back onto the bed, letting her shorts fall back into place, and she lets out a soft sigh as I tug my pants back up and fix my clothing. "I'm going to get in the shower," she says softly. "Tell Isabella I'll be down in a few minutes."

And just like that, it's over, and everything is back to normal.

I nod, turning back to finish packing as I hear her walk to the shower. There's a fresh stab of arousal as I hear the water turn on, and I think of her stripping off her clothes, her skin wet and soapy under the spray, the inevitable memory of all the times we fucked in showers in Rio, and how it's become inextricably linked in my mind with pleasure. I think of her purposefully avoiding washing away my cum, thighs clenched together to keep it inside of her, and my cock swells against my thigh.

Fuck. You're going to be right back where you started if you're not careful.

I force the thoughts out of my mind as I finish packing and go downstairs, leaving my bag by the door as I let Isabella in. She gives me a terse smile as she walks inside, glancing over my shoulder. "Is Elena still in bed?"

"She's showering. She said to tell you she'll be down in a minute. I can try to fix you both breakfast, if you like?"

Isabella shakes her head. "It's fine. I'll do it for us both. The sooner you get to the airport, the better."

She says it with a smile, as if she's telling me to get there ahead of time so I'm less stressed out for my flight, but I hear it for what it is —*the sooner you're away from Elena, the better.* I know the only reason that she might not be actively hoping that I don't come back is because of how much it would hurt Elena, and even so, I think she might have an idea that Elena would just get over it, and we'd all be better off.

Isn't that what you think, too? I ask myself as I get in the car, driving to the airport. I can feel the distance acutely with every mile, wanting to turn around and go back to her. I haven't been back to New York since the wedding, and I should be excited to go back, to visit some of my old haunts and be back in the place that I've considered home for over a decade.

It's telling that I'm already looking forward to the moment when I'm going to be on the return flight home.

It's not until I'm there and at work that I'm able to push thoughts of her away. Nico greets me, filling me in on what he's been doing in my absence and giving me the files of the six trainees that I'll be overseeing. "You've given me some big shoes to fill," he says with a chuckle as he follows me down to Viktor's office. "I thought I had a lot to do before, but the list got twice as long when I took over."

"Tell Viktor you need a new version of you to replace yourself," I tell him wryly as we walk into the office. "Shouldn't all be on your shoulders. And once the baby comes, I won't be able to come up here but once every so often."

"I heard. Congratulations," Nico offers, and I give him a tight smile as we step inside, and he stands back a little, letting me talk to Viktor in semi-privacy.

Viktor fills me in on the trainees, his opinion of them, and what he wants me to look out for. When he's finished, he pauses, as if considering something. "Get a drink with me tonight," he says finally. "I'd like to hear how things have been going for you. Talk a little. If you don't have anywhere else to be."

My evening plans had involved drinking, although I'd intended to be alone. I have a feeling I know what questions Viktor might have for me, what he wants to talk about, and it's not a topic I want to address. But I also know he's been more than accommodating, letting me go to Boston instead of insisting that I move Elena here, as he'd have been well within his right to do. After so many years of working together, he's more my friend than an employer, and I don't have the heart to tell him no.

"Sure thing," I tell him as I pick up the files. "I'll meet you after."

—

By the time I get there, Viktor is already at the bar, seated in a booth further back with a glass of vodka in front of him and a book open on the table. He looks up as I walk in, motioning to a passing waitress and nodding at his glass to imply she should get another.

"There'll be a drink for you momentarily," he says as I sit down in the leather-backed booth. The bar is one we've drank at in the past–high-end and polished, all leather and mahogany, the faint scent of tobacco creeping in from the smoking room at the back. "How are things?"

"As far as the trainees?" I accept the glass from the waitress, taking an immediate sip. It's smooth, expensive vodka, and I can feel it starting to burn away a little of my tension almost immediately. "They're all excellent choices, I think. They all passed their tests with flying colors, and I can't see anything in their files to indicate that they might not be assets, either to you or to the Syndicate. Although," I chuckle, taking another drink, "I think you ought to give one of them Nico's job, before you run him into the ground."

"I'm already looking for someone to fill his position, now that he's doing more of your work," Viktor says wryly, "I expect that once the baby comes, I might get you up here every four to six months for a while, at best. I know from experience how the time gets away from you with a newborn."

"More than most, I'd expect," I tell him with a laugh. Caterina had twins, and it's surprising to no one that she hasn't gotten pregnant again yet, with two stepdaughters *and* twins.

"You're not wrong." Viktor sips the last of his drink and motions for another. "But that's not what I was asking about. I wanted to know how things are with Elena."

"As well as can be expected." My response is purposefully terse, hoping I can stop the conversation in its tracks. I don't want to tug apart the threads of everything going on in my marriage and examine them more closely, but I have a feeling that Viktor might not be willing to give me a choice.

Viktor is quiet for a long moment, until his drink arrives, and then he sits there for a moment longer, pondering the clear liquid as he swirls it. "I know you better than most," he says finally, his voice low and serious. "I've known you for years, since Vladimir reassigned you to my family. I know more about your past than anyone, except maybe your wife. And I understand what you're struggling with."

"Do you?" I ask the question baldly, both because I know we're here as friends and I can speak plainly—and because I want Viktor to know just how little I want to have this conversation. If he's going to press, then I want him to understand I'll push back.

"I think so." Viktor takes a sip of his drink. "I lost my first wife too, Levin. You know that. I found her dead, too."

"Your marriage was in a bad place when she died." I look at him. "I'm not trying to compare, Viktor. But you know it's not the same. My marriage with Lidiya was just beginning. It was hopeful. It was the start of something. Vera—"

"Vera was different. I know that. She took her own life; it wasn't taken from her. Our marriage was volatile by that point. But I loved her, Levin. I loved her even when I hated her." Viktor's expression is tight, old grief pressing at the edges of it as he remembers. "I found her in a bathtub full of blood. I found out that I'd lost a wife and a child in that moment. There are things that are different, yes, but also things that are very much the same. And I grieved her, Levin—deeply."

He takes a breath and another deep drink of his vodka. "You know as well as I do that I intended to never make a marriage for love again. That I determined that any woman I married would be for heirs and the good of my Bratva, not because I'd fallen prey to my own emotions. I tried to make Sofia my wife, to gain territory from the Romanos, and when that failed, I took Caterina. It was never meant to be for love. I fought against it, hard. I fought against the changes that she wanted from me. I fought against the feelings I had for her. I fought and fought—her and myself, until it nearly destroyed us both. Until it nearly *killed* her and my children that she was carrying."

A heavy silence falls over the table between us. "Do you see what I'm saying, Levin? I need you to hear this, because I see you making many of the same mistakes, and no one else seems to be able to pierce that stubbornness that makes you so very good at your job. You are excellent at violence, both against others and against your own happiness, and you deserve some peace after all these years."

"What happened to Vera wasn't your fault." My hand tightens around my glass. "You're not to blame for it. Whereas I—"

Viktor snorts. "Levin, I have just as much blame as you. I neglected Vera when our marriage started to fall apart and pushed her away. I let our marriage fray in places when I could have patched it up. There were long stretches of time when I blamed myself for so much. And you—" He shakes his head. "I've watched you blame yourself for years for something you couldn't have stopped."

"I could have left her alone. I could have kept my desires to myself, not married her, not fallen in love with her—I could have made her hate me so she'd leave—"

Viktor lets out a long, heavy sigh. "Levin, you can't make others' choices for them, and you can't blame yourself for their choices, either. You married her so that she'd be safe from the cartel boss who thought he might take her as payment for the losses he suffered—"

"I could have divorced her when we got back. Made it a marriage only to keep her safe. I could have ended it—I *asked* her to stay with me in Tokyo. I practically fucking *begged* her. I wanted her, and that got her killed—"

"No." Viktor's voice hardens. "Levin, our lives are dangerous and hard. It's easy to say that we should shun everyone to keep them safe. But that takes away the agency of those who find themselves in our lives. Lidiya made a choice to love you—and you can't say she made that choice blindly, when she experienced firsthand from the day the two of you met how dangerous and fraught with violence this world that we live in is. She could have walked away, and from what I've heard you say in the past, she considered it. She made a choice to stay, and—" He shakes his head. "I haven't said this before, Levin, because it's your life, and I haven't felt it was my place. But I see you destroying your only remaining chance at happiness, and I've known you far too long and consider you too much a friend to not do what I can to stop it."

He sets his glass down, looking frankly at me. "By blaming yourself and only yourself all these years, you're taking away Lidiya's choice to love you. You're imagining that you somehow forced her into a happy marriage with you, and you're taking away her agency in all of it. It does her and her memory a disservice, Levin, to imagine that she would have been happier if you'd forced her away. If you'd broken her heart to keep her safe. She walked into your marriage with her eyes wide open, and she deserves to have that choice honored."

Viktor pauses for a moment, draining the last of his vodka, and motioning with his hand for two more, one for each of us. "You told me what you did to the men who murdered Lidiya, once. Now I'm telling you, if you stay in this purgatory of a marriage with a woman you love and who loves you, if you push her away again and again, if you destroy what chance either of you have for a happy life

—you will end up like that old man, the one who plotted to kill Lidiya. You will throw yourself into your work, only allowing yourself moments with the one you love when neither of you can bear the space any longer. You will end your life on the other end of someone else's gun, regretting all the days between this one and that, all the wasted time when you could have been happy."

He pushes my drink towards me. "It's not a betrayal of what you had with Lidiya to be happy now. She would *want* you to be happy. And before you tell me that I don't know what she would want, you're right in a way. I never met her; I didn't know her. I only know what you've shared with me, the bits and pieces over the years. But I know the kind of woman who would love you, Levin, despite all the danger and all the roadblocks. I know that kind of woman, because I've married one, too. And I know that Caterina would never want me to punish myself the way you've punished yourself all these years." He takes a deep breath. "Not to sound like Max, but you've done enough penance. Get off your fucking knees, and tell the woman you love that you want to be her husband. None of us know how much time we have left in this life that we live. Don't waste it grieving someone who would be heartbroken to know how you've torn yourself apart for something that was never your choice to make for her."

I listen to all of it, my hand wrapped so tightly around my glass that I think at one point that it might shatter, and at first, all I can feel is a searing, stubborn anger at everything he says—at the idea that he might know what Lidiya would have wanted, that I might have spent all these years suffering needlessly, that I might have handled everything in my marriage wrong thus far. It makes me furious to hear it, but somewhere in the middle, I start to realize what Max and Liam had only been able to get me to ever so briefly consider.

He might be *right*.

It had been easy to tell myself that Max and Liam didn't understand. That they'd never had to deal with anything like this. Max had suffered loss—the violent death of his brother that caused him to leave the priesthood for his revenge, but not the loss of a spouse. Neither had Liam, who had never been in love with anyone before he fell head over heels for Ana. I'd told myself that their advice, while well-meaning, missed the mark. That they couldn't grasp what I'd struggled with for so many years.

But coming from Viktor, it's different. His comparison of his own loss to mine had irked me, but he had a point. His loss *was* similar in many ways. And while his second marriage had been out of necessity, rather than an accident, I can't deny that he and everyone else has been the better for him falling in love with Caterina, and her with him. She's *good* for him. They have a happy marriage, one that anyone would envy. He found a way to make his life a happy one, even after loss and grief.

What he said about taking away Lidiya's choice sticks in my mind, burning a trail of fire through me. It makes me angry—but again, I can't shake the feeling that he isn't *wrong*. Even if it hurts to admit it.

I swirl the vodka in my glass, frowning, and then look up, narrowing my eyes at him. "This is why you dragged me up here, isn't it? Not because you really needed me to look in on the trainees for you."

Viktor shrugs. "I did need your opinion. But I'll admit to wanting to have this conversation with you, before your marriage went on too much longer. It felt—necessary. You should be happy, Levin. You're a good man—better than most of us. You don't deserve the things you've suffered. You certainly don't deserve to suffer for the remainder of the life you still have to live."

He clears his throat, taking another sip of his drink. "Now, what else do you have to tell me about my trainees?"

By the time I head back to my hotel room, my head is pleasantly fuzzy with expensive vodka, and swirling with everything Viktor said to me. It feels like a violent struggle within my mind, between the part of me that thinks that he might be right, and the part that wonders if I'm only listening to him out of my own selfishness, because deep down, I *want* an excuse to give in to Elena, to let myself love her, to let myself be happy.

Call her, the small voice in my head whispers, emboldened by the alcohol. *That's what a good husband would do, call his wife while he's out of town. See how hearing her voice makes you feel. You should have called her when you landed, and you didn't. Call her now.*

I make it up to my room and pull my phone out, sinking onto the edge of the bed. I should call her, to be a good husband. I shouldn't call her, because I'd planned for this trip to be a test of putting distance between us. I should–I shouldn't–I go back and forth, over and over, until I find myself searching for her name in my contacts, pressing my finger to the screen before I can stop myself.

The phone rings. It rings again, twice more, and I expect to hear her voice—but I don't. It rings until it goes to voicemail, and all I hear is the sweet chirp of her voice saying that she'll call me back.

I can't explain the feeling that goes through me. There's disappointment, followed by a sharp rush of fear—which makes absolutely no sense. We don't text and call each other like a normal married couple; I've made a point of *not* doing that to keep some of that distance. There's no reason to think something is wrong just because she didn't pick up the first time I called her.

But she doesn't pick up the second time, or the third. I wait a half hour, drinking another glass of vodka from the minibar, and call her again, with no answer. The fear grows, settling like a rock in my gut, and I have to physically stop myself from calling an Uber to the airport and going back to Boston tonight.

Maybe call someone else, like you have some sense, instead of rushing home because she didn't answer phone calls from the husband who has made a point of offering her space.

I call Isabella twice, and there's no answer. *Maybe whatever she and Elena are doing, it's keeping her away from her phone, too.* My head is full of panicked thoughts of Elena in the hospital again, Isabella at her side, and I call Niall next. When he doesn't pick up, I call Max, and then Liam, and when no one answers, I nearly throw my phone across the room in frustration.

What the fuck is everyone doing?

I call Niall again, and this time, to my eternal relief, he answers.

"Levin? Is everything alright? Sorry, I was in the shower and didn't get your call."

"I—yeah. Everything is fine. I just wasn't able to get ahold of Elena earlier and wondered if you knew what she and Isabella were up to. I was worried about her. You know, after—"

"Of course." Niall pauses. "As far as I know, they were staying in tonight. They went out shopping earlier, I think. Now that I think about it, actually, I haven't heard from Isabella, either."

The fear comes back in a choking rush. "For how long?"

"Ah, shite. I don't know. Aisling has been keeping me busy all day. I haven't had time to think about it, honestly. I assumed she'd call me if she needed me. Are you sure you're alright?"

"Just a little worried." I'm more than a little fucking worried, but I don't want to let on just how much. "Can you try calling her?"

"Sure thing. I'll let you know what I hear."

Thirty minutes later, I get a text from Niall that makes me very nearly jump on a plane all over again.

No answer. Maybe they turned in early? I'm sure it's nothing. Isabella is probably enjoying her time away, honestly.

I grit my teeth, trying to compose a return message that doesn't make me sound like an absolute lunatic. **Can you go and check on them? I'm sorry for the inconvenience, but after what happened—**

A moment's pause and my phone goes off.

If anything happened, I'm sure Isabella would have called me. But sure, man. I know you're far away. I'll go check on them.

Thank you. I was about to hop on a plane and fly back tonight.

No need for that. I'm sure it's fine. I'll let you know.

I toss my phone onto the bed, reaching for another shot of vodka from the minibar. This time, I drink it directly from the bottle.

I won't be sleeping until I hear back from Niall. And if anything is wrong—

My hand tightens around the small bottle, nearly cracking it in my fist. What Viktor said to me tonight could change things. I need time to think, time to consider—but for the first time, I find myself truly wondering if I've been wrong about all of this.

What if it's too late?

Elena

Levin is gone by the time I come down from the shower. No kiss goodbye, no *goodbye* even, and I have a feeling it has something to do with Isabella when I walk downstairs, and I'm immediately greeted with the smell of breakfast—specifically things battered and fried.

"Levin told me you've been keeping food down," Isabella says cheerfully as I walk into the kitchen, sitting down heavily at one of the barstools by the large island in the center. "So I made you your favorite." She strides across the kitchen to the island, setting a plate with French toast, bacon, and cheesy scrambled eggs in front of me, along with water and orange juice. "I'm not exactly the cook we had growing up, but I think I do alright."

"Levin's been trying to learn to cook breakfast for me." I don't know why that comes out of my mouth, but I blurt it out as she hands me a fork. "He's terrible at it, but he's been trying."

Isabella looks at me as she fills a plate with food for herself, letting out a small sigh. "You don't have to try to sell me on him, Elena. I see what's going on, and it's not endearing him to me. It's also not making me feel any better about you being married to him."

"What do you see?" My tone is sharper than it should be, but I'm feeling on edge. The whiplash from the quick, hard, lustful fucking followed by him leaving without so much as a goodbye is hitting me harder than usual, knowing he won't be back for two days.

It's the kind of behavior I'd expect from a friend with benefits—worse than that, actually, I'd expect a friend to at least tell me they were leaving. Not that I've ever had one—and I never will. My own husband is determined to treat me like a one-night-stand, and—

"Elena." Isabella snaps her fingers. "Are you alright?"

"As well as I can be." I cut a piece of the French toast. It's delicious, and I've never been so glad that I seem to finally be able to keep food down. "You didn't answer me."

"I tried to, but you weren't listening. You were somewhere else." Isabella sets her own fork down with a sigh. "He's trying to mollify you. He's trying to do just enough that you aren't miserable, while still trying to keep up this whole thing that he can't help being one foot in and one foot out of this marriage." She frowns. "Niall doesn't tell me *all* his business, but he tells me enough for me to understand what's going on. And I don't like this, Elena. Let me guess, he fucks you once every couple of weeks, pretends that it's to keep you happy, but actually, it's because he can't stand anyone else having you, even if he doesn't want you?"

My mouth drops open, and tears spring instantly to my eyes. Isabella has never said anything so bluntly hurtful in her life. I feel them welling up, spilling over before I can stop them.

"Oh, shit." Isabella's face falls. "I'm sorry, Elena. I didn't mean to say it like that. I just—" She clenches her jaw momentarily, pushing her plate away as if her appetite is entirely gone. "I've been seeing this for weeks. I didn't mean to hurt you. I've been trying not to say it for so long. I just—you're my little sister, and I can't stand this. Marriage is so long, Elena. Having a baby with someone is years and years of something really fucking hard. It's hard even when you love them to absolute distraction. And I see this happening to you and how Levin is acting, and I just—you deserve so much better."

Isabella sucks in a breath, stopping herself. "Look, I don't want to spend these two days fighting with you. I'm looking forward to getting uninterrupted time with my sister."

There's a long silence, and then I let out a breath, deciding to be the one who makes peace. I'm not sure that I want to be the one to do that right now, but I also don't want to spend these two days fighting with my sister, either. I want to enjoy her company. I know once the baby comes, I won't get to see her as often.

"You're right, too," I tell her quietly. "We shouldn't fight. What do you want to do today?"

We toss a few ideas around and finally settle on going into the city. I haven't been since before I was put on bedrest, and I've been feeling a little stir-crazy. If Levin were here, he'd probably come up with a reason for me not to go, worry me back into bed—or at least into staying in the house—but he's not here, and this is the one good thing that I can see coming out of it.

So we settle on shopping and lunch.

"I need to get some things for Aisling," Isabella says as we settle into the back of the car. There's no chance of us driving ourselves—the two security guards who insist on coming along with us make sure of that.

"I should probably pick up a few things for the baby," I manage as the car pulls into traffic. "We have the basics, but not everything yet—"

"We should do some shopping for ourselves, too," Isabella says firmly. "I can't remember the last time I bought myself anything."

"I don't really need anything—"

"It's not about *need*, and you know that." Isabella flashes me a smile. "Let's have some fun. I know Levin isn't going to care if you spend a little, and neither will Niall. It'll be good for us both to relax."

She's right, and I know it. My doctor would tell me the same thing—that stress isn't good for the baby. I should try to enjoy the day, the time with my sister, and not think about how much I miss Levin, or that I don't *need* a shopping trip, or anything else weighing on my mind.

Once the car is installed in a parking garage, we head to a coffee shop with the guards following us. Isabella gets a coffee, I get a decaffeinated tea, and we head down the street toward the shopping district. We spend the morning trailing through stores—a jewelry store for Isabella, where she buys a pair of heart-shaped ruby studs that catch her eye and a silver bangle bracelet, and a bookstore for me, where I buy more than I technically have time to read in a month. She picks up a few new outfits for Aisling, and we coo over baby clothes, choosing a few neutral things for the baby.

"Let's get lunch," she says finally, checking her watch. "What are you in the mood for?"

"You pick," I tell her. "You've lived here longer."

Isabella settles on a cute French-style cafe that she likes, one where we can sit outside under an awning. She orders a glass of wine, and I get sparkling water, with an appetizer of bread and fondue, and I feel myself relaxing a little more in the warm sunshine.

"What is it like after the baby comes?" I ask her suddenly, tearing apart a piece of bread. "Being married with a baby, I mean. You said it was hard, even if you're in love."

Isabella laughs, dipping a piece of bread in the cheese. "It is," she says frankly. "You're both sleep deprived, and you've never done anything like it before, and there's suddenly this whole other person who has no one to depend on other than you. It's a lot of worry and stress. You don't have sex for ages—" she laughs, breaking off. "I'm sure that's too much information, though."

"What do you mean, *ages?*" One of my fears has been that Levin will use my needing to recuperate post-baby as a reason to stay out of our bed, a reason to put more distance between us that intimacy can erode. "A really long time?"

Isabella shrugs. "It depends. There's a set time the doctor gives you, but after that, it's really up to your comfort level. I was fine pretty much once we were cleared, which Niall was eternally grateful for." She laughs. "But you've had a pretty hard pregnancy so far. It just depends on how you feel. And Levin, despite his insistence that he doesn't love you, seems to err on the overprotective side. So there's that, too."

"That's what I'm worried about." I bite my lip. "You were right about what you said earlier—about it not being that often that we—and just to keep me happy. Or at least, that's what he says. That it's for me, so neither of us goes outside the marriage. But I don't really believe him. When we—" My teeth sink deeper into my lip, and I can feel my cheeks flush.

"I wouldn't worry about it," Isabella says gently. "You're both going to be exhausted. There are plenty of reasons why that part of your marriage might get put on the back burner for a little while that have nothing to do with anything other than needing sleep whenever you can get it. And that stress is going to put pressure on your marriage in other ways. I'd focus on that."

I feel my chest tighten with anxiety. I'd thought in passing about what the strain of a new baby might do to my and Levin's already frail connection, but I hadn't let myself dwell on it. Now it feels like a sudden and crushing anxiety.

"You'll get through it," Isabella tells me gently. "I know you will. Your marriage isn't something that can be undone, not without causing huge problems. So there's that, at least. You don't have to worry about it splitting you up."

"We don't have to be divorced to be split up," I mumble, and Isabella narrows her eyes at me.

"Is that something you've talked about?"

"Not exactly. I—" I bite my lower lip. "We had an argument, after he went out on a job without telling me. He offered to give me space after Diego is taken care of and the baby comes if I needed it. To split time between New York and Boston, live in a different apartment, whatever I needed."

"And what do you feel like you need?" Isabella asks gently, and the words come out before I can stop them.

"I need my husband," I whisper, and I see her face soften.

"Maybe when the baby comes, it will change things. Make him see that the worst didn't happen—that your baby is here and you're both safe."

"That's what I'm hoping for."

Isabella changes the conversation after that, asking about the nursery, what we've done to it so far, our plans to decorate— anything that doesn't circle back to my relationship with Levin. I know she's trying to distract me, but the truth is that *everything* makes me think about him, and how much I miss him, even though I'm beginning to feel very sure that he doesn't miss me the same way in return.

Maybe he's even glad for a couple of days away, without the strain of trying to make me happy. Maybe that's why it was so easy for him to leave without saying goodbye.

"I need to grab one more thing," Isabella says as we leave. "Why don't the two of you bring the car around?" She nods at the security. "We'll be here."

"I'm not sure I can do that, Mrs. Flanagan—"

"Oh, for fuck's sake." Isabella lets out a frustrated breath. "We're in the middle of a busy downtown. I just need to run in and grab some things." She nods towards the store to our right. "We'll be in there.

Just get the car, so we can get Elena home before she gets too tired. I'm sure Levin and Niall wouldn't want her overdoing it."

She narrows her eyes at them, and they both hesitate, but finally turn to go and get the car. "It's not even that far away," Isabella mumbles, clearly irritated. "I'm so tired of being followed all of the time. I thought we left that behind in Mexico."

"I know." I give her a small smile. "It won't be too long, I'm sure. Liam and Connor will figure out what to do about Diego, and—"

The security has barely rounded the corner as I speak, just out of sight, and a heavy hand clamps around my arm, yanking me back. I open my mouth to scream, wrenching towards Isabella, and another hand presses over my mouth, stifling it. I see someone else manhandling Isabella, dragging us both backward, and I wait for someone to help, someone to scream, anything.

I twist in the thick arms of the man holding me, trying to get free, desperate to get free. I don't know what's happening, but all I can think is that Diego has caught up with us. That one moment of carelessness is going to cost Isabella and me our freedom, and Levin—

"Stop struggling, bitch," the man hisses in my ear, his arm pressing against my throat, and I hear Isabella's screech, see her trying to claw at the man holding her as she's shoved into the van, two men following her as the two holding me heave me towards the open door.

It feels like a bad dream. I feel a cloth against my face, and I struggle, fear spreading through me like ice in my veins at the thought of being helpless, of being suffocated, of the possibility that they're drugging me, and what that could do to my baby.

Which is exactly what they're doing. I know it the minute the world starts to go fuzzy, white around the edges, and I know that I've only been running away from the inevitable all this time.

I've been caught, and there's nothing I can do about it.

Levin

When Niall calls me, I already know something is wrong.

For one thing, if it had been fine—if my worries had been unfounded—he would have texted. But I can hear it in his voice from the moment I answer.

"They went out for the day," he tells me, his voice taut and full of helpless anger. "Security went with them—it should have been fine. But they left the girls for a few minutes to get the car, and that's all it took. Someone must have been watching them."

It feels like my entire world is coming crashing down all at once. It's like it takes me back in a single moment to the day I found Lidiya, walking into our apartment and knowing something was wrong before I even saw her body. I'd smelled the blood—a scent I knew so well, and known something terrible had happened.

For a moment, I feel frozen in place, the blood pounding in my ears, a sick sense of pending loss twisting my gut as I feel, for a brief second, as if I'm going to crumple from the inside out, like paper crushed in someone's fist. That I can't take this again.

And then I snap, the anger rushing outwards.

"What the fuck do you mean, they left them? What the fuck is their job, except to *not* fucking leave them?" I shout the words, not at Niall, but at the security that I can't shout at in person—which is for the best, because I'm not sure that I wouldn't strangle them if they were in front of me right now.

"I know," Niall says, anger lacing his tone. "They've been fired. Trust me, they won't ever work a security gig again. But there's nothing we can do about that now. Liam and Connor are calling a meeting. As soon as you get here—"

"I'm leaving now. Viktor will let me use his jet. I'll come straight to the headquarters when I land." I already know where they'll be meeting, and I intend to make certain I'm there for every second of it. I want to know what the fuck is going to be done about this.

I want my wife back.

I'm shaking with rage when I get off the plane.

It's everything I can do not to go hunt Diego down this minute, alone, and take Elena back. But I know better. I know going in alone, even if I knew exactly where he is—which I don't—would be suicide. I've run a thousand missions alone, but this is different. This isn't a target I can snipe, or sneak up on, or bait into a trap. This is a man with an army of other men at his behest, waiting for me to do something exactly that stupid. To treat this like a Syndicate mission and not what it is.

Not only that, but Isabella is gone, too. This is Niall's fight as much as mine. He deserves to be with me when we rescue them.

I knew something was wrong. I knew it. The guilt hammers at me, for going to New York, for once again not being there, and it would be easy to let it take over. To let it swamp me, render me helpless. To see this only as the past repeating itself, exactly as I'd feared it would.

I refuse to let it this time.

I'd planned to come home and tell Elena what Viktor had told me. To tell her that I still have no idea if I can be the husband she wants and needs. That I don't know if I can ever fully exorcise the ghosts of my past enough to move on fully with her, to not pull away when I get too close—but that I'm willing to try. That if she can be patient with me, I'm willing to take the first steps. To try to accept that I love her, and that doesn't mean I have to punish myself for it.

The idea that I might never get a chance, that this all might be taken from me again before it has a chance to blossom, feels like the most horrifying purgatory, as if I'm doomed to repeat the same cycle, again and again. I refuse to believe it.

I go straight to the Kings' headquarters, where I know they'll be meeting.

I find Connor, Liam, Niall, and Jacob there, gathered around the table with a laptop open. "We're calling Beth," Liam says the moment the door opens, and he sees me stride in, Nico at my back. Viktor sent him with me, saying that if he couldn't come himself, Nico was the next best choice. I couldn't argue, nor did I have it in me to refuse. Not when Nico eagerly agreed, and I knew we'd need the backup. "No one better to try to track where they've gone."

"Max is on his way," Niall adds. "He said he wasn't going to let us do this alone. Not with Isabella and Elena's lives on the line."

"You've got to be fucking kidding me." I look at them. "*Max?* Out of the question. He can't risk leaving Sasha a widow—"

"We're all risking ourselves. Max is as much one of us as you are." Connor's voice is flat, anger burning at the edges of it. "Diego wants a war; he'll get one. And we'll end it with one fight." He frowns, seeing Nico over my shoulder. "Who is this?"

I open my mouth, but Nico steps forward instead. "Nico Davis," he says with an easy grin. "Viktor sent me with Levin as backup. A little help, since he couldn't be here himself."

Connor snorts. "More like he wasn't willing to. Are you capable?"

It might offend anyone else. But Nico is an easygoing man, at least on the surface, and his grin doesn't falter. "Sure," he says, still casually. "I've been running Viktor's operation with the Syndicate since Levin here got himself wife'd up, so I think I can manage. I've been running mercenary operations for a decade before I came to work for Andreyev."

The screen comes to life, and Beth appears, already tapping away at a keyboard. Her pretty, heart-shaped face is set in lines of concentration, her black bob pulled back at the front in a small knot at the back of her head. She is, as always, dressed in jeans and a grey T-shirt. I've never seen her wear anything else. And I see Nico, who is at my shoulder now, looking at the screen with sudden interest.

"This someone who works for you?"

"Beth Wan," I tell him in a low voice. "She's the best hacker we've ever seen. A friend of Liam's from way back. She's helped us track down targets we needed to find a number of times. If anyone can get us Diego's location quickly, it's her."

Nico nods, a low, appreciative whistle coming from between his lips as he watches her fingers fly over her keyboard. "I'm no good with technology," he says with a low laugh. "But I'll be damned if that isn't the quickest I've ever seen anyone with a keyboard."

Beth hasn't so much as glanced at the camera, although I'm sure she can hear the conversation. She's staring at the screen in front of her, going through result after result, swapping through tabs faster than any of us can follow. "You gave me the location of the abduction, although your guards couldn't get a license plate read—it was gone before they got back." There's a derogatory note in her voice that says exactly what she thinks of their competence. "So I'm pulling street camera views to try to pinpoint it. It'll take longer, but that's all we've got. If I can get a shot of the license plate—" Her fingers fly over the keyboard, and her eyes narrow. "Just give me a minute."

"We're just going to wait on you," Liam says. "You've never failed us yet, Beth."

"There's always a first time," she says wryly. "But let's hope it isn't this one."

"Have you sent anyone to the house?" Niall asks quietly. "I left Aisling at the estate, but—"

"Once you said Aisling was with Ana and Saoirse, we re-routed all security to the estate," Connor says firmly. "That place is locked down with half an army. No one is getting to them. Not a fucking chance."

It feels like an eternity as we wait on Beth. I know she can't work any faster than she is—it's already impressive—but I feel as if every muscle in my body is wound tight, waiting for her to say *something*. I know there's a very real possibility that this might be the time that she can't help us, and if she can't, then we're looking for Diego like looking for a needle in a haystack. He could be anywhere in the city. We can try to track his movements, and Beth can help with that as well, but there's no guarantee.

"Here!" Beth crows her success as she points at the screen. "There it is. A van, four men, two women. The women were on the sidewalk—and then they're not. No clear view of their faces, but dark hair—it could be them. And the location matches. As for a license plate—"

A few more taps, and she nods. "I doubt the records of it will have any names attached. Probably bought with cash. But now I can try to follow where it's gone—" She hums under her breath as she looks at the screen. "Give me a few more minutes. I'll figure this out. I just needed one lead, and now I have one—"

The minutes tick by, and I can feel my hands clenching into fists, my muscles aching with tension. All I can think about is what might be happening to Elena right now, to our child—to Isabella, too. What Diego might be doing to them, how he might be taking his anger out on them.

I need to get to her. I never should have left. The two thoughts repeat over and over, tumbling through my head, until I feel like I could go mad from it. Like I *am* going mad, standing here waiting to be told where we might be able to find the woman I love.

It feels like an eternity before I hear Beth's voice again.

"I have a location." There's satisfaction in it, and a smile spreads across her lips. When I glance sideways at Nico, I can see his gaze is fixed more intently on the screen than any of ours—and that's saying something.

Looks like Viktor's new second-in-command is smitten with our hacker.

I don't have time to give that any more thought, though. Another beat passes, and then Beth claps her hands. "Here. This house. I'll send Connor and Liam the coordinates." She pauses, frowning. "If you're going to go in, let me know. I'll see what I can do about hacking into their security system if they have one. Might make things go a little easier for you."

"Thank you—"

Liam starts to speak, but we never hear the end of that sentence. There's a sudden, explosive sound, and the entire building shudders, sending the table and computer flying, knocking Connor off his feet, and sending the rest of us stumbling backward into walls and chairs as what is undoubtedly an explosion ripples through the building from somewhere—close enough to hurt us, but not close enough to instantly incinerate us all.

There are alarms going off everywhere. Liam picks himself up from the carpet, reaching for his brother, and looks at me with a pale and panicked face.

"We need to get the fuck out of here."

Elena

When I wake up, my first instinct is to fight.

I don't even know where I am before I start struggling. Something is holding me, and I think it's still a person at first, but when I try to lurch forward and can't, it slowly dawns on me through the lingering fogginess that I'm tied up.

To a chair.

Slowly, the world starts to come back into focus around me. I'm in what seems to be a warehouse, rope wrapped around me, sitting in a hard metal chair. There's a horrible taste in my mouth, and my tongue feels stuck to the roof of it, and my head is pounding. Despite that, I twist to one side, looking for Isabella.

I only see a huge, dark-haired man in fatigues and a black shirt sitting on another metal chair, a gun balanced in his lap, and his gaze raking over me. I don't like the way he's looking at me.

I don't like any of this. *I was drugged.* Panic sears through me all over again, not just because of the situation I'm in, but because I don't know what the drug might do to the baby. Visions of the blood-soaked sheets a few weeks ago tear through my mind, except this time, I have no way of getting to a hospital, no way of getting to Levin—

Levin. A sharp pang strikes me in the chest, realizing what this will do to him. To *us*, if I'm so lucky as to get out of this trap and back to him, which feels horrifyingly unlikely. This is his worst fear all over again—his wife and child in danger, in a situation where he can't help.

How long will it be before he knows? He's in New York. The guards would have come back to find that we weren't there and raised the alarm. I have no idea how much time has passed—he could already have gotten a call and be on his way back to Boston by now. But I have no idea what Diego's plans are. I could be on a plane somewhere else before Levin can ever get to me, and Isabella—

"Where is my sister?" I demand, the words coming out more slurred than I'd like from the aftereffects of the drug. "Where's Isabella."

"None of your fucking business," the man tells me, his gaze raking over me again. "Don't worry, I'm sure you'll get to see her again before the boss is done with what he's got planned."

I feel a cold chill at that, down to my bones. "What do you mean?"

"You'll find out soon enough." He grins, reaching down to adjust himself as he looks at me. "You know," he adds conversationally, as if I weren't tied to a chair in the middle of a room with a gun pointed at me, "I think you're the prettier of the two. The other one looks like she'd bite your dick off, but you—" he licks his lips. "You look like you'd suck it real good."

"Don't bet on it," I snap at him. "What have you done with my sister?"

"Me? Nothing. Diego said we can't touch the two of you, more's the pity. Something to do with buyers and all that, although I don't see what it matters, since neither of you are virgins. But boss man's orders are orders." He grins again. "He said you were the priority.

He's gonna be real fucking pleased that we managed to grab you both."

"So you do have Isabella." I feel sick at the thought. I'd seen her grabbed before I passed out, but I'd had some small hope that she might have fought her way free, that somehow she might have avoided this fate. There's a possibility that the man is lying to rile me up—there's always that possibility—but I don't think that's what's going on. I think he's telling the truth.

"Diego is gonna be fucking thrilled," he repeats, as if I hadn't spoken. "Real fucking happy to get his hands on both of the sisters who made a fool of him. That's all he talks about, how much he hates the both of you. How you made a fool out of him. Not what I'd say in front of the men who work for me—but hey, maybe that's why I don't have men who work for me." He laughs, a deep, rolling laugh from his gut, as if he's said something especially funny.

I don't laugh, and that seems to piss him off. He stands up, striding towards me, the gun in one hand. Somehow—maybe because I know Diego will have plans for me, and that means this man can't actually hurt me—I manage not to flinch when he stops right in front of me and grabs my chin between meaty fingers.

"It's a real fucking shame he won't let us do anything to you girls," the man growls. "I'd show you what happens when you don't laugh at a man's jokes." He lifts the gun, pushing the muzzle against my lips, and this time I *can't* flinch, because the terror that spreads through me is so absolute. Diego might have given them orders not to hurt me, but that can't save me from an idiot with a shaky trigger finger. It also can't help me if I move and startle him.

"I'd make you wrap those pretty lips around this gun, see how well you suck it off," he hisses. "And then, if your face was still in one piece, you could do a repeat performance on my cock." His hand slides down, rubbing himself lewdly. "Either way, I'd be coming in your pretty mouth."

I think I'm going to throw up. The only thing that keeps me from it is knowing what could happen if I do, and the fact that I have no idea how long I'm stuck here for, how long I could be sitting here in my own vomit.

"Hugo, what the *hell* are you doing?" Another voice comes from the doorway, and this time I do flinch. I can't help it, and I brace myself for the gunshot, for the oblivion that comes after, especially when I feel Hugo jerk too, the gun twitching against my mouth.

God help me. This is not how I want to die.

"Get that out of her fucking face." The man who stalks towards us is thinner than Hugo, but with an air of authority that Hugo doesn't have, an intelligence in his face that the one standing in front of me is missing. "Diego's plane just landed. He's going to want to see them. Come the *fuck* on, and don't fucking try me, or I'll tell him I caught you with your gun to the face of the one he wants the most."

The thinner man circles around me as he speaks, cutting through the ropes tying me to the chair. "And you used ropes, not plastic ties, on her wrists. Fuck, man. You better fucking hope she doesn't have burns—"

"She just woke up," Hugo says defensively. "She didn't have time to struggle."

The thinner man ignores him, pulling me up from the chair and looking me over in a detached sort of way, without any of the lewdness that Hugo had on his face. He pushes the sleeves of my t-shirt up, inspects my arms, lifts the hem, and checks my thighs for marks, all with a clinical detachment that tells me he's more worried about Diego being pissed than he is about any attraction he might feel for me.

"Go get the other one," he snaps at Hugo. "I'll handle her."

And with that, I'm marched out of the room.

"Don't bother struggling," he tells me as he leads me down a hallway. "Just get in the car like a good girl, and you'll see your sister soon—for a few minutes, anyway. If you struggle, I'll have to drug you again, and I don't think you'll like that. For one thing, they used a cloth for the sake of time. I'll put a needle in your neck, right in a vein, and you'll sleep like the dead until you wake up. Feels way shittier when you come to."

Another wave of nausea hits me, and despite the fact that everything in me *screams* that I should be fighting back, trying to escape, I walk with him, doing my best to keep up with his pace even as my muscles cramp and my numb feet trip over each other from what I can only imagine are the lingering aftereffects of the drug.

I'm not dead yet. I am, as far as I'm aware, not out of Boston yet. And if there's the slightest chance that I can make it out of this, I have my baby to think about. I can't risk this man drugging me again and increasing the chance that something might happen to them.

So I do my best to keep pace with him, and I don't fight. I get into the car, my stomach knotting and heart sinking, because it feels like doing so is another step further away from safety, further away from the chance that I'll ever see Levin again.

The only thing that keeps me from dissolving into a complete panic is both the hope that the man is telling the truth, that I'll see Isabella again soon, and that if I fall apart, there's a chance that he might drug me anyway.

The car ride feels like it takes an eternity. I sit stiffly in the back, my hands bound in front of me with a plastic tie, not too tight to cut off circulation, but tight enough that I'm well aware that I'm at someone else's mercy. I have no doubt that it's intentional. When the car pulls up in front of a large house, the man who took me out of the warehouse opens the door and reaches for my wrists, pulling me unceremoniously out of the car.

"Don't struggle," he warns me again. "Diego will be angry if I have to subdue you, and he has to wait. It won't be me that he takes it out on."

Fear pools in my stomach, because the way he says it makes it sound as if Diego intends to hurt me. As if he'd be *okay* with hurting me, and a lot of my courage is coming from the idea that Diego still sees me as having some value, that he has plans for me. That I have time, and I'll be physically okay for a little while, still.

The house appears to be a mansion, one that has either been taken over by Diego or acquired for him, and I'd honestly be willing to place bets on either. I'm marched into a large room that looks as if it's used as a study, with bookshelves lining the walls and a huge desk, and my stomach cramps with fear as I see Diego sitting behind it—the first time I've seen him since the afterparty following the auction that Levin bought me from.

That feels like a lifetime ago. Like it happened to an entirely different person.

He stands up, setting the cigar that he was smoking aside and dusting his hands off on his chinos as he rounds the desk and walks toward me. "Elena Santiago." Diego makes a *tsk*ing sound with his tongue as he comes to stand in front of me. "Jorge, give me a moment with her. You can check on Hugo, make sure he hasn't gotten too handsy with the other one. I expect her here in a few moments as well."

"Of course, *señor*." The thinner man—Jorge—backs towards the door, and I feel another cold rush of panic as it closes behind him, and I realize that I'm now entirely alone with Diego.

I don't see the slap coming. Diego hits me, palm open across the face, but so hard that it knocks me to the floor. I end up on my hands and knees, heaving from the pain, very sure for a moment that I'm going to vomit all over the expensive rug in front of me as I stare down at it, my mind absently tracing the pattern as I struggle to regain control of myself.

"Get up," Diego snaps, his voice disgusted, but I'm not sure that I *can*. My stomach is still heaving, my face burning and aching by turns, and I feel as if I'm going to pass out.

"So fucking weak," he snarls, grabbing me by the elbow and dragging me back to my feet. "How did such a weak little bitch manage to run my men on a merry chase all through Rio? I wouldn't believe it if I didn't see you standing here in front of me."

He slaps me again, on the same side of my face, sending me to the floor again. I hit my knees hard, scraping them against the rug, and my eyes burn with tears. *Don't cry*, I shout at myself in my head. I don't want to cry in front of him. I don't want to give him that fucking satisfaction.

"Where is my sister?" I hiss between breaths, trying to grab some air in between the bursts of pain from my now-bruised cheek and jaw. "Where is she?"

"You'll see her soon." Diego pulls one foot back, just in time for me to nonsensically notice that he's wearing crocodile leather boots, and kicks me in the ribs. In the stomach, in the ribs again, and I wrap my arms around myself, tears welling in my eyes as I think over and over, *oh god no, not my baby, no, please no*.

I can't tell him I'm pregnant. I have no idea what he would do. If he plans to sell me, as I still think he might despite his treatment of me, he would probably force an abortion on me. He might anyway, just for the pleasure of hurting me, regardless of what his plans are. No matter what, I can't tell him that. I can't give him anything else to use against me.

His foot is drawn back again when the door opens, and I see Hugo and Jorge walk in, Isabella between them. Her lip is split, but she has that defiant look that I know so well on her face, and I'm sure she gave one of them hell before they finally broke and slapped her—probably Hugo. I don't think Jorge is stupid enough to do that.

Diego's face goes dark as he takes it in, at the same moment that I see Isabella look down at me in absolute horror, the way I'm curled on the rug, my hands protecting my stomach.

"What the fuck did you do to her, you *fucking* monster?" she shrieks, wrenching out of Hugo's grasp before he can stop her. As if by instinct, he grabs her hair, wrapping it around his fist as he yanks her backward, and she screeches.

Jorge opens his mouth to say something, but he doesn't have time. Diego draws a gun faster than I can blink, and a gunshot temporarily deafens all of us as Hugo hits the floor, bleeding from a hole in his forehead.

"I told you not to touch them," Diego says coolly, setting the gun down. "I assume it was Hugo who did that to her lip?"

Isabella is shaking, crumpled against Jorge, Hugo's blood splattered on her arm. She jerks away from him the moment she realizes that she fell into him, and Jorge nods, looking the slightest bit pale.

"He was. Sounds like she gave him some trouble—but of course, that's no excuse," he adds quickly.

"Of course, it's not a fucking excuse," Diego spits. "One girl gave *him* that much trouble? No, he wanted a reason. I hope it was worth it."

Diego steps past me, to Isabella, and he grabs her chin as he turns her head this way and that, ignoring Hugo's body next to his feet. I can't stop staring at it, at the blood leaking from the gunshot wound onto the rug.

"Make sure we compensate the homeowners for their rug," Diego says idly as he inspects Isabella's face. "It wouldn't do to be rude to our hosts."

At least they're alive. It's all I can think as I lie there, wracked with pain, a dead body only a few feet away from me, and my sister being held in the grasp of the man we both hate and fear the most in the world.

"It's not too bad," Diego says finally. "I'll have to delay her sale until it heals, but the man I planned to sell her to said he couldn't meet until a few days later than planned, so it might work out." He lets go of her face, turning back towards me. "As for you—"

Isabella opens her mouth to say something, and I stare daggers at her, hoping she sees the look on my face. I don't think she would say anything about the baby—I think she would come to the same conclusion that I have—but I also know she's likely as panicked as I am and twice as likely to let her tongue run away with her.

Diego reaches down, dragging me to my feet again. I can't help flinching, and he laughs, as if he's truly delighting in the whole thing. "Don't worry," he says carelessly. "I won't hit you again. Not yet, anyway."

He motions to Jorge, who brings Isabella to the side of the room, and then leads me over to stand next to her. She immediately fumbles for my hand with one of hers—both of which are bound with the same sort of ties—and I cling to her fingers, needing something, *anything* to ground me, to keep me from falling apart.

"You've made a fool of me," Diego says harshly, looking back and forth between the two of us. "Your *family* has made a fool of me. Or at least, you've tried to. But I've persisted. I've continued to look for ways to ensure that the Santiago family comes to understand that Diego Gonzalez is *not* a man to cross." His eyes narrow as he comes to a stop, facing us. "And now, I've succeeded."

"In what?" Isabella spits. "You have us here. Congratulations. You've captured two women, and not even yourself, but by sending your goons after us. Big, terrifying man you are. And that doesn't mean it's over. My husband rescued me from the bride-tamer. Elena's husband worked for the goddamn fucking *Syndicate*. You think you're scarier than that?" She laughs, a rough, rasping, cackling sound that I'm not sure I've ever heard from my sister before. "You're *nothing*. And when they come for you, you'll die nothing."

She rears back, spitting in his face, and I see the way Diego stiffens, the clench of his hand as he physically stops himself from assaulting her for it.

He reaches down, fishing a handkerchief out of his pocket. Slowly, he wipes the spittle away from his face, tucking the handkerchief back in, and then as casually as if he were reaching for something off of a shelf, he steps forward and punches me in the jaw.

The pain bolts through me, the force of it temporarily making the room swim as I collapse back into the bookshelf. Books tumble off behind me, clattering onto the floor, and I slump as Diego stands there, watching me with a careless expression on his face as Isabella cries out in shock.

"Brave words from a brave little girl," he sneers. "I can't lay a hand on you, since I intend to sell you. But that doesn't matter. It's better, in fact, I think. You could take the blows. I know some of the things the bride-tamer did to you, the stories he's known for. I'm certain you would take the pain and still spit it back into my face—unless I did something truly terrible to you, something that would render you unfit for sale, and I don't want to do that. I can't take a total loss."

Dimly, I hear what he's saying, and fear creeps along my skin, settling into my bones with a sick realization of what that means. If he's taking his violence out on me, if he's willing to hit me and not Isabella because he plans to sell her, then that means he *doesn't* intend to sell me.

That means he has something else planned for me. Something that I feel sure will be much worse.

"Seeing your sister hurt, though," Diego continues, flexing the hand that he punched me with, "I think that hurts you more than your own pain. And I'm very much going to enjoy watching you stand there, helpless, while I inflict whatever pain you earn on her. So if you want to spare your pretty little sister, then keep your own pretty little mouth shut. Understood?"

Isabella sucks in a breath, and as my vision clears, I can see the barely restrained fear on her own face. She nods, slowly, and Diego smiles.

"Good. I'm glad that we've come to an understanding. Now, if you'll let me finish explaining."

"I don't care about your villain monologue." I slowly push myself up from the floor, feeling as if every part of my body is beginning to hurt. "Just tell us what you're going to do."

Diego lets out a long, slow sigh. "Please do shut up before I gag you." His dark eyes land on me, full of a venom that sucks the air out of me. "And what I give you to fill your mouth with won't be something that you want in it in front of your sister." He looks at Jorge as he speaks.

To my surprise, there's no look of anticipatory lust on Jorge's face at the inference that I might be forced to suck his cock as a punishment. If anything, he looks faintly sick at the idea, a momentary flinch that he instantly steels himself against before his boss can see it. It gives me a flicker of hope.

Whatever it is that has led Jorge to be working for Diego, he doesn't seem to enjoy violence against women. He doesn't seem to *want* to hurt me, and he especially doesn't seem to want to violate me. I have a small, infinitesimal hope that might work in my favor before the end of this.

"You are going to pay for what you've done," Diego continues, looking at the two of us. "Your *family* is going to pay for the time you've cost me, the sales you've cost me, the respect you've cost me. I was meant to be given a bride, and instead, I've been bled of resources, of men, of time. Isabella was stolen from me, and then your family had the gall to try to refuse me Elena, and then for her to be stolen as well. I tried to recoup my losses by selling her, and I was *tricked*." His cheeks are turning red, flushing with anger as he recounts the sins my family has committed against him. "I will have my recompense. And it has already begun."

I see Isabella pale slightly at that. "What do you mean?" she asks in a small voice, trembling at the edges, before I can. "What are you talking about?"

I know she's thinking of Niall, of Aisling. My stomach twists at the thought of my niece being harmed, but I don't think Diego would balk at that. In fact, I feel certain that he wouldn't.

Diego turns away from us, crossing to the desk as he opens a file, pulling out a stack of glossy photographs. My stomach turns at the thought of what they might be of.

I don't have to wait long to find out. "Jorge," he calls over his shoulder as he spreads them out on the desk. "Bring the girls over here, so they can see."

Neither Isabella nor I struggle this time when Jorge nudges us toward the desk. I understand now why Diego has felt that he only needed one man to guard us both. I won't fight back for fear of what further violence Diego might inflict on me—even if he doesn't know that it's more out of fear for my baby than myself—and Isabella won't fight back because she knows he'll take his anger out on me. It's a perfect plan, in his own twisted way.

We approach the desk, slowly, and as I see what's in front of me, I hear Isabella's strangled cry, and bile rises up in the back of my throat, acidic and burning.

"No," Isabella whispers. "Oh god, what is this?"

The first photos are of a mansion that looks like our childhood home, burned and shattered in places from gunshots, looking like the ruins of a wartime attack. But the others are far worse.

They're of guards, mutilated, burned, and shot. And then a couple, a man and a woman in their late middle age dressed in what look to be very fine clothes, mutilated beyond the point of facial recognition, and very clearly dead. No one could survive what has been done to them.

The bile burns at the back of my throat, and I can't stop it. I double over, retching onto the carpet as Isabella gasps, a sobbing moan coming from her lips as I see her stare wildly at Diego out of the corner of my eye.

"This can't be, it's not—"

"Your parents?" Diego looks at her with a self-satisfied smile. "It is. This is your home, your guards, your parents. The beginning of my revenge. While you were out shopping, enjoying the freedom that these men you claim to love—the Irishman and the Russian—bought you, your parents were being tortured. Told that their children would be next. Their grandchildren. That I would not stop until the Santiago line is wiped from the earth and the ground salted behind it." His hand shoots out, grabbing Isabella by the chin, his gaze dark. "Do you understand what I am saying?"

"You're going to kill us," Isabella whispers, her voice cracking with barely held-back tears, and Diego laughs, a deep and rumbling laugh that seems to fill the room around us.

"Hardly." He smiles broadly. "At least, not you. But I will make you pay. And since these Irish Kings were foolish enough to make an alliance with your father, they will pay too. I will wipe them out and take their territory. Boston will belong to the Gonzalez cartel when I'm finished."

Isabella laughs, not the rasping, mocking cackle of before, but a hollow and broken sound. "You *are* a fool," she says contemptuously. "A stupid fucking fool to think you can take the Kings' territory, that *you* can beat the McGregor brothers, the family whose patriarch nearly took away the Bratva and mafia territory in New York, before Viktor found out their plan. You are *nothing* compared to them. Connor and Liam will eradicate every man you have and piss on your corpse before you take Boston—"

She breaks off as Diego pushes past her, his hand wrapping in my hair as he drags me forcefully to one side, forcing me to my knees on the carpet as I cry out.

"One more rant from you," he hisses at Isabella, "and we'll all have a little show as I get your sister to pleasure my guard. Is that understood? And if you don't learn your lesson from that, it'll be my cock I stuff her mouth with next. And after that—"

"Alright!" Isabella shakes her head, her teeth sinking into her lower lip. "I get it."

"Truly, I hope you don't." Diego grins menacingly at her. "I hope you mouth off again, so I can enjoy watching your pretty sister cry while she's forced to pleasure Jorge here.'

Isabella's jaw clenches. I can see all the words dammed up behind her gritted teeth, everything she wants to spit at him, but she doesn't. She remains silent, and Diego makes that *tsk*ing sound again.

"A pity. But we're not done here yet, so there's still time." He releases my hair, but doesn't make a move to pull me up from my knees, and I don't dare move.

"You see," he continues, with that same malicious smile on his face, "your Kings and their associate, the brave former assassin who was so taken with pretty Elena here, are being walked into a trap. In fact—" he checks his watch, "that trap may have already gone off."

Isabella stares at him, her face ashen, and I know mine must look exactly the same. I feel as if I'm trembling in every part of myself, down to my bones, quivering with fear as I kneel there, wondering what terrible thing he's going to say next. I should be crying, dissolved to tears by what we saw in those photos, but I can't even cry. I'm past that, shock spreading through me until all I feel is numb, shivering cold.

"What are you talking about?" Isabella demands, and Diego chuckles.

"The timeline of events is this. My men picked you up, just as they were instructed. You were kept, held, and drugged while we waited for the pieces to assemble themselves. Of course, as soon as your hapless security found that you'd been taken the moment they turned their backs—and we *were* watching for that moment when they would—they notified Niall, who in turn called Levin, who immediately took Viktor Andreyev's private jet back to Boston, by which point Niall has begun to mobilize the Kings—all of which we expected. By the time my plane landed and you girls were brought to me, the men who wish you both protect you and their territory—to varying degrees of concern, based on who you ask—have gathered to try to come up with a different plan than the one they'd originally put together. And, of course, I was prepared for that, as I've been prepared for all of this."

"What do you mean?" This time it's my turn to say it, my turn to whisper it in a hushed, shaking voice. I'm not sure that I want to know what he means—but I *need* to know. I need to know what's happening, just how bad this is.

"There is an explosion set to go off in the Kings' headquarters. It may or may not kill them." Diego shrugs, as if he's talking about the possibility of rain. "It may kill some and not others. That's the beauty of it—you have no idea if the men you love are alive this very minute or not, as I expect the explosion will go off any moment now. It is my hope that at least Levin survives, for my own purposes, although I would be pleased if the rest are dead. Especially Niall, as it would be the sweetest of vengeance for you to know that your husband, who thwarted me in the beginning, is dead by my hand." Diego smiles at Isabella. "But of course, either way, they will all be dead eventually."

"They've survived worse." Isabella tips her chin up, but the words don't carry the venom they did before. I don't know if it's out of fear for me, or because she's no longer as certain as she was, but the possibility of the latter only makes me feel all the more afraid.

"Of course they have. But as I said, it doesn't matter. I have men en route to your home, to take out your remaining security and collect your daughter. If Niall survives, then he can watch with you as I ensure your child is dead, the beginning of the steps I plan to take to ensure there is no surviving Santiago blood. I'll kill him afterward, and then you can be sent on to your new owner, who will delight in making sure your remaining days are as painful and humiliating as they can possibly be."

"You're a monster," Isabella whispers, and when I look up, I see tears rolling down her cheeks. I can see the slump in her shoulders, the fight draining out of her, and that's when I know we're well and truly fucked. My sister, the one who refused to give up no matter what Diego put her through, who survived until Niall could get to her, who all her life has defied anyone and anything that dares to tell her that her life should be anything but under her own control, is broken.

Tears spill down my cheeks, too, my hands knotted in my lap until I can no longer feel them, the steady thump of the pain in my face and body mirroring my heartbeat. I feel Diego's hand around my arm, dragging me to my feet, and I don't fight. I can't. I know he's going to tell me what will happen to me next, and I don't want to know. My heart is breaking for Isabella, for Niall, for their family, and ours—and I know that when I hear what comes next, it will shatter.

Diego reaches out, and I can't help flinching this time. He chuckles as he touches my face gently, this time, fingers skating over the already-bruising flesh where he struck me. "Beautiful, innocent Elena. You would have made a lovely bride for me, since I was denied your sister. You would have made me a great deal of money, sold to one of the men who wanted so badly to break Santiago's daughter, to rob her of her innocence in every violating way they could imagine. You stole both from me. Your Russian assassin stole both from me. And now I will steal everything from you."

"Please don't hurt him." The words come out in a whisper. "Please. I–I don't care what you do to me. But please don't hurt Levin."

Diego laughs. "Such a sweet sentiment. But the thing is, sweet girl, hurting you *will* hurt him. I've done my research on your brave assassin. I know quite well what will make him tick. And I know what was done to his first wife—and child."

My knees nearly buckle at that. I can't imagine what expression is on my face, but whatever it is, it clearly delights Diego.

"Oh, you think I didn't know?" He motions to Jorge to pull Isabella back, away from me, so there's space between us. So I have nothing to cling to as he steps forward, one hand still on my bruised face as he presses the other to my stomach. "I'm quite aware that your assassin was very busy in Rio. Busy enough to put a baby in your belly—one that I'm going to take out."

This time, my knees do buckle. I feel them give way, feel myself start to sink to the floor, and Diego catches me, his arm going around my waist and pulling me against him in a mockery of a romantic hero. "I'm going to let brave Levin relive his past horrors all over again. Of course, my treatment of you today might have already made you lose the baby, but that's not what really matters. What matters is the *visual.* If Levin has survived that explosion, then once he and the others find out where you're being kept, they'll come here. Of course, it should take them a while to figure it out. By the time he does, he'll walk into a trap of my own making—just in time for my guards to catch and subdue him, so he can watch the tableau of his first wife's murder—but in real-time, this time."

Diego's fingers run through my hair. "I'm going to have my guards cut you open while he watches, so he can see you bleed out on the bed. I'm going to make him watch every painful moment of it, just as I've been told his first wife was killed. And then, just before the last bit of life leaves your eyes, I'll have him shot, so you can see him die as he's watched you." Diego grunts, pulling me tighter against him, and to my horror, I can feel that he's rock-hard, aroused by the entire long-winded speech he's made. "Isn't it poetic, sweet girl? The two of you, dying together. Your sister will be left, of course, but don't worry. I plan to make certain she can't have another child before she goes to her new owner, and he'll eventually brutalize her to death, too, at any rate. I'm aware of his—unique tastes. I've sold girls to him before."

I feel like I can't fully comprehend the horror of what he's told me, that I can't wrap my head around it. "You are a monster," I whisper, tears still streaming down my face, pooling between my lips and dripping off my chin. "You'd kill *children*? Aisling? I can't—please don't do this. Please. I'll do anything you want. Anything. I'll—do you want me? You can have me. Please."

"Elena—" Isabella whispers my name from the other side of the room, but it's not a warning. I can hear in her voice that it's nothing more than a tired plea for me to put myself through this when it doesn't matter. I know it doesn't matter before Diego even says anything, because I realize that if it did, Isabella would have offered herself up to. We both would. We'd submit to anything, if it meant our children, the men we loved, lived.

"I have what I want," Diego says, echoing the realization I came to moments ago. "I have *exactly* what I want. The two of you, under my power, the tools of my revenge. When I destroy the men you love, your families, when I put an end to every Santiago, when I have exacted my vengeance in flesh and blood and tears, I will have what I want." He smiles down at me. "There's no pleasure you could offer me, either of you, that could compare to that."

He nods to Jorge, who steps forward to wrap his hand around my wrists, tugging me back to stand with Isabella. "You'll be kept in separate rooms, of course. I won't have you plotting—and of course, simply for the reason that the separation will make this all so much harder on you both." The smile still hasn't left his face. "I'm so looking forward to watching this all play out. You've all assembled yourselves so perfectly for me."

With that, he nods to Jorge again, who pushes us both toward the door. I feel the firmness in his hands, urging us forward, and I know with another wave of despair that he isn't going to be convinced to help us. He might not want to hurt us more than necessary, and he might push back if ordered to violate either of us—but he won't be the tool of our escape.

At this point, I don't think there is one. I think this is over. That there's no hope left, except that Levin and Niall and their backup come for us—and even then, I know Diego is expecting that.

I think hope is lost. I've never felt that way before.

It feels worse than anything. It feels like dying.

And very soon, there will be nothing left for me to do except exactly that.

Levin

I know all too well what Liam is reliving right now—a fire in one of the Kings' warehouses that nearly ended with him and his brother killed. "Let's go," I say sharply, striding for the door, Nico on my heels. "Get Connor up as best as you can."

I see Niall stumbling to his feet, bleeding from his arm where something struck him, and Jacob is groaning as he rolls to his hands and knees. There's no time to assess injuries right now, not when no one is dead, but I can hear Connor's grunt of pain and know for sure that he's the worst off out of all of us.

That's something, at least. No one is dead, no one is critically injured. I have no idea if the explosion was supposed to kill us—if it was incompetence that led us to make it out of it—or if it was meant as a threat, but it doesn't matter right now. All that matters is getting out.

When I open the door, I see immediately that we're going to have to find a different way.

We're on the fifth floor, and part of the lower floors and the way to both the stairs and the elevator have been blown apart. I see smoke starting to billow up, the alarms shrieking in my ears, and I feel a sick fear in the pit of my stomach as I retreat, motioning for everyone to get to the window.

"See if the fire escape is intact. I don't think we can get out any other way."

Liam curses under his breath, Connor's arm slung over his shoulder as he nods to Jacob, who goes to look out of the window. From the unnatural way that Connor's leg is turned, it looks as if it's broken.

"It'll take two of us to get him down," Liam says flatly, as Jacob turns and nods.

"The fire escape is still intact. Must've blown up on the other side. I'll help get Connor down," Jacob adds, motioning for Liam to bring Connor towards him. "The rest of you lads bring up the rear."

Nico and I nod, Niall keeping close to Liam and helping maneuver him towards Jacob and the window, as Jacob covers his hand with a part of his sleeve and knocks the remainder of the broken glass out of it. It's going to be slow going, I know that, and I'm all too aware of the alarms still shrieking from outside the door.

"There's a fire down there," I tell the others, keeping my voice as calm as I can. "So be careful with him, but we need to hurry. The windows will have blown out, and depending on how far the fire has spread, it might be hard to get down the fire escape."

Jacob nods, glancing at me as he takes Connor by the upper thighs, careful not to touch the lower part of his injured leg as he starts to climb out of the broken window. The glass is sharp at the edges, and one wrong move could end with the person moving through cut in a number of unpleasant ways.

We don't have the time that we need. Jacob winces as the glass catches his sleeve, tearing through it and his skin, sending rivulets of blood streaming down his arm, but he doesn't stop. He moves backward through it, balancing Connor, and Liam passes his brother the rest of the way through to sit atop the fire escape with Jacob as Liam starts to climb out.

"Wait!" Jacob says, wincing as the fire escape shifts. "Shit. It's not all that stable. Three people can't be on this platform."

"You can't get him down alone." There's the beginnings of panic on Liam's face, and I know he wants out of here. I saw his expression when I mentioned fire. "You need—"

"Like hell I can't," Jacob growls. "I'll fireman carry him down. I've got this. Wait until I'm a few rungs, and then you come out. One person at a time on the platform."

I can see that it takes everything in Liam not to argue. He nods, entrusting his brother's life to Jacob's hands—a man who Liam has only known for a short while, but who followed Connor for years, when he ran his gang in London under the name William.

"Nico and I will go last," I tell Liam, who shakes his head.

"It's your wives Diego has, you and Niall. Go next."

I open my mouth to argue, but Liam gives me a look that shuts me up instantly, and I nod. "Alright," I concede, and Liam steps back, giving Niall and me room to wait for Jacob to call up the signal that the next one of us can go out.

When he does, Niall motions for me to go, and there's no time to argue. I get out onto the platform, and I immediately discover exactly what Jacob meant. It feels rickety, as if the explosion might have partially dislodged it, and I look down to see Jacob halfway to the ground.

"I'll call up when I'm the only one on the rungs," I tell Niall, who nods, looking a bit pale himself. The alarms are loud enough that we have to shout to be heard over them, and the air is beginning to fill with smoke. We don't have a lot of time.

When Jacob hits the ground, Connor still slung over his shoulder, and I'm halfway, I call up. I see Niall step out—only for the fire escape to sway dangerously.

Fuck.

I climb down faster. There's no other solution for it. When my feet touch concrete, I back up, the heat from the building and the fire crackling inside coming off in waves as I move towards Jacob and Connor, who looks as if he's close to blacking out from the pain.

Niall makes it down, and then Liam. Nico goes last, and he's a foot from the concrete when the fire escape suddenly groans, screws popping loose as it sways to one side.

He jumps. His feet land, and he grunts, stumbling to his hands and knees before pushing himself up and rapidly backing away, looking as ashen-faced as the rest of us.

"I called a car," Jacob says. "Two of them. We'll regroup at the estate. Beth will have to resend us the coordinates; I don't think Connor's phone made it out. Liam might still have them—"

"I do," Liam confirms, checking his phone. "Let's get to the estate, and we'll talk."

—

Once we're there, we get Connor into a bed, with Saoirse already calling the doctor to come and make a house call. Ana looks as if she might pass out when Liam explains what happened, but he tells her to stay with Saoirse and Connor, and to keep an eye on Aisling. "We don't have time to go over it all now," he tells her gently. "We'll talk more when this is done."

I can tell that's hard for her to accept, given the brief version of the events we explained. But Ana has had time to grow accustomed to this life, and she nods, although I can tell she's biting back her worry and fear.

We regroup in Liam's office, and he rubs his hand over his face, looking at the coordinates on his phone.

"I'll go," I say immediately. "I'm used to infiltrating a building. I can—"

"You're not going alone," Liam says firmly, before I can get any further. "There's not a chance. It's too dangerous."

"Absolutely too dangerous," Niall agrees. "And besides, I'm not letting you go alone. You know that, man. It's my wife in there too. My family at risk."

"I know." I run a hand over my hair. "It's why I didn't go looking for him the minute wheels hit the tarmac, and I was back in Boston. This is your fight too."

"It's all of ours," Liam says quietly. "He sees the Kings as an adversary too, responsible for what's happened since we made the alliance with the Santiagos. You don't think he'll come for us too? For my family and for Connor's? He'll wipe us all out if he can. It won't end with Elena and Isabella—"

My phone buzzes in my pocket, once and then twice, and I pull it out, jaw clenching when I see that it's from an unknown number.

I raise a finger to my lips, answering it, and a sharp, accented voice comes over the line.

"I see you're alive, assassin. Did they all make it out, or just you?"

I don't reply, teeth gritted, and there's a deep chuckle from the other end.

"Fine. Keep your secrets. It doesn't matter to me; I'll know soon enough how many I still need to kill. You're the one I hoped would make it out alive the most—you're the essential piece to my little game of revenge. So here are the rules, Levin Volkov. I imagine you've found where I'm staying by now, the clever band of criminals that the men you run with are, but if not, I'm sure you'll figure it out shortly. Come to find me, and come alone. And if you don't follow instructions—well, I can't promise that your pretty wife will die quickly regardless, but as I'm certain you know, there are *so* many ways to make someone die much more slowly. I hear you've even employed a few of those tactics yourself, in the past. And yet they all think you're a good man." The voice *tsks*. "Come alone, Levin." The words are repeated, flat and heavy. "Or we'll play another game—how much flesh can a human live without before they start to die?"

It makes me sick. All of it, every word. I don't say a single one throughout any of it, my hand clenching the phone so tightly that I think it might snap, and I hear one final laugh before the line goes dead.

It takes me a moment to lower the phone. I'm shaking with a fine, furious rage that permeates every part of my body, and I can see it reflected in the faces of the others that they, too, can tell just how angry I am.

"That was Diego." Niall doesn't frame it as a question. "What did he say?"

I relay the call to the others, and I can see the same fury reflected in Niall's face, and to a lesser extent, the others as well as I finish speaking.

I can feel the fog of rage and grief crowding in, how close this is to how I lost Lidiya and our child, pressing in on me until it feels as if I could be crushed by it. This is too personal, as Jacob once warned me, but I can't let them go without me. I can't entrust this entirely to others.

I have to be there for her.

"We'll all go," Liam says firmly, after a few seconds have passed. "Except Connor, of course—I don't think he'll be mobile for some time yet. But you, I, Niall, Jacob, and Max will go to the coordinates Beth provided."

"We need to find a way around his insistence that I come alone."

Liam nods. "I have a plan for that. Beth mentioned that she could manipulate the security system. You will go in first, making it look as if you're alone, offering to exchange yourself for Elena. Get to her, however you can talk Diego into that. And then once Beth has ensured they won't pick us up, the rest of us—with backup—will follow behind." He looks around the room. "Does that sound amenable to everyone?"

It's the best plan that I can see. We go over it a few times, looking for holes or potential ways that it could go wrong, looking for alternatives. There's not a great deal of time to hash it out, though, and once it feels like we have a solid enough grasp on what will give us the best chance, using Liam's plan, there's nothing to do but get ready to go.

"Jacob will send a message to the other men," Liam says. "Let's go and get geared up. There's no time to waste."

―

We can't, of course, drive directly up to the house where Diego is keeping them. The car is parked a far enough distance off that if Diego has any patrols making rounds, they're unlikely to find it. Liam and the others hang back as I start to make my way towards the house.

I only have my usual gun with me. I have a feeling I'll be disarmed shortly after I get to the house anyway, so there was no point in gearing up. I just intend to make sure I get it back when this is all over.

There are several burly guards at the front of what can only be termed a mansion. I walk up, feeling tension tight in every line of my body, but keeping my expression as blank-faced as ever. If I could keep a poker face in Rio, I can do it now.

The guards move forward instantly as I approach. "What the fuck do you want?" one of them snaps, and I give him an easy grin that's entirely at odds with the rage and fear coiling tight inside every inch of my body right now.

"Levin Volkov, here to see Diego. He called and asked for me personally. As you can see, I came alone, as instructed." I motion to the empty space around and behind me, and the guard narrows his eyes.

"Hold on."

It's all the usual. They radio ahead, they get the response that I'm telling the fucking truth, and they march me to the house. I've been through the same song and dance before, and although I well and truly hope to hang up this hat after I get Elena out of here, I also hope that I live long enough to make that choice. It's as familiar to me as an old choreography. I follow their lead, allowing myself to be led into the foyer. I even give up my gun, remembering the face of the man who takes it from me.

I'll be putting a bullet in it before the night is over.

The thought calms me. This I can do. This I'm familiar with. Pretend to go along with it all, pretend not to have any ideas—although I think Diego is savvy enough to know I wouldn't walk into this without any plan. Then again, he might be betting that I'm worried enough for Elena *not* to have a backup plan.

That would be the best outcome.

The guards take me all the way to a study on the left of the house. There's blood on the rug, and I feel my fists tighten, hoping against hope that it's not Elena's or Isabella's. *If it is—*

Easy, Volkov. There will be time for violence later. This is the time for talking.

The guards keep me to one side of the room, and a moment later, the door opens, and Diego walks in. He sees me immediately, a satisfied grin splitting his face, and he stops in front of me.

"Volkov. How good of you to make it. Of course, I thought you would, considering that we have your wife."

"She better still be in one fucking piece," I growl at him, my eyes narrowing. "If you laid a finger on her—"

Diego gives a one-shouldered shrug. "Well, you'll see she has a few bruises. They were necessary—she was quite defiant. Her sister even more so—and I quickly figured out that the best way to silence her sister was to hurt Elena. Don't worry," he adds as my jaw clenches, "she's not badly harmed. A few bruises here and there never hurt anyone. What else happens to her remains to be seen."

He glances at the guards. "Did he come alone?"

They nod, and a small bit of relief trickles through my veins. That, at least, they've bought. It's the first part of our plan, and if it's working so far, then we have a chance.

"I want to see Elena." I try to keep my voice flat, hard, but it's difficult. The need to see her is beating under my skin like a second pulse, a frantic, desperate need. I have to see that she's alright for myself.

"Of course you do," Diego says, almost patronizingly. "She is alive."

"You'll forgive me if I don't believe your word."

Diego lets out a breath, eyeing me. "What's your plan here, Volkov? What have you come to offer me? What will you do, for your pretty wife?"

Anything. It's not what I say, but it's the truth. It always has been, from the moment I saw her and recognized a strength in her that I hadn't expected, even if I couldn't admit it.

"I'm the reason for what's happened since you took Elena from her father. I posed as someone else to buy her from your auction. I killed the men on that plane and got her out of the wreckage after it crashed. I kept her alive—on the beach in Rio. I got her to Boston. I'm the one you should be furious with. So let her go, and you can have me. Do what you want with me. Torture me to death; I don't care. I hear you cartel types have some creative ways of going about it—do your worst. Show me how much worse you are than the fucking Syndicate, because let me tell you, I have seen them do some *awful* fucking shit."

It's bravado, all of it. I don't want to find out what ideas Diego has about how to make a man die slowly. I sure as hell don't want to die at all, especially not in some creative and extended manner. But if it means getting Elena out of here, I will. I'd do anything in the fucking world for that. I'd suffer anything. And I think Diego sees that—believes me—because an odd expression crosses his face.

"Impressive," he says, clapping his hands slowly. "Truly the speech I hoped for. Come on then." He nods to the guards. "Escort our brave assassin upstairs."

I'm not immune to fear. Even the fear of dying, which I've long since lost, can reappear when the means of doing so is in question. But I'm good at handling it. At *managing* it. I shove it down, deep into the recesses of myself, to deal with later if I have time. I think of Elena, and only her.

She's all that matters.

We go up a tall and winding staircase, up to the third floor of the house, all the way to a back room down a long hall of rooms. The door is opened, and what I see when I step inside feels like a punch to the gut. The air is literally sucked out of me for a moment, as if someone has reached inside of me and squeezed. It's like seeing my worst nightmare in front of me, and I must have gone pale, because Diego gives a delighted, maniacal laugh from behind me.

"I heard about your poker face from Vasquez," he says in a satisfied voice. "I wondered what it would take to get even a flicker of emotion out of you. I'll remember this moment for a long time."

"Levin—"

Elena isn't gagged. Her lips part, my name whispered, and it breaks something inside of me, just as the sight of her does.

She's on the bed, stripped naked and tied by her wrists and ankles to the posts of it. There are three other men in the room—two guards watching her with openly lewd expressions on their faces, hungry as dogs staring at a plated steak, and one taller and thinner man who looks as uncomfortable with the whole situation as he's likely allowed, given that his boss is in the room.

It would be bad enough that these men have seen my wife naked. *Mine*. That they likely stripped her themselves. That they—

"Did they touch her?" I look at Diego, and I think he hears the bald rage in it, the barely restrained violence, because he answers without hesitation.

"No," he says simply. "She was not touched in that way. I haven't allowed it. And Jorge here has a distaste for rape—" he motions to the thin man, "—so I trusted him to ensure that nothing happened to your pretty wife while I was gone. Now, as for what they do to themselves when they leave with the memory of this—" Diego licks his lips. "I can only imagine how many times they'll imagine what we see in front of us right now."

I've never been so thankful for my years of training in the Syndicate as I am right now. It's only that that keeps me from coming unraveled, from lunging for Diego and undoing all the work I've done to get up here, to stall. It's not only the casual way he says it, or Elena's nudity, but it's the bruises I see on her. On her face, marring her cheeks and jaw, on her ribs, on her *belly*, and fear for our child spreads through me like a sickness as I look at her.

"It's okay," Elena whispers, her voice breaking a little, and I know very well that it's *not* okay. But she's trying to comfort me. *Her*, comforting *me*, when she's the one naked and tied to a bed.

It makes me see red with fury.

"I'm here." It's all I can do to keep my voice even. "You can do with me as you please. Let her go."

"Levin, no!" She gasps my name, but I don't look at her. I *can't*. If I do, I'll lose control, and all of this will be at risk. I need him to let her go.

Diego smiles, and I know that the other outcome, the one I feared, is going to be the result. "No," he says simply, and the guards grab me.

"Levin!" Elena shrieks, yanking against her bonds, and I hear one of the guards groan at the sight of her naked body twisting in the bed. It makes me furious, my vision narrowing as I fight the guards holding me, knowing even as I do that, I'm not going to get free. Not until there's a distraction.

Liam and the others need to hurry.

"Well." Diego looks pleased. "Hold him, men. This will be in two parts," he explains to me, as coolly as if he were reading me an instruction manual. "First, I'm going to let these two guards enjoy her while we watch. They've been promised a reward for exceptional service, and this is it. When they've finished with her—and I've promised they can have her as many times as they can manage it—then we'll begin the rest of the night." He smiles broadly. "I've been very well-informed as to the manner of your first wife's death, Volkov. I think we'll be able to do quite the reenactment of it tonight."

I can't describe what I feel. The rage, the horror, the helplessness, and guilt all roaring through me until all I see is red, my blood pounding in my ears, and I hear myself make a nearly animal noise, fighting against the hands holding me as I lurch towards Diego, lunging for him in a fury that feels as if it comes from some part of me I've never fully let myself access before.

I've lost my mind, and I don't fucking care.

They drag me backward, two more guards coming to assist, pulling me back against the wall and hemming me in. One puts a hunting knife to my throat, and I feel the warm trickle of blood as I jerk against the men holding me again, seeing the two guards by Elena's bed starting to unclip their belts, setting their guns aside in preparation to fuck her.

"I'm going to kill all of you," I snarl. "Every fucking one of you."

"No, you won't," Diego says simply. "You're going to watch your wife be violated in every way a man can, and then you are going to watch her be torn apart. And then, just before the life leaves her eyes, you will die. Just as you should have died twelve years ago when you failed your first wife, you useless piece of shit." He smiles broadly. "Oh, have I done my research on you, Volkov. And I have played you like the finest of violins."

The guards are flipping a coin to see who gets what part of her first. One has his pants halfway down his hips, his cock in his hand, and I'm no longer a man. I'm a slavering, furious beast, twisting and snarling in the hands of the men holding me back, the knife at my throat drawing blood, and I don't feel it. I don't feel anything except a blind, burning rage.

It's a nightmare playing out in front of me, and I can't fucking wake up.

There's no physical torture Diego could have devised that's worse than this, and he knows it.

And then, just as I realize that I can't get free, that I'm about to watch two other men touch my wife in ways no one else besides me has—I hear gunshots from downstairs. Rapid fire, a volley of them, and I have only moments to react.

There's a brief second where everything comes to a stop in the room, the occupants startled by the gunfire from below, gunfire they hadn't expected. Once again, I'm endlessly thankful for my training, because it kicks in instantly.

I lunge forward, breaking the hold on me, grabbing the wrist of the man holding the knife and twisting it, hearing it crack and his sudden, shocked cry of pain as I turn his arm unnaturally and drive the knife into his throat. Blood sprays over me, and I leave the knife there, grabbing for his gun and disarming him as I bolt to one side, dodging the other guards drawing their weapons and blocking Diego from my view.

There's confusion. They don't know what to do—whether to go down and help or stay here and protect him. I take full advantage of it.

The first two to die are the ones who were about to touch Elena.

I shoot them both in the groin. The one who already had his cock out loses it in a spray of blood and flesh, and the other falls to the floor, moaning and clutching himself. Elena screams, blood spattering her skin, and I want to tell her that it will be alright, that she'll be free soon, but there's no time.

I leave the two on the floor to bleed out, rapidly firing at the guards surrounding Diego. Two of them fall, and the others return fire, narrowly missing me as I drop to the floor, rolling and getting up again, snatching the gun from the man whose dick I blew off and firing again, dropping the remaining guards one after another. The bodies fall, *thud, thud, thud*, blood spreading across the floor, and I stalk toward Diego.

His weapon is drawn, pointed at me. Mine is leveled at him. I walk straight up to him, until he's nearly touching me with the muzzle of his pistol, and I smile.

"Do you think you can shoot before I do?" Diego asks, his eyes gleaming, and I shrug.

"Who the hell knows?" I look at him, wanting to savor this moment. "But I don't have to shoot you."

He has a knife at his hip, too. I saw it when he came into the office. He hadn't expected me to go for it. But I do, snatching it free as I knock his hand holding the gun away. His shot goes wild as I shove him with my entire body backward and against the wall, driving the knife into the hollow of his throat.

"I wish to god I could do this slower," I tell him, rage coloring every word as I twist the knife, hearing the guttural, bubbling noise as blood froths from his lips. "I wish I could take you apart piece by piece in every way I know how. But at least you're going to die like this, far from home, knowing that you've been outwitted yet again. And there's not a goddamn thing you can do about it."

I jerk the knife free, and then drive it lower, into his gut, and again, into his groin. He coughs, gargling blood, and I grab both of his hands, pinning them over his head against the wall as I drive the knife through both of his palms, pinioning him there while he bleeds out.

"Go ahead and die," I tell him, and I rear back, spitting in his face.

I don't know how long it takes. I would have liked to watch, but what I want more is Elena to be freed from the bed and in my arms. I cross to her, sawing the bonds holding her free, and she sags against the bed as she's released, just before I gather her into my arms.

"Are you hurt?" It's a nonsensical question, but we don't have time to think things through. I don't know what the state of what's happening downstairs is, and I need to get her out of here.

"Not as badly as I could be," she whispers. "I just want to go home. And Isabella—" She pulls back, looking at me with naked fear on her face. "They have Isabella. In another room—you need to get her—"

"Niall is here," I tell her gently. "And Liam and the others. They'll get to Isabella."

"They're alive?" Relief washes over her face. "Diego told us about the explosives he planted—he made it sound like you were all going to be dead—"

I've rarely in my life wanted to kill a man all over again, but at that moment, I wish I could bring him back so I could repeat it. "They're alive," I promise her. "But we have to get you out of here."

I can still hear gunshots downstairs, but fewer of them. I grab the sheet from the bed, wrapping Elena in it before gathering her into my arms, holding her against my chest with one arm as I hold my gun in the other. "Just hold onto me," I whisper to her. "And we'll be out of here in no time at all."

I hope it's true. I hope everything I've said to her is true, that this time I won't fail. I hold her close, moving down the hallway slowly, and I flatten myself against the wall as I see someone come out of one of the rooms—only to realize a moment later that it's Niall, with Isabella close behind him.

"Isabella!" Elena gasps her name, and Isabella twists to face us, a relief like nothing I've ever seen washing over her face.

"Oh god, you're alive." She breaks free of Niall, rushing towards us, and Elena turns her head to look at her.

"I'm fine, Issi. I just want to get out of here. Are you—"

"I'm okay." Isabella swallows hard. "Diego wouldn't let them touch me since he wanted to sell me. I want to go home too." She looks at Niall. "What's the plan?"

"We stormed the place," Niall says, looking at me. "There might be a few guards left, but we've almost cleared them out. We can go. Max went to get the car. Diego?"

"He's dead. I killed him myself."

"Good." There's a satisfaction in Niall's voice that mirrors what I feel, too. "Let's get them home."

Elena curls against me, her head against my shoulder, and I know at that moment that there's nothing more in the world that I want than to be home with her.

She is my home. No matter where we are—on a lonely beach or in a Rio motel, or in the house we chose together.

I've fought against it too long, but that wasn't the war I needed to win. Now I've been given a chance to make that right.

I won't squander it twice.

I can't make it down the stairs fast enough. Niall and Isabella are behind me, Niall still on guard for anyone else who might be left, and I find Liam, Jacob, and Nico on the first floor, bodies scattered.

"We're going to run a check on the house," Liam says. "Make sure everyone here is dead. We're not leaving anyone to go back or try to use whatever knowledge they have to infiltrate us." He nods at Jacob. "Jacob will call for a second car. You four go with Max—get Elena and Isabella home. They don't need to be here a second longer."

The part of me that's done this sort of work for long years feels like I should stay, clean up with Liam and the others, ensure their safety and watch their backs. But I'm not leaving Elena, and I'm not making her stay in this house. I want her in a bed, safe and sound, where a doctor can look at her and tell us both that she'll be alright.

I need that as much as she does.

"Just go," Liam tells me firmly. "We've got this. There's more backup outside, combing the grounds. We'll check in with Connor when it's done." He looks at me, at Elena curled against my chest, very close to passing out. "Be with your wife."

I can't find it in myself to argue. Because right now, that's the only thing I want to do.

Elena

I sleep for a long time.

I don't know how long passes exactly, not until Levin tells me that I slept for almost two days. The doctor made a house call, coming to check on me and reassure us both that the baby was safe and that, other than my bruising and exhaustion, I'd suffered no ill effects. She told us there was no need for extended bed rest—I needed sleep, and once I got it, to trust myself and how I felt.

I managed to stay awake long enough to find out that Aisling was safe at the estate with Ana and Saoirse, and that everyone survived the explosion. Isabella filled Niall in on the photos Diego had shown us, and Liam had immediately contacted our parents, saying that there'd been no intelligence that there was an attack on the Santiago compound and that they had enough men there that there should have been.

As it turned out, there never had been an attack. The photos were staged, bodies made to look as if they'd been mutilated and murdered without enough identifying features for us to know better, intentionally meant to prey on our terror. It made me furious, and I was glad to know beyond a shadow of a doubt that Diego was dead. That I'd seen him die with his own eyes.

I managed a shower to get the blood off, with Levin helping me, and then I fell into bed. Into a deep, thankfully dreamless sleep, until I wake up in a haze, apparently nearly two full days later, to see Levin sitting on the other side of me.

He turns towards me instantly. "You're awake." There's relief in his voice. "I was going to give you about another six hours, and then I was calling the doctor. You slept like the—" he clears his throat. "You barely moved. You slept harder than anyone I've ever seen."

"I'm awake now," I croak, sitting up slowly. "I need to pee, and I need a shower."

"I can help with the second if—"

I shake my head slowly, smiling at his attempt at a joke. "Just give me a minute, okay? I'll yell for you if I think I need help."

I feel like the walking dead. After two days of sleep, I desperately need to feel clean, and I want to do that on my own. I stumble to the bathroom, and once I'm under the hot water, I start to feel a little like a human again.

Which is good, because there's something else I need, too.

I wrap the towel around myself as I come out of the shower, leaving my hair dark and wet down my back. I see the way Levin looks at me as I step out of the bathroom, the heat in his eyes, and the way he restrains it. A shiver of disappointment goes through me, because if there was one good thing I had hoped might come out of all of this, it was that Levin might realize that he loves me after all. That he might realize that we're wasting precious time in this stalemate of a marriage.

Of course, I also knew that it could be the opposite. That it might reinforce his fear of loss all over again, especially with the lengths that Diego went to in order to play out the tableau of his first wife's death. And seeing the way he struggles with the desire that flickers over his face, I have a sinking feeling that it's the latter.

Slowly, I approach the bed. I crawl onto it, holding the towel close to my chest, and meet Levin's gaze.

"Can you tell me what happened?" he asks quietly. "You don't have to, if you're not ready. Niall and Isabella have filled me in on a lot of the details. But—I'd like to hear it from you. If you're ready."

Am I? I'm not sure. I'd like to never relive that period of time again. But I don't want what Levin knows of what happened to all be from others. So slowly, very slowly, I tell him what happened.

I tell him about how Isabella sent the guards to get the car and how we thought we'd be safe. I tell him not to blame her, that I'd been just as sure that nothing would happen. I tell him about Hugo and Jorge, about Diego hitting me, about him shooting Hugo in front of us. I tell him how Diego outlined the plan. And I tell him that I believed he would come for me.

Because it's true. I hadn't been sure if it would work—if he could pull it off, or if Diego had at last engineered a plan that even Levin couldn't beat...a hand of poker he couldn't win. I don't say that, because I know what Levin needs to hear, the *only* thing he needs to hear, is that I believe in him.

And I did. I *do*.

"As soon as I saw you come through that door, I knew I was saved." I move closer to him on the bed, leaning forward to touch his face. "I knew you would get us out of there."

"That makes one of us." Levin catches my hand in his, folding his fingers around it. "Elena, I—"

"You don't need to say anything." My heart races in my chest. I'm not sure I *want* him to say anything. I don't want to hear how this has broken him all over again, how it's reminded him how easily he can lose what he loves, how it's reinforced the walls around his heart, barbed wire atop hard stone. I can't bear to hear it just yet. But looking at his face, I don't think I'll have a choice.

"I know," Levin says quietly. "But I *need* to say this, Elena. I need you to know."

He wraps his hand around mine, bringing it away from his face and clutching it in his lap, his other hand covering both of ours. "I could have lost you, Elena. I'm grateful you believed in me—but the truth is, it could have so easily gone another way. It could have—" He breaks off, clearly unable to follow that thought to its conclusion. I can see that he's struggling with how close he came to losing me. How horribly this all could have ended.

"It's alright." I clutch my hand around his, looking at him gently. "It didn't end that way. We're home, and we're safe. Diego is dead. Our baby is fine. It didn't play out the way it did before, Levin. I'm safe. *We're* safe." I repeat it, wanting him to understand. Wanting him to know that there's nothing to fear. That we can start to try to put the past behind us, if only he—

To my shock, I see his blue eyes start to mist over with tears. "Elena—" my name comes out choked, sticking in his throat. "Fuck. I meant to say all this to you when I got back. And then I found out that you—"

He sucks in a deep breath, steadying himself, clinging to me as if I'm a life raft and he's adrift. "I talked to Viktor, in New York. I didn't mean to have the conversation that we did, but he—well, he kind of forced me into it." He gives a small, dry chuckle.

"What was it about?" I ask carefully.

"He talked to me about you. About Lidiya. About the past and how I've clung to it." Levin takes another deep and shaky breath. "He's not the first to try to get through to me in that way. Max and Liam tried, too, the night I came home to find you bleeding. We might have had this conversation sooner, if not for that. It scared the living hell out of me, Elena. All I could see was being helpless again, losing our child, maybe even losing you, and there being nothing I could do to stop it. I felt that way this time, too, with Diego. That history was repeating itself. And it would be so easy to shut myself off, to hide away in my grief and fear. But I—"

I feel the tiniest sliver of hope. I'm afraid to cling to it, just yet. I'm afraid that I might let myself believe in something that will never happen. But I listen, and I have that small spark of hope.

"Viktor lost his first wife, too," Levin says slowly. "It was different—she took her own life. Their marriage was different by then, too—it was fraught, difficult. They weren't in love the way they had been. But he found her in their bathtub. And he found out she was pregnant. There were—similarities."

"Oh my god," I whisper. "I had no idea. That's awful."

Levin nods, swallowing hard. "He told me a lot of things. The one that stuck out the most was that by clinging to the idea all of these years that I could have made Lidiya's choice for her, that I could have pushed her away and therefore given her a long life and happiness, takes away her agency in all of it. It diminishes her love for me, by pretending that she couldn't make that choice for herself, knowing as well as she did how dangerous the life I lived was. It took Viktor talking to me to make me see it, to hear it from his perspective, knowing what he's lost too—and how he's found happiness again."

As Levin speaks, I feel that spark of hope catch. I feel it flicker. And I wonder—

"I left that conversation wanting to come home and tell you that I wanted to try. To give this a chance. Only to almost lose you and our baby, in such a similar—"

His voice breaks, and I feel my throat tighten with grief, an overwhelming feeling of loss at the thought of what we almost had. What I feel certain is lost now, after what Diego did. But I won't let him blame himself for it. Not this time.

"I understand," I tell him softly, still holding on to his hands. "I've always understood; I just—I hoped things would be different. But I knew that after this, there was a chance they couldn't be." I take a deep breath, sucking in the air. "I understand if you can't love me. It won't change how I feel about you—that I love you—but isn't that what love is? Loving someone for who they are, no matter what they can give you in return?"

"Elena—"

"No, it's my turn." I force a small smile. "I know you'll do everything in your power to be a good father. And I know that will only make me love you more. I know you'll do your best to be a good husband to me, even if you can't open your heart up. And I'll be glad for what we do have together. All my life, I'll be glad for it. I promise—"

"Elena." His voice is strident, pushing through mine. Interrupting me. "Elena, that's the problem."

I stare up at him, confused. "What is?"

Levin reaches out, his fingers tracing over my cheekbone. "I do love you," he says gently. "I've been trying for so long not to, but it's been a losing battle. I've loved you for so much longer than I've been willing to admit. And I can't fight it any longer."

It takes a moment for the words to sink in. When they do, I feel my chest tighten, a glow washing over me like nothing I've ever felt, a happiness that I never expected suffusing every inch of my body. "You love me?" I whisper, and Levin cups my face in both of his hands, tumbling me backward in the bed, his body stretched over mine.

"I love you," he repeats. "I love you."

I arch upwards, kissing him. My fingers curl around the back of his neck, pressing his mouth hard to mine, and my legs wrap around his, the towel coming loose between us. My other hand is already fisting in his t-shirt, dragging it upwards, and Levin breaks the kiss long enough to look down at me with worry in his eyes.

"The doctor said it was fine. I remember that." I look up at him, pleading. "Don't say no, Levin. I need you."

I wait for him to fight it. To struggle against what we both need. But to my shock, he doesn't.

He runs his fingers through my hair, and he kisses me. Long and deep and slow, his tongue tangling with mine, his hands sliding down my body as he tugs the towel away and throws it to one side.

"You're so beautiful," he breathes. "So fucking beautiful."

I can't get his clothes off fast enough. There will be time for foreplay later, time for us to spend hours in bed exploring each other, for him to give himself the unfettered freedom that he's fought so long against. Right now, I need him inside of me.

I don't realize that I murmured it aloud, against his lips, until Levin laughs.

"My filthy girl," he murmurs, his fingers trailing through my wet hair. "So innocent when I met you. And now—" he grins against my mouth. "Listen to you. Begging for my cock."

He shoves his pants the rest of the way off, his cock hard against his belly, and he reaches down, angling it so that the swollen head brushes against my clit. "Come for me like a good girl, and I'll fuck you. Come on my cock, Elena. Get it nice and wet so I can fuck you as hard as you deserve."

I moan helplessly, hips bucking, rubbing my clit against his cockhead. I'm helpless in the torrent of my desire for him, and when he talks to me like *that*, his accent thickening, his words low and dark and filthy, there's nothing I wouldn't do for him.

It doesn't take long. I can feel the wet heat of his pre-cum against my clit, slick as he rubs himself against me, teasing me until I'm arching and panting and begging, and then he pushes himself tightly against my clit, fucking it with the head of his cock, and I scream his name as my nails dig into his shoulders and I come hard.

"That's it. That's my good girl. Take my fucking cock," he groans. Halfway through my orgasm, I feel him push inside of me, his fingers replacing the tip of his cock as he rubs my clit, pushing himself hard into my clenching depths.

The pressure, the fullness, the unrelenting friction on my clit—it sends me over the edge into a second orgasm immediately on the heels of the first. I arch upwards, thrusting myself onto him, impaling myself hard on his length so that he's as deep as he can go in an instant, and Levin groans, his hips snapping against mine as he sucks in a breath.

"Fuck, you feel so *fucking* good—" He presses his forehead to mine, his hips moving in a steady rhythm, thrusting into me in long, hard strokes that leave me gasping and moaning with every single one. Even as the orgasm recedes, it feels exquisite, like my every nerve is raw, his cock driving me wild. His fingers rub my clit relentlessly, his tongue tangling with mine, and he groans as he fucks me harder, his cock throbbing inside of me.

"I'm not going to last long. *Fuck*—" he moans, driving himself into me again and holding himself there for a moment. "I'm not letting you out of bed for a week. I'm going to fill you so full of my cum, *god, fuck, fuck*—"

I feel him jerk, feel his mouth slant over mine, the arch of his back as he rubs my clit faster still, desperate to push me over the edge one final time before he loses control. "Come for me," I moan into his mouth. "I'll come when you do. Fill me up, Levin, *please*—"

"God, I love when you fucking beg for my cum." He rears back, slamming his cock into me with the force that I know he's wanted for a long time. I nearly scream his name as I feel him swell and harden. The hot rush of his cum fills me as I unravel around him for a third time, clenching and rippling along his cock as I drag every drop of cum he has for me out of him.

Levin sags against me, shuddering—and then he goes very still.

"What is it?" I turn my head, trying to look at him. "What's wrong?"

He laughs, a low, hoarse sound. "This never happens."

Slowly, he leans back, sliding out of me. I realize what he means as I feel him, still hard and thick and solid, as erect as if he hadn't come. But he did—I can feel it on my thighs, dripping out of me as he slips free. I can see it on his length, my arousal and his cum, streaked over his straining flesh as he wraps his hand around it, a look of bemused surprise and lust mixing together on his face.

"What should I do with this, *malysh*?" he murmurs, stroking himself slowly, and a sudden, dark rush of arousal goes through me.

"Fuck me in the ass."

"What?" Levin falters, staring down at me. "Elena—"

"I asked you to in Rio. Don't you remember?" I spread my legs invitingly, letting him see me, well-fucked and exposed for him, his cum dripping out of me. "And you said you couldn't. But now you can. You said you love me. You want me—*this*. So there's no reason to protect that last bit of my innocence any longer." My voice drops a little, low and husky. "And I want to be all yours. I want to belong to you, Levin. *All* of me."

I've never seen such raw lust on anyone's face. "Oh god, *krasotka*—" he groans, and I see his cock throb visibly in his fist. "You drive me insane. Begging me for my cock everywhere, even—"

"I want it," I whisper. "*Please.*"

I know that's always the magic word with him.

He leans forward, covering my mouth with his. He kisses me long and slow, his hand sliding over his cock between us, teasing my clit with it until all I feel is pleasure burning through me again, bringing me close to another climax, readying me for what I've asked him to do. And then, as his tongue tangles with mine, I feel his cockhead dip inside of me, sliding out as he uses his cum and mine to ease the way lower down, making me slick with it as he presses his cock against my ass.

"If you say stop," he says softly, "I'll stop. I don't care how good it feels or how close I am. You tell me, and I stop."

I nod, swallowing hard. I'm a little scared—his cock is *huge*—but I want this. I want him—all of him. And as dirty as the act might sound, I feel like this makes me his, entirely. Like there's no part of me that he won't have.

I cry out when I feel him push forward. There's resistance at first, tight and burning as he pushes his swollen cockhead into my ass, and then I feel the resistance give, and the first inch is inside. It's like losing my virginity all over again, but just like that—there's no one I want to have this more than him.

"More," I whisper, and Levin closes his eyes, sucking in a breath. His fingers find my clit, rolling over it as he kisses me again.

"I won't last," he warns me. "Your ass feels so tight, and just the fact that you're letting me do this—" he groans as he pushes deeper, another inch. "God, Elena. My good girl. My good fucking girl—"

I moan, arching as he pushes deeper, deeper, until all of his cock is buried in my ass, and I feel as if I'm going to come apart at the seams. My clit throbs under his fingers, and I clutch at his shoulders, bucking on his cock.

"I'm going to come when you do," I gasp. "Fuck my ass, Levin. Please. Fuck me and let me come with you—"

He groans, an almost animal sound of lust, as he starts to thrust slowly, shallowly, his body shuddering with pleasure. His fingers are tight against my clit, rubbing in exactly the way he knows I like, and I cling to the edges of the orgasm, waiting for him, waiting—

"Oh *god*—" Levin's hips snap forward, burying himself in my ass. "God, I'm going to fucking come in your ass, fucking come on my cock, *fuck*—come for me, Elena—"

He doesn't have to tell me twice. My nails rake furrows in his skin as I come hard, clenching around him as his fingers drive me over the edge, his cock buried in my ass, and I feel the hot flood of his cum for a second time as he fills me with it, his cock throbbing. The sound he makes is one of such absolute pleasure that it drives my orgasm higher still, until we're both clinging to each other, shuddering with the force of our combined climaxes.

Levin stays there for a long moment, rolling off of me at last, his cock finally wilting against his thigh. "I would never have thought you'd be such a little deviant," he says, looking over at me, his voice hoarse. "You never cease to surprise me."

"I'll try not to stop." I curl into his arms, my head against his chest. "Tell me that you love me again, Levin."

His arms go around me, sure and certain, without the slightest hesitation as he holds me close. "I love you," he says, and as his fingers run through my hair, I know he means it. I can hear it in his voice—and besides that, I've never known Levin Volkov to commit to something he didn't intend to see through.

What he says, he means.

"Forever," he whispers softly, pressing a kiss to my forehead. "I will love you forever, Elena Volkov. It should have started sooner—but it starts now."

I lean up just a little, pressing my hand to his cheek as I turn his mouth into mine, whispering against it as I kiss my husband, the man that I love—the man who, at last, after all this time, loves me too.

"That's all I could ever ask for."

Epilogue
Elena

"I don't know how anyone has more than one child!'"

I screech those words at no one in particular in the delivery room, truly wondering what the answer is as I cling to Levin's hand, feeling as if I'm dying. I thought I knew pain, but nothing prepared me for this.

Just yesterday, I'd been complaining about how I was past my due date, that I was ready to hold my baby, instead of what felt like interminable waiting. There had been a period of a few months where I'd actually enjoyed being pregnant—where the nausea had receded, but I hadn't felt like a walking house—but by the time eight months rolled around, I was ready to be done.

Until the contractions started in earnest, and I was absolutely certain that I'd rather go back to the early months of throwing up every morning, rather than do this for hours.

They'd told me I had plenty of time, that I could get an epidural, but our daughter clearly wants to see the world as soon as possible. "As adventurous as her mother," Levin tried to joke when we first realized it, only to be silenced by a withering glare from me.

I'll apologize later, but for now, all I can think about is how goddamn much it *hurts*.

It feels like it goes on forever, even though later they tell me it was a fairly quick birth. I tell myself, and Levin, a thousand times over, that we're never doing this again.

But when I hold our daughter in my arms, I forget all about that. When Levin leans over me and whispers her name, kissing my forehead, I forget everything except the absolute, glowing joy that I feel.

"She's beautiful," he whispers. "Little Mila." The name we'd chosen, while wallpapering and decorating the nursery, while I'd gotten to live moments that I had once thought I'd only dream about. Levin had thrown himself into preparing for the baby, doing everything he could to make sure I never felt that he was walling himself off from the future that we were planning for our family. There were times when he couldn't help it—times when I saw the old grief creep in, times when he needed space and patience. But it was easier, knowing that he wanted to try. Knowing that those moments would pass, and he would be back with me, hopeful for what was coming—and no longer fearing shadows that had been dispelled.

She cries, and it feels like my heart cracks open in the best way. Like there's room for all the love in the world in it and not enough all at the same time. "Let's make another one," I croak, looking up at Levin with tears in my eyes, and he laughs, smiling down at me as he rubs a thumb gently over Mila's head.

"Let's give it a little while," he says, chuckling. "But I want more, too. As many children as you want. We'll fill the house up with them. Build another wing."

Tears spill over my cheeks, because I remember all too well when I'd wondered if I could give our baby even one sibling. Now he's promising me anything, just as he always has tried to—but now it's what we both want. Now it means everything.

"I love you," Levin whispers as he kisses my forehead again, and then hers, his hand wrapped around mine. "I love you both more than all the world."

It feels like days before I can leave my room. The birth took a toll on my body, and I'm confined to my bed with Mila for almost a week before I'm cleared after a follow-up appointment to move around. Isabella watches her for a little while so I can get some air, and I go out to the back of our house, to the small garden I started to plant. It's nothing like Isabella's yet—not nearly as lush or as beautiful, but it's a start. There are roses climbing up the wall of the house, and I've planted seeds for peonies and pansies and violets and other flowers that will bloom in time. I'm so busy taking it in, enjoying the fresh air on my face, that I don't hear the footsteps behind me until Levin clears his throat.

When I turn around, I stare at him in shock.

He's on one knee in the grass in front of me, a velvet box in his hand. He holds it out, open, and I see the ring that he proposed to me with that night that we decided that we would get married. It feels like a lifetime ago now, as so many things do, but I still remember it.

"Levin—"

He looks up at me, his face as soft as I've ever seen it. "You told me that you couldn't accept a proposal that I didn't mean," he says, his voice full of what sounds like yearning—and hope, too. "I mean it now, Elena. You've changed everything for me. I love you more than I will ever have words to say, and you've given me a future that I didn't believe I could ever have. I want forever with you. Tell me that you want that too."

He slips the ring free of the box, holding it in his fingers. "Say you'd marry me all over again, Elena."

Tears fill my eyes, hot and bright. I hold out my hand, my finger with only the slim wedding band from the day we said our vows and the tears spill over my cheeks. "Yes," I whisper, looking down at the man I love beyond all reason—that I have loved, for far longer than I was ever supposed to. "I would marry you all over again, Levin. Today, and tomorrow, and every single day. I love you."

He slips the ring onto my finger—a perfect fit. Just like we've always been.

It just took a little while longer for him to see it.

He stands up, gathering me into his arms. "I will love you forever, Elena. Today, and tomorrow, and every single day. You are everything I never knew I needed."

They're the wedding vows I wanted. The wedding vows I've been dreaming of, said here in our own little patch of garden, in the backyard of our home. It's better than any grand ceremony.

And it means everything to me.

"We can have another wedding," he murmurs, pressing a kiss to my forehead, my nose, my lips. "We'll do it all over again."

"I don't want another wedding," I tell him firmly. "I didn't even really want all the pomp and circumstance of the first one, but Isabella insisted. I would have been happy saying our vows at a courthouse."

"You deserved much better than that," he says, and I laugh.

"You and Isabella are more alike than either of you know." I tilt my chin up, taking in the sight of him. "I would take a honeymoon, though. When Mila is a little older, maybe? Somewhere romantic and secluded, just the two of us. Where we can stay in bed all day and wander around cobblestone streets at night and eat in a little restaurant like that one in Rio—" I trail off, feeling a warm glow just at the idea of it. "I would like that. A trip for the two of us."

"No wedding, then. And a honeymoon that I am more than happy to take with you. What else?" He presses his lips to mine again. "I'll give you anything you want," he vows. "This house. More children. Anything you ask for, Elena, it's yours. You only have to say the word."

I lean up, kissing him, and I smile against his lips. "I already have everything I want," I whisper, and this time, I know it's the truth.

It's all I've ever needed. All I've wanted. And now, with the past firmly behind us and the future wide open, it feels like we can have anything.

"I have you. Forever"

Want more dark mafia romance featuring an alpha hero and a feisty heroine who fall in love har? Keep reading for a sneak peak of my next full-length standalone Poisoned Vows, a true enemies to lovers, age-gap romance with a happily ever after!

Poisoned Vows

Lilliana

"This all depends on you. And you can't even remember which fucking fork to use."

My father's voice cuts through the air, sharp as a knife. A whip crack, lashing at me. I should be used to it by now—he's talked to me this way all my life. Being loved by a parent, cherished—that isn't something I've ever known or experienced. There have been no moments of kindness or closeness. The moments I look forward to are the ones where he forgets I exist.

In the past few weeks, those have been nonexistent.

In his eyes, I have a chance to fulfill my purpose—the only purpose I've ever had. The only reason for him to ever be grateful that he has a daughter and not a son. I'm something to be molded, shaped, and bent to his will. That's all I've ever been.

My beauty was the luck of the draw. The rest of it—any grace or intelligence or good manners I possess, any charm or seductiveness—has all been instilled in me. Taught, for this moment.

What I can't seem to learn is how place settings work at a fancy dinner.

"Do you really think they're going to care?" I blow out a harsh breath, exasperated. I'll likely pay for that later, but my nerves are stretched taut, humming with anxiety. "I'm meant to be this man's fuck toy, not his wife. What does it matter if I know which spoon is for soup and which fork is for dessert?"

I can see the moment my father wants to hit me. He might have, if we weren't so close to the day of reckoning. But he can't risk anything marring my face. No redness or bruising. Nothing that leaves a mark, and he can't be trusted to stop himself, if he unleashes that control. So instead, he makes a fist, glaring at me with piercing dark eyes.

I've been told I have my mother's eyes, soft and blue. But I wouldn't know. I don't remember her, and there are no pictures of her in the house. Nothing to remember her by.

"He may want you for more than one night," my father snaps. "And sometimes Bratva men take their mistresses to functions. You will impress them more if you behave like a mistress, and not a whore. A woman who can hold her own among their associates."

Ah, yes. That distinction. I've heard it a thousand times. A whore lies on her back for one night and gets paid. Easy, simple. One and done. A *mistress* is beautiful. Polished. Elegant. For my father to succeed in installing his daughter as a mistress and not a whore means *more* for him. More of everything—but mostly the potential to rise higher…the only thing that's ever mattered to him.

"All daughters in these families manage to learn these lessons," my father snipes at me, as I look down at the place setting in front of me again, struggling to commit to memory what I'm meant to do with the silverware. As far as I'm concerned, I'd rather shove the butterknife in one of these men's eyes than politely eat soup with them.

But it's not my choice. It never has been.

"I'm not one of those daughters." The words catch in my throat. "I'm no one." *You're no one*, I want to say, but that might earn me a beating no matter how hard my father tries to restrain himself. And then later, when he's realized what he's done and blames me for pushing him to it, days locked in my room without food or entertainment, only the charm school books that reinforce my place in the world.

That whether I'm on my feet or my back, I'm here for the pleasure of the men around me. To serve their whims. To make them happy.

"You're right," he says, his voice still cold and cutting. "You are no one. But you will make me into someone. You *will* please the *pakhan*, and you will earn me my rightful spot in the ranks. And then, when he's finished with you—"

He trails off, and I wait for the end of that sentence. The only thing that's kept me from stealing a kitchen knife and slitting my own wrists long ago, to escape the absolute hell of my own existence.

"Then you can do as you damn well please," he finishes. "And good fucking riddance."

At least there's no pretense. That's the only relief I have. My father doesn't pretend to be a good or kind or loving man. He isn't horrified that I'm afraid of him, rather than loving or respecting him. He relishes it, because no one else is afraid of him, and he so desperately wants to be a man that others fear. A man whose name makes others tremble.

I want to laugh at him. To tell him how pathetic it all is. But I have a healthy dose of self-preservation, and so I don't.

I endure the rest of the lesson, and his berating, and then I go back to my room. Hungry, which is ironic, considering that we spent the last two hours discussing silverware and dinner platings.

But my father wants me slender, which means I eat very little, and what I do eat is restricted. I'll have to come down for dinner later, where he'll eat as he pleases, and I'll be served the usual—a spinach salad, grilled chicken, and a medley of vegetables. Water, not wine, or anything else more exciting. I've never actually had a drink other than the few times I've been brave enough to sneak it from my father's liquor cabinet or an open wine bottle—on the occasions that he has others over for holidays or other celebrations, he makes the excuse that I'm too young.

Twenty *is* technically too young, but I don't think anyone else gives a shit. Neither does he, really, other than it's something else to prevent me from doing. Another edict, another form of control.

I close the door to my room behind me, leaning back against it, letting out a long breath as I allow the exhaustion to sink in. I've been up since five in the morning—exercising, doing my lessons, going to my hair and beauty appointments, coming home for more lessons, and more exercise. It's the same thing day in and day out, with the exception of the appointments on a biweekly rotation. I know my father doesn't really have the money that he spends on me, but he considers it an investment.

An investment that, should I fail to deliver the return he expects, will be taken out of my own flesh. I can't imagine what's in store for me if I fail to please the *pakhan*, the man that I'm going to be presented to very soon. What will happen if he doesn't want me—if he doesn't give my father what *he* wants.

Slowly, I walk to the bed, sinking down on it. There's little to do when I'm alone—I have a few books, but I've read them until the covers are falling off. Outside I can see the Chicago skyline rising in the distance, and I know there are streets full of people, living their bustling, full lives—on their way home, or to see friends, or to go out on a date. The things that ordinary people do, in their ordinary lives.

I would like very much to be ordinary.

I *should* have been ordinary. My father is no one. As far as I know, my mother was no one, too. My father is a rank-and-file man in the Chicago Bratva, someone whose life means very little to the men far above him, the men he seeks to please and cozy up to. I was never supposed to be one of those girls bred and groomed for the pleasure of a high-ranking man, for marriage, for providing heirs. My future was supposed to be wholly unwritten.

Of course, I won't be marrying anyone. I won't be providing any children, thank *fuck*. I'll be *getting* fucked, and then once that's done, once my father has gotten what he wanted and I'm free, I can choose a different life.

I get up, open the window, and lean out. Our apartment is high up, on the twelfth floor, and there have been many nights where I leaned out just like this and imagined what might happen if I simply…tumbled out. I ran the calculations, trying to determine if there was a chance of survival. I was fairly sure that there wouldn't be.

Isolation and loneliness will do that to a girl. Growing up with a father obsessed with pushing his daughter into the bed of the most advantageous man will do that. *Everything* I've endured has pushed me to the very brink.

But now, if I can hold on just a little longer, my freedom might be very close. And with it, what will I do?

I'll get the fuck out of Chicago, that's what. I'll go as far away as I can—Florida, California, fucking Alaska, for all I care. I don't give a shit *where* I end up, as long as it's not this room, this apartment, this *fucking* city. As long as I never have to hear the words *pakhan* or *Bratva* again. As long as I get to choose who I fuck and when.

All I have to do is give up this one last thing. Endure for just a little longer. And then my value to my father—to all of these men—will be gone. I won't be a virgin any longer, and none of them will give a shit about me.

I have no idea what I'll do after that. I have no real plans, because it doesn't matter. Anything is better than this.

All that will matter is that I'll get to *choose* what I do next.

If I can survive.

Nikolai

The man's screams and pleas are meant to move me. I know, objectively, that they are. But I feel nothing as I stand there, hands bloodied, setting the pair of pliers I'm holding aside as I stare at the man trussed up in front of me.

He's missing most of his teeth at this point and several nails, both on his hands and his feet. His answers, the ones I've managed to coax out of him, are spoken through blood and spittle, sobbed gummily as he cries between words.

The man is utterly pathetic, and I'm ready for this to be over.

"Tell me again," I say patiently, reaching for a filleting knife. "And perhaps I'll believe you this time. How many men did you say that we have watching tomorrow night's shipment? And what time did you tell them that it will be landing? And to whom?"

It's too many questions for a man in this much pain to remember, so I repeat them again, in between shaving off thin strips of skin. I know he's lying, and at this point, I'm not sure what it will take to get him to tell the truth. But lies are useful, too. If he's enduring this much, it means his treachery goes deeper than we knew. It means he's afraid of something more than my father and I—which could be very few men in this city.

I am brutal, but my father is terrifying. Merciless, even to those he loves. This, to me, is a job. A rote duty that I'm expected to carry out. My father has often told me that he leaves interrogations to me because while we're both equally skilled, my father enjoys it far too much.

That, and he's getting older. His hands are no longer as steady as they once were. But he would never admit that, and to suggest it would mean ending up where this poor bastard is, trussed up above plastic sheeting and being killed an inch at a time.

His end is quick, at least. When I'm sure there's nothing more to gain from him, I slit his throat. A gunshot would be quicker still, but I left my weapon on the other side of the room, and he only told me lies. He didn't earn the effort it would have taken for me to get it.

As I'm washing my hands afterward in a side room, rinsing the blood from around my nails while I listen to the steady thump of my father's lackeys removing the body and cleaning the room, my phone buzzes in my pocket. I dry off my hands and see a message from my father.

Meet me in my office as soon as you're finished.

Brief, and to the point. I chuckle to myself as I dry off my hands, because my father is nothing if not consistent. He could want to speak to me about anything, and the message would be the same, no matter his mood. He could be pleased or furious, hopeful or despondent, have good news for me or bad, and I would receive the same text.

Emotion, in his eyes, is something for a man to quell. To kill, lest it gets him killed. And I have learned, over the years, to keep whatever emotion I feel buried, to a fault.

Fortunately, it hasn't seemed to matter much. My life is a pleasant one. I have whatever I desire. I live in a Chicago penthouse, I want for nothing, I drink and eat what I wish and fuck who I please, and go where I want. One day, my father's empire will be mine. And all I have to do in return is follow his commands and, sometimes, spill a little blood.

A small price to pay for the life I lead.

My father, Egor Vasilev, is in his office as promised. He's leaning back in his broad leather chair, flicking through papers with a cigar burning in an ashtray next to him and a glass of vodka at his right hand. My father is a man who rarely stops working, and so he enjoys his pleasures when he wishes to take them, rather than saving them for the end of the day. If it had been anyone other than one of his children coming to meet him, he likely would have had a woman under the desk. I'm almost surprised that he doesn't, anyway. It's only my sister, Marika's sensibilities that he concerns himself with, mostly.

"Nikolai." He doesn't glance up, waving at a chair with one hand as he reaches for his vodka with the other. "We've had an offer."

His expression doesn't change, but there's a hint of amusement in his voice. He sets the papers down, taking a long sip of his drink, and then looks up at me, at my blood-spattered shirt and trousers. "No time to change?"

"You asked me to meet you as soon as possible," I say calmly. There was a choice to be made, between receiving that text and coming to meet my father in his office. I could change my clothes and come to him fresh and appropriately dressed—or I could follow the letter of his instructions and come as soon as I was finished. Knowing my father, I chose the latter.

"Very good. You're a good son, Nikolai."

Coming from him, that's the very highest praise.

He leans back, steepling his fingers as he looks at me. "The man you interrogated, he's dead?"

I nod. "As the proverbial doornail."

"And did he give us anything useful?"

"Not plainly. But he lied, right up to the end. Nothing broke him. That kind of pain is only endured when the fear of telling the truth is worse. Which means whoever he was reporting to, it can only have been a few of the men in the city."

My father nods. "Theo, maybe. Or Haruki."

"It's possible. We can try to find out more. Some of his friends may be more—forthcoming, once they know what happened to him. They'll be eager to avoid the same fate, or be perceived to have helped him."

"We'll have to be careful to separate lies from truth. To make sure they aren't offering up false information to save their own skin."

"Someone will," I tell him confidently. "And that man's punishment will be enough to dissuade the rest."

My father nods approvingly. "Spoken like a true Bratva *pakhan*. No man among us, of our rank, should be afraid of blood on his hands. You bathe in it, and don't flinch."

The pride in his voice is evident. A rare thing from him, and only in private. It's no secret that my father values me—as his only son and heir, it goes without saying. But anything else is kept between us, and in this room.

There is no room for caring in our world. No room to love what can be lost.

"You said there was an offer." I clear my throat, banishing any thoughts of regret, that I might like to be closer with my father. To feel more affection from him. Those sorts of thoughts are a pointless weakness. "From who? And about what?"

"I'm getting to it." He takes another sip of his vodka, nodding to the decanter on the gilded bar to his right. It's a clear offer for me to pour myself a glass, and I take him up on it. An afternoon like the one I had makes a man need a drink.

I pour two fingers into a crystal glass and sit back down.

"One of our lower-level men has an offer for us. An Ivan Narokov."

The name doesn't ring a bell. "I haven't heard of him."

My father shrugs. "I don't know who the fuck he is, either. But he clearly heard that someone in our inner circle betrayed us. How he came about *that* information, I'm curious to know. Ordinarily, I might have had you simply torture it out of him. But his offer was—intriguing."

Now I'm all ears. My father's curiosity is rarely piqued, and he has a penchant for violence. If he's chosen to hear this Narokov out rather than simply taking pieces off of him until he gives up how he came to find out about this vacancy, *I'm* curious to know why.

"Apparently, he has a daughter. A very beautiful one."

"Oh?" I take another sip, even more curious now. "I'm sure many men who work for us have daughters. What does that have to do with anything?"

My father chuckles. "She's a virgin. Twenty years old. And he's offered us her innocence, in exchange for the place that the traitor you tortured today so recently vacated." He pauses, finishing his drink. "He offered *me* her virginity, specifically. Suggested that I might use her in any way I pleased, for as long as I pleased. No parameters on it, either—no pleas that I not harm her. Honestly, I think I could have said I planned to strangle her after I fucked her, and he would have agreed."

"Hm." I take another sip, hiding the shudder that goes through me. The only kind of violence I abhor is violence that targets women. The idea of killing this girl, whoever she is—particularly in such a way—makes my skin crawl. But I don't let it show. "And you don't want her?"

He shrugs. "I considered it. A beautiful, innocent young woman entirely at my mercy? It's a pleasant thought. But you've done well. You are an exemplary son, a worthy heir. And I think you deserve a reward. It's good timing, actually. I'd been wondering—what does a father get a son who has everything? Well, now I see." An uncommon, satisfied smile spreads over my father's face. "A virgin that you can use as you please. That's quite a reward, isn't it? And if her father proves to be useless, as I expect he might, we'll simply have him killed after you've had the chance to enjoy her."

I'm not sure it's a reward that I want. I'm not in the habit of harming women, and I doubt that this girl is going along with this scheme willingly. But I also know better than to refuse my father, especially when he's clearly so pleased with how it's all worked out.

I drain the rest of my glass. "And when will I be meeting this girl?"

"Tonight. Her father is bringing her here. I knew you'd like the suggestion, so I accepted the offer." My father's pleased expression spreads across his face, a jubilance I've only seen once or twice before.

The last time, there were more bodies than I could count around us.

"Well then." I stand up, setting the glass aside. "I suppose I'd better change clothes."

Want to get Poison Vow a week early? Purchase it here and use code 'Vow' to save 15% off!

Buy now and you'll automatically receive an email on August 20th with a link to download and read the ebook on your favorite app. It's the perfect way to support me as an indie author while still reading the stories you love!

Printed in Great Britain
by Amazon